HEATHER McCORKLE

I0524560

BITTEN &
BEHOLDEN

CHILDREN OF FENRIR BOOK ONE

CITY OWL
PRESS

This book is a work of fiction. Names, characters, places, and incidents either are products of the author's imagination or are used fictitiously. Any resemblance to actual events or locales or persons, living or dead, is entirely coincidental and not intended by the author.

BITTEN & BEHOLDEN
Children of Fenrir, Book 1

CITY OWL PRESS
www.cityowlpress.com

All Rights reserved. Except as permitted under the U.S. Copyright Act of 1976, no part of this publication may be reproduced, distributed, or transmitted in any form or by any means, or stored in a database or retrieval system, without the prior consent and permission of the publisher.

Copyright © 2020 by Heather McCorkle.

Cover Design by MiblArt. All stock photos licensed appropriately.

Edited by Yelena Casale.

For information on subsidiary rights, please contact the publisher at info@cityowlpress.com.

Print Edition ISBN: 978-1-64898-022-0

Digital Edition ISBN: 978-1-64898-021-3

Printed in the United States of America

For the Viking who keeps me warm at night.

PRAISE FOR HEATHER McCORKLE

"Kickass women, Icelandic warriors, and plenty of action!"
– *Kait Ballinger, Bestselling Author of The Execution Underground Series*

"The characters have lots of depth to them and are strong, sexy and fun. A fabulous story line full of magic and danger that I was pulled into from the first page. I can't wait to read more of this series. I loved it."
– *Petula Winmill, Book Reviewer*

"Holy werewolves, Batman! What did I just read!! A winning combination of romance and heat, action, and drama, not to mention plenty of Norse lore and mythology to make a paranormal lover combust! This story was unique and quite different from the shifter stories we've come to know and love. Ms. McCorkle did a marvelous job with weaving her story and I am so looking forward to what's coming next."
– *Katrina Berry, Book Reviewer*

"Excellent book!! Not your average shifter book. I really like the Norse bent to the storyline. Couldn't put it down and anxiously awaiting book 2 of the series."
– *Susan Hall, Book Reviewer*

"What a great story this is! One of the best things about it is that I can't think of a book to compare it too. The reason why I love that, is because the story is just so unique. Which is why I kept turning the page! Loved it!"
– *Ali Cross, USA Today Bestselling Author of Young Adult Fantasy*

"There's trouble in the Dragon Empire, the kind that could start a war between dragons and the races of people...For those who love fantasy, dragons and a sweet love story, this book is definitely a must read for you!"
– *Geeky Book Gal*

"Channeler's Choice is definitely my choice for a fantastic story. Heather McCorkle turns the heat up in her second novel of the Channeler series... McCorkle is an outstanding storyteller, and she totally blew me away again."
— *I Heart YA Books*

CHILDREN OF FENRIR

RECOMMENDED READING ORDER

CHAPTER ONE

SONYA

C aught up in the moment as I was, I didn't see fate coming for me. I should have. There were signs. Like the animalistic growl rumbling in his chest as he kissed a wet line down my jaw to my neck. I wasn't about to protest. The primal sound of it was sexy as hell, even if it did remind me of all the strange things I'd seen over the last week. His incredible amber eyes developed a shine that seemed unnatural, but I figured it was the drinks we'd had earlier getting to me. It had to be that, along with my wild imagination. His hips ground against mine, pushing me into the door of my downstairs apartment.

Again he asked to go inside, and again I refused. I certainly had nothing against premarital sex, but casual sex was another thing altogether. Especially with a guy I had only met two weeks ago. What had I been thinking when I'd invited him back here? It was bad enough that we were making out in the dark alley in front of my low-income apartment where my sketchy neighbors could come out at any moment. But then, Twin Falls, Idaho wasn't exactly a hopping town after midnight. And seeing as my apartment building was only a little two-story number that housed less than fifty, the odds of anyone being around were slim to none. All the more reason not to go inside where temptation would lead me somewhere I wasn't willing to go yet.

At least I wasn't anymore. I needed to process the weirdness of our date and make sense of it first. Something strange was going on here. I felt it deep in my bones.

The gentle nips at my neck grew harder. Walking that razor edge of pleasure/pain made my blood pump so hard the cool Idaho night felt more like Arizona in the midst of summer. Until impossibly sharp teeth grazed the sensitive skin of my neck. People did not have razor sharp teeth!

"Ouch!"

Those teeth broke through my skin and sank deep into the muscles and meat of my neck. I screamed and writhed in pain but he had locked onto me with the strength of a boa constrictor. After an excruciating second, his teeth withdrew from me in a rush.

One moment he was pressed up to me, the next he leaped back and stood against the building across the alley as if using it to brace himself. His mouth hung open and within it, not one set of fangs shone in the streetlight, but two, a set on the top and a set on the bottom, much like a canine. The worst part: they were covered in my blood. My *blood*.

"What the hell?" I yelled, a hand going to my neck.

My fingers came away slick and sticky with blood. He stood there, staring at me with those gleaming eyes, blood trickling over his bottom lip. Slowly, like a cat's claws, his fangs retracted until they looked like no more than overly pointy teeth. Before tonight I had thought his toothy smile looked sexy. Now, not so much. If it weren't for the blood making a steady trail down his chin, I would have thought I'd imagined the whole thing. Then there was the pain.

Keeping my eyes on him, I fumbled in my pocket for my keys with one hand while the other searched for the mace I kept on me. My fingers settled around the metal canister. Hand so steady it surprised even me, I took it out, flicked my thumb under the safety cap, and pointed it at him. The bastard just grinned, though it was a sad smile instead of one filled with humor. A cold chill of fear threatened to extinguish my anger.

"What. The. Hell?" I demanded slower, emphasizing each word, desperate to hang on to the anger that gave me courage.

His shoulders sagged, his defined chest caving in on itself as if he were trying to melt back into the wall. The button-up shirt he wore lay splayed open, giving me a good view of the blood that dripped from his chin onto his pale pecs. Only moments ago I had opened that shirt in my eagerness to touch his bare flesh. The memory made me shiver with revulsion. That gorgeous, fit body of his suddenly seemed to sport more hair than I remembered. Hair covered his bare chest where I didn't recall him having any before, and the line of it from his belly button down into the waistband of his jeans had definitely thickened. The hand holding the mace began to shake, and I loathed myself a little for the weakness. He looked past the mace at me with something close to contempt.

"I'm sorry it happened this way. I didn't want it to, I swear." He glanced down the alley, then back at me. "Sonya, please, come with me and I'll explain everything."

Straightening, he adjusted the erection pushing against the fly of his jeans, as if I weren't pointing mace at his half-naked body. The front step swam a bit. Damn, how deep had he bitten into me? I pressed one hand to the wound and kept the mace trained on him with the other. Freaked out and feeling exposed, I wanted nothing more than to dig my keys out of my jeans pocket and open my apartment door, but I didn't dare. Dropping my guard even a little wasn't an option.

Hot, sticky blood oozed through my fingers and ran down my neck. "You *bit* me, you son of a bitch!"

"I'm so sorry. I ran out of time." Going stiff, he stood up straighter, eyes darting down the alley in both directions.

The alley swam, and not in a pleasant, too-much-Jack-Daniels kind of way.

"Get away from me, Raul. Now," I said, doing my best to sound like the badass I totally did not feel like at the moment.

"No, Sonya. Listen, I'll explain everything, but you need to come with me now," he urged, reaching a hand toward me.

Soft yellow light from headlights outlined his spiky brown hair. Someone had parked at the other end of the parking lot, beyond the small bit of green space that edged the building. When the lights didn't switch off, I realized whoever it was wanted to see us. I called out for help. The blinding bright light hid Raul's expression from me until he turned his back to it. Damned if he didn't look a bit toothier—and worried. The second part I liked; the first made me even more concerned than I already was.

He backed away and started down the sidewalk, moving away from the headlights. "Damn him. I will come back for you and explain everything," he said in that sexy voice of his that made me want to vomit.

Light bounced off the green thread of the top rocker sewn to his black jacket. No matter how many times I had asked, he'd never told me what AVW—stitched onto the top rocker—stood for. The bottom rocker read Montana, revealing he belonged to some kind of group out of that state. Beyond that, I knew very little. Between the rockers sat a patch with strange symbols of circling knotwork woven into the shape of a canine with Norse runes all around it. That told me even less. Damn it, I should have known better.

"Not a chance, you freak. You ever come back here and I will kill you."

I couldn't even bring myself to kill spiders, but he didn't know that.

White teeth flashed in a snarl that was directed at something behind me before he dashed off. I wanted to follow him, make sure he left, but I couldn't move. Hell, I couldn't hold the mace up anymore. Before it could fall, I shoved it in my pocket, having to try twice. Soft footsteps padded from the direction of the headlights. While my fuzzy mind regretted having pocketing the mace, part of me realized it was probably a concerned neighbor who had heard me yell. But none of my neighbors were as tall and muscular as the man who came running down the alley toward me. I wasn't sure if it was the light, or if he had short golden hair, but one thing I couldn't miss were his ice-blue eyes. A woman could get caught in eyes like that. The man looked like he'd walked right out of one of the old Norse legends my dad had liked to tell me when I was a kid.

Everything swayed. Or maybe it was me; I couldn't tell. Strong hands gripped my arms, holding me upright. The skin of his hands tingled against my arms, growing warmer the longer he held on, until it felt like we might melt together into one. Something in my fuzzy brain tried to tell me that wouldn't be a bad thing, not at all. Those ice-blue eyes snagged my gaze and held on with a vengeance. Heat to rival that of an inferno lay behind those glacial blues, and it pulled at me as if it wanted to consume me.

"You should get inside and lock the door behind you. I will go after him." His voice was accented with the right timbre to set my nerves vibrating in a very good way.

Survival instincts broke through the haze caused by blood loss. Yeah, that had to be it, the blood loss. I thrust my hand in my pocket and pulled out my keys. As I turned them in the lock, I forced my weary head up so I could look at the blond man one more time. I wanted to remember his face, and not just because he was the only witness to the assault on me.

"Careful, he's dangerous," I warned.

"So am I. Do not worry about me. I will be back to make sure you are all right," he said.

I turned the knob and nearly fell as the door opened inward. Just before I closed it, I heard the man curse in a language I didn't recognize but that tickled at my memory. Several sets of footsteps pounded on the pavement. I slammed the door shut, threw the deadbolt, and bolted the other two locks for good measure. On weak legs I made my way to the bedroom, using the walls and furniture to keep myself upright. Coagulating blood forced me to peel my hand from my neck so I could use it.

Blood ran in a hot trail from the wound, down my neck and between my breasts. In this light I couldn't tell by the color alone how bad it was, but the flow was entirely too steady for my comfort. The fact that my heart was working overtime from the stress didn't help. Halfway there, with my stomach threatening to revolt and my vision swimming, I realized I should have grabbed my cell phone off the coffee table. Too late now. Besides, I didn't want the cops involved. Damn police only made things worse, a lesson I had learned all too well growing up. I'd go back for the phone in a moment and call Nikki from work. She'd take me to the hospital faster than an ambulance could get here. First, I had to stop the bleeding, and I was closer to the bathroom than the living room. Shock would soon slow my heart and with it my blood flow, giving me plenty of time to get to an ER. With six years into my medical degree I could do just as much—or more, in most cases—to stop the bleeding as an EMT anyway.

Hoping I didn't split my head open on the doorframe, I let go of the wall and took a leap of faith by crossing the open space to the bathroom. My hand left a bloody streak on the door as I stumbled through. The vanity offered me something stable to lean on and was thankfully at the right height so I didn't have to lift my hand to do so, because at that point, I didn't think I could.

From within the vanity mirror my ghost stared back at me. Or at least that's what it looked like. My bronze skin looked sickly pale, a hue I strove hard to avoid with as many hours in the sun as I could manage while working full time at the bar and studying for college with plans to go back the next semester. Blood stained my straight-as-an-arrow black hair, making it cling to my neck and left breast. I didn't want to peel away the hair, didn't want to see, but I had to. Swallowing my fear, I pulled my hair away. The pain caused my vision to go dark, but it came back after a few blinks.

Bright red blood flowed from not one but four holes, two above and two below my carotid. They weren't deep enough to show muscle or bone, but the sight of them was enough to make my stomach twist. I definitely should have grabbed my cell phone. I could have at least called one of the waitresses from the bar to come get me. With one hand bracing myself against the sink, I opened the vanity with the other and grabbed the hydrogen peroxide. The way I figured it, a biker guy with a bizarre biting fetish and weird teeth was likely to carry some kind of germs. Even if he didn't, I wanted to boil the freak's saliva from my skin and this was the best way I could do it without actually using boiling water.

White-hot agony exploded into my neck as I poured the bottle of peroxide onto the wounds. My vision went black and this time it didn't clear.

CHAPTER TWO

TY

The apartment buildings rising to either side zipped by in a blur as my feet ate up the pavement, but it was not fast enough. He was pulling away. Eyes gleamed from the darkness as he chanced a look back at me. Damn, but the wiry little bastard was fast. A solid thud resounded as he leaped up onto and over the wooden fence at the end of the alley. To get more air, I bounced a foot off the concrete block wall of the closest apartment, then landed on top of the fence. I could have jumped straight up and cleared the six-foot height, but someone could have been watching. Better to make it look like I was just a fan of the move from old kung fu movies rather than have someone suspect the truth.

As I descended I scanned the area. An open green space stretched in all directions with a lawn that went for acres dotted with trees and bushes. My gaze cut through the dark easily enough, locating him already halfway across the lawn, the metallic green threads of those damn rockers of his gleaming in the moonlight. No one but him was in the immediate area.

"Raul, stop now and I'll go easier on you!" I yelled. I didn't need to see his face to know it was him. I'd know that detestable pine, nylon, and exhaust stench anywhere.

He flipped me the bird. I jumped from the top of the fence with everything I had, launching myself close to thirty feet. Wood splintered and cracked but it didn't sound like the fence came down, so I didn't bother to look back. The moment my feet touched the grass I took off. The whites of Raul's eyes reflected the moonlight as he stumbled backward, mouth agape. He only got a few paces before I caught him within the shadow of a huge fir tree. I grabbed the back of his nylon motorcycle jacket—and a bit of his hair—and tossed him to the ground. He landed on his back and froze halfway up on his elbows. His breath came in gasps that had more to do with the stench of fear wafting off him than with being out of air. Rank as it was, the fear smelled better than that nasty cologne he was wearing. No doubt that had been a ploy to throw me off his scent. And it had worked, for a while.

"You just bit a woman. The Council will have your hide for that," I said.

Not just any woman, but one with eyes like tiger's eye gems that felt like they had tried to pull my soul into them. Even now I could not get her out of my mind.

"Stay out of this. It doesn't concern you," he demanded as he started to rise to his feet.

Fists closing, my chest rumbled with a sound that made him freeze before he could even get both legs beneath him.

"You are in my territory, which means it concerns me. And you broke one of the oldest laws, which means it concerns the Council. I am taking you back to Hemlock Hollow," I said.

Light footsteps approached from all sides, but I didn't dare take my eyes off Raul. Lips quirking up into a smirk, he rose into a crouch.

"I don't think so. Like I said, this doesn't concern you," he said, voice filled with that damn bravado of his again.

But it was a misplaced bravado, because the ones I smelled in the darkness were not his people. Raul stood and crossed his arms while others leaped at me from the shadows. Dodging, I avoided the man coming at me from my right. I planted my foot into his back, right on the patch of his jacket, and sent him sprawling. Another came at me from behind. Lunging back and crouching at the same time, I grabbed his leg, yanked, and sent him flying over my back. Grunts and curses told me he had collided with either Raul or the other one. A fist flew at me from the left, my instincts pulling my face out of its path a second before it could connect. I grabbed ahold of the wrist attached to it, yanked it forward and down, and flipped the man onto his back.

They came at me again, slower but no less determined. I took them down yet again, bloodying a few lips and blackening a few eyes in the process. If they kept it up they would soon force me to do much more than that. The way they panted and heaved meant they would get desperate during the next round, which meant things were about to get bloody.

Off to my right, Raul battled with two of his own opponents. Whoever these people were, they planned to take both of us out.

From the shadows, another erupted, swinging what looked like a baseball bat. It connected hard with my left shoulder and knocked me off balance.

"Go the hell down, Viðarsson," he said, voice little more than a growl.

He swung again, but this time I grabbed it in mid-swing and tore it from him. His eyes shot wide open, but to his credit, he did not cower. That was, I was certain, mostly because of his buddy trying to sneak up behind me. Without looking, I sidestepped and ducked, then whipped the bat around behind me to connect with the man's midsection with a swing that would have earned me a home run. The others hesitated like they did not want to go another round. One of them suddenly slumped to the ground as if the very thought made him faint dead away.

The stories about me were not that scary.

Raul suddenly slumped as well, falling to the ground with the gracelessness of one who was completely out of it. *Shit.* A sharp sting in the side of my neck took my voice and my consciousness a moment before I could tell the others that I was one of the good guys.

CHAPTER THREE

SONYA

The incessant beeping of my alarm pulled me from a foggy sleep. Since it was on my phone I could have it set for a tone or a song I liked, but then chances were it wouldn't wake me. The sound was hollow, as though I was hearing it in a tunnel or from another room. Cold, hard tiles beneath my cheek yanked me back to what had happened with a clarity I'd rather not have. The stench of bleach, pine-scented cleaner, and dried blood nearly burned my nose it was so strong. That beeping soon birthed a headache that felt like it was trying to split the two halves of my brain apart.

I *had* to shut it off.

Muscles protesting like I'd run a marathon I didn't bother to train for, I pushed myself up to a sitting position. Expecting to see blood, I searched the floor around me but found only a small pool near where my head had been. Base drums began to pound with the insistence of a war party inside my head, the volume increasing with each pulse of my alarm. The left side of my neck ached, but not as bad as I thought it would. Using the vanity, I pulled myself up, half expecting my legs to be shaky. But I felt steady, almost strong even. The nausea was gone too. Maybe he hadn't bitten me as bad as I thought he had. Or maybe he had slipped something into my drink and the entire night was a drug-induced nightmare.

The mirror revealed four scabbed-over wounds surrounded by crusty blood that trailed down between my breasts, gluing locks of my black hair to my shoulder. It was hard to tell how bad it was under all the blood, but one thing was for certain: the bastard had actually *bitten* me.

I should have known better than to mess around with a guy who belonged to some kind of speed freak group he liked to compare to the Toretto family from the *Fast & Furious* movies. Though he had called them a pack instead of a family. It had seemed exciting at the time, but now it made me feel like an idiot.

Libido chalks up another point. Brains still remain at zero.

Alarm shot adrenalin through my veins, blowing my eyes wide open. Forgetting about the possibility of being weak from blood loss, I dashed into the living room, grabbed my phone off the coffee table, and shut the alarm off. For a split second, I thought about calling Nikki from work. But I felt all right. A quick scan of the room revealed it to be empty. Daylight streamed through the thin curtains, making me wonder how long I had been out. Bumps rose along my bare arms. I had to make sure no one else was here.

Speaking of my libido, what had happened to the Norse-god-looking guy? Concern nagged deep inside. I tried to tell myself it was only because he had come to my rescue, but I wasn't making a very convincing argument.

Pulling out my mace, I worked my way systematically through my small apartment. I didn't think Raul would come back, not with that big blond guy chasing him off, but I had to be sure. I knew the sense of security the mace gave me was false—and that I wouldn't use it on anyone anyway—but it made me feel better. Mostly I carried it because it was the last thing my dad had given me, and he had told me to always keep it close. Hell, the shit had probably expired.

The daylight made me worry about my rescuer a bit. He had said he'd come back to check on me. But considering that he looked like he could pass for Thor, I figured he could probably hold his own against Raul. Just in case, I peeked out the peephole in the door. After adjusting to the blinding light of day, all I saw was an empty walkway. The concern in my stomach blossomed into an H.R. Giger–sized alien. Part of me wanted to know what happened to him—needed to know—but first I had to take care of myself.

In the absence of the cacophony of the alarm, I could hear the buzz of the refrigerator along with a low droning that I thought may have been electricity. Maybe a transformer was going out somewhere. That had to be it. Concentrating, I tried to hear beyond it, to make sure no one waited around the corners or doors in the few rooms that made up my small apartment. Only when I was certain each room was clear and the deadbolt was engaged on the front door did I finally retrieve some clothes from my bedroom and return to the bathroom.

Hot water cranked as high as I could stand it, I climbed into the shower and let it pour over me, washing away the smell—if not the memory—of Raul. For some reason the floral scents of my bodywash and shampoo were so overwhelming that I had to use half the normal amount. Even then, the scents burned my nose, forcing me to rinse until I had washed as much of them from me as I could. Above them I could smell the soap scum clinging to what I thought had been a clean shower, and the hints of mold in corners here and there.

I returned to the bathroom mirror to inspect the bite marks again. The small exhaust fan clunked along like a wounded animal, scarcely clearing the mist. Pulling the towel—which smelled entirely too strongly of fabric softener—from my long hair, I used it to wipe the mirror clean. That was the last time I was buying the cheap shit. The spendy stuff had to smell better, or at least not as strong. Ugh. In a few moments the exhaust fan cleared away the film that remained. The four holes I remembered were covered with scabs that looked several weeks old. Around them my skin was only slightly pink, as if the wounds had been healing for some time.

"Impossible," I murmured, not liking how loud my own voice sounded.

It occurred to me that maybe I had been passed out from blood loss a lot longer than I had thought. The ravenous grumbling of my stomach suggested that was a good possibility. What if I had been on the bathroom floor for days? No way. Then again, that entire night seemed impossible now. One of my first stops had to be the hospital so I could get a tetanus shot, because damn. Aside from the ick factor of being on the bathroom floor for who knew how long, another thought pulled a groan from me.

"I am so going to get fired." Okay, maybe the hospital would have to be my second stop.

I dug my phone out from beneath the pile of clothes I had thrown on it. It hadn't occurred to me to check the date when I had shut the alarm off. The display read June 12th, two days after the date with Raul. No fucking way.

"Yep, fired."

Shuddering, I pulled my clothes on with a resigned slowness. I was *so* remaining celibate after this. For good measure, I slapped a few Band-Aids over the wounds. I would deal with the weirdness of what had happened with Raul later. Right now I had to face the music and prepare to beg to keep my job. Yeah, right, as if I could debase myself like that. After rushing through my morning routine and glancing in the empty fridge, I thought maybe I should try to grovel, at least a little. I tucked my cell phone in my pocket and opened the door.

On my way out I grabbed an apple and wrapped a silk scarf around my neck to hide the Band-Aids. I couldn't stand the thought of anyone seeing the wounds and asking what had happened. Not until I figured it out. Midafternoon sunlight heated the concrete, bringing out the smell of tar and the moss that clung in the cracks and along the edges. A quick glance both directions revealed what my ears already told me: I was alone. No sign of Raul or the blond stranger. Designer cowboy boots—found at a thrift store—clicking out a rock song rhythm, I made my way down the shaded walkway between my apartment and the one crowded next to it. While I was possibly the furthest thing from a cowgirl, the boots made me feel badass, and right now, shaking in my boots as I literally was, I needed to feel a little badass.

Sunlight pierced through the gloom, forcing me to put my sunglasses on before I stepped out of the walkway between the buildings. The overwhelming tangy scent of freshly cut green grass tickled my nose so badly I had to suppress a sneeze. Damn if I couldn't still smell the exhaust of the lawn mower. The groundskeeper must be close by. But I didn't hear a lawnmower. Thankfully, the almost sweet scent of the tall pines that loomed over the three-story apartment buildings helped dilute it enough to be tolerable. The catchy, high-pitched tune of meadowlarks singing in the trees sounded particularly loud today, almost piercing. I tossed my apple core at the base of the nearest tree and watched the yellow-breasted birds descend upon it like a pack of dogs. Big though the Red Delicious had been, it hadn't even taken the edge off my hunger. No surprise, considering I had been passed out on the bathroom floor for two days.

My mind started going over all the species of bacteria in a human mouth, then promptly launched into the diseases that could result from a bite. I walked faster.

Trying to look everywhere at once, I crossed the sidewalk at a brisk pace and leaped into my topless black 1975 Jeep CJ. Chills of trepidation raced up my back even though the streets were empty. I couldn't shake that crawling sensation of being watched. Paranoia most likely, but that didn't banish it. With one hand I twisted my long black hair up while the other reached for my ball cap from the center console. Hair tamed, I pushed the latest Stephen King novel I was reading aside and grabbed the screwdriver from the glove box, stuck it in the altered ignition and started the Jeep. Passionate as I was about restoring this rig, fixing the ignition was the one thing I hadn't gotten around to yet. Reliable as ever, it purred to life despite my fear that it would fail like in a bad horror movie.

Common sense told me to go to the hospital and get checked out first. Regardless of how good the wounds looked, I had been bitten by a person and had been passed out for two days. I would need to get tested. Clearly all was not copasetic with me, what with the auditory heightening. But, it was hard to pay medical bills and college tuition while unemployed. Testing would have to wait. At least until after I tried to salvage my job. So several miles later, I turned left toward work at the intersection instead of right toward the hospital. After all, aside from being hungry and my sense of smell and hearing being totally out of whack, I felt fine.

The urge to speed was hard to fight, but I managed. No matter how early I got there, it wouldn't make up for missing two days without calling. As the primary buildings of Twin Falls began to recede in my rearview mirror I relaxed a bit. Mostly hilly scrubland stretched out to my right, and fewer roads intersected with the highway I cruised down. Only a few cars shared the road with me, and none of them were sports cars like Raul's.

Steeling myself, I took the side street off into the tree-covered hills that led to the bar. More than hunger rumbled in my stomach when the single-story dive bar came into sight, standing like a lone hitchhiker alongside the road. Two cars sat in the gravel parking lot: the owner/cook's beat-up pickup and Nikki's sedan.

The biting incident with Raul had shaken me in a way I really didn't want to think about. Love-biting wasn't something I was opposed to, but tearing into flesh with fangs, yeah I was against that. Part of me—hell most of me—wanted to believe the fangs had been a delusion created by some drug the bastard had slipped me, that or purchased from a costume shop. But wouldn't cheap plastic fangs break before doing the kind of damage that left me passed out on the bathroom floor? Likely, but maybe Raul had them specially made, which made him kinkier—and creepier—than I had imagined anyone could be.

Having stalled as much as I could, I removed the ball cap and ran a brush through my hair before leaping out of the Jeep. The brisk pace I kept while approaching the bar was out of a need to make up as much time as possible, or so I told myself. It had nothing to do with the way the scent of the pine trees bordering the parking lot drew me like a magnet, or the thought of someone that could be hiding in the shadows there. Someone in particular. Digging my keys out of my jacket pocket, I shook the notion off. Raul had gotten his twisted rocks off and was likely long gone by now thanks to the blond stranger. What had happened to Blondie, who knew?

Stale beer, salty pretzels, and the sweetness of strong alcohol assaulted my nose the moment I stepped inside the dimly lit building. Trying to breathe through my mouth, I wove my way between the tables and upside-down chairs that sat atop them. Jeans cut so short they barely covered the skinny cheeks of the ass they were meant to contain met me as I approached the side entrance to the bar. The blingy pockets didn't help make that ass look any bigger, like I knew the woman hoped they did. Mousy-brown ponytail bouncing, she turned around with mop in hand. Her eyes went wide and she dropped the mop with a scream when she saw me. The sound pierced my hungover ears like arrows.

Hands over my ears, half to shut out the sound, and half so I didn't smack her, I shook my head. "Damn, Nikki!"

Fingers clutching at her heart as though she feared it would burst out of her chest, she stared at me with wide eyes. "Sorry, but you snuck up on me. And, girl, we thought you were dead."

"So did I."

I picked the mop up and handed it to her. Needing to get away from the overpowering stench of the bleach water, I started toward the kitchen. Not that it would be much better in there, but at least there wouldn't be a bucket full of the stuff.

"Okay, not dead. I figured you took home takeout. You did, didn't you? You never do that," she said.

I cringed. *Takeout*—the waitresses' polite term for taking home a guy they met in the bar that night. To split hairs, that wasn't exactly what I had done. Raul had been coming in to see me every night for two weeks, tipping heavily, cranking up the charm, and even leaving a rose on my Jeep each night last week. While that was far more time than most of the women in this place took, it was far less for me. In fact, I had never done it. One-night stands weren't my thing. But I thought we'd had a connection, and he led me to believe it wouldn't have been just one night. At least I hadn't let him in. Who knows what he would have done if I had. After all the odd shit that happened, I should have known better.

"It was that hot guy in the Jag, wasn't it? I want to hear all about it!" she called after me.

Ignoring her, I pushed through the swinging door into the kitchen. The rapid clicking of a knife on a cutting board drew me around the fryers to the prep counter in the back. Bald head shining with sweat, my boss stood hovered over a half-chopped head of cauliflower. His white apron strained to hold in his bulk as if he expected the thing to double as a girdle. So as not to repeat the incident with Nikki and potentially have a knife thrown at me, I rattled my keys in my pocket as I approached.

The chopping ceased and a pair of muddy brown eyes shifted over to glare at me. "Sonya. You're alive."

The fact that he didn't sound happy about it was going to make the necessary groveling almost impossible. But it was grovel or get another month behind on my tuition loans. If I hadn't skipped out on enrolling this last semester, I wouldn't have had to start paying them. But I had to get my head together and figure out what I wanted rather than just aimlessly chalking up debt on classes I didn't need for a major I wanted to change. "I had an accident, couldn't make it in."

"Or to a phone?"

"I was knocked out."

Lips pursing, he shook his head. "Well, no one called in for you."

Stiffening, I had to force my teeth apart so I could answer. "I don't have anyone. You know that."

The chopping commenced. "Not my problem. You not coming in, now that's my problem."

Slow, steady breaths helped cool my temper a little. "I'll work double shifts, no days off, whatever it takes to make up for it."

Again the chopping stopped and he turned halfway toward me. A grin revealed nicotine-stained teeth. His gaze crawled up my body. "Whatever it takes?"

Anger so hot it hurt scorched its way through me. My teeth ached as if I had been grinding them again, but I hadn't. "Fuck you."

The vehement words came out sounding strange, as if something were in the way. Something pricked inside my mouth and I tasted the coppery flavor of blood. On instinct, my tongue rolled forward, feeling my teeth. What felt like fangs stretched both down and up. Two on the top and two on the bottom, exactly like I had seen on Raul. *No way.* The world swam a bit as I worked my way up to a panic attack. Maybe some of whatever Raul had slipped into my drink remained in my system. Unlikely, highly unlikely, but I couldn't wrap my mind around the alternative. I took a few deep breaths to push the panic back.

"What the fuck?" I whispered.

Thankfully, my boss's eyes were on my breasts instead of my mouth.

"That's what it will take," he said.

Pressing my lips together, I spun away from him. "Not a chance in hell, you son of a bitch," I said as I stormed away.

The chopping commenced.

"Oh no, did he fire you?" Nikki asked as I blew through the swinging doors.

Tongue working against the impossible fangs in my mouth, I tossed my keys onto the bar and kept walking. "No, I quit," I said without looking her way.

Upon reaching the door I realized I had locked it. If I waited, I risked Nikki seeing the fangs that may or may not be a delusion left over from the attack. Was it the delusion, or was I fooling myself that he may have drugged me? I couldn't risk having her answer that for me. Without even thinking about it, I popped the lock of the doorknob with one easy twist and pulled the door open. Fear fueled my steps as I did my best not to run to my Jeep. The whole "Raul drugged me" excuse was starting to seriously lose credence. My mind did not want to go where the symptoms were trying to take me. I was a rational girl after all.

An envelope tucked beneath my driver's side windshield wiper stopped me dead in my tracks. My gaze attempting to dart every which way at once, I snatched the envelope and jumped into the Jeep. My surroundings appeared as vacant as when I had arrived. Leaning forward, I pulled my lips back from my teeth and looked in the rearview mirror. Unless the delusion had graduated into hallucinations, there really were fangs in my mouth. A set on the bottom and a set on the top, like a canine. I had seen something like this before, a long time ago, but I had written it off as a trick of the shadows and moonlight. It took several deep breaths to drive back the rising panic that threatened to make me throw up.

The smell of Raul's subtle but expensive cologne wafted up from the envelope. How had I found that crap sexy? I wanted to toss the envelope away from me, but I couldn't. There could be answers inside the damn thing, hopefully answers that wouldn't sound as insane as I was beginning to feel.

Before opening the envelope, I grabbed the screwdriver from the glove box and started the Jeep. Trying to keep one eye on my surroundings, I pulled out the letter with hands that shook like a junkie's. It was written with an actual pen. I was surprised he hadn't just texted me. Of course, that wouldn't have had the same creepy factor this did, and this guy seemed to be all about the creep factor now.

Sonya,

For what it's worth, I'm truly sorry things happened the way they did. That wasn't how I wanted this to go. Hurting a woman, taking her choice, those are things I never wanted to do. And you are so special. I'm sorry. You will have questions about what you're becoming. I have answers. Come find me, please. Until you do, may Odin watch over you.

Yours,

Raul

"Becoming? What the hell?" I grumbled a few more choice words while looking inside the envelope again.

Such a familiar closing to a letter hardly seemed appropriate after having only known him for two weeks, despite the mediocre make-out session that ended with far more kink than I'd liked. And "becoming"... What the hell was that supposed to mean? I chanced another look in the mirror, raising my upper lip into something like a snarl. The fangs were still there. But then I knew that already; I could feel them. There had to be a medical explanation. But if that were so, why did I feel so lucid? I went over all the drugs I knew of, over the counter and otherwise, but couldn't come up with any that possessed such a strong psychotropic and yet left the victim functional. Or maybe I just thought I was functional.

Wait, had he seriously said Odin? I reread the note to make sure.

"As in Odin from the Norse legends," I murmured to myself.

I knew the guy was into Odinism like my dad had been. We'd talked about it briefly. But he'd never actually mentioned his Gods or said much about it beyond that discussion. I thought it had been only a weird coincidence. More and more people embraced the old religions nowadays. It had nothing to do with my dad. It couldn't. Tears blurred my vision. Either I was going mad or something seriously messed up was happening to me, something impossible. I was leaning toward madness, or a delusion brought on by a roofie or those crazy stories my dad had told me years ago.

You're special, Sonya, chosen by Odin. Someday it will all make sense, he used to say. But this couldn't possibly have anything to do with that. Those had been stories to entertain a young girl. Some girls got Cinderella for a bedtime tale; I got the Norse eddas. Some were princesses in their daddy's eyes; I was touched by Loki and chosen by Odin. Tears made hot tracks down my cheeks.

Maybe this sick bastard had known my dad somehow, met him in prison or something, and was messing with me. If that was the case, I was going to tear him a new one. No one messed with the memory of my dad.

My fingers closed around a business card inside the envelope.

The Staybridge Suites, Missoula, Montana.

"Montana?" I exclaimed as I shook my head and threw the Jeep in reverse.

The bastard expected me to meet him in Montana. Suddenly all those conversations about places we wanted to travel, his questions about where I had been, seemed decidedly pointed. He had not only done this on purpose, but it seemed he had planned it. And the sharp points of two pairs of fangs pushing against my lips meant I had no choice but to seek him out.

CHAPTER FOUR

TY

Thoughts still fuzzy from the aftereffects of the horse tranquilizer they had used on me, I glared across the table at my captors. Or rather, those who had ordered me to be brought in with the other delinquents. Six people sat on the other side of the solid oak table, three men and three women. A mixture of tension and power rolled off them. The tiny room was choked with it, making it seem all the smaller. One of the men wore a police uniform, the others were casually dressed, but they had no less of an authoritative air to them. Sunlight spilled through a window behind them, reminding me of how long they had knocked me out and held me up with their questioning.

"I have already informed you that I knew nothing about what Raul was doing in my territory, that is why I was hunting him. If I had, I assure you, he would not have been successful. Now let me go so I may check on the woman. I will not ask again," I warned.

If I had known what he was up to, Raul never would have succeeded. That poor woman... I had to get back to her. Not only was it my responsibility because she was in my territory, but something about her would not let go of me. Could I fight all six of them off to get away? I was not sure. But I was sure I would try if I had to, and I let that show on my face. I knew I could take a few of them down at least, which would be devastating to them in more ways than one.

One of the men in a black leather jacket sprawled a spider-like hand onto the desktop as he leaned forward. He glared down his hawkish nose at me, pinprick pupils dark behind his dirty blond hair, which was shaved to the scalp on the sides and long on the top and back like the Vikings of old. It took all my restraint not to lunge across the desk and tear into him. I could have broken my bonds easily and done so, but I was not about to give him the satisfaction of knowing he had riled me with no more than a look.

"As you shouldn't. You are in no position to ask for anything," he practically hissed at me.

The man in the police uniform shot the speaker a harsh glance. "Enough, Bain. I think we can all agree that Mr. Viðarsson had nothing to do with the woman getting attacked. He clearly tried to stop it. And you stepped out of your bounds of authority by tranquilizing him and bringing him in." He gestured to someone standing behind me. "Remove his bonds and let him go. We have the matter of the woman's *kennari* to discuss, and we must decide on it quickly."

Bain shot the man a sharp glare. "No, Isak, I had every right. The man was present during an unsanctioned biting. He wouldn't have come in on his own, and you know it. We can't let him go until we're sure he had nothing to do with it."

"Agreed," came a woman's voice from beside him.

It was a voice I had once found sultry. But now I heard the derisive, judgmental tone it truly held. Through the carefully styled wave of brown bangs, she tried to glare a hole through me. The disdain in eyes set above cheekbones so sharp they looked like they could cut made me wonder how I had ever found her lovely. To say Morene disliked me—and I her—was putting it far too gently.

Pulling at the collar of his police uniform, Isak turned a hard look upon Bain. "We can, and we are. The majority has ruled."

I tensed as footsteps approached from behind. Steel rasped through sisal and my bonds loosened. The rope stuck to my blistered skin in places, forcing me to peel it off. The bastards had soaked it in wolfsbane. I could not say that I blamed them, especially knowing now that it had been Bain who brought me in. He and I had a monumental score that he feared I would settle someday. Having the Council rein me in would make him feel safer. If they hadn't taken such drastic measures with the wolfsbane-soaked ropes, this would have ended quite badly for him. But I had control of my temper now, and a reason not to act out. Yet.

Tossing the rope aside, I rose from the chair, rolled my shoulders, and took a step toward the desk. The group across the table from me tensed as one, several of them moving to rise as well, Bain even baring his teeth. Not wanting to seem too aggressive, I halted. The three who had started to rise sat back down. Relief flashed across Bain's hollow face.

"Allow me to be her *kennari*," I said, making it more of a demand than a question.

Bain's beady eyes narrowed at me and he pulled his lips up farther from his teeth. "Why on Helheimr would we do that?"

"Because I am the closest one you have. And because she has met me. I tried to save her; she will be more likely to trust me," I said.

It was more than that, but I wasn't about to admit it out loud. Hell, I didn't want to admit it to myself. Something about that woman pulled at me. The instant I laid eyes on her I knew she was special. Whatever it was, it was likely what had drawn Raul to her, which meant I had to keep him away from her at all costs. But being her *kennari* would be a double-edged sword, because I would have to keep my distance from her emotionally. The code demanded it. At least she would be safe in my care, though. And a spark was just a spark. I was a grown man in full control of my emotions and libido. Control would not be an issue.

Morene scoffed and rolled her eyes toward the ceiling. The jealousy I saw flash over her sharp features made my stomach roil. Bain muttered something derisive in Icelandic, but I missed part of it due to the others erupting into conversation. They turned to one another, huddling in to speak in hushed, hurried tones. Even from halfway across the room I could hear them, no matter how quiet they tried to be. The fact that they even tried to be quiet spoke of their disbelief in my power. Their eyes darted among one another, to me, and back again as they spoke. As many argued for me as against me. I was not sure whether or not I should take comfort in that. What I did not like was how four of them were arguing to send *kennari*s of their own.

I took another step closer to the desk, bringing their conversation to a screeching halt. "This is not about your reservations in regards to me. This is about a young woman who was bitten in against her will by a wayward pup who was likely trying to avoid an arranged marriage." I paused and nodded toward two of the Council members. "Seeing as Raul is your son"—I paused and nodded toward another pair—"and he's engaged to your daughter, a *kennari* sent from either party would not be impartial. This woman deserves the right to be brought through the *verða* by someone without an agenda. It is the law."

The conversation started back up, but I was encouraged by the nods I received from two of the members who had been arguing to send their own.

"You sure you don't have an agenda of your own?" Morene spoke above the others.

"Careful, Morene. You sound jealous. You dishonor yourself as a Viking woman and your pack if that is the case," I warned.

Her eyes filled with so much hate it looked as though it would spill over. In a way it did. Power rolled off her in a biting wave that raised the temperature in the room. Using my own power, I whipped it away as easily as a summer breeze. She glared harder at me, but it lacked weight this time. Hateful though she was, she knew she couldn't best me and she wouldn't try. I heard the others reach their decision before they announced it.

They fell silent. This time, the woman sitting between Isak and a broad man with a scar across half his face leaned forward. She was a petite thing with long, wavy blond hair. But her demeanor did not fool me. I knew Gyda was more Viking shield maiden than fragile stereotype.

"The majority has ruled. You shall serve as this woman's *kennari*. Please approach her immediately to begin your duties. It is her choice whether or not she attends Raul's trial the day after the next full moon, but we hope you will encourage her to do so," Gyda said.

I nodded my head to them as a whole. A deeper bow was customary, but I did not owe allegiance to any of them, and I was not about to honor them by pretending I did. "I thank you for your wise ruling."

With that, I turned to go. The young man standing between me and the door skittered to the side. Whether it was something he felt in my power, or something he saw in my face, I was not sure. But he cowered in the corner as if I had whipped him within an inch of his life. Helheimr, I half expected him to lose control of his bladder by the look of terror on his face. Then again, maybe it was not my power or my demeanor. Maybe the stories about me truly had grown that bad. I did not care about that or about the Council that once again erupted into conversation the moment my back was turned. All that mattered was getting to that woman and helping her before the *verða* took hold.

CHAPTER FIVE

SONYA

O nly after I had ransacked my apartment for the few belongings I couldn't live without was I finally able to make the fangs go away. The key seemed to be relaxing, something I was not very good at. All those years studying control in *glíma*—the Scandinavian martial art my dad insisted I learn—were what finally helped me do it. For the first time, I wished I had paid more attention to those lessons. Fighting just wasn't my thing. The lack of desire to hurt anyone had always held me back. Or maybe that was because my dad had wanted it to be my thing so badly. My big rebellious idea had been medicine. Go big or go home was my motto, even in rebellion.

Once I choked down the noxious mixture of anger and fear and got my heart to return to a normal rhythm, the fangs simply retracted. They were still there, longer than normal canines—much like Raul's had looked. Nothing too out of the ordinary unless you looked hard. And I couldn't help but look hard. The seemingly ever-present tears in my eyes made me hope I was seeing things. I had no idea what any of this meant, what was happening to me, but I knew I had to find out. And after I did, I was going to kill that crazy son of a bitch, monster or no monster.

A co-worker of mine at the hospital had tested me for drugs and gave me a tetanus shot. Nothing had shown up in my system. The only other thing that made sense was hallucinations caused by rabies. But rabies would have taken longer to set in and damage the brain enough to cause hallucinations. Which came right back around to nothing making sense. Whatever was going on, I had to get it cleared up before fall semester. The fierce competition in the medical profession meant I couldn't afford to miss any time at all. If I did, someone else would get the internship I had been working my ass off for. It was hard enough for a half-Cherokee woman to get ahead in my field. Over my dead body.

Well, I hoped not.

Everything I needed fit inside two duffel bags: a few changes of clothes, my favorite shoes, and my copy of *The Lucifer Effect, Understanding How Good People Turn Evil,* and my extremely worn paperback of Stephen King's *The Stand.* Taking one last look around at my thrift store furniture, I sighed at the sad state of my apartment. In the four years since I had left Washington and landed here, I hadn't accumulated much beyond the necessities. It was hard to while putting yourself through school. There was no dog, cat, or even a goldfish to worry about. Nikki, the closest thing I had to a friend, would only notice my absence because she'd have to work extra shifts. After a month she'd probably forget my name.

The few acquaintances I had in school had probably already forgotten about me since I took a semester off.

The finality of the deadbolt clicking into place as I turned my key brought an unexpected rush of excitement. No matter what Raul was, I looked forward to meeting up with him and grinding his balls into the dirt for what he had done. That, and it didn't hurt that I quit my shit job, was leaving a crappy apartment behind, and was getting out of this sleepy town for a while. One duffel bag over my shoulder, the other in hand, I made my way to where my Jeep was parked on the street.

I tossed my jacket and one duffel bag in the backseat, and the other in the passenger seat. Standing at the door, I paused, wondering if I should wait for the blond stranger who had helped save me in the alley. Worry for him nagged at me. Raul was clearly dangerous. Who knew what he might try to do to the guy. But he had been a big guy, clearly capable of handling himself. Still, the thought of Raul trying to hurt him bothered me, a lot. On the other hand, it had seemed like he knew Raul. If he knew him, he might know what the bastard had done to me, might know a way to fix it.

Or he might be just like him, which meant he could be dangerous too. Best to face the danger I knew rather than the one I didn't. If Raul had wanted to kill me, he clearly would have. No, he wanted something else.

Maybe I would get to see the blond stranger again. I hoped so.

Thunder boomed overhead, followed by a crack of lightning. Longing to play in the storm filled me. But I didn't have time. Forcing thoughts of what all the crap about Raul meant down somewhere deep, I climbed in, started up the Jeep, and grabbed an apple from the duffel bag full of food. Tight red skin gave way to juicy crispness that helped distract me as I turned my radio to a satellite station of hard blues. With Ram Jam screaming about Black Betty from my speakers, I laid rubber down on the asphalt of Twin Falls, Idaho for what might be the last time.

Aside from a few rest stops and fast-food breaks, I drove nonstop for over six hours until I reached Missoula. The fact that I could stay alert that long shocked the hell out of me. Being behind the wheel for over an hour had always made me sleepy. Dad once told me it was because any time I wouldn't stop crying, Mom took me for a ride in the car. It put me right to sleep, every time. The long drive made me think about them, something I hated doing. It hurt too much. He'd been dead and gone for years, and she might as well be.

Despite being a sprawling city with over twenty thousand more people than Twin Falls, the scents of vegetation and water hung here and there on the air, making it almost tolerable. Cities really weren't my thing, having grown up in a remote part of Northern Washington and all, and this one was too big for my liking. The four-story brick building of the Staybridge Suites thrust up into the night sky like a glowing, impenetrable fortress. All right, that was probably my nerves getting the better of me. In all fairness, most of the hotels all around it were as tall, though not nearly as imposing because they didn't hold Raul within their walls.

I parked beside an SUV, shut off the headlights and ignition, and took a few deep breaths. It was going to take every ounce of control I had not to pound the bastard's face in the moment he showed it. Even if he was a monster, I was determined to get a few good hits in before he overcame me. I had to keep my head enough to find out if he had known my dad, if he was using that to get to me. If I met him in the lobby, then I really wanted to be able to control the temper that now raged through me like a blaze well on its way to an inferno.

Several slow, deep breaths later, my teeth stopped aching and the four fangs pulled back up into my gums. For now, that would have to do. The feel of them didn't bring tears to my eyes or nearly throw me into a panic attack anymore. I had mastered enough of my fear during the long drive that I didn't lose it every time the damn things sprang, which was all too often. Not one to carry a purse, I grabbed my jacket, the two duffel bags that held everything I cared about, and started through the dark parking lot for the entrance.

Polished hardwood floors led the way to a modern yet classy-looking reception area. Halfway to the desk, someone stepped in my way. At easily six and a half feet tall, he was the tallest man I had ever seen this close up. Broad shoulders filled out a black T-shirt like they were trying to burst from it. Huge biceps coiled like snakes waiting to strike. This beast of a man had at least fifty pounds of muscle on Raul, and Raul was nicely built. Eyes so blue they looked as if they had been chipped from a glacier regarded me with veiled interest from a clean-shaven face framed by pale blond hair. And dammit if he didn't smell absolutely amazing, like pine and clean water. Not the overly sweet pine scent that came from aftershave or cologne, but the pine of a forest and the clear water of a snow-fed river. Though the last time I had seen him had been on my dark porch step, I recognized him immediately.

How could I not? The thrill that raced through me when I met those icy eyes brought back the memory of his burning touch.

"You're not Raul," I said a bit breathlessly.

Despite his effect on me—or because of it—anger started to boil inside me, making my jaws ache.

One side of his lips curved up. "Thank the Gods. He is...detained at the moment, and I have been sent in his place." The first part was a whisper said through a sneer. His voice reverberated along my bones like chords played on an amplified base guitar. It was a very nice feeling.

Clearly, he didn't like Raul, and that made me like him a little bit more.

Yeah, like that was possible. What the hell was I thinking? My attraction to anyone right now could not be trusted.

He held out a hand. "May I get your bags for you?"

Manners and good looks, a dangerous combination, one I did not trust. Fingers wrapping tighter around the straps, my eyes narrowed. "No, you may not. What do you mean, 'sent'?"

Turning sideways, he motioned to a hallway. "May we at least take your things to our room and go somewhere more private to talk?" His speech wasn't so much old-fashioned as it was the precise wording of one whose first language wasn't English, and had taken their lessons a bit too seriously. But it was nice. Really nice.

My eyes danced across his broad chest. Going somewhere private with him was a bad idea in a colossal way, but I didn't have much choice. I couldn't take him if it came down to a fight. It had been years since I'd attended a *glíma* class, and I hadn't exactly been a model student. I motioned toward the luggage carts behind the reception desk. "Fine, but just send my bags up, that way we can get this over with." I was determined not to go upstairs with him until I had made up my mind about whether or not I'd be safe alone with him.

It did not escape my attention that he had said "our room" with a casual air that implied he was confident it wouldn't bother me. To be honest, with a body and a face like that, it almost didn't. I must have taken a blow to the head somewhere between my porch step and bathroom to even entertain the idea of trusting some big, good-looking guy again. I wasn't ready to trust anyone. But I was picking my battles, as my dad had taught me. Tall, Light, and Handsome cocked his head and raised his blond eyebrows.

"Fair enough." He held his hands out toward my bags with an expectant look.

This time I had no choice but to give them up. He accepted them with a slight nod and carried them over to the desk. The dark-haired female receptionist smiled a little too large for my liking. I didn't care that she was flirting with him. Sexual relations were the last thing on my mind right now. Or so I told myself as I watched his perfectly shaped ass. They exchanged words that I barely paid attention to. Instead, I peeled my eyes off him and scanned the hallways, making note of the rooms and doors.

Only the door I had entered through seemed to lead back outside. Far from ideal if I needed to make a break for it.

"Shall I have them park your Jeep? We can go for a walk," Not-Raul called over his shoulder.

I clutched the keys inside my pocket tighter. "Hell no. We'll take it to wherever we're going." If I had my Jeep I could flee and leave his ass behind if things got too spooky.

"Fair enough. I am all for a lady behind the wheel," he said, quiet and low, making it sound sexier than I wanted it to.

I tried not to shiver, but his effect on me was too strong. Dammit.

Sure, this man seemed nothing like Raul, all polite and proper where Raul was edgy and daring, but that didn't mean I could trust him. My libido was not going to get the best of me again. But, he had helped save me from Raul, so he couldn't be all bad. And then there was the way his skin had felt against mine... True, it had just been his palms on my arms, but the fact that had felt so amazing made me wonder what more would feel like.

He shrugged, laid a few bills on the desk, and strode back toward me. He held his hand out and I stared at it like the snake it could very well be. Slowly, he lowered it and nodded as if this was a perfectly acceptable reaction.

"I am Ty. I am sorry we had to meet like this. If I had known Raul was after you, been another step ahead of him, I could have prevented this entire thing."

My spidey senses began to tingle. "You're not a cop, are you?"

Every muscle in my body tensed in preparation to run. It was a stupid instinct when I hadn't done anything wrong, but I couldn't help it. Heart in my throat, I waited for his answer. Brows scrunching together, he shook his head, the motion releasing some of my tension, but not all of it. Just because he wasn't a cop didn't mean he wasn't an authority. Cops could be funny like that. Detectives, PIs, DEA, some of them didn't call themselves cops, but that didn't make them any less of one in my eyes, which was only a small part of why I didn't trust them. Having watched them haul my dad away at a young age had forever tainted my view of them.

"No, I am a professor."

That was so not what I had been expecting that it rendered me speechless. Part of me relaxed a bit. All those years of sitting in lecture halls had given me a healthy respect for professors. Still, self-preservation made me hang on to my suspicions. For one, I'd never seen a professor this hot. He could be lying. We started to walk for the door.

The moment we were out of the receptionist's hearing, I asked, "A professor that was following or tracking Raul? Why? And what do you mean you could have prevented what happened? What do you think happened?"

Ty held his hands up before him. "Easy. One at a time. Yes, I was following him, trying to find out what he was up to. The rest we will need a bit more privacy to answer."

I ground my teeth as he opened the door for me. I wasn't against a man being gentlemanly, but I didn't want him at my back. The casual way in which he did it made it seem like something ingrained in him. Great, a true gentleman on top of being hot. Just what I needed. They were an endangered species that I had a soft spot for. One thing I didn't need right now was soft spots. I walked backward through the door, keeping my eyes on him. "Why should I let you in my Jeep? How do I know I can trust you?"

The cool night air swept around me.

"Fair enough after what happened to you, and you should not trust anyone right now. That said, you are behind the wheel, in control of my fate. And I did try to save you. If you do not trust me after we talk, you can leave me there and return to your life."

"Fair enough." I threw his own words back at him. It wasn't enough, but the cold metal of the mace pressed against the waistband of my jeans was.

Once outside, he walked straight for my Jeep as if he knew it was mine. Then I realized he had probably watched me pull up. Yeah, that wasn't creepy at all.

"Nice classic you have here. Seventy-nine?" Ty asked. The impressed tone of his voice sent a thrill through me.

I didn't want to warm to him, but his appreciation of my rig hit yet another soft spot. "Seventy-five. It's unlocked," I said as I walked around to the driver's side.

Somehow, he beat me there and opened the door for me. My

traitorous heart thudded harder. Brows raised, I stared at him for a moment before climbing in. He closed the door after me and strode around the Jeep. Dressed all in black as he was, he blended with the night in a way that set my nerves on edge and on fire at the same time. With those long legs of his, he didn't even need to use the rocker bar as a step to climb in. The grace with which he folded his tall, broad frame into my Jeep was a bit distracting, causing me to forget my anger for a moment.

Doing my best to hide my blush behind my long hair, I picked the screwdriver up out of the cup holder and started the Jeep. Being that he seemed to be a jeans and T-shirt kind of guy, I shouldn't have been worried what he would think of my low-budget way of starting my ride. But he had an air of sophistication about him that made me uncomfortable. The way he perused the inside of my Jeep with a boyish smile spread across his face softened me and eased my embarrassment a bit.

"This is amazing."

I smiled and motioned toward the modern stereo. "It isn't exactly stock. But I try to keep it close. Where do you want me to drive?"

He pointed. "To Clark Fork Park. Only a few miles away."

"No. We should go somewhere more public."

He gave me a side-eye look. "Trust me, you do not want to talk about this within earshot of anyone. There are things I have to tell you that will sound insane."

"You aren't exactly imbuing me with confidence right now."

One brow rose in a charming look that I was determined not to let work on me. "I did not save you from Raul only to murder you later. You are safe with me, I promise on my honor."

Damn if he didn't sound convincing as a trickster god. While I had little choice if I wanted answers, that didn't mean I would turn my back on him for a second.

"Fine, but one wrong move and I will make you wish you'd never met me." Pulling out into the light traffic, I followed his directions.

"Did you catch Raul the night...that night?" I asked. I'd almost said the night he bit me, but the words wouldn't come out. Even though this guy had seen it, knew what happened, it still felt too crazy to say out loud.

"I did."

Damn his voice was sexy. Like, slide over your skin and turn your nipples to ball bearings sexy. I gripped the steering wheel harder.

"But he left a note on my Jeep, telling me to meet him here."

Ty shook his head. "A friend of his left it there. They were going to meet you here, take you to his family." He didn't look happy about that.

I raised a brow at him. "And you what? Intercepted them?"

"Not exactly. Shortly after I caught Raul, the authorities caught both of us. When they let me leave, I tracked down one of Raul's men and persuaded him to tell me their plan."

Their plan. I did not like the sound of that. The traffic around us suddenly didn't seem thick enough. More people would be better.

"What did you do to him?" I asked. Blunt though it was, I had to know what kind of man I was dealing with.

Brows furrowing into deep grooves, Ty sat up a bit as he turned to look at me full on. "Nothing untoward, I assure you. Though he would have had it coming." Yeah, English was definitely not this guy's first language. The way he phrased things was as much of a clue as his slight accent. But as much as I hated to admit it—even to myself—that part of him was kind of charming.

"Okay. Sorry, I had to ask. English isn't your first language, is it? That, or you aren't from this century," I said with a snort. My skin along the back of my neck tingled at that thought. But no, I couldn't go there. Not yet. I'd been reading too many horror novels.

A slightly crooked smile tugged his lips up in one corner. "I get that a lot. No, English is not my first language. But I like to think my grasp of it is not that atrocious."

I shook my head. "Not at all. It's impeccable, which is how I could tell. That and the lack of contractions."

He let out a short, humorless laugh. "Yes, well, contractions are the downfall of any language. They are often not even a combination of the proper words one means to speak."

So many more questions burned in my brain, too many. If I kept asking them, there was no way I'd be able to concentrate on driving. Hence the whole detour into the language subject. But that was all the small talk I could take. I allowed a tense silence to fill the Jeep. Well, tense for me. Ty leaned back into his seat and watched the scenery pass by. After a bit, his manner started to relax me, too. It was nice to drive with a guy who didn't feel a need to talk, or worse, to critique my driving. The universe was clearly against me ignoring my libido. I mean, seriously, what kind of guy could be so charming while not doing or saying anything?

Over four miles later, we pulled into a parking lot within a grouping of trees. Through the open window I smelled water—a lot of it. A few people milled about carrying various bags, couples and individuals mostly, all going about their normal lives as if nothing were amiss in the world. But then, I supposed nothing might be amiss in theirs. I was the one who was about to receive news I didn't want to hear. No matter if it was something from a horror movie like I suspected, or simply that I would never see Raul again and miss my chance to pulverize his scrotum.

I leaped from the Jeep, walked around the front of it, and stood with my arms crossed, tapping a foot on the sidewalk. It seemed to take Not-Raul an eternity to unfold his huge frame from the Jeep and join me. I didn't want to think of him as Ty. The name made it more personal, and I didn't want to get personal with this guy. Well, part of me did, but I was ignoring that part.

He moved with an air of confidence that suggested he was a fighter: slow, steady, and aware of everything around him. Not good. Yet very sexy. Swallowing down my impatience and sex drive, I followed in silence as he started down a tree-lined sidewalk. Questions burned my mouth but I didn't dare ask with all the people milling about us. Everything I had to say was going to sound crazy as hell and I didn't want anyone to overhear. He'd been right about that. But it freaked me out that he thought the answers would sound crazy.

"I am sorry we had to meet this way, Sonya." They were the first words he had said to me since I'd stopped asking questions.

That he knew my name was only slightly disturbing considering all the other disturbing things that had been happening to me lately.

"Me too. So what happened to you that night? You said you were coming back; when you didn't, I figured you were a delusion caused by whatever drug Raul slipped me."

Delusion, yeah, fantasy was more like it, of the Thor in clingy Under Armor variety. But I wasn't about to say that. Why did this guy affect me so much?

"The authorities took me in, thinking I was the one who had attacked you. I set them straight and came back for you," he said.

"But I never called the cops."

No one did. I was sure of it. If someone had I wouldn't have lain on the bathroom floor for two days in a pool of my own blood.

"Not your authorities. Mine," he said.

The hushed tone along with the way he looked away from me made it clear he didn't mean the Montana State Police versus the Idaho State Police. No, he meant something else entirely, something that had to do with the fangs that sprang from my jaw every time I got pissed. Just thinking about it made my heart race as though it were trying to escape the truth. A huge part of me fantasized that he was with the DEA and was after Raul because of some wicked new psychotropic drug he was pedaling. That would make far more sense to my scientific mind, which was exactly why I knew that wasn't it. Being raised by a dad who practiced Odinism, and a Cherokee mom who believed in the old ways, meant sense and logic weren't places I often got to visit.

The sound of moving water drained some of my tension away as we wound along a riverside dotted with trees. The further we walked, the more scarce people became. Whether it was due to the lack of people, or the shadows in which I could hide, the trees soothed me, eased my anxiety. Once we reached a part of the path void of others, I stopped and moved into Ty's way. We were alone and I was done with all the eluding. Damn, but he was tall. And that chest looked really hard. My fingers wanted to dance across it. I had to step back and crane my neck to see his face.

"Your authorities, Montana police, you mean? If the police knew about the attack, why didn't anyone contact me?"

Blond brows rose. "Those are the first questions you have for me?"

My patience wore as thin as rice paper. "Yes." It came out sounding like a growl, a growl that freaked me out more than a little.

My gaze flicked to the nearest couple walking some distance away on the path. Maybe coming all the way out here with him had been a bad idea. I took a step back in the direction of the oncoming people.

He held his hands up in surrender then leaned against the trunk of a tree. "As you suspect, the police do not know. I meant my kind's authorities, not Montana's. What Raul did to you broke our laws. He will stand trial for it. I was sent by them to be your *kennari*."

I swallowed hard and decided to go for the first tough question I could take. "What exactly did he do to me?"

Guarded eyes shifted from the undulating green river to me. "What do you think he did to you?"

One side of my top lip curled up, exposing the fangs that had sprung forth on an instinct that I could only assume was born of my anger and fear. "Don't play games with me," I snarled.

His gaze didn't waver from mine. "I am not. I need to know how much you are ready to accept so I know how fast to take your instruction."

So much was wrong with that. But the words confirmed my suspicions. I was going to have to sound like a crazy person and see where this led. "He bit me and it...*changed* me. I thought he had drugged me at first, but then..." I motioned to the fangs.

The world started to sway a bit, growing fuzzy around the edges as it closed in around me. Tears stung my eyes, again, dammit. I couldn't explain it away with science and that made me feel crazy, made my world feel crazy.

"Look, I'm ready to hear it. I need to know what's happening to me. It's just all a bit insane, you know?" My voice broke, making me want to crawl into a hole and hide. I hated letting others see when I felt weak.

"I know. I am sorry."

Suddenly Ty stood before me. His big arms wrapped around me, pulling me in against his chest. Going stiff, I held my breath. The warmth of his hard body soon melted through my resistance. Without meaning to, I relaxed against him, sinking into his arms and molding myself against his chest. The scents of sweet pine and an aloe glycerin soap enveloped me. The tide of my troubles receded. Somehow this stranger put me at ease in a way no one else ever had besides my dad. Something about him tugged at something inside me. I both loved and hated the feeling at the same time. After a long moment, I forced myself to pull away.

The thoughtful, surprised look in his eyes suggested maybe he had felt the tug too. I lifted my chin and crossed my arms beneath my breasts. His left hand opened and for a second I thought he was going to reach out to me, but then his arm dropped to his side.

"Aside from the fangs, your senses are also stronger—smell, hearing."

Though it wasn't a question, I nodded. The fact that he went on while I was so obviously close to losing my shit made me like him even more. A guy that respected a lady's wishes even if he didn't agree with them couldn't be all bad.

"Did he tell you anything? Did he ask your permission?"

In the shadows it was difficult to tell, but his expression looked serious, as though my answers held a lot of weight. Suddenly that weight pressed down on me as I realized the unfathomable depths of what I had gotten myself into. I had an overwhelming feeling that the world—mine in particular—was about to get far more complicated and interesting.

I had to take a long breath that shuddered through my chest before I could go on. "Not much. He said he wanted to see the world, travel, and that I seemed like someone he could do it with. As for permission, why the hell would I give him permission to bite me? I'm not into that kinky shit."

Sighing, Ty ran his hand through his hair. "So he did not tell you anything about what the bite meant? He did not ask you if you wanted it?" The precise way he worded things told me the answer would be important.

Blood scorched its way up to my face. Normally I wasn't one to blush, but the flashback of Raul's body pressed against mine, hands all over me as he asked me if I wanted it, was too much. Or maybe it was the hot mountain of a man standing next to me asking about it that really did it. I turned my own gaze out over the slow-moving water so I wouldn't have to face him. The attraction to Ty was starting to bug me. Sure, Raul had left me far from satisfied, but I wasn't one to drool after a man because he was hot as Hades.

"No, he didn't ask if he could bite me, or if I wanted him to. And he definitely didn't say anything about what it would do to me."

A low, rumbling growl unlike anything I'd ever heard come from a human throat issued from Ty. The glow of the distant streetlights was barely enough to gleam off the edge of what I thought might be fangs exposed by his curled upper lip. Knees growing weak, I stumbled back heavily against a tree. Part of me wanted to get as far away from all this craziness—and Ty—as fast as I could, while a much bigger part wanted right back in his arms. Whatever was wrong with me, was wrong with Ty as well. It made me afraid of him and drawn to him at the same time. Hell, I was kidding myself and it was getting old.

"That bite changed me into something, something both you and Raul are, didn't it?" I asked. Voicing it made it hard to breathe. I became light-headed and things began to blur and sway.

From behind a fringe of blond hair that reached below eyes filled with concern, Ty's piercing blue gaze found me. He smiled, the hint of fangs gone save for a few pointy canines. "Yes, you are in the process of changing. You seem to be taking this rather well."

"Sure, if you consider being on the verge of a panic attack *well*." My voice shook as much as I did. I sucked in a deep breath to give my brain some air so I could think. "I've seen a lot of things as a med student, some that couldn't be explained away. And I'm not naive. I know even more exists in this world than I have seen with my own eyes."

The reality of that statement made it easier to breathe and stopped things from swaying a bit. Some part of me had always known there were worlds within worlds, things that couldn't be explained away with logic. The self-preserving instinct in me made me hold my tongue about my dad. I didn't know this guy from Raul, so there was no way I was going to tell him that my dad had told me stories about Viking werewolves my whole childhood. He didn't need to know my dad had believed the stories, talked about Loki and his wolf-child Fenrir as if they were real. If Ty knew something about my dad, I wanted him to be the one to say it. I wasn't about to give him any information about me he didn't need.

Ty made that low, rumbling sound again that vibrated through my core in a very pleasant way. "Hmm, wise and beautiful. No wonder he chose you."

Stifling the feeling both the rumble and his words awakened, I fought the impulse to turn away. Such feelings were what had gotten me into this mess in the first place. Well, not quite. With Raul it had been more about how terribly long it had been since I'd had sex. That and his slippery charms, if I was going to be completely honest with myself. I opened my mouth to ask my next question but promptly shut it when I heard footsteps on the bridge. A glance back toward the parking area revealed a couple stepping onto the bridge some fifty feet away.

"Shall we walk over to the park where we can find more privacy?" Ty asked.

With a nod, I shoved my fisted hands into my pockets to keep from looking like I was itching for a fight—which I was at this point—and followed him. What could I say? It was a defense mechanism of mine that reared its ugly head when I got stressed.

The questions burning a hole through my tongue had to wait as we walked farther down the path and wove our way through couples and a few families. After walking beside a bend in the widening river, we veered off onto one of the paved paths that led deeper into the trees. Soon we were shrouded in shadows even the distant streetlamps didn't reach. Ty stopped and sat down on a bench that looked out over the river, inviting me to sit beside him with a wave of his hand. Getting as far to the opposite end of it as I could, I sat, turning sideways with one leg pulled up partially beneath me. The position not only gave me a good view of his nice profile, but would help launch me to my feet faster should I need to run.

"What do you mean 'in the process,' and what am I changing into?" I asked. The world started to close in again. Recognizing the signs this time, I took several deep breaths to stave off the tunnel vision that came before a panic attack. It worked, a little. The dark tunnel trying to close around me opened up.

Even in the dim light I could see the calculating look in his eyes as they met my gaze. He stretched an arm up onto the back of the bench, fingers just barely brushing my shoulder. The light touch banished my panic far better than a few calculated breaths ever could. "Your DNA is changing; that takes time. You are changing into a *varúlfur*, but you will still be you, only enhanced."

"Wait, I'm changing into a...*varúlfur*? What is that, even?" Coming out of my throat it sounded like a completely different word.

Half of his mouth quirked up into what I had to admit was a handsome grin. "*Varúlfur*, or in English..." He paused and stared hard at me before finishing. "A werewolf."

Though I had been expecting something like it, the words hit me like a hard slap. It explained the fangs, and it meant some of my dad's old stories were true. I'd always written them off as the ramblings of an overly religious man. Head dropping into my hands, I leaned forward until my elbows rested on my knees. It was too much. Could my dad's stories seriously have been true?

It had never bothered him that I didn't embrace his religion. He always said I'd understand someday. Was this what he'd meant? More than ever, I wished I could talk to him again. Tears began to drip between my fingers. Jeans brushed against steel as Ty slid over next to me. His arm came to rest on my shoulders, warm and heavy. He didn't pull me in against his chest this time, but I wanted him to, oh how I wanted him to.

That was twice tonight I had let a practical stranger see me weak. I leaped to my feet and began to pace before the bench.

"That bastard. All the leading questions and conversation... Dammit!" It served me right for being attracted to a man with a fast car. Whether all this shit was true or not, and I wasn't sure it was yet, that I had made a colossal mistake with Raul was clear.

Spinning on Ty, I fixed him with a hard look. It might not be his fault, but he was the only one I had on hand to focus my anger on. "Why would he do this to me?"

Sadness filled Ty's eyes. "To make you his."

A feral-sounding growl tore from my throat, frightening me almost as much as the fangs that sprang forth. Now I really, really wanted to hurt this bastard. Moisture stung my eyes. I looked down before Ty could notice. Pinecones and goose droppings littered the sidewalk, but I was able to avoid them by mostly smell alone. This fact only disturbed me more. My mind searched for conditions and disorders that heightened senses, but everything I came up with was almost as improbable as becoming a werewolf. I kicked hard at one of the pinecones, sending it flying off into the night. It took a lot of deep breaths to get my fangs to go away.

Fangs. Fucking hell.

In mid-pace, I stopped before Ty. "I'm going to turn into a monster on the full moon?"

He shook his head. "You will still be who you are. If you are not a monster now, neither you nor your wolf self will be a monster. Forget the legends. Very little of them are true."

Resuming my pacing, I took a few strides to breathe before asking my next question. "So I won't feel the overwhelming urge to eat people?"

Laughter erupted from Ty, the deep kind that vibrated along muscles at my apex of my legs. "Gods, no. Can you imagine how bad humans must taste? With all the garbage they put into their bodies?"

I was not convinced. "No overwhelming urge to feed every full moon? You're sure?"

"Do you have an eating disorder now?"

"No," I snapped.

Was this a game to him? The touch of humor in his voice suggested it might be. Just when I thought this might all be some big joke, my teeth began to ache again. "What about these fangs growing every time I get mad?"

He shrugged one broad shoulder. "Emotions evoke instincts in your wolf. You must simply learn to control them."

I ran a hand through my hair, forcing myself not to clutch at the long black locks and pull. It wasn't easy. The struggle made me remember something he said. "You mentioned you were here to be my *kennari*. What does that mean?"

"Roughly, it means teacher. I am here to help you through the *verða*—becoming—then to take you to Raul's trial, if you wish to go." The guarded tone in his voice made me stop and take a long, hard look at him.

My mind spun with a million different thoughts, questions. Even though I had suspected such creatures existed for years, it was too much to take in, too impossible. "I take it there's no cure."

"No."

Hands gripping my hair, I sat down on the bench—hard—and rested my elbows on my knees. "Of course there isn't. Just my luck."

No tears would come, though it felt like I should lament the life stolen from me. Crying wasn't working, so there was no point. Screaming...now *that* I really wanted to do, and was close to it.

"So much for being a doctor," I mumbled.

"You wanted to be a doctor, like a surgeon?" Ty asked, eyes wide.

My own gaze hardened. Why did people always find that so hard to believe? "Not exactly. I was close, dammit. One more year of med school..."

"A surgeon. Truly?"

"At first, yeah. But after so long in med school I'm more interested in the inside of a person, mentally. But none of that matters now."

Ty leaned a bit closer but didn't reach out to me. "I am sorry this was forced upon you. Such things are not done anymore. Raul was out of line and will be punished. You can still have a normal life after this is over."

Bones ached as fangs grew within my mouth. Normal, yeah right. Only if crazy was the new normal. "I want to be the one to punish him."

To my surprise, Ty nodded. "That is your right. You will be given the opportunity to do so after his sentencing, and you will be able to pass down his sentence, with the Council's approval."

Anger spread out from my center as if riding on my very blood itself. The sensation reminded me of hard whiskey burning all the way down to one's stomach, only in reverse. My skin crawled as if the tiny hairs along it had been stirred by a breeze. Sitting back against the bench, I rubbed my arms. The crawling magnified, turned into a burning, as if that breeze were now brushing against sunburned skin.

"Easy, there, easy," Ty soothed, a hand reaching out to touch my arm.

His cool fingers helped ground me, bring me back to myself a bit. That glacial gaze of his pulled me back from the brink of rage so completely I found myself leaning toward him as if those eyes were magnetic. But it had to be more than that because he began to lean toward me as well.

"It is best not to focus on anything that makes you angry for the first week or so," he said, breaking the spell.

Inches from his face, I leaned away quickly, feeling utterly foolish. "What if I don't want your help with the becoming?"

His big fingers wove through each other as if he needed to keep his hands busy. "That part is not an option. Every new *varúlfur* must be guided through the *verða* by a *kennari*. That is the law, and for good reason. There is a lot to learn that will keep not only you, but those around you, alive."

I sat up straighter, palms pointed skyward. "So I *will* feel compelled to kill people?"

Blond hair light as wheat flashed in the streetlights bouncing off the river as he shook his head. "No. But your emotions are heightened and they will be harder to control. If you get angry and lose that control…" His voice trailed off as he shrugged.

Sighing, I nodded as I tried to take it all in. "I get it. So I can control this thing with help. Will I actually turn into a wolf?" My voice dropped to a whisper on the last part.

A gentleness entered his eyes, softening them like spring melt. Oh damn, now his pretty eyes had me thinking all poetic. "Yes, but it isn't like the movies or books. You will be able to change at will. Emotions will be heightened during the full moon, but it will not force you to change. You will want to that much more."

Hell, why not dive head first into the crazy? "Will it hurt?" I was no stranger to pain, and a hard life had given me a high threshold, but I wasn't looking forward to more.

"Only if you fight it, like how your jaws ache when you try to hold back the fangs. I will teach you to control your emotions, and that will help curb the instinct to shift."

The fact that he knew about that made it seem more real, more plausible that he wasn't pulling my leg. Obviously, he wasn't. The fangs made that clear. But still, part of my mind couldn't let go of the possibility that this was all a hoax. Sadly, that part grew smaller by the moment. The breath in my lungs eased out. There was one more thing I had to know sooner rather than later.

"You said something about being sorry you didn't get to Raul before he bit me. Did you know he was going to do this?"

He shook his head. "I suspected he was searching for a woman to bite in to be his mate, and since I knew he did not have the Council's permission, I was following him to keep an eye on him. I had no idea he would go to the extreme of biting someone in without their permission and knowledge."

After a long moment he stood and offered me his hand.

"I have overwhelmed you enough for one day. What do you say we get you something to eat, then let you rest?"

My stomach growled at the words. The bag of food I had filled from my pathetically stocked kitchen had run out and it had been hours since I'd eaten. Even then, that had been a granola bar. I accepted his hand and let him help me to my feet. The warmth of his rough palm felt amazing, like a hot tub I wanted to sink into. It was all I could do to force myself to let go. I needed to get this over with, get back to med school, and most importantly get away from this guy before I made another poor decision.

"All right, let's go. But, Ty, will you promise me one thing?"

He grinned. "Only one?"

My expression hardened. "Only one. Don't keep secrets from me."

His smile vanished as if blown away by my words. "I promise."

We walked back to the Jeep in silence, if I didn't count the chaos of thoughts going off like fireworks in my head. Part of me wished Ty hadn't been the one to be here, hadn't told me all of this. But not knowing wouldn't change it. The world had upended, leaving me drowning in a foreign universe. I was bad at being human. How I was going to be a werewolf, I had no idea.

CHAPTER SIX

TY

W e rode back from the park in a tense silence broken only by the buzz of traffic around us. From across her classic Jeep, I did my best to sneak looks at her without getting caught. I could not help it. Everything about her, from her slightly pouty lips and remarkable brown eyes to her long, jet-black hair, drew me in. Amazing. But I was not as shallow as all that. More pulled at me than her knockout looks.

The way she was handling all this, for one, was pretty impressive. I had never known a newly bitten, but I did not imagine any of them took it in such easy stride. True, anger radiated off her, but she was not afraid. Even if she had been able to hide it from me, I would have smelled it. But all I smelled coming off her was her unique spicy scent that managed to be feminine and sultry at the same time. From her adaptability to her spunkiness, none of it was what I had expected out of a woman chosen by Raul. She surprised me, and I liked that more than I cared to admit. But I had to admit it to myself, if only to strengthen my resolve to keep my distance.

It was not just that she had been traumatized by Raul. From what I had been taught, over half of the newly bitten did not make it through the *verða*. They lost their sanity, meaning they could not control their wolf selves, which resulted in them having to be put down. Any big distractions, like family, friends, or attachments could mean the difference in her surviving or not. I would not be the reason my first assignment did not make it.

I wanted to be a gentleman and allow her to be the one to break the silence, but there was so much I wanted to know about her. There were things I *needed* to know.

"We will be away for a while. Do you have anyone you need to contact?" Not the most subtle way to find out if she was involved with someone or would have complications with the *verða*, but it was a legitimate reason. We could not have anyone looking for her.

She snorted and damn if it was not cute as hell.

"No."

Her voice slid over me like mist, tingling and hair-raising. The sensation traveled all the way down to my cock, threatening to make it stand up and take notice. I forced my mind to recall the most boring thesis I had the displeasure of reading last year. By the third chapter I had stopped my blood from flowing to my groin. A crude method, but effective. *Nemi*, she was my *nemi*, damn it.

"No family or friends that might worry?" I asked once I could focus again.

We rolled to a stop at a red light.

Her voice dropped in both volume and energy as she glanced out the driver's side window. "No. You don't have to worry. No one will come looking for me."

That statement held a world of pain and unsaid words. I tried to catch a glimpse of her expression, but she would not turn back to me.

"I apologize. I did not mean to pry into painful territory, but I had to know if there might be complications."

She shrugged and looked back at the road as the light turned green. "Don't worry about it. I'm a struggling college student who tended bar in a town far from the place I grew up in until yesterday. College students don't have time for complications," she said, voice carefully controlled.

A *War and Peace*–sized novel of unsaid words lay within her tone, but I was not going to press, not yet. The comment did make me wonder, though. Did I need to rethink my first thought of Raul choosing her because she was special? That she was special, I had no doubt. But Raul was a bit too shallow and dim-witted to put that much thought into his choice. It was easier to believe he had chosen her because she had very few connections to her community and might not be missed for a while.

"That is most certainly the rest of the world's loss," I told her, unable to not say at least something. It was hard to imagine anyone not missing this woman.

She shot me a sideways glance filled with a mixture of distrust and appreciation. Someone had hurt her, badly, and I was guessing it was not just Raul. She did not reply and I did not press the issue. To do so would only make it worse. I could tell by the way her eyes narrowed. Trust was a long way off yet.

We pulled into the parking garage and walked through the darkness back to our hotel room in silence. She peered into every shadow as if expecting something nefarious to leap out of it. But she did not look ready to flee. She looked ready to fight. I had to hide a smile as I opened the hotel room door for her and stepped aside to allow her entry first. She cocked an eyebrow at me as she entered, never quite turning her back to me. A breath eased from her as her eyes scanned the two queen beds.

"I took the liberty of changing the room Raul had reserved to one with two queen beds. I tried to get a suite with a sofa sleeper in a separate room, but one was not available," I said.

"Thanks," she snapped.

I hoped the sharpness in her tone had more to do with the idea of meeting Raul here than it did with anything I had said or done. Unless, of course, she was disappointed in the idea of not sharing a bed with me... No. I couldn't let my mind go down that road. She was attractive, yes. But I was to be her *kennari*. Which meant I would have to be on my best behavior. Ancient law forbid *kennari* to get involved with—let alone copulate with—their *nemi* for good reason. Going through the change heightened everything, emotions included. Taking advantage of her, let alone being a potentially deadly distraction, was not something I was willing to do. No matter how delicious those large breasts looked or how alluring her strength and resilience were, it was not worth the pain such an indulgence would cause.

I took my time at the door, allowing her to choose which bed she wanted. She dropped her bag—which she had vehemently refused to allow me to carry from where the valet had left it inside the door—onto the bed farthest from the door. Such good instincts made me smile, and I had to quickly turn away so she would not see and misinterpret it.

The peel of her bag's zipper seemed infinitely loud in the silence that fell. After pulling a number of items out of it, she looked up at me. Though her mouth was set in a hard line, a softness in her eyes told me her anger was dissipating.

"I didn't mean to snap. I'm sorry. Just hearing his name kind of pisses me off," she said.

This time I let the grin pulling at the edges of my mouth show a bit. "I understand." Oh, did I ever.

Toothbrush and paste in one hand and clothes in the other, she started for the bathroom. "I hope you don't mind if I crash right away. I'm kind of wiped out," she called over her shoulder as she entered the bathroom.

"Of course. I understand," I said.

The door closed behind her and I did my best not to picture her changing. Those long, darkly tanned legs, that perfectly shaped ass... Yes, I completely failed.

Sleep remained elusive and sporadic, and not only because I was worried about Raul sending some of his friends after her. Despite the Council's ruling, he was bound to try. The arrogant *asni* would not give up after going through all the trouble of biting her in. He had taken a huge risk. Incarcerated though he was, he would fight to finish making her his. If he did not, he would be condemned to an arranged marriage. And that was the last thing Raul wanted, player that he was. Of that I was sure. But that was not the main reason I tossed and turned all night.

Sonya's soft, steady breathing might as well have been brushing across the sensitive skin of my ears. She slept heavy due to the *verða*. Her spicy scent crept down into me, warming me and stirring my blood. I could not stop thinking about the spark that lit her eyes, the strength that kept her together when so many others would have crumbled. The way her hair shone in the light that filtered through the hotel curtain made it look like spilled silk around her curvy silhouette. A constant hard-on made it difficult to sleep, to say the least.

I just had to hold out through the full moon, when the *verða* was over. Then, if I still felt this way and she was interested, I could possibly pursue something with her. The strength of my reaction to her surprised me. After what had happened with my last girlfriend, I had not expected to feel this way about anyone again. A professional distance was best not only for her sake, but my own as well.

Less than an hour before dawn, I could not take it anymore. I rose, made my bed, and grabbed a fresh change of clothes. After placing a chair in front of the motel room door just in case, I started for the bathroom. One last glimpse at Sonya revealed the thin sheet covering her had been cast aside. The tantalizing curve of her ass cheeks was more exposed than covered by her incredibly short cotton shorts. My blood rushed to all the wrong places, making me hurry to the shower. Cold though the water was, it could not cool the heat radiating from within me. I turned it down even colder. The water pounded against me, running down the sensitive skin of my cock, making me harder. I could not take it. To go back out there and show any modicum of professionalism, I was going to need release.

I grabbed a bar of soap in one hand, my cock in the other, and went to work.

CHAPTER SEVEN

SONYA

The sound of a shower running yanked me from the slumber of the dead. All right, not quite the slumber of the dead. I was becoming a werewolf, not a vampire. Eyes opening to take in the hotel room crowded with two queen beds, I froze. Sunlight seeped in to frame the curtains drawn over a huge window on the opposite side of the room. Not more than three feet from the side of my bed, Ty's bed lay empty, made up perfectly. If not for the sound of the shower and the sight of his hiking boots sitting on the floor at the foot of his bed, I might have thought yesterday had been a dream. But then, there was no way I would have dreamed up such a sexy guy only to have a disturbing conversation with him.

Yawning, I sat up, eager to get away from the overwhelming smell of the flowery fabric softener that had been used on the sheets. The scent made me want to hurl. Muscles stretching with ease, I yawned and raised my arms above my head. Blood pumped through my veins at the thought of all Ty had told me yesterday. At least, I tried to convince myself it was our conversation and not the memory of how he had filled out the clingy muscle shirt that caused the reaction. Why did he have to be so fine?

It didn't matter that he was nice, polite, was a career man, and had just a touch of a sexy accent. I needed to focus on myself right now. Getting through this craziness and being strong on my own had to be my priority. The sooner this becoming stuff was over and I had a handle on everything, the sooner I could get back to paying off my student debts enough to return to school.

I realized I felt good, well rested, and almost eager. When I had lain down last night, I hadn't thought I'd be able to sleep at all. Not only had my head been buzzing with all I had learned, and wanted to learn, I had been in a room with a stranger I didn't exactly trust yet. A stranger who was a werewolf.

The water shut off, but even over the bathroom's exhaust fan I heard the *drip, drip, drip* of the showerhead. A towel bar rattled, filling my mind with a delicious image I had no time to be picturing. In only a little tank with a built-in bra and cotton shorts that barely covered the cheeks of my ass, I wasn't exactly dressed for company. It made me wonder, had I been under the blankets when he'd walked to the bathroom? The idea of him getting an eyeful excited me in ways I wasn't ready for yet. I couldn't trust my judgment after Raul.

A groan slid from me as I jumped from the bed, retrieved my bag, and dug out something to wear. A pair of black panties followed by my favorite blue jeans—they were all I had left that was clean—made me feel a touch less vulnerable. As I pulled the last shoulder strap of my lace bra on, soft footsteps padded on the carpet.

A sharp intake of breath followed by what I thought might be a curse word in a foreign language came from Ty in a husky whisper.

"I am sorry," he said after a moment. Yet he didn't leave the room.

Like the ghostly fingers of seduction, his scent drifted to me: soap and shampoo that had the bare scent of those natural shampoos people make at home. Beneath it, like a present waiting to be unwrapped, lay his alluring male musk. I knew I shouldn't have been able to smell such details, but then, I shouldn't be sprouting fangs every time I got pissed, either. He smelled so enticing that I didn't mind the former.

Back turned, I tried to pretend I wasn't worried too much about modesty. I picked up my T-shirt and pulled it on. "No need. So what is that language? I'm guessing it's the same one as those words you spoke last night, am I right?" I could almost place it, but I needed to hear him say it to make it real.

I turned around and moved to sit on the edge of the bed. Despite the half-naked mountain of muscle standing there, I managed to keep the movement natural looking as I eased onto the bed. As if the sight of him with only a towel wrapped around his waist didn't completely fluster me— yeah, right. It was a very good thing I had gotten the words out before I turned around, because my tongue was immobile in my mouth. The man's six-pack was outshined only by pectorals and arms that would make the most dedicated gym rat jealous. And the tattoos. Oh my God, the tattoos. Swirls and intricate knots wove around his arm and partway across his chest, accenting his muscles in the most delicious way. All this time I had been trying to convince myself that what lay beneath his T-shirt wasn't nearly as good as the cloth made it look. I had never been so happy to be so wrong.

"Icelandic."

With all those planes of hard flesh before me, it took a moment to remember I had asked him a question, and a few more to remember what it was. After an embarrassingly long pause in which I regained my composure, I asked, "You're from Iceland?" It would explain the tattoos that made him look as though he'd stepped off a Viking ship. Yet another tie-in to my dad's beliefs and all those stories he told me when I was a kid. A shiver tried to run through me.

"No."

Slowly, as if taunting me with all those delicious valleys and mountains of muscle, he crossed the room, picked up his bag, and walked back to the bathroom. My eyes widened as they took in the knotwork tattoo that continued from his arms, across his shoulders, and down his back. On his right biceps was a circle with Norse runes around it like the numbers on a clock, and in the center of that was a wolf's head done in knotwork. It was the same symbol from the back of Raul's jacket. The one that I had found so eerily similar to one of my dad's tattoos. It had to be connected.

Ty didn't close the door. I couldn't see him, but that didn't stop my mind from picturing that towel dropping to the floor a moment before I heard it hit.

"I am originally from Hemlock Hollow, Montana. My ancestors were from Iceland."

Not far removed by that tantalizing hint of an accent. Unlike Raul, who sounded very American. But then, for all I knew, he worked on sounding that way. Anger, shame, and an unhealthy dose of self-loathing flashed through me. Since both had ancestors from Iceland, and both were werewolves, it made me wonder what else they had in common. Though I had no intentions of the horizontal variety on this guy, I still didn't want him to be a thing like that bastard. "Do you belong to the same pack Raul does?" I snapped.

His head poked out around the doorframe. Furrowed brows pinched his blue eyes. "Definitely not. The mark from his jacket, the one on my back, it is the symbol of our ancestors."

Chills danced along my skin. My dad had said something like that.

His head disappeared into the bathroom again.

My mouth opened, but the words wouldn't come out. I didn't know this guy well enough to trust him with info like that yet. The fact that I was ridiculously attracted to him made me want to trust him less, not more.

I tried to focus on something else. "What do the rockers on Raul's jacket mean? Is he in a gang?"

"AVW stands for American Viking Werewolf. Montana is the state he hails from. Many of our kind belong to a secondary organization—an umbrella pack some call it—in addition to their pack. It helps keep them connected to our kind all across the world and adds strength to their pack."

The water came on and I waited for it to shut off before asking my next question. "Do you belong to an...umbrella pack?"

Silence stretched out so long, I didn't think he was going to answer.

"I am a lone wolf," he finally said, voice husky with vulnerability.

That he wasn't a member of an organization—umbrella pack, whatever he wanted to call it—was a huge relief. Yet, I couldn't lie to myself. Seeing him behind the wheel of a muscle car or straddling a racing motorcycle would be hot. Again, my mind had to beat back my traitorous imagination and recall what we were talking about. "Is that where Raul's trial will be? Hemlock Hollow?" The anger caused by speaking that man's name helped burn away my desire, bringing focus.

"Yes, and that is where we are going, eventually, if you wish to go to the trial." Ty's voice grew louder as he walked out of the bathroom, unfortunately fully dressed. Even the way the man talked was sexy, all grammatically correct and scholarly. Oh God, I had never been hot for a teacher. Med school didn't leave time for such juvenile things. What the hell was happening to me?

Jeans and a dark blue T-shirt, both tight enough to suggest the wonders that I now knew lay beneath, clad all that gorgeous skin. Well, I didn't know *all* that lay beneath... I had to drag my eyes up from his crotch to meet his gaze. Along the way I couldn't help but notice the smug smile on his face. And was that a hint of desire in his own eyes?

"I wouldn't miss it," I said as I stood, hands curling into fists.

Ty shook his head, his wet locks sending droplets flying. "Beautiful and dangerous." He blinked twice, hard, and forced his gaze away. "I apologize, that was inappropriate."

A thrill shot straight down to my groin. I grinned. "Flattery will get you everywhere." I hadn't meant for it to sound so dirty, but it was out and taking it back would only make it worse.

A grin flashed before he turned away.

At twenty-seven years old, I wasn't about to swoon over a sexy guy calling me beautiful. Quite the contrary. Or so I told myself. It gave me power, a power I might have to use later. While he gathered his things I pulled my shoes on and tried not to watch him too much. It was difficult. He moved with a grace unusual for a man his size. All the body builders I had seen at the gym had a stiffness to their movements, as if their muscles weren't used to much more than lifting weights. Ty moved with a fluidity that was almost mesmerizing. Now who had the power? *Ugh.*

"I'm ready to hit the road. Where is this Hemlock Hollow?" I asked as I put my jacket on and slung my bag over my shoulder.

"Northwest, far north."

He opened the door and stepped aside for me. Charming as it was, prickles of caution traveled across my back as I bared it to him when I walked past. Only after he stepped alongside me in the hall did the tension drain from me.

"So what's the plan then? We head for Hemlock Hollow?"

His face went stoic as a shadow passed over it, one that told me he wasn't eager to go to Hemlock Hollow. He shook his head. "The trial is not until after the full moon, so we have a few weeks. We must get you through the *verða* by then, anyway. You do not want to go to Hemlock Hollow until after that."

"Why?" I couldn't keep the suspicion from my voice, and I didn't try.

Eyes locked on the long hallway ahead, he answered, "Three packs inhabit the town and right now they are...at odds. Your creation has only amplified the tension. You need to be at your full strength before meeting any of them."

Three packs. I wasn't sure which bothered me more: knowing there were that many, or hearing them called packs. It made it all feel like a fantasy. But fantasies didn't sprout fangs that were all too real, fangs that were pushing at my lips right now. "Why do I need to be at full strength?"

Though we had reached the end of the hall, he stared at the elevator. From the distant sound and the vibrations coming through the floor, it was clearly several floors down. Still, he stared at the closed steel doors and did not answer. I grabbed his rock-hard biceps, and with a show of strength that surprised me, turned him toward me. If I was going to take the trip to crazy town, I had to know more.

"Why?" I demanded.

His chest collapsed inward a bit as a long breath blew from him. "The answer will infuriate you, and being newly bitten, that could force you to change. I will tell you, I promise, but not until you have had a chance to get more control over your wolf. It is not safe."

Whoa. My mind conjured up every horror movie I'd ever seen in which a werewolf changed violently and painfully. I so wasn't ready for anything remotely close to that. The answer wasn't worth it, not yet. The elevator arrived with a hollow *ding*, opening to an empty chamber. We stepped inside and leaned against opposite walls, staring at each other.

My anger receded enough that the burning beneath my skin cooled and the ache in my jaws faded. "Will I look like something out of a horror movie, or just like a wolf?"

"A wolf, unless you count the fangs and claws you can grow while in human form."

Pushing away the panic, I thought about that for a moment. "If I can control it, those could be useful."

His lips turned up into the beginning of a grin, and he nodded. The elevator settled on the lobby floor with a jolt that wrenched my gaze from his captivating eyes. Part of me wanted to know if the pull I felt toward him was a werewolf thing, but I didn't dare ask in case it was something far more basic. With a nod and a look, he invited me to leave the elevator first.

He walked straight for the exit. The desk clerk didn't even look up as we passed.

"Already settled the bill?" I asked as we reached the doors.

A full—oh-so-handsome—grin dimpled both of his cheeks. Seeing it made me ache on a level I didn't want to think about. "Yep. This one's on Raul."

Laughter spilled from me as we stepped out into the bright morning. Served him right. He had that and so much more coming. The scents of concrete and exhaust fumes assaulted my nose. And was that garbage I could smell? Crinkling my nose up and attempting to breathe through my mouth, I led the way toward the parking garage.

"Wow, this city smells bad," I said.

Stepping up beside me as we entered the shade of the many-tiered garage, Ty nodded. "That is the *verða*. Your sense of smell is stronger than it has ever been, and it will get stronger still."

Voices drifted to me, along with the sounds of keys jingling and luggage being dropped into a trunk. Though the people were nowhere in sight, I could almost swear I heard the groan of the car's shocks as they got in it.

"Right, the canine thing," I said softly.

If a lot of werewolves occupied this Hemlock Hollow, I could see how I might be at a disadvantage. "How many..." I searched my memory for the Icelandic word he had used, in case anyone overheard us, "...*varúlfur* are there in Hemlock Hollow?"

"Just under fifteen hundred."

The morning suddenly felt far too warm. I unlocked the passenger door of the Jeep for him with a shaking hand before going around to the back to throw in my bag. "How many people are in the town?"

"Just under fifteen hundred."

Shock reverberated through me as if I were a tuning fork. For several seconds I couldn't breathe. The Jeep shook a bit from the impact of the tailgate slamming shut too hard. "Sorry, baby," I muttered as I walked around to the driver's side.

As I settled into the seat, started the Jeep, and shifted into reverse, I couldn't speak. Foot still on the brake, I looked over at Ty filling up my passenger seat like a wall of muscle. That wasn't fair, I supposed, but everything about him made me nervous, muscle included. The sight of him was a reminder of how deep over my head I was in. Finally, I found my voice.

"So where are we going until the full moon?" I asked.

"My place outside of Missoula."

"Don't you have a car?" I asked.

One hand on the side of his seat, I turned to look behind me and backed out of the parking space. Heat radiated off his body as if he were a furnace set on slow burn. I wanted to reach into that heat and see if it would scald me. The temptation was so strong I almost let my hand slide down onto his shoulder. As I shifted into first gear, I quickly withdrew my hand with a silent vow to keep all my body parts on my side of the vehicle.

"Not here. A friend brought me," he said.

Was that a touch of humor I heard in his voice? My teeth clenched at the idea he might know the effect he had on me.

"You were that confident that I'd leave with you?" I asked.

He dipped his head to the side in a sort of shrug. "That hopeful. And I knew if you did, you would likely not want to leave your own vehicle behind."

Thoughtful and hot. Was it too much to ask for this guy to have a few flaws?

"So packs, huh?" As my shock subsided, a deep need to know everything filled its place.

He made an affirmative noise. Sunlight reduced my eyes to slits as I pulled from the parking garage onto the street. Ty touched my arm, nearly making me jump. I glanced over to see him handing me my sunglasses that had been hung over the passenger grab bar.

My skin burned in a nipple-hardening way from where his fingers brushed mine. "Thank you. Tell me about the packs," I said, feigning an indifference I didn't feel.

His smile faded and his attention moved to the road. "How about we save that for when we get to my place? You will not like what I have to say about Raul's pack. We cannot have you losing your temper while driving."

I ground my teeth together—an act made more difficult by the fangs that had extended. The damn things made it hard to argue the point. "Fine. In that case, I'm turning the radio on because just about everything I want to ask you is likely going to piss me off or freak me out."

Zen as a damn monk, he crossed his arms over his chest and settled back into his seat. "That is probably a good idea."

Reaching for the stereo, I started making a mental list of all the things I would demand to know the moment we pulled up to his place. The soulful voice of Buddy Guy began to wail from my speakers, soothing my irritation instantly. Swaying my head to the music, I bit my bottom lip to keep from singing along. Ty's eyes settled on me with a weight I couldn't ignore.

"What?" I asked.

Eyebrows rising, he shook his head slowly. "Blues. I would not have guessed you liked the blues."

I gave him as hard a look as one can through one's peripheral vision. "If you don't like blues, I'm afraid you're going to have to get out of my vehicle right now."

Laughing, he threw his hands up in the air. "I love blues. It surprises me that you do."

Part of that was hot, and part of it pissed me off. Was he surprised because he didn't think I was cultured enough to enjoy great music? "And why is that?"

Tight lines formed around his lips as he smiled, almost as though it pained him. "You surprise me, that is all."

Tired of the lack of forthcoming answers, I shook my head, turned up the stereo, and focused on the road. Regardless of what was happening to me, I began to wonder at the wisdom of what I was doing. A strange guy in my car leading me to a strange place where no one knew I was going was a monumentally bad idea. No matter how I fought it, though, something about Ty put me at ease. I loved and hated it, craved and wanted nothing to do with it.

Less than ten minutes later, my growling stomach shattered any plans of silently enduring the drive. With the way it felt like it was trying to eat me from the inside out, there wasn't a chance I was going to make it without stopping for food, no matter how close his place was. As if to strengthen the point, my vision began to swim. I reached up and turned the stereo down.

"I'm starving," I said.

Ty nodded. "The *verða* is making your body burn through fuel at an accelerated rate. There is a diner a few miles ahead."

I rolled my window down, the motion of the old-style hand crank only making things sway worse. Before me, the road blurred. Cool air rushed in, driving back the dizziness that threatened to overtake me.

"Raul is not known for choosing women with depth. That is why you surprise me so much," Ty said out of the blue.

The very mention of Raul's name sent a shard of anger shooting through me. My vision cleared. "Yeah, well, I'm not known for choosing guys like him. I had a moment of weakness," I snapped.

For some reason, the idea of Ty thinking badly of me because I had been so close to inviting Raul into my apartment rubbed me all kinds of wrong. Maybe because what I had said had been such a blatant lie. I *was* known for choosing guys like Raul. Not werewolves, of course, but bad boys that you didn't take home to the family. Though it wasn't as if I had a family to take one home to. The thought of Ty knowing that about me stung. He was the first person in many years to reach out and try to help me. Despite the fact that I didn't trust him, I didn't want to mess that up like I did everything else.

"I am not judging. I know Raul. He could probably charm the pants off a nun."

Laughter erupted from my lips, surprising me, helping me focus. Grinning, Ty guided me off the main road with a few directions and into the parking lot of a diner. I let out a long breath as I shut the Jeep off, then met his gaze.

"Thank you for helping me focus. I was pretty close to passing out back there," I said.

Brows pinched together, he nodded and looked down as if the seatbelt required his full attention. "I know. I am sorry. I should not have let you leave the hotel without eating."

Hand on the door handle, I paused to give him a hard look. "I'm a grown woman. I should have said something earlier about being hungry." I didn't want to admit that I liked the idea of him looking out for me.

"Fair enough."

The warm morning air filled with scents of the city wrapped around me as I climbed from the Jeep. So many smells mingled together that it was overwhelming: the unpleasant acidic asphalt, sickly sweet garbage mingled with the metallic tang of a dumpster, warm steel of car engines, all beneath the seductiveness of eggs, meat, and hot cooking oil. One hand held over my nose, I tried not to gag as I made my way to the sidewalk in front of the diner. I would have thought the overwhelming scents would steel away my appetite, but my stomach growled even more fiercely than before.

"Do not worry. You will be able to control your sense of smell eventually. Try breathing through your mouth and concentrating on one scent," Ty said.

Partially because he was the closest thing, and partially because he smelled amazing, I focused on him. Beneath the scents of soap and shampoo were those of fresh pine, river water, and a very pleasant musk. I leaned into him a bit as we walked. The urge to rub along him, against all that tattooed flesh, made me step closer. My breast brushed his arm as he reached up to open the door. Nipples standing at attention as they were, I was suddenly very glad for the layers I wore. Shaking my head to clear it, I entered the diner. Perhaps his scent wasn't the best thing to focus on.

The quiet din of a hundred conversations punctuated by the clashing of dishes distracted me almost as much as all the wonderful odors of different foods. To his credit, the host behind the desk showed us immediately to a booth in a far corner and hustled off with the promise to return with coffee. Moments later I had the delicious aroma of coffee to focus on so that I didn't get drawn in by Ty's scent. For an entirely different reason, I leaned across the table.

"How did you come to be a *kennari*?"

Creases formed at the corners of his eyes and they pinched together so tightly it almost looked painful. The stormy look passed as quickly as if a gale force wind had swept it away. "I am a professor at the University of Montana. It came naturally to me."

The promise of stormy skies lingering in his eyes told me there was much more to that story, but it also warned me not to press in the wrong direction. "Let me guess, English?"

Sipping his own coffee, he relaxed a bit. "History, but I do have a strong love for languages."

My breath nearly caught at the mental image of his muscular frame packed into a suit and tie, pacing the podium as he lectured. He would fill out a suit oh so well. Muscles that had nothing to do with shapeshifting tightened low in my body, and suddenly I was forced to stare deep into the depths of my coffee.

"Obviously. Your English is impeccable," I grumbled.

Even his eyes seemed to smile as they caught mine. "Only because it is my second language and I am a bit of a perfectionist in that aspect. Until I reached twelve years old, I only spoke Icelandic. My parents wanted to make sure our ancestors' language was my native tongue."

Sexy as hell and cultured. Damn, I was in for it.

Thankfully our waitress—who smelled like she bathed in some overly flowery perfume—arrived with our food, saving me from having to try and speak. Cute as she was, Ty didn't spare her a glance, even when she giggled seductively at his compliment on the sight of the food. Perhaps he played for the other team. I could count on one hand the straight guys I'd met who would pass up a chance to flirt with an attractive woman. In the male species' defense, I did have a way of meeting all the wrong kind of guys. Then it occurred to me that Ty could be involved with someone. Stomach dropping, my eyes flicked involuntarily to his ring finger. It was bare of a ring or even a tan line from one.

Fork in one hand, knife in the other, I decided not to care. I had more important things to think about, like the mountain of food before me that my body screamed for. We ate in silence, waving away the waitress from time to time as she dropped by to flirt with Ty. I hardly noticed, let alone cared. Right.

In truth, the mediocre food captivated me. Food had never been overly important to me. Having grown up a mixture of poor white and American Native trash, I wasn't used to eating much and didn't need much, until now. The omelet, ham, hash browns, and toast went so fast I scarcely tasted them. When I found myself staring at the toast left on Ty's plate, he surprised me by ordering another side of ham and toast for me. I wanted to kiss him for it. The petite waitress gave him a sympathetic look, then glared at me like I was an embarrassment to all of womankind. She was so not getting a good tip.

Before she had even walked far enough away to be out of hearing range, Ty waved a hand. "Ignore her. The *verða* takes a lot out of you. During it you have to eat and rest a lot."

Without so much as a comment, I inhaled the ham and toast before the waitress could even bring back our check. I reached for it but Ty got to it first.

Shaking my head, I grabbed his hand and did my best to ignore the sparks that flew inside me at the contact. "No way. As much as I ate, I'll pay."

Humor sparkled in his eyes. "This one is on Raul."

"What'd you do, mug him?" I asked. Imagining it brought me far more pleasure than it should have.

Ty laughed. "In a way, I suppose. I snagged his wallet because I knew it might hold some clues." His smile grew. "It held more than that. And the man owes you."

I let go of him. "I won't argue with that," I said through a huge grin of my own.

The moment I stood my knees went weak. Ty was at my side in an instant, an arm around my waist, supporting me before I could fall. His hard body felt oh so good against me.

"Whoa," was all I could manage to say.

"That would be the second essential part of the *verða*, the way it draws energy from you. I hope you are okay with me driving."

It took a monumental amount of effort to lift my arm high enough to go around his waist. Hooking my fingers through a belt loop on his jeans was all that kept it there. Exhaustion dragged at me as though it were an anvil tied to my soul. It was a good thing it did, considering how tempting being this close to him was.

"Don't think I have much choice. But if you hurt my Jeep, I'll end you." My weak voice made the threat sound terribly hollow.

Ty's chest rumbled. "Fair enough."

All I could concentrate on as he settled the bill and led me to the Jeep was one step after the other. Without his arm around me I wouldn't have stayed upright. The one advantage was that my sense of smell was dulled back down to normal and I was spared the reek of the parking lot. When he reached over me to help with my seatbelt, I tried to bat his hands away and failed miserably. I wasn't too proud to accept his help. It was his hard body leaning over mine, his scent pouring down my throat like fine whiskey, that I couldn't handle. If I had the strength I would have risen up off the seat and nuzzled against him. Thank goodness for small favors. Warmth flooded across my skin as he laid my arm in my lap and tucked my leg over. Such simple touches had never affected me so. It had to be part of the *verða*, or at least a werewolf thing.

He withdrew and the door closed a moment later. Half out of a need for fresh air, and half to go with him, I leaned toward the open window. Footsteps followed by angry voices swept away some of the fog of sleep that was trying to crawl over me. Forcing my eyes open, I tried to track the sound. At the other end of the parking lot, Ty stood beside a black Harley arguing with a leather-clad man nearly as broad as him. How Ty had gotten over there so fast, I had no idea. Voice no more than a harsh whisper, the man thrust a finger in my direction before shoving Ty back a step. I tried to reach for the door handle but my arm wouldn't lift.

Left with no other choice, I focused on their voices, trying to bring the sound to the forefront like Ty had mentioned. Along with their conversation, their scent rushed toward me. The stranger smelled of leather and fine linen, but beneath that lay a woodsy scent—like peeled bark and rain mixed with some kind of musk. It was similar enough to Ty's pine scent that I knew with undoubtable clarity that the man was a werewolf. Their voices became as clear as if I stood next to them, only I couldn't understand a thing they said. Then I caught two words, *kennari* and *verða*, and I realized they were speaking Icelandic.

My attention wavered as the world swam out of focus. When I blinked rapidly to clear my vision, I saw the stranger bent over, a hand covering his nose, blood seeping through his fingers. Though his words were harsh and muffled, I didn't need to know Icelandic to understand them. Somehow cursing sounded more menacing in the Norse language. Fists clenched, Ty strode back to the Jeep without even a glance over his shoulder. He had climbed in, put his seatbelt on, and started the Jeep by the time I was able to roll my head to the other side so I could look at him.

"What... Who..." Each word carried the weight of an elephant.

The Jeep moved, causing a wave of exhaustion to rise up and pull at me. "A *lögreglu*, or policeman, if you will, from Raul's pack," Ty said.

Head lolling back against the seat, I struggled to find the strength to speak. But I had to know before I passed out. "What did he want?"

"You."

"But..." I couldn't finish the thought, let alone the sentence.

"No need to worry. He does not have any authority. He is here against the Council's decree to merely try and plead Raul's case, as he put it. He will not risk challenging me." The protective tone of his voice soothed me more than his words did. It felt good having someone looking out for me. Strange, but good.

The Jeep picked up speed until it felt as though I was being whisked along on a roller coaster. So many more questions raged within me, but they didn't have the strength to burn back the exhaustion. My tongue stopped working and my eyes slid closed. I had no choice but to entrust my life, and more importantly, my Jeep, into Ty's hands and hope I didn't end up somewhere worse than where I had started.

CHAPTER EIGHT

TY

I let my foot rest heavier on the accelerator. The change in engine noise from a steady hum to a high rev woke Sonya with a start. Eyes on the rearview mirror, I saw her gaze shoot to my white-knuckled hands on the wheel. She sat up so fast the seatbelt jerked her to a stop. The exhaustion that had been dragging her down was gone, leaving her looking alert and more than a little panicked after her eyes shot to the speedometer.

Even out of my peripheral vision, I could appreciate the way the seatbelt pushed her breasts apart and tugged down her low-cut shirt. A fleeting glance was all I had time for. That was a good thing, for more than one reason.

"What's going on?" she asked as she turned to look behind us.

A yellow Porsche and two black BMW racing motorcycles hugged the ass-end of the Jeep.

"Why aren't they passing?" she asked.

"Because they do not want to go around us," I said.

"More of Raul's friends?"

"Afraid not. Can you fight?"

I eased my foot off the gas and the speedometer started to drop, leveling out at eighty for a moment. Despite being a classic, the Jeep handled quite well at high speeds. The stiffer suspension and slightly souped-up motor suggested Sonya had done a bit more than simply restore it. Though it had been a long time since I had been behind the wheel of such a vehicle, it did not mean I could not appreciate one. It was the woman more than the vehicle I appreciated.

"A little, and not very well. Why?" Her voice went up an octave on the last question, which I would have found cute as hell if I was not so worried.

A glance back showed the bikes were not backing off.

"We cannot outrun them," I admitted.

"Don't you dare ram them. If you hurt my Jeep..."

I shook my head. "I would not dare. Besides, it is not as clean or easy as the movies make it look. We could flip, and you could get hurt because you are not through the *verða* yet. It is best to stop and face them on our own terms."

"Point made. You're sure they're not Raul's guys?" she demanded, eyes on the dropping speedometer.

We were at seventy miles per hour now.

"I am sure. They are from another pack. I will explain later. Get ready."

Her breathing quickened, making mine quicken—though not for the same reason. Heat radiated off her as she leaned back into the seat and squeezed her eyes shut. The spicy scent unique to her intensified, became musky as her wolf started to rise. Mine stirred in response to it. *Shit.*

"Breathe, just breathe, Sonya," I said in a soothing tone.

Slowly, she relaxed back into her seat, closed her eyes, and did as I instructed. From her open mouth I saw the gleam of her fangs retract. I tried not to think of how sexy that mouth looked, lips parted. My ability to distance myself needed work.

"Good. Feel that calm center?" I asked.

She nodded.

"Excellent. Hang on to that, because we are about to stop."

Gods, I hoped she could handle this. It was a lot to ask of a new wolf—too much. But we did not have a choice. I slammed on the brakes, took a hard left that rocked the Jeep up on two wheels, and rocketed down a dirt road. I barely got up to fifty before slamming on the brakes again, bringing us to a jarring stop inside a group of tall pine trees. In a flash, too fast for her new wolf eyes to follow, I took off both my seatbelt and hers.

She was not going to like what I had to say, but it had to be said. "Keep that calm center, and hide, but be ready to fight if they sniff you out."

"What? But—"

In the middle of her questions, I leaped from the Jeep, hoping beyond hope that she would comply. Cursing, she flung her door open and made a considerably less graceful exit that I found completely charming. I did not hear her walk away, but I could not risk looking, either. Arms crossed over my chest, I stood in the middle of the overgrown road, staring at the oncoming speeding car. If I made a big enough target, maybe they would not see her. Plenty of trees that would make a good hiding place lined the road and stretched out behind us. She needed to find her way into them, fast.

"I told you to hide," I said out of the side of my mouth.

"Not happening."

Though I cursed inwardly, I did not say a thing out loud. No sense in aggravating her further and testing her control. Her bravery impressed me more than I wanted to admit.

Dust barreled toward us as the Porsche and bikes braked to a stop so hard the ass-end of the Porsche slid out. A man poured out of the car to join the two off the bikes storming our way. Each of them stood over six feet tall, and though they were not as built as I was, they were big Nordic-looking lads like most of our kind. The one in front carried a baseball bat, the one to his right a tire iron. Nothing I had not seen before, and nothing that worried me overly much.

"Don't make this harder than it has to be, Tyler," the dark-haired man walking slightly in front of the others said.

I stiffened at my full name. He was not the biggest of the three, but by the way the other two men hung back, it was clear he was the one in charge. From the stench beginning to waft off him, he clearly was not happy about facing me. Good. Slowly, I unfolded my arms, slid my feet out into a fighting stance, and curled my fingers into fists.

"It is not going to be hard, James, it is going to be impossible. You know me, and you know how this is going to go down."

Head tossed back, James let out a barking laugh before exchanging a grin with his two companions. His eyes shot back to me like two hazardously flung darts. "You aren't what you used to be, *kennari*. Just hand her over. She won't be harmed."

The way he twisted the word *kennari*, as if it were a bad thing, made me want to do the same to him.

Anger flowed like a heat wave from Sonya. "Who are you and what the hell do you want from me?" she demanded.

His eyes darted to her. "Raul really did leave you clueless, then, didn't he?"

The heat coming off her grew in intensity. *No, no, no!*

"Ignore him, Sonya. He is trying to make you angry," I said.

Hands spreading out, James shrugged. "I wasn't trying really. I'm told I have that effect on people. Now that you mention it, though, we really don't care if she turns early and goes insane. Either way she'll serve our purpose."

That did not make any sense. I must have been wrong about why they wanted her. It did not matter. They were not getting her. I heard Sonya taking slow, measured breaths and hoped they were helping. The two men behind James fanned out, flanking us. This put one of them too close to her for comfort, but at least it was the one without a weapon.

"Now you are trying to piss me off, and that is dangerous," I said in a voice that sounded far calmer than I felt.

James and the man to his left moved in, weapons rising. The man with the tire iron lunged in and swung for my head. Fast as a snake, I ducked, shot a foot out, and took the man's legs out from beneath him in a sweep. Air expelled from him in a loud rush as he landed hard on his back. Not waiting, my right foot slammed down onto his chest and I heard a crack. I snatched the tire iron from him and brought it up to block a blow from the bat James swung at me. Twice more he struck and twice more I blocked.

Too far away I heard a deep, grating voice that I knew was talking to Sonya. "Best worry about me, pup."

It was almost impossible not to get distracted from my own struggle when I heard flesh hit flesh.

"No, asshole, you'd better worry about me," came Sonya's spunky reply. "Move again and I'll see if werewolf balls detach as easily as human ones."

I grinned, ducked James's latest swing, and swept his legs out from under him. Before he could hit the ground I cracked the tire iron hard against his head. Nothing broke from the sound of it—no surprise when it came to the strength of *varúlfur* bones, but he'd be out for at least a few moments.

A small whimper that I would not exactly call masculine, but was clearly a man, came from Sonya's direction. I turned to find her standing over her attacker with a death grip on his balls. Damn, she was kind of amazing. How she did it, being so new and undisciplined, I had no idea. But I was intrigued. Shaking my head and laughing, I approached.

"And here I had been worried about you," I said.

"I'm not the kind of girl who needs fussing over," she said, sounding out of breath and in pain.

"I can see that. You should probably let go of his balls before you catch something."

Lips curling up from her teeth—I was kind of proud that they did *not* sport extended fangs—she let go of his balls and wiped her hand on his yellow T-shirt before stepping back. He bared his teeth in return, a low growl starting in his chest. I shot between the two of them. Grabbing him by his shirt, I lifted him up with an ease born of fury and *varúlfur* strength. Feet dangling above the ground, the man sagged in defeat, head dropping.

"Drag your sorry-ass wolves back onto those bikes and get the fuck out of Missoula. Tell your alpha if he sends anyone else into my territory, I will kill them," I said, letting the desire to do that fill my voice.

The man nodded quickly. Grunting in disgust, I tossed him to the ground and turned to Sonya.

"Just for the record, Isak didn't send us," the man said as he got to his feet with as much dignity as he could.

Ignoring the man, I put a hand on Sonya's back as we started to walk to the Jeep. Blood flowed from three deep gashes on her left arm. She opened her mouth but didn't say anything, so I did not take my hand away because I knew what was coming. From the time of my first change as a child, I remembered the *verða* all too well. Her knees gave out and she collapsed.

Before so much as her jeans could brush the ground, I swept her up into my arms and cradled her against my chest. Long black lashes fluttering, she let out a little moan that did things both wonderful and terrible to me. Then she slid once again into unconsciousness.

CHAPTER NINE

SONYA

The crunch of a gravel road woke me. Blinking away the haze of sleep, I yawned. The almost sweet scents of spruce and lavender ·drifted through my open window. Their smell mingled with Ty's in a way that was close to heaven. Evergreen trees rose up to the sky on both sides of a winding road. Around a bend, I saw a house peeking through the green needles.

"You are awake just in time. I was afraid I might have to carry you in," Ty's deep voice came from the driver's seat.

Stifling another yawn, I sat up and stretched the kink out of my neck. "No such luck." While I made it sound convincing enough that it was him who was missing out, tingles of a very naughty kind worked their way through my abdomen at the thought. His deep chuckle made the damn feelings spread lower. Glancing over, I noticed he was shirtless. Damn, if that didn't make me ache with desire. Pressure on my left arm made me look down. A strip of his blue T-shirt was wrapped around my biceps. Dried blood darkened it. Only a twinge of pain remained.

"Your shirt. I'm so sorry. Told you I wasn't a very good fighter," I said through a half smile.

He waved the comment away. "Not to worry. It served a better purpose in halting your bleeding. And you did splendidly, considering you fought off a seasoned *varúlfur*."

Talk about being able to charm the pants off a nun. Raul had nothing on this guy. "Thanks. Where are we?" I asked.

The Jeep rounded a bend as I spoke, revealing the little house that had been peeking through the trees. A mixture of an alpine-style A-frame and stone siding insured the place was well-equipped to handle harsh winters. At least ten feet off the ground, a raised deck wrapped around it, creating a dramatic entryway to the wooden door inlaid with a huge oval of stained glass. The place couldn't be over two thousand square feet, especially not with the extreme angle of the roof, but that still made it at least a thousand square feet bigger than anywhere I had ever lived.

"Home," he said. The conflicted tone of his voice made me curious, but the closed-off look on his face told me I wouldn't get any further info out of him at the moment.

"Wow," I murmured as the Jeep rolled to a stop.

Without a word, Ty stepped out of the Jeep and went around to open the back. Realizing he was getting my bags for me, I jumped out and hurried back there. The songs of at least half a dozen different types of birds serenaded me and I thought I smelled water of the lake variety. It would have been relaxing if I weren't freaking out about arriving at a werewolf's private cabin. A hot, intriguing werewolf, but a werewolf nonetheless.

"I'll get those." I tried to take them from him but he tossed them over his shoulder, which was way out of my reach. Not that I didn't want to climb up there and get them. I wanted to. Oh, did I ever.

"That is all right. I have it."

The argument died on my lips as he strode off toward the house, leaving me standing alone. The view of his backside in those jeans was well worth losing the argument, and then some. Left with little other choice, I closed the Jeep's tailgate and followed him up onto the porch. Electronic beeps broke the mountain retreat stillness, followed by the metallic sound of a deadbolt disengaging. He opened the solid wood door and strode inside. The door alone had to cost as much as all my first year med books combined. Standing on the cedar deck, I hesitated. This place was so far beyond anywhere I had ever lived that I was reluctant to cross the threshold in my off-brand hiking shoes. Not only did I feel a bit like out-of-place trailer trash, but entering that house felt like the point of no return. Stupid, considering the bite had been that point, but knowing that didn't make it feel any less real. I had little choice. Even if I did, I wasn't sure I'd choose anyone else to guide me through this. And he had my worldly belongings slung across his back, so what else could I do?

Marveling at the tile entryway, I stepped inside. The tile floor continued into a large, open floor plan filled with far more modern furnishings than I expected to see in such a place. Beyond the foyer stretched a long marble bar that separated the kitchen from the living space, which boasted some kind of dark fur rug—real from the smell of it —and a gathering of furniture around a tiled fireplace. Above it all hovered a loft with a steel cable and glass railing. The place smelled like wood, leather, stone, and a diluted pine cleaner. Not a bad mixture of scents, really.

"Wow," I said again, feeling completely inarticulate.

"Thank you, I think." Ty's voice was filled with a humor that put me at ease. Hell, everything about this guy put me at ease. He had that special aura about him that some people had, the one that makes everyone around them comfortable. Unlike a lot of guys who worked that too hard, his was easy, natural.

I checked the coat rack, the shoe bench, but didn't see any signs of other people. I tried not to sound hopeful as I asked, "Do you live here alone?"

"I do." A slightly guarded undertone hid beneath his cheer.

I decided to press a bit. "No Mrs. Werewolf or pups frolicking in the woods out back?"

He laughed, but it was a strained sound. "No. Lone wolf, remember?"

"I do, just clarifying what that means exactly."

Without the further explanation I'd been hoping for, he started for a closed door to the left of the kitchen. "There is a small guestroom back here. Sorry, it is not much, but at least it is private, and there is a bathroom right next door."

Whatever was in this guy's past, it was clearly painful. Nice as he was being to me, I didn't want to cause him any pain, so I decided to let it drop, for now.

The door opened to a room with a daybed nestled beneath a bay window framed by walls of bookshelves. Sunlight spilled through the windows, giving the bed with its fluffy comforter a dreamlike appearance. Not much room was left when he stepped inside, but with the ceiling that stretched up forever into open beams, it gave it a cozy feel rather than made it crowded.

"It's fantastic," I managed.

Inclining his head toward a dresser that was cleverly recessed in the wall, he set my bags down on the floor. "Clean linens, of course, and you are welcome to use the dresser."

"Do you bring all the new *varúlfur* here?" I gave the foreign word my best shot.

I tried to convince myself I was asking just to tease him, and not because I wanted to know if I was special. Red brightened his cheeks, sending an unexpected shot of jealousy through me.

"You are my first," he all but whispered.

Shock washed the jealousy away in one fell swoop. But he didn't seem embarrassed, he seemed...shy. Pink cheeks were a very good look on him. It was adorable that he could blush over such a silly thing. "The first you've brought here?"

Standing up straighter, his eyes lifted to meet mine. "Yes, and no, my first *nemi*, student. There has not been a new *varúlfur* in over thirty years and I have only just been appointed a *kennari*."

"In over thirty years? Really?"

With a nod, he left the room and invited me to follow with a sweep of his hand that was more beckoning than commanding. The stubborn part of me wanted to plop down on the bed and refuse to move, but the curious part of me didn't dare. Then there was the fact that the nap during the ride here had left me feeling charged to the point of crawling the walls. I had the urge to go for a run, something I hadn't done since starting college. Trying to keep my pace from seeming hurried, I followed him out into the kitchen, gaze fixed to his hot backside.

"Really. The laws against turning *varúlfur* are very strict. Raul broke nearly every one of them when he made you." His voice sounded hollow for a moment as he opened the refrigerator and stuck his head inside.

"Sounds like you and Raul have a bit of history," I prodded.

"We do indeed. But it is more than just that. He took your choice away and that is unforgivable." The passion in his voice sent a hot flush into me. This time it was more than just base attraction, though. A guy that passionate about someone taking a woman's choices away was something special. I suddenly felt very lucky he had been appointed my *kennari*.

So many questions came to me that I had no idea which one to ask first. My mind threatened to spin out of control, a sure sign that I needed to take it slow and digest things.

"Would you like a beer?"

I crawled up onto one of the white cushioned steel barstools. "What kind?" What could I say? I was a bartender; it had made me picky.

He said a name I didn't recognize. The look on my face must have made it obvious.

"It is a micro-brewery out of Montana. I usually try to pick up the good stuff while I am in Oregon, but it has been a while."

"A man with great taste in beer. I like that."

He placed two brown bottles on the bar and popped the tops off with his bare hand. I gazed hard at him from beneath my brows. I could tell by the tops of the bottles they weren't twist tops. Broad shoulders rising in the semblance of a shrug, he slid one of the bottles toward me.

"Strength is one of the perks of being a *varúlfur*."

He took a long pull from the beer as he walked around to my side of the bar.

"Yeah, 'cause that had nothing to do with your monstrous biceps." Oh God, had I said that out loud?

Rather than bury my head like I wanted to, I took another long drink. The alcohol was beginning to calm my restlessness so I figured I was ready to hear some tough answers.

"What are the laws that Raul broke?"

Putting one barstool between us, Ty sat down and spun to face me. The way he sat with his heels up on the stool's bottom bar, legs parted to give a nice view of the bulge at his crotch, was more than distracting.

"The creation of any new *varúlfur* has to be approved by the *ráðið*. And the chosen person must go into the *verða* knowingly and willingly."

Glass clanked against marble as I set my beer down on the bar a little too hard. "Wait, the what now? I didn't catch that middle word. Do your people say every other word in Icelandic? What the hell?"

"Sorry, it is our way of remembering where we come from. It translates roughly as 'council.'"

My mother hadn't allowed me to have any contact with either her family or my dad's, so I got the need to connect, more than I wanted to admit. My ire cooled. "I can understand that. So am I going to need to learn Icelandic?"

Already the desire to do so began to build in me. I spoke a bit of Swedish. Dad had insisted on me learning it since his parents were from Sweden. I wasn't very good at it, but I had practiced hard because it had made my dad happy. He'd said I would do big things one day and would need to know different languages. Now I couldn't help but wonder if he had known something I didn't. I wish I had taken the lessons more seriously, for more reasons than one.

Ty shrugged. "It would not hurt. Everyone in Hemlock Hollow speaks it, so you will be at a disadvantage if you do not. But there is no rush. We have a lot of other things to cover first."

Thoughts of Raul stirred the anger back to life in my belly. Any advantage he had over me was one I had to get rid of. Learning Icelandic would be an easier first step than shifting into a wolf. I rinsed the feeling away with another long drink of my beer. At this rate the damn bottle would be empty in no time. I braced myself.

"Why did someone from Raul's pack come to the diner? And who were those men on the road? Why did they attack us?"

Ty sat his beer down and looked me straight in the eye. "To answer the first one: Because Raul thinks you belong to him now, and his pack feels as if a *kennari* of their choosing, from their pack, should teach you."

The ache of my teeth told me my fangs were beginning to extend, but at that moment, I didn't care to stop them. "I don't belong to anyone. Why would they think that? Because he's the one who bit me?"

Head tilting to the side, Ty's shoulders rose. "It is a bit more complicated than that."

"Tell me," I actually growled. The sound surprised me. It wasn't something I thought could come out of a human throat, let alone mine. But it didn't frighten me, not anymore.

The callused palm that settled atop my hand sent sparks shooting up my arm. Leaning closer, Ty ensnared my eyes. "Slow, deep breaths. Let the anger flow out of you."

I realized my lips were pulled back to bare my teeth—or more to the point, the four fangs that were now fully extended. It flowed out of me all right. Right on a wave of desire so strong I almost leaned into him. The weathered skin of his hand against my arm felt amazing. And he smelled delicious enough to lick. Desire and anger went to war with each other, leaving me oddly balanced. Breath more controlled, I forced my lips to relax over my fangs.

"Okay, tell me."

His hand didn't retreat from mine and I didn't pull away. The touch helped keep me grounded and not only because of the desire it stirred low in my abdomen.

"When we bite a human with the intent of turning them, our venom comes up. That venom enters the person's bloodstream and slowly changes their DNA until they become one of us."

Tingles of unease crawled across my scalp as my mind started to put it together. "Changes our DNA, you mean to reflect that of the person that bit us, specifically? Making us almost like siblings?"

He nodded.

I cringed, face contorting. "That's disgusting." Before he bit me I'd been about to let him into my apartment—and my bed. I had to swallow down my revulsion before I could go on. "Why would he want to make me practically his sister?"

Ty sat back. "It is an ancient way of choosing a mate and tying them to you, forcing the pack to recognize and accept you."

Disgust made my stomach do flips. "A...mate, after he made our DNA close enough that he could be my brother?" I couldn't help but stumble over the word *mate* a bit. It sounded so primal.

"If he had bitten you during sex, it would have been as good as marking you as his mate. No one could have contested it. Like I said, it is an ancient custom that is not practiced anymore, for that reason."

"Why would he do that? I'd only known him for two weeks." Insta-love was something I so did not believe in.

A nasty mixture of embarrassment and that ever-present fury worked its way through me, making my skin burn. Caring what Ty thought about me before I really even knew him was horrible, but I couldn't help it. He was the first person that had cared to help me in...well, ever. Creases formed between his brows, making me think I was going to like this next bit of information even less than the last.

"I am almost certain it is because he is engaged to be married to someone he does not want to marry. Changing you into *varúlfur* pretty much guarantees he does not have to marry that woman. And those men on the road are from the pack his intended belongs to."

The words struck me like grease from a fryer, igniting and exploding through my body. Not because I was "the one" or even because he cared about me. He had flipped my life over into the crazy lane because he didn't want to be forced into an arranged marriage. The bottle of beer in my right hand suddenly exploded, sending shards of glass flying everywhere as well as stabbing into my palm. I didn't feel it until blood began to drip from my clenched fist. The pain took the edge off my anger, but not enough to stop my skin from feeling like hornets were crawling under it. My breathing sped and my stomach churned. The world swayed.

Suddenly Ty stood over me, his hands taking mine. Slivers of more pain stabbed through my hand as he began to pick glass from it. The world swayed and I ended up in his arms. I tried to look up at him, but he was no more than a blur.

"What's happening...?"

I tried to stand and only ended up pressed against Ty's hard, broad chest.

"You are losing control of your anger and it is triggering your body to shift, a defense mechanism." The worry in his tone was far from comforting.

"Will I shift so soon?"

"Yes." The certainty even less so.

Panic wrestled with the outrage at all I had been through. Aches the likes of which I hadn't felt since my last growth spurt during adolescence echoed through me. An out-of-control feeling, much like the dizziness of being truly good and drunk, grasped me. I hated it. It was one reason I never drank to excess.

"But I'm not ready," I murmured.

Holding me back at arm's length, yet still holding me up with ease, Ty stared hard into my eyes. "No, you are not. Focus on me. Take slow, deep breaths."

Those gorgeous, glacial-blue eyes made it easy to comply. The hint of a blond five o'clock shadow shimmered across his cheeks and chin, making me forget my anger. I didn't just focus on him, I became captivated by him. Comfort and concern radiated off him, but I realized it was more than that. It was almost a physical thing, like the wind, or the feel of water, only this wasn't an element. This was power, his power. I knew that beyond a doubt. It wrapped around me like the warmth of a fire on a cold night. I never wanted it to let go. My vision cleared and a bit of strength returned to my legs. I remembered the second part of what he'd said and forced myself to draw in a deep breath and let it out slowly.

"Good, now match my breathing," he said.

My gaze dropped to his lips. They were just full enough with a distinctive raised edge separating the sensitive pink skin from the cream-colored skin of his face. The desire to press my own lips to them doused the last of my anger. The crawling sensation beneath my skin faded away, but I still couldn't get my fangs to retract. I breathed as he instructed, trying to find a calm center that simply did not lie within me and never really had. Eyes dropping to watch the rise and fall of his chest, I tried to focus harder. Realizing the distraction of looking at him was no longer helping, I closed my eyes. A few breaths later, my fangs retracted.

Ty's grip on me relaxed, and I opened my eyes and leaned back against the bar. Concern pulled his brows together.

"I take it shifting right now would be bad?" I asked, acutely aware that he still held my arms—and really hoping he wouldn't let go.

"Yes. You must be in control of your emotions first. Emotions and instincts are tied together. If your emotions are out of control, your instincts will be as well. If you do not know how to control them before you shift, you will have a very hard time shifting back, among other things."

Still working on my breathing, I gave him the toughest look I could manage while being so frazzled. "Other things?"

"With your instincts out of control you are more likely to kill, or worse, go mad. New *varúlfur* are supposed to be prepared before they are changed. It is part of why they must be approved by the *ráðið*."

I swallowed hard. "Can you prepare me before I change for the first time?"

He dipped his head. "If you are strong enough. The full moon is about three weeks away. At least Raul had decent timing when he bit you in. We have until then, and the urge will be so strong that you will need to change, prepared or not. Come on, let's get that hand cleaned up."

The cryptic words soaking in slowly, I allowed him to lead me to the kitchen sink and hold my bloody hand under the cold water. For several moments I watched the silver-hued liquid run from the arched neck of the tap, transfixed. Some of the cuts were deep enough they looked like they needed stitches, but I couldn't feel more than a dull ache.

"Do not worry, you will be healed by morning," he said.

I wasn't as concerned by that as I was fascinated that I'd had the strength to shatter a beer bottle in my hand. My thoughts caught on something he had said.

"Why would going mad be worse than killing someone?"

His eyes grew hard with a new depth of seriousness. "Because then you would not stop killing. New *varúlfur* that go mad have to be put down."

I swallowed hard. "How often does that happen?"

That power I had felt in him stirred, grew anxious. It made the hairs on my arms rise.

"From what I am told, at least a third of all new *varúlfur* go mad."

Head dropping into my hands, I groaned. Ty's fingers wove through mine. "But they were not as strong as you are, and they did not have me as a *kennari*." The softness of his voice was almost intimate.

"What makes you think I'm strong?" My quavering voice sort of drove the point home.

His free hand stroked my left cheek. Unable to resist, I leaned into the warmth of his skin.

"Your power is as bright as Odin's lightning. I have not encountered a *varúlfur* that felt this powerful, not even the alphas," he said.

He might just be trying to make me feel better, but it was working. More than that, it charmed the hell out of me. I fought the impulse to lean toward his hand as it withdrew from my face. Desperate to retain a touch of the distance I had been trying for, I stood up straighter. After all, I had to focus now more than ever. Going insane wasn't an option.

"Mad psychologists aren't exactly all the rage right now, so let's definitely try to avoid that happening. Those guys that attacked us on the road said something about not caring if I went insane, that I would serve their purposes either way. What were they talking about and why did they attack us?"

His brow crinkled over his blue eyes. "I must admit, I am a bit puzzled by that. I had thought they wanted to steal you and make you a member of their pack—the Arnoddr pack—but when James said that, it did not make sense. For one, his alpha, Isak, is a good man who would never approve of a member of his pack attacking and abducting someone." Scratching at his blond five o'clock shadow, he contemplated. "It does not make sense. Pardon me a moment, please."

He pulled out his phone, dialed a number, and waited as it rang. I heard it plain as if I held the phone to my own ear. A man answered. They discussed whether or not the man knew about the attack. He assured Ty he did not and that he would hunt down the wolves of his pack who were involved immediately. They said formal-sounding farewells and ended the call.

"Something else is going on here. I suspect it has to do with the unsanctioned bitings."

My head spun. Wasn't it enough Raul wanted me as his mate and other packs wanted me as their member? What the hell else could there be? "Are we safe here?" I asked.

"Yes."

His lack of hesitation made me feel a bit better, but something else became painfully clear. "I take it we aren't immortal."

Glancing sideways at me, he half grinned. "No, just very hard to kill."

"So we don't live forever?"

"No, but we do live a very long time. And we do not start to really age until our last decade."

I forced myself to pause a moment so I didn't sound too eager. "How long?"

"About five hundred years."

Knees going weak, I had to grab the counter with the hand Ty didn't have a hold of. Considering I had expected to live to maybe eighty, five hundred might as well be immortal. I had no idea what to do with the short lifespan I'd had, and now this. Not only could I be a psychologist, I had time to go into orthopedics, or hell, I could even be a brain surgeon. With the time I had, maybe I'd even cure cancer. I could really, truly help people. If I didn't go insane and be put down first.

"I think I need some air."

Blotting at my hand with a paper towel, Ty turned off the water.

"That is a good idea. We will go for a walk in the forest, it will help you ground and center."

He folded my fingers around the paper towel and relinquished my hand. Instantly I missed the feel of his skin against mine.

"That may as well have been in Icelandic," I told him.

Deep laughter rumbled in that hard chest of his, making me miss his touch all the more. He started for the door.

The glass all over the floor and counter made me pause.

"Do not worry, we will get it when we come back," he called over his shoulder as if he had noticed my hesitation without even seeing me.

Of course he had. The guy was like Yoda. Only problem was, watching his muscular back and perfectly shaped ass as he walked out the door, I realized control was the last thing I wanted him to teach me.

CHAPTER TEN

TY

T he scents of spruce and pine flowed down my throat, soothing me and helping me focus, as I knew they would do for Sonya. Beneath my feet a pine needle–strewn path provided a cushion that made it feel like walking on exercise mats. Trees reaching over two hundred feet high rose up on both sides of the path, stretching their feathery bows across it overhead here and there. From them came a gentle energy that soothed the wolf inside. Sunlight poured through the branches, dappling the path—and Sonya's lovely face—with promises of warmth. Birds chirped and sang overhead, some musical, others urgent, as if they knew predators walked below them. Each sound, smell, and sight eased my mind, helped me center. Whether she realized it or not, it would do the same for her.

"Better already, am I right?" I asked.

"Much."

I made a sweeping gesture. "Nature helps. *Varúlfur* feel the tie to it more than most humans, but it is more than that. Manipulating our atoms to shift draws energy from the Earth and the moon."

Her delicate dark brows rose. "Why wolves? Or are there other kinds of shifters? Or vampires? Or, hell, zombies for that matter."

Her refreshing honesty and curiosity charmed me. I threw my head back and laughed long and hard. "I love how well you are taking this. Zombies are an impossibility, as far as I know. Other types of shifters, yes. I have never met a vampire, but I have heard stories."

She did not even miss a beat. "How did Raul know I'd end up being a wolf shifter? Does everyone who is bitten change?"

And direct as hell. Damn if that did not send a thrill to places that had been hibernating for some time. Or rather, I may be damned that it did. "We can sense our own. When someone has the ability to be a shifter, we know, and we know what kind. And no, those who are bitten who do not have the ability do not change, they die."

Her eyes widened but that was it. "So, I was born with this ability?"

"With the potential. It took the bite awakening it in your DNA to make you a *varúlfur*, though."

"Like an environmental trigger that awakens cancer," she mumbled. Her heart sped up and the scent of anxiety—dark and thick—rolled off her. The expression on that lovely face was too guarded to make out. She was holding something back, or hiding something. But I did not want to push her too hard or too fast. Trust had to be earned. The scent of anxiety blew away as her focus shifted. I felt the weight of her gaze making its way across my body, though I pretended not to. It felt very, very good.

"How old are you?"

Was that the only reason she stared?

"How old do you think?"

She slapped my biceps. "Don't mess with me. Seriously, how old?"

My gaze dropped as I pulled my bottom lip between my teeth. Would she think me too old? Twenty-somethings had a way of seeing my age as a point of no return. But the way her eyes shot from my lips to the trees on the other side of the path made me think maybe she would not. And could that be the hint of a hard nipple poking at her tank top? Even if it was, it could be due to the breeze. She was not through the *verða* yet, which meant she felt the cold far more than I did. It was not right to think of such things. More than not right, it was forbidden. It might not be such a bad thing if the truth made me sound old and boring.

"I am thirty."

Her attention shot back to me. "Seriously? Just thirty? Not two hundred and thirty or something?"

Well that was a relief. It should not have been, but it was, nonetheless. Eyes widening, I put a hand against my chest as if appalled. "Do I look that old?"

Rolling her eyes, she smacked my arm again. I did not mind at all.

"Of course not. You don't look a day over your prime. I half expected a *kennari* to be a few hundred years old."

"Let me guess, you were thinking that because in all the books and movies the werewolf or vampire is always older than the girl—like pedophile older," I said.

She laughed so hard I knew I had hit the mark dead on. "Yes. Though you don't strike me as the type to watch a lot of movies."

Did that mean she thought of me as the romantic hero who would sweep her off her feet? Did she want me to? Feigning ignorance to the reference, I raised a brow at her. "That is where you are wrong about me. I am a huge fan of movies, especially horror movies," I admitted. Not many people knew that, but telling her felt so natural that it slipped out. And I had to say something.

"A werewolf who likes horror movies. I kind of love that. So how did you draw the short straw and get the new clueless girl? Surely there are tons of other *kennari* that could have gotten saddled with me," she asked, something hidden in her tone.

My back went rigid before I could stop it. "Not many. Our numbers have greatly depleted due to both our strict laws about changing others, and because of our nature."

"Our nature?" she asked gently.

I could not keep the sadness completely from my expression—nor would it be fair to her, or honest, to do so. "Our instincts often rule us, and our strongest instinct is to fight. It is based off a need to protect our packs, but we are not just wolves, we are human too, so that instinct becomes skewed. Our kind flock to war like ravens, especially when it gets close to our homeland."

"Why don't you change more people? I imagine there are plenty that would be willing."

A meadow of brilliant green grass dotted with groups of bell-like blue columbine flowers opened up to our left. The grouping of trees beyond it drew Sonya's attention. Her gaze went distant, almost trancelike, and her feet started in that direction. Was it a coincidence, or was she drawn to the place? She glanced back at me. Head cocking to the side, lips pursed, I watched her a moment before following.

I answered as we walked through the tall grass. "Changing others is very dangerous. Not everyone can handle being so in touch with their instincts, even if they are born with the potential to be a shifter. It makes murderers out of some, rapists out of others. Over the centuries we have discovered the risk is too high. Too many had to be put to the reaper."

Her face scrunched up in concentration and damn if it was not cute enough to make me ache. Gods, I hoped she made it through the *verða*. If she did not, I feared it would crush me. "Why wolves? I mean, what determines what type of shifter we are?" she asked.

Some of the tension eased from me when she did not ask about the reaper. That was a story she was not ready to hear. Mentioning it had been a mistake. I almost managed a smile as I shrugged. "That is debatable. All we really know is that if your ancestors were wolves, you will be a wolf. If they were cats, you will be a cat. Some think we are touched by Fenrir, yet loyal to Odin, others think we are children of Loki."

She swallowed hard and the scent of anxiety drifted up from her skin once again. Her brows scrunched together. "Fenrir and Loki?"

"Loki is a Norse god who battles against Odin and his sons, bringing about Ragnarok—the end of the world. Fenrir is a wolf who is the son of Loki."

She let out a long breath. "I know the legends. My dad... He told them to me when I was a kid. What do you believe?"

We began to work our way up an incline. Her pace put her slightly uphill from me, allowing me to catch a really nice view of her backside. No harm in looking, except for the physical ache the sight of her caused deep inside me. The urge to run my hands up those long legs, over the curve of that ass... Damn, I was failing at keeping this professional. Distance and focus were paramount. Giving in to my desire was not an option. I was one of the first *kennari* in hundreds of years. To foul this up would not only put an even darker mark on my honor, it would mean her death.

I forced my mind back to her words. Clearly she was leaving something about her father out, but it could wait. Did I dare tell her my beliefs? Most people had very strict views on gods.

What the hell. I wasn't going to hide who I was or how I felt. I had promised her no secrets and I would not go back on that. If I wanted her to be open—and I very much did—then I needed to offer the same. "I believe we are touched by Fenrir, but should be loyal to Odin."

"Really? You believe in all that old gods stuff? In Odinism?" She sounded surprised, but not judgmental.

We crested the small hill and kept going. I increased my pace to walk beside her, because if I did not, I was not sure I would be able to fight the urge to touch her much longer.

"Religious studies was a minor of mine. The closer you look at the religions of the world, the more you realize they are all based on the same basic story. And the Norse story is older than most, so yes, I believe it to a degree. What about you, were you raised to be religious?"

We went several strides before she answered. "My dad believed in Odinism. He taught me the eddas, told me the stories, but he never pushed it on me. My mom is of the Cherokee Nation, so she taught me a little of the beliefs of her ancestors. After Dad was gone..." Laughter chirped from her, but it was humorless, filled with pain. "I pretty much raised myself. My next meal and getting to school took priority. After that I never put much thought into religion."

I tried to hide my shock with a compliment. "Well, you did a fine job." The old religion was gaining popularity in small pockets of the world, but it was still too rare for this to be a coincidence. I was going to have to research her family.

She stopped and craned her neck back to look up at me. The light spilling through the trees over her, making her eyes look like sunbursts of gold, distracted me so much I almost forgot what we were talking about. Now that she had mentioned her mother was Cherokee, I did not know how I missed seeing it in her.

"Really? I'm a struggling student on hiatus who was a bartender in a hole-in-the-wall bar in Nowhere, Idaho. A moment of weakness led to the worst decision of my life, which pretty much ended it as I knew it."

I shook my head. "Could have done worse. You could have ended up a drug-addicted prostitute living off the system. And your life has not ended, it has just moved into the next stage."

Openmouthed, she stared blankly at me for a moment before nodding and turning away. "Thanks," she said, then sighed deeply. "It has to be connected. But what could this have to do with my dad?"

I shook my head. "No idea. You talk about him in the past tense. Can I ask what happened to him?"

Her jaw tensed and I smelled the musk of her wolf trying to rise. She calmed it into submission with an ease that I would not have thought a newly bitten could manage. Impressive. And very sexy.

"He was killed in prison by white supremacists who didn't like him having Norse tattoos when he wasn't one of them."

My own wolf stirred along with my anger. I wanted to touch her, to try and comfort her, but her stiff shoulders warned me against it. "My deepest condolences for your senseless loss. Our kind are not like that, not at all. In fact, *varúlfur* are from every race. Many Icelandic *varúlfur* are of African descent."

Her brows rose. "How's that?"

"Their ancestors were slaves that our ancestors stole or acquired, then freed, and they were bitten in by one of us. *Varúlfur* do not discriminate based on skin color, just like wolves do not discriminate based on coat color."

"Interesting." The impressed tone of her voice gave me hope that she might be starting to accept us a little at least.

She began walking off the path into the shade of the trees. Birds sang a piercing siren song overhead as she passed beneath them. Something about her stance and demeanor became almost trancelike again. She stopped next to a waist-high boulder with a flat top that was set within a hundred-foot circle edged by twenty-four spruce trees, each nearly a hundred feet tall. Her fingers trailed over the knotwork carved into the concave surface of the boulder, touched the dried lavender piled in the center. It was as though she felt the power of this place. But that should not have been possible, not before she was through the *verða*.

"You can feel that?" I asked.

"Yes..." Her voice trailed off, gaze turning to the trees.

The circle we stood within was so big that sunlight poured down upon Sonya despite the long boughs that stretched out. The limbs did not start until eight feet or so up the trunks. Those trunks drew her attention. The scars of old carvings marked each of them. She started toward one.

"This is amazing," she murmured.

Amazing about summed it up—her and whatever drew her to this place that is, not the crude carvings my father and I had done over twenty years ago. I remained a step behind her, feeling as though we were tethered together. Disturbing as that was, I could not question it or stop. I tried, oh how I tried.

Flaky bits of brown bark surrounded the raised edges of a scar in the rough shape of an *S*. She ran her fingers over it, slowly, reverently. I stopped several feet away, not wanting to interrupt such an important moment.

"You are drawn to the *Sowilo*. Interesting," I murmured. Maybe she really was starting to accept what she was.

Pulling her hand slowly from the tree, she turned to me. "I don't remember what it means."

I lifted my head in the direction of the tree she hovered near. "The *Sowilo* is the Norse rune for an elemental force, or a cleansing power. It signifies a deep connection between one's unconscious and higher self."

When she did not scoff or roll her eyes, a breath eased from me—taking the tension that had been building with it. Telling someone you housed obscure beliefs was one thing, exposing some of the details of those beliefs and not having them judge you was another altogether.

"These are all the runes, aren't they?"

My arm swept out to indicate the circle of trees. "They are. When my parents found out they were going to have a baby, they had these trees shipped over special from the old country. My dad and I carved the runes into the trees when I was ten years old."

Her eyes sparkled with fascination. "Why?"

I looked up into the trees, enjoying the feeling of their pull, and half hoping they might shield me from her scrutiny. "To create our own place of power."

"Place of power? And what is that exactly?"

Though no judgment or doubt colored her tone, worry still nagged at me. But I could not stop now. I had promised not to keep things from her. "In certain places the power of the Earth intensifies, becomes concentrated, if you will. For *varúlfur*, such places become places of renewal, healing, and recharging. And, many say, these places can become gateways to the other eight worlds."

Fascination lit up her eyes, filling me with encouragement. She gestured toward the next tree. "Remind me what they all mean."

Grinning, I grabbed hold of her hand and led her to the next tree. The warmth seeping off her smooth skin and into me distracted me so completely I had to take a moment to gather my words. I described what the arrow-shaped rune meant, but all I could concentrate on was the way she licked her lips as she watched my own. We moved from one tree to the next, the next, and the next. She followed the tug of my hand, and I was grateful she never let go but dreaded what that meant. When we reached the rune shaped like a trident, I leaned over her too much and my chest brushed against her arm. The sensation sent a hot trail of sparks all the way down to my groin.

Forcefully, I turned my thoughts to anything but her. The trees, the birds singing overhead, to the history of the rune. What did it mean? Oh yes, *Algiz*, protection, shield. That worked for all of a moment before the sound of her voice responding sent blood to my groin. The most delicious part was, I knew from her heavy breathing and the way she pressed closer than necessary that I had the same effect on her. My hand slid lower on her back, just above the swell of her ass. The brush of her waistband tempted me to go lower. Her tongue darted out and licked a line across her upper lip. Her breathing quickened, making me hard as iron. Yet I did not sense her wolf rise up. Impressive. She brushed against my arm and I felt her nipple standing at attention. Too much more of this play and I would be overly aroused, which, with her new heightened senses, she would likely smell.

Term papers! My mind retreated to the most boring term paper I had graded that I could think of. After I reached the outline I had myself under control. Dammit, I could not allow her to affect me so. The stakes were too high. If I did not make light of this quickly and discourage her, things might progress to a dangerous point of distraction.

"Well done," I said.

"What?"

I caressed the back of her hand. "Suppressing your desire."

She jerked her hand from mine and took a half step back. "Excuse me?"

Damn. That had been too much. I held my hands up. "Sorry, but with the promise you have shown today, I could not resist testing you a bit." A poor excuse, and a lie, but a small one. Or so I tried to tell myself.

Despite the cute upturn of one corner of her mouth, anger burned in her eyes. "Promise? What the hell are you talking about?"

For a moment I leaned forward, but then gathered my control and leaned back against the tree instead. "You were drawn to this place, you felt its power. Most *varúlfur* would not be able to do that until they had shifted for the first time."

"I happened across it."

"No, you walked straight to it. There is something special about you..." My voice trailed off as my gaze traveled up her body. "I am not sure what it is yet. But I think it is why Raul chose you."

She stiffened, fangs extending. "Yeah, well, you 'testing' my control by flirting with me isn't much different than him choosing me for the wrong reasons. Just another man with an agenda."

She spun away and began to storm off. In two quick steps I caught up to her and gently gripped her arm. She stopped, but did not turn. It was one thing to discourage her, but I did not want her upset—and not just because it might force her to shift.

"I am sorry, Sonya. I did not mean to offend you. Everything I am doing here is for your sake, not my own. I promise."

After a moment, she turned toward me. I did not let go of her arm, but I was hoping by the look on my face, she would know it had nothing to do with testing her.

"How do I know that for sure? You're virtually a stranger to me."

"I was chosen to be your *kennari* because I am neutral." My eyes dropped to my feet. I really did not want to tell her the next part, but after how I had botched things up, I did not see a way around it. "I have no pack."

"Is that strange, to have no pack?"

She sounded like she did not consider that a bad thing. Which made me want to kiss her. The desire made me feel like possibly the worst *kennari* in *varúlfur* history. It was a very good thing the Council could not read my thoughts. I was a history teacher, dammit, I should be used to this role. No student had ever affected me this way. The Council would have my head if they knew what was going on inside of it.

"Extremely. Both humans and *varúlfur* are pack animals."

A delicious humming noise came from her. "Explain how flirting with me tests me."

Not the smoothest change of subject, but I was not about to complain. There were some things I was not ready to tell her. Helheimr, I may never be.

"Before you shift you need to be in control of your emotions because they trigger instincts. If you lose yourself in instincts, well, then you have lost yourself. We will focus on your strongest emotion, the one that you find hardest to control, and master it."

"And how will you go about teaching me to control these things?" There was a teasing note to the suspicion in her tone.

Keeping my expression blank as possible, I tried to look like her flirting did not affect me. "We will start with meditation."

She nodded. "Makes sense."

My eyes widened. "Really? No arguing about getting down to the real learning?" Considering how eager she was, I had thought meditation would be too slow for her.

"Nope. It makes sense that I would need to be able to control my breathing and focus first."

"You sound like you are no stranger to meditation."

"Like I said, my dad tried to teach me the art of *glíma*. Just because I wasn't good at it doesn't mean I didn't listen."

My mouth dropped open. The humility, the intelligence... This woman kept surprising me. I could have sworn I saw what looked like a thrill of victory shoot through her eyes. The mischievous grin she tried to hide made me think she was beginning to enjoy shocking me. If only *I* was not enjoying it so much. Thinking of how very much was at stake, particularly for her, I forced my expression to go blank.

"Good. That will make this a little easier on you. How about running?" I asked.

"Running?"

A smile slipped through before I could stop it. "Do you enjoy running?"

Shoulders rising in a half shrug, she cast her gaze to the path. "I used to do it for exercise when I started college, but I can't say I ever really enjoyed it."

I stepped out of my shoes while my fingers reached for the hem of my shirt. "You might be surprised to find that has changed. Shall we test it out?"

Looking down at her hiking shoes and jeans, she shrugged. "Sure."

With her eyes heavy upon me, I undid the buttons on my shirt as quickly as I could, giving her just a flash of my chest and tattoos. As I started to turn away, her eyes caught on my pendant—three interlacing triangles hanging on a steel and glass beaded chain. Odin's symbol. No judgment or surprise hid in her expression, only curiosity. The reaction thrilled me and I really did not want it to.

Under the guise of stretching, she bent over and let her hair fall down to obscure her face. Through the ebony curtain I felt her gaping at me. Her heart picked up a fast rhythm, but her breathing stayed controlled. Already she was getting better at this. Pride swelled in me. I let my own gaze travel to the nice curve of her ass as she stretched. The swelling of pride moved from internal to somewhere very external.

Part of me wanted badly to believe the thing I felt growing between us would not interfere with her *verða*. But I could not give in, could not take that chance. I had to remind myself that almost half of new *varúlfur* went mad. One-third odds were nothing to play around with.

Clearing my throat, I shook my head. "If at any time you start to feel out of control, just let me know and we will stop." My voice had dropped an octave and become husky. Dammit, now who needed to work on their control? I could not allow such distraction right now. With the full moon growing ever closer, I knew her instinct to hunt and kill would be growing stronger with its approach.

It must have affected her because I felt her wolf stir much like the pressure before a storm. She breathed deep and it settled back down. Acting as if nothing had happened, she pulled a hairband from her pocket, put her hair up in a ponytail, and gave me a drop-dead-sexy look.

"Let's go then." She took off before the last word crossed her lips.

I settled in and let her pick the pace. The wolf inside thrilled at running with her. It urged me to go all out, but I resisted. Good as the wildness felt, I could not expect her to show control if I did not. And control was the vital element she had to learn. I concentrated on my breathing and the sensation of oxygenated blood pumping through my veins. Moments later our feet were gliding across the needle-strewn path. It gave way like a cushion beneath my toes. My tough skin assured I did not even feel the needles. We ran and ran, continuing long after Sonya thought she should have tired. She remarked upon how surprised she was that she did not become winded, and her legs did not tire. Then she remarked upon the very ability to be able to make remarks without breathing hard after running for so long. She made me laugh. It had been a long, long time since anyone had been able to do that.

We followed the path that stretched around the edge of the lake framed by hills covered in evergreens, across a foot bridge spanning a crystal-clear creek, and back around to where we had started. When I stopped to put my shoes back on, Sonya buzzed with so much energy she could hardly stand still. It was so cute I could hardly stand it.

"That was amazing, I'm not even winded. How is that possible? That had to be like five miles," she said.

I slung my shirt over my shoulder and walked back to her, trying to act like I did not want to rub my skin all over hers and lick her in hidden places. How could she affect me so powerfully when no one else had been able to even stir my interest in years?

"One of the perks of being a *varúlfur* is great stamina," I said as I fell into step beside her.

The gleam in her widening eyes told me the double implication of my statement did not escape her. I let the flirting drop. Helheimr, I should not have said that much. Together we returned to the path and walked back toward the house. Sonya literally bounced on the balls of her feet.

"How long can I run before tiring?"

"After the *verða*, days."

That stopped her in her tracks. I kept walking, needing desperately to look at anything but her. A moment later she bounced into a slight skip to catch up to me. "Seriously? Can we test it out?"

I gave her a hard look. "Not yet. In a very short time you will be starving again and, as you discovered, that can come on rather suddenly." Not to mention any more might trigger her desire to hunt, which would in turn trigger her need to shift. I could not allow things to progress to that before she was ready.

Her legs stretched out into a long, swift stride. "Tell me more about the runes."

With the eagerness only a teacher could possess, I did as she asked. All the way back to the house we chatted about what the different runes meant, written both normally and inverted, how they were cast like tarot cards by some to see the future (though Sonya interrupted with skeptical questions on that one), how they were used in language, and on and on. She was a bottomless pit of them, but I liked that about her.

When the house came into view she had finally managed to slow to a walk. I opened the front door for her and stepped aside. My eyes traveled over her curves when she walked past, lingering on her backside when she could no longer see me. The woman was downright intoxicating. I had to get away from her and collect myself.

"You can hit the shower if you would like. I will get lunch started for us."

She placed a hand upon her shapely hip. "Why, Tyler, are you saying I smell?"

Eyes squeezing closed, I cringed. "My uncle was the only one who called me that."

The widening of her eyes told me she caught the past tense part. Her features softened into sympathy. My pain melted as I leaned in close, drawn to her. Nearly touching her hair, I breathed in deep. "And yes, you do smell incredibly sexy. Which is why you need to shower." A mistake? Probably. But I could not handle her asking about my uncle. Not yet.

Letting my *varúlfur* speed drive me, I withdrew quick as I could, stirring her hair as I left, which only served to pull her scent after me. One moment I stood beside her, the next I was ascending the stairs to the loft all the way across the room. The distance was not nearly enough, though. I needed to get a door between us. Something about this woman completely undid my restraint. Considering I was supposed to be teaching *her* restraint, it was going to make for a very long couple of weeks.

And if she did not make it... I could not think that way. She *had* to make it.

CHAPTER ELEVEN

SONYA

Left in shock by his words, I couldn't even formulate a snappy comeback. The attraction being mutual came as no comfort. If anything, it could make it harder for me to keep my distance. But only if I let it, and I had no intention of doing that. After Raul, I wasn't about to jump into anything again so soon—if ever again. Clearly my attraction to men was not to be trusted. I had to be able to stand on my own two feet—or four for that matter—through this. I still didn't know whom I could trust in this strange new world, if anyone. Then there was the whole possibility of going insane and being put down. As if this wasn't bad enough already.

Tearing my eyes from Ty's impressive half-naked retreating physique, I started for my room. I desperately needed to wash that image from my mind. From my bag, I grabbed what clean clothes I had left. I made it halfway across the room before I realized I hadn't even tried to lock the door. Something about Ty made me drop my defenses, and I didn't like that. Or so I tried to convince myself.

Like the house, the bathroom had a modern look to it with more glass and travertine than wood and leather. Decorated in white, cream, and shades of beige, it was easy on the eyes. A huge mirror spanned one wall, along which ran a counter that looked to be of solid frosted glass, with a colorful blue and green hand-blown glass sink perched atop. The surprisingly large room opened up with more open floor space than I could imagine any practical use for in a bathroom. The guy had fantastic taste on top of being gorgeous, thoughtful, and successful. No matter how hard I tried, I couldn't find a flaw in him.

Opposite the sink stood the glass doors to a huge shower. Along the wall behind the door I found several towels rolled up and placed artfully upon what looked like a brushed stainless steel shelf. Setting my clothes down on the counter, I grabbed a bar of soap that was either of the homemade variety or from an expensive store that liked to make it look that way. Next to the soap sat two glass containers with hand pumps. One was labeled shampoo, the other conditioner. Clearly, Ty wasn't into store-bought toiletries. Lucky thing my hair was relatively easy to manage, straight as an arrow no matter what I did, but easy nonetheless. An experimental sniff of the containers brought only subtle scents and made me realize how much I smelled like sweat.

And he had thought that was sexy. Even that was charming, dammit.

"Ugh."

I peeled off my clothes and dropped them on the floor. One brush against my arm and I tried to tell myself that my nipples stood at attention because of the cool air, not the memory of Ty half naked. Heat rushed down my stomach toward my groin as if to mock me. Time to wash that sight from my mind. Tucking the toiletries under my arm, I reached for the shower doors. They opened up to a space that looked better designed for an orgy than cleaning oneself. But then, that could be my present state of mind. The thing was ten by ten at least, more of a room than a shower, really, with four showerheads on two different walls. A bench of stone built as though it were part of the floor and walls stood at a height perfect for all kinds of interesting uses.

I shook my head and set the armload of toiletries on a shelf built into the wall. After several tries that ended in me soaked in a mixture of warm and cold water from three different sides, I finally figured out how to turn only one showerhead on. Warm water poured over me from a showerhead designed to feel like rainfall, and damn if it wasn't amazing. Long breaths eased from me as my muscles relaxed and my energy finally came back under control. Eyes opening, I looked down as my hand skimmed down my stomach and over my hip. Just above my pubic hairline, my fingers stopped to caress my birthmark. It was a splotchy pink mark that resembled a crudely drawn *S*. The similarity to the *Sowilo* rune was not lost on me.

Dad had always told me the birthmark meant I was special. How or why, he hadn't said.

I wanted to deny that I had been drawn to that rune, that maybe I had seen it from a distance and recognized it as similar to my mark. The shadows had cloaked it until I was nearly upon it, though. What drew me to it wasn't the similarity, but something much deeper. Part of me wanted to tell Ty, to ask him about it, but I wasn't about to. Not until I understood more. And more importantly, not until I knew I could trust him, at least a little. Like he said, something more was going on here, something more to do with me.

CHAPTER TWELVE

SONYA

Three solid days of nothing but running and meditation and I'd had enough of taking things slow with my training. As Ty had stated days ago, I was beyond ready to "get down to the real thing." The full moon was getting closer. Each day that passed I could feel it tugging at me more and more. Nature as well pulled at me like never before, making me want something I didn't understand. This new desire frightened me almost as much as the idea of shifting into something I wasn't sure I could control and possibly going mad in the process. The running was beginning to stir a need in me to hunt, to kill. That part freaked me out almost as much as the idea of shifting.

Not to mention my attraction to Ty pulling at me more each day. I was actually handling the moon better than the man. Flaws weren't exactly something he had in spades, or at all, that I could tell. Everything about him made me want to drop my defenses—and my undies. But dropping my defenses was what had landed me in this mess and ruined my plans for a future as a doctor. Still, if I was going to die... No, I couldn't think that way. I had to make it.

Standing on the back deck looking out over the lake not far from the back of the house, a restlessness came over me that had me literally jumping

BITTEN & BEHOLDEN | 101

in my skin like an espresso junkie. Now that I thought about it, espresso sounded really good. Maybe that's what I needed, to be around people for a bit. Having gone through over a week of the *verða* now, I wanted to see if being around people felt different. I needed to know I wouldn't hunger for their flesh. True, I hadn't so far, but what if it was something that developed further into the transformation? I wanted to trust that Ty wouldn't lie to me about something like that, but I hadn't known him long enough.

So soft they barely made a sound, Ty's footsteps brushed against the deck in a pattern that was becoming quite familiar. It was like my thoughts had conjured him out of thin air.

"This is the view I long for when I'm in Hemlock Hollow."

For a split second I almost thought he was talking about me. But of course he couldn't be. I turned to see him looking out over the lake with a wistful expression softening his freshly shaven face.

"You don't live here all the time?"

Sighing heavily, he shook his head. "I wish I could, but duty calls me back there often during the summer, and sometimes on the weekends."

"Duty?"

He rested his elbows on the steel deck rail, gaze never leaving the still blue water. "*Varúlfur* politics that require my input."

I touched his arm and gave him a hard look through narrowed eyes. The almost magnetic feel of his skin beneath my palm stirred things in me I didn't want stirred. His long lashes fluttered and he leaned into me, telling me he felt it too. "I need to hear more about the packs, but can we please go into town? I'm dying for a good espresso, and I'm restless," I forced myself to say.

He gave a slight shrug that failed to look as casual as he tried to make it, then moved away from the railing, but not so far that it would take my hand from his arm. Until then I hadn't realized I'd left it there. I pulled it back a little too quickly. Thankfully, he pretended not to notice. The disappointment and shame in his eyes ruined the attempt.

"Yeah, I need to pick up some things from the store. That's a good idea."

Was that a touch of humor in his voice? I tried not to grind my teeth as I walked alongside him back to the house. The aggravation stirring within didn't cause my fangs to extend, or even make my jaws ache with the need. Much as I hated to admit it, the meditation was helping.

While in the bathroom putting my hair up, I heard an engine start. After grabbing my wallet, keys, and tucking my mace into my pocket, I made my way to the front deck. At the bottom of the stairs, Ty waited next to a forest green Chevy Colorado. The vehicle shone in the sun as if recently washed and waxed, yet the scars of a few scratches and small dents proved it was also well used. For a man of his stature I had expected a Hummer, or at least a full-size truck.

"What, no big rig?" I asked as I descended the stairs.

Blue eyes sparkling, he grinned. "I have no need to compensate."

Damn if those words didn't burn a trail straight to my core and make me wonder exactly what lay behind the fly of those nicely fitted jeans of his. Feigning exasperation, I rolled my eyes and climbed in when he opened the passenger door for me. I became so caught up in ogling the pristine interior with its spaceship-looking console jammed full of electronics that I jumped when he opened his door. This truck was pretty much the polar opposite of my classic Jeep, so much so that it might as well have been a Maserati. I couldn't have felt more out of place as it was. Fumbling with the threadbare hem of my shorts, I stared at my filthy hiking shoes and realized I was going to have to rely on him a bit more than I wanted to.

"When we get back, do you mind if I use your washer and dryer? I'd be happy to do the cooking in exchange."

The truck purred to life and eased out onto the gravel drive so smoothly it had me aching with envy. It wasn't that I wanted a new vehicle. I didn't. I liked my old classic. But I'd never had anything new. The dash felt like real leather. The smell wasn't quite right, but it was close enough.

"Of course, but you do not have to work for it. You are my guest. Offering basic amenities is the very least I can do."

My hand jerked back at the sound of his voice. "Is that what I am, a guest?"

"Of course."

"So I can leave at any time?"

For a moment, his hand froze over the gear shifter, moving only when the engine revved so high it sounded like a growl. "You can, but I would not advise it. The *verða* is something you need to be guided through. And I hope you would not want to." The last part was low and gentle, as if he knew he shouldn't say it, but couldn't help himself.

I chose to ignore the last part, because if I didn't, I'd swoon. "But it's more than that, isn't it? It's Raul's pack, and that other one."

One long moment stretched into another until I feared he wouldn't answer. The truck glided down the road so quietly it was hard to tell we were on gravel. Trees zipped by, giving the occasional view of a cloudy sky.

"Yes," he finally said.

The next question had to be forced past my constricting throat. "Am I part of his pack now?"

Ty's eyes never left the road, but by the way he tensed, I could tell the question bothered him. "Not unless you want to be."

Somehow I knew that if I said I didn't, he'd relax, but something in me wanted to keep that information close to my chest for now. If he relaxed too much around me, then I'd relax around him, and then things would progress to a place I couldn't afford for them to go and didn't want them to. Or so I told myself. Lying to oneself is no easy thing. When I didn't respond after a moment, he went on. "I did a bit of online research, cross referenced it with *varúlfur* records, and found that your dad descends from a Swedish pack."

"That can't mean my dad was a werewolf. We were close. I would have known." It wasn't just denial. He would have told me something like that.

"No, but I think he knew about the Swedish pack."

He handed me his phone. On it was a picture of a man with a roaring wolf formed of knotwork covering his back. Above the wolf was a phrase in Norse runes: Seeker Wolves. I knew it from memory. At first I thought it was a picture of my dad's back, but the man's build was wrong. The tattoo, though, was dead on.

"That's my dad's tattoo," I whispered.

"I know. I also found his admission photos. Sonya"—he looked at me from across the truck—"that's the crest of the Swedish pack your dad's family descended from. That is where you get your *varúlfur* blood."

The world swam. My stomach heaved. "I thought all the stories of werewolves and Vikings were only that, stories. But he knew. He loved those stories. He would have wanted to be a werewolf. Why wouldn't he have gone to the pack and asked to be bitten in? It makes no sense," I protested, unable to wrap my mind around it.

Ty gave me a long, meaningful look. "Because he loved you. The odds of surviving to become *varúlfur* are not good, remember? I do not think he wanted to leave you alone, or take the chance of you wanting to follow in his steps and try to become one too."

Like I could forget. "He would have asked before I was born," I argued, unable to accept it.

"I do not think he knew until after you were born. I spoke with the alpha of the Seeker Wolves pack. He said a seer of theirs predicated your birth, and that they reached out to your father when you were born, offering your family the chance to join the pack if they would go to Sweden. When he declined, they offered him their mark—their tattoo—so all would know his family was protected by them."

I dropped my head into my hands. "My mother wouldn't have wanted us to live that life, to take those risks."

That would have meant my dad denied himself the one thing in life he would have wanted more than anything. Well, almost anything it turned out. Tears stung my eyes and I couldn't blink the damn things away.

"There is more," Ty warned.

"I want to know. Tell me everything," I demanded without hesitation.

"He went to prison for murder, right?"

I nodded.

"The man he killed was not a drug dealer like they said. He was a member of a tribe of skinwalkers who tried to kidnap you. The Swedish pack found out and threatened the tribe, they kept you and your mom safe."

The world swayed. Gripping the dash in front of me didn't help. Things were starting to click into place that I didn't want to believe. I grasped onto the one thing I did want to believe. "My dad wasn't a murderer."

Ty's hand came to rest on my leg. "No he was not. A no-touch creed was issued on your family after that. It is all in the *varúlfur* records."

Half the reason I had wanted to become a doctor was to balance the scales—in my mind at least—for what my dad had done. "This is insane." I might have yelled; I couldn't tell.

All this time I had thought my dad had been involved in drugs. Now...

But Ty wasn't done blowing my mind. "It seems the tribe believed your mother had skinwalker blood in her. That might be why they targeted you. Being half *varúlfur* and part skinwalker, you could have ended up going either way based on who found you first."

My mind couldn't wrap around the fact that skinwalkers were real too. But they couldn't be in my mother's blood. That would mean she wasn't full Cherokee like she had always told me. Skinwalkers were a Navajo legend. But then she had told me stories of them. The stories said they could wear the skin of just about any animal big enough to turn into and use it to transform. Why would she tell me those stories if she wasn't part Navajo?

The guilt of knowing it had been her own people—well, sort of—that had tried to kidnap me, resulting in her husband going to prison, might have explained her descent into a haze of drugs after my dad's death in prison. I'd never blamed her for her fall. She lost the love of her life. But I'd also lost my dad, and she always seemed to overlook that part. If this was true, it meant she had reason to blame me for everything. And I hadn't spoken to her in years because *I* blamed her. What kind of person did that make me?

"You think they wanted me so they could make sure I turned into a skinwalker instead?"

"That I do not know. The alphas of the Swedish pack would not tell me, but they want you to get in contact with them. Their wolves lost track of you when you moved to Idaho and they have been worried about you," Ty said.

Taking slow, measured breaths, I laid my head back against the seat and closed my eyes. I took a while to process it and fought back tears. Once I got the lump in my throat down, I told him, "Not until after the *verða*. I want to be at full strength before I have to deal with anyone else who expects something of me. You didn't tell him where I was, did you?" I wanted to know, I needed to know, everything that alpha had to say, but right now I needed to focus on getting myself through this.

He squeezed my leg. "Of course not."

"Good. When I left Washington, I made sure I'd be hard to track so my mom couldn't find me. I had just put her into a rehab facility, again. I was hoping that my leaving might actually be enough to make her think she'd really hit rock bottom this time. In psychology, I learned they have to believe that or else they'll just keep falling off the wagon. At the time it had seemed like the only option," I said, the last bit dropping to a whisper.

Without a word, Ty grabbed my hand and held it. His power flowed over me, cradling me. I relaxed into it for a mile or so before pulling my hand away. I owed my mom. Making it through this wasn't just about me or the people I could help as a doctor anymore. It was about family.

"You still haven't told me about the Hemlock Hollow packs." They were an immediate threat that knew right where I was. Forewarned was forearmed.

His jaw tensed, making me wonder if he was struggling to keep his fangs retracted. An interesting reaction to a simple statement.

"Don't keep me in the dark, Ty. I don't like it," I warned.

A long breath blew from him, and he sagged a bit. "That is not my intention." He drew in an equally long breath before going on. "There are three packs in Hemlock Hollow: Reinhard, Draupnir, and Arnoddr. While they live in a relative sort of peace for the most part, they each have their own...politics, and there are politics between the three of them."

The tension tightening his features told me *varúlfur* politics weren't the same as normal world politics.

"Is that why you spend so much time in Missoula?"

"Partly."

His following silence told me the conversation would end there if I didn't push. So I pushed. "Did you ever belong to one of the packs?"

"Once, yes," he practically growled in a low voice.

Tension filled the cab of the truck like fog, so thick I could taste its acidity on the back of my tongue. His hand withdrew from my leg. The absence of his heat made my heart sink. No, not my heart, exactly, more like the rush that waited in my chest. It wasn't just attraction. This rush had hovered within ever since I woke up on the bathroom floor. I think it was my power. What did it mean that he made not only my body thrill, but my *varúlfur* power as well?

The pain that pinched his brows together made me want to stop there. But I couldn't. If I made it through the *verða*, I would need to know things. "Sorry, I didn't mean to hit a touchy subject. Which one is Raul's pack? What are they like?" I asked.

I knew throwing too many questions together tended to make him clam up, but we were starting to come across more houses than trees, which meant we were nearly to town. Time was running short, and once he stopped talking about this subject, it would be hard to get him going again.

"His is the Reinhard pack, and they are...driven."

"Do they all belong to the AVW organization or whatever you call them? And is that just a huge group of speed-loving werewolves?"

He chuckled. "Someone watches too much TV. We do not use the term organization, just pack. The AVW is considered an umbrella type of pack, one that encompasses many with the cooperation of their alphas. And no, not all of the Reinhard belong to the AVW, mostly those of Raul's generation and newer. And yes, I guess you could say they are all speed demons." He shrugged. "Most of our kind are. We love to run, and driving something fast is the next best thing."

"Is the AVW the only umbrella pack?" I asked.

The look of approval he gave me made me feel like teacher's pet. That thought took me to all kinds of dirty places.

"No. There is also the AVV, the American Viking *Varúlfur*, though they tend to be the older generations. I used to be one of them," he said, voice growing quiet with the last sentence.

I wanted to know more, but I could tell by the distant look in his eyes that was all I would get on that subject. "The other pack that came after me, on the road. Which one are they?"

"Arnoddr."

His short answers suggested a new direction was called for. "How do the packs work? Is there, like, an alpha that everyone follows?"

To my surprise, he answered quickly. "Two, a male and a female, lead the pack together. Their family is considered *konunglegur*—royalty. The sons or daughters, whichever proves the best leader, usually rise to the position after their parents reach a venerable age and become elders."

"Usually?"

Again his jaw clenched so hard that if he weren't a *varúlfur* (I was finding that term was more comfortable than werewolf, maybe because it made it less fantastical), his teeth may have cracked. Through his parted lips I could see that both his top and bottom fangs had extended a bit.

"Sorry, you don't have to—"

"No, you need to know what you are getting into. Struggles for dominance between the three packs is always ongoing, though it is usually kept to a minimum. Struggles for dominance within the individual packs is another matter. The elders consider that pack business and they do not get involved in it." Voice drifting off, he swallowed hard and looked out the driver's side window for a moment.

After almost a minute, I didn't think he was going to go on, and at this point, I wasn't going to push him. Finally, he did. "Raul is the alpha's son. His pack arranged a marriage for him to solidify an alliance with the Arnoddr pack, and if they are forced to recognize and accept you, then that alliance crumbles."

The breath knocked right out of me as if I had been struck. It took a minute to recover. I shifted sideways, needing to see Ty better.

"Why would Raul want to ruin that alliance?" And arranged marriages? Seriously?

When he answered, I definitely saw the flash of extended fangs. "I honestly do not think the whelp cares. Ever since we were children he has only ever been concerned with what affects him directly."

That led down an avenue of self-loathing I really didn't want to travel right now. How could I have been attracted to a man like that, again? Anger built and built until I felt like a tea kettle about to blow. Then I did. It hit me in a wave so powerful I gasped and slammed back into the seat. I became acutely aware of the moon, far below the horizon and hours from rising, but there nonetheless. It was getting much, much closer to being full. That awareness resonated through me until it was all I could focus on.

"Whoa, Sonya, relax, take it easy," Ty's voice soothed from somewhere far away.

The vehicle slowed. Gravel crunched. We stopped. Before I knew what I was doing, I flung the door open and spilled out onto the ground. My insides burned like they were going to combust. I had to get somewhere cooler. Down on all fours, I crawled toward the forest edging the road. Soft earth against my palms soothed me. Using a tree trunk, I braced myself and stood. The colors of the forest took on new depths, greens becoming more vibrant, browns deeper, and whites brighter. My teeth ached something fierce, as did my fingers. Before my very eyes my fingernails lengthened, hardened into claws. I screamed.

BITTEN & BEHOLDEN | 109

Instincts raged as if against an internal cage: run, hunt, kill. Where the instincts and my human conscience met I felt the edge of the madness I'd been hearing so much about. It felt like a massive storm waiting to swallow me whole and never spit me out. And it was *inside* me. Panic pushed me closer to the edge of that storm.

Ty's shadow fell over me, his hand coming to rest on my back. "Let go of your anger," he urged.

My lips drew back from my teeth, several of which had become exceedingly sharp. "Can't," I growled.

The storm within whispered about how wonderful it would feel to tear into Ty's flesh, feel the heat of his blood spraying over me, taste his meat in my mouth. Oh Gods, it saw Ty as a threat. The growing panic pushed me another step closer.

"You have to. Do not let the anger control you. Control it instead. It is not your fault that you were drawn to Raul. He was the first of your kind you met. It was natural to be drawn to him. It is not your fault." The second time he said it, the words sank in.

I became aware of the warmth of his hand on my back as he stroked up and down, the nearness of his body, so tall and strong looming over me. I didn't want to hurt Ty. He was my friend, my teacher, someone who cared about me, someone I cared about. My claws became fingernails once again. A long breath eased out of me, my anger along with it. Not quite ready to trust my judgment yet, I moved around the tree and took a step away.

"Well done," Ty said. The pride in his voice made me stand a bit straighter. But then, he hadn't seen my claws, or been privy to my thoughts.

Those horrible thoughts made me want to vomit. Holding a hand up to keep him away, I took several more steps into the forest. "Give me a second, please."

The cool breeze moving through the trees felt good on my face. I lifted my chin into it. Several breaths later I felt grounded, in control. For good measure, I waited another few seconds before turning and walking back to where Ty stood waiting.

The concern on his face made my chest tighten. "Would you like to go back home?"

That made me smile; home. I shook my head. "No. I need to do something normal, mundane. A coffee shop is exactly what I need right now."

He smiled and nodded, falling into step beside me, close enough to be comforting, but not quite touching. It meant a lot that he respected my need for boundaries at the moment. It meant even more that he cared about what I needed and was so willing to give it to me. If only Ty's chivalry could save me from the madness.

CHAPTER THIRTEEN

SONYA

"So, if you aren't working for one of the packs, was it this Council you mentioned that sent you after me?" I asked after the drone of the tires on the asphalt became too loud.

His blank expression revealed nothing, but tension filled up the cab of the truck as if it were thicker than air. I hated that I was bringing up so many sore subjects for him, but these were things I had to know. His reactions had me worried about the packs for more than one reason. And I desperately needed a distraction from the memory of the madness waiting just on the other side of the precipice I balanced over.

"Yes, the Alpha Council. They are comprised of alphas from all three packs and they sent me because they know I am neutral."

I had just regained enough focus to process what he said and ask more when he pulled into the parking lot of a coffee shop. Damn. Before I could get my seatbelt unbuckled, he shut the truck off, got out, and was halfway around to my side. Like a gentleman of old, he opened the door for me and offered me his hand. My body screamed at me to take that hand, revel in the feel of his skin, his warmth. This damn attraction had to be a werewolf thing, part of the *verða* maybe. Because Gods knew my emotions were not to be trusted where men were concerned—particularly if I were going mad.

Yes, a heightened sexual instinct. That made sense. The other option didn't even warrant considering. I was not going mad. I *would* not. Raising an eyebrow at the offering, I ducked under his hand and stepped from the truck in one easy leap. He shrugged and closed the door. Swallowing the desire to apologize, for what I had no idea, I strode around to the sidewalk at the front of the truck. The heat of his body tried to wrap around me as I passed by him. Resisting its pull almost took more resolve than I had. The devil was in the distraction. But hell, at this rate, resisting my attraction to him alone was threatening to drive me mad.

"If you would like to go ahead and order, grab a table, I have to run to the store across the way." With a thrust of his head, he indicated a grocery store down a few buildings from the coffee shop. "I will meet you back here in a few minutes."

"Sounds good."

Nose in the air, drawing in a deep breath, he started to back away, eyes scanning the parking lot as he went. Was he worried about Raul showing up here? Seeing as he was being detained, I didn't think that was possible. I was about to ask when he turned and started to stride away at a swift pace. Shrugging his weirdness off, I started for the coffee shop. My eyes only betrayed me once or twice, sneaking a peek at his fine backside as he walked away. Fine, maybe three times.

The bell hanging on the glass door jingled as I entered, a clear tone that rang above the swishing and banging of coffee drinks being made. Ten or so tables filled with college-age students chatting or typing took up the floor space, leaving a small aisle clear that led to the counter in the back. Three baristas worked with what was no doubt a caffeine-induced speed, hands a blur as they mixed up drinks for the four people standing at various points along the counter. The rich, wonderful aroma of fine coffee, flavored syrups, and milk made my mouth water in anticipation.

One step inside the door and the euphoria that began to settle over me tore away like duct tape being ripped from dry skin. Something—no someone—in this room set my nerves to screaming. Bumps rose all over my skin and chills spread out from my center. Every smell and sound amplified until I was drowning in a sea of sensations. Then one suddenly banished the others. The beating of a heart that I knew with a terrible certainty was a *varúlfur*, terrible because something about them wasn't right. Drawn by both a need to help and a force I couldn't fight, I walked toward their table.

Or, her table, rather. A young brunette with a bright stripe of purple in her hair, who had to be under eighteen, sat alone at a table, wide eyes staring out the window. The paper coffee cup in her hand shook so badly it was a wonder there wasn't coffee all over the table. Next to her chair sat a beat-up backpack, one of its straps hooked through her right leg. Her clothes were rumpled and slightly dirty and she smelled as though she hadn't bathed in at least a week. Compelled by a force I didn't understand, I sat in a chair across the table from her.

"Mind if I sit here?" I asked. A bit late, yeah, but my mind was still trying to catch up with where my body was leading me.

One twitch and her gaze shot to me, her body going tense.

When she didn't respond I leaned my elbows on the table and whispered, "Are you all right?"

She made a strangled sound and shook her head.

"Are you from Hemlock Hollow?"

Confusion clouded her eyes and again she shook her head. "Never heard of it," she said so quietly it was scarcely more than a broken whisper.

Prickles of alarm began to work their way up my arms. Ty hadn't mentioned any other *varúlfur* being in Missoula, or anywhere for that matter. It seemed he and I had a lot more to talk about. But right now I had more pressing matters to worry over, like why something about this young woman felt *wrong*.

"I know what you're going through. I think my friend and I can help," I said.

She made a sound between a snort and a laugh and fixed half-crazed eyes on me. "I seriously doubt that."

"Trust me, I do and I can."

"Really?" she growled, baring fangs at me.

Now her whole body shook, as if she were struggling to control something and was quickly losing.

For the first time, I willed my fangs to grow, and they did. Hiding my surprise, I smiled, exposing them to her. "Really."

The girl pulled back so fast her chair rocked back onto two legs. She teetered, arms flailing. Faster than I ever imagined I could move, one of my hands shot out and grabbed her right wrist. I steadied her, holding tight to that wrist and rising with her as she stood, making it look as though I supported her. A few eyes turned our way.

"Enough caffeine for you, time for some air," I said aloud for the benefit of the onlookers.

Thankfully, she resisted only long enough to grab her backpack and toss it over her shoulder before walking to the door with me. A breeze carrying the scents of blacktop and fast food hit me like a slap as we walked outside. How something I had once loved could now smell so foul, I had no idea.

"You're one of them," the girl whispered in a harsh tone.

Her darting wide eyes told me she would attempt to run the first chance she got.

"Them?" I asked.

She tried to pull her arm from my grasp but I held tight easily. "Like the son of a bitch that bit me, that turned me into...this."

I walked her over to stand beside the bed of the truck, putting it between us and the windows of the coffee shop. "I'm nothing like that one, trust me. I was bitten and turned against my will too."

Some of the fear leaked from her eyes, but the tightness around them betrayed her wariness. "You were?" Hope tinged her quiet voice.

I nodded. "They aren't all like him. We aren't all like him."

The hope I had heard in her voice blossomed in her eyes, brightening them from brown to an almost golden hue. I let go of her arm. She immediately crossed her arms over her chest, but it did little to hide how much she shook.

Her eyes darted about, not as if she were looking for an escape route this time, but more like she was looking for witnesses. "We're werewolves, aren't we?"

"We are. You haven't been through the—well, your first shift yet?" Though I was growing comfortable with the Icelandic terms, I figured she wouldn't have a clue what they meant.

She shook her head. A breath eased from me. For some reason that felt important, as if part of me knew that would change matters considerably.

"My name is Sonya."

Her shaking slowed and her shoulders relaxed a bit. "I'm Candice."

"I'm glad we met, Candice. There are people that can help you through this. You aren't alone." Saying the words aloud made me face the fact that I wasn't alone, either.

The idea both thrilled and terrified me. My entire life I'd been alone. It was easier that way, less people to worry about, to disappoint.

She snorted. "Hmm, well that would be new."

Soft though they were, I heard the distinct rhythm of Ty's footsteps coming across the parking lot. To keep her from growing alarmed, I turned and motioned in Ty's direction with a thrust of my head. "Here comes my friend now."

Looking at his tall, broad frame striding with a confidence few possessed, I realized it would be difficult to look at him and not become alarmed. The man had a presence about him, one that brought Norse Gods to mind. Why the sight of him thrilled me instead of alarmed me, I wasn't sure. Maybe I was well on my way to madness after all. Though he stopped at the tailgate and leaned against it with a casual air, the lines between his brows and around his eyes revealed his tension to me almost as much as the tang in his scent.

"Who do we have here?" he asked through a forced smile.

"This is Candice, and she needs our help. She's like me," I said, though from his demeanor I could tell he already knew she was a newly bitten. But the words were for her sake, not his.

Running a hand through his blond locks, Ty blew out a breath. "I am sorry this happened to you, Candice. Our kind are forbidden to do this to anyone who is not willing."

The girl tightened her arms around herself and thrust her chin higher. "Yeah, that's what she said, yet here we are."

"You hungry? Shall we go grab something to eat and talk?" he suggested.

The casual shrug she gave couldn't hide the way her eyes lit up.

Eager as she was, she refused to get into the cab of the truck with us. Despite only being about sixty-five degrees outside, she insisted on riding in the bed. Still on the edge of wanting to trust Ty myself, I couldn't blame her. She didn't know us, and from the looks of her she was a runaway who had been on her own for a while. Those types didn't tend to trust anyone, something I knew all too much about. After going through a fast food drive thru, Ty took us to one of the half dozen or so parks that made Missoula feel more rural than city. It was easy to see why he chose this city to live near.

In somewhat of a state of awe, I listened as he told Candice most of what he had already told me, using a tone and manner that put the girl at ease. Once in a while she would lower her burger to ask a question, but for the most part she simply devoured the food he put before her and listened. Her ability to absorb it all in stride impressed me, and the fact that she ate two mega-size meals—double cheeseburgers and fries—made me feel a little less guilty about eating an entire one myself. After a bit of careful prodding, Ty and I determined the person who bit her wasn't Raul, which only made me feel slightly less murderous toward the bastard. From the pinched look of confusion on Ty's face when she gave her vague description of her attacker, he couldn't place who it was. She had been attacked at night while walking back to her "pad" as she put it, which sadly turned out to be a place beneath a bridge. When she finished her second meal and began eyeing the fries I had left, I pushed them her way. The hesitant, almost ashamed smile she gave me brought up memories I quickly stifled.

For the first time since I had been bitten, I felt normal. No, better than normal. Helping her felt natural and right on a level that went deeper than even my desire to be a doctor. I couldn't explain it. With a certainty that was a touch disturbing, I knew I had been drawn to that coffee shop, to her. Could it be madness creeping in? Worry over it ate at me, but I didn't let her or Ty see it.

An hour or so after we'd started chatting, a blue Xterra pulled into the parking space behind Ty's truck. Set back some way from the road as our table was, I couldn't see who got out. Leaning back to look around a tree, I saw that it was a woman. Before her first foot stepped on the grass I knew she would come our way. Everything about her from her energy to her stride revealed her to be a *varúlfur*. Whether it was that energy, or just her, I wasn't sure, but something made my proverbial hackles rise. Ty fell silent and sat up straight and stiff. The tightening around his eyes made it obvious he was fighting for control of his temper. Was that veiled anger in his eyes? I couldn't quite tell, but I didn't like what it meant about the woman walking across the grass.

An athletic body was clothed in gray slacks and a darker gray top that revealed quite a bit of cleavage. A plait of long brown hair swung as she walked. Severe brown eyes glared at me from a face that might have been pretty if it didn't look so hostile. The glare only deepened when her gaze shifted to Ty, turning into something almost feral. That look told me all I needed to know about her animosity toward me. And damn if it didn't make me hate her.

"Hello, Tyler," she said coldly.

"Morene." Ty's tone was neutral, careful.

In a flash too quick to be real, her energy changed and she smiled as she looked to Candice. "On behalf of the Alpha Council of Hemlock Hollow, I apologize for what has happened to you. I will take you to people who will help you through this, you have my word." She had that same quality to her voice that told me her first language wasn't English.

She sounded sincere enough, but part of me still didn't like her. Before she arrived Ty had explained to Candice that she needed a teacher of her own to get through this. To my surprise, she had asked for me to do it. When he had explained I was still going through the *verða* myself, she had asked him to do it. Though it seemed like the best option to me, he had insisted she needed a *kennari* of her own, one who could focus solely on her. I didn't know what I had expected, but this woman was not it.

I couldn't help but notice her nails were short and stubby, some clearly having been chewed, as she stuck her hand out to Candice. Like everything else about her, that rubbed me the wrong way.

"I'm Morene," she said.

Candice only stared at her hand as she finished chewing a mouthful of fries. Her hard eyes scanned the woman from top to bottom. Swallowing, she cocked her head. "Yeah, I got that. I'm Candice."

Pulling open the wrapper that held the fries closer, she stuffed another handful in her mouth and leaned back to cross her arms over her chest. "And what happens after you get me to people who will 'help me through this'?"

Morene sat down on the edge of the bench as far from Ty as she could get. "Then you get to decide whether you want to stay with us or leave." The words were tight and the tone controlled, leading me to believe they weren't entirely truthful.

Candice turned to look at me. "Will I be safe with her?"

The question struck a protectiveness deep inside me, making me turn a questioning gaze to Ty. By his pinched look, he clearly wasn't happy about it, but he nodded. Determined not to scare her, but to get the whole story later, I met Candice's eyes again. "Yes. I trust Ty's judgment." I looked to Ty again. "Got a pen and paper?"

Like any good teacher, he produced both from a pocket of his jacket. I wrote my cell number down and handed it to Candice. "You can call me if you need anything, or if you just want to talk."

"I don't have a phone."

Elbows resting on the edge of the table, Morene leaned forward. "We'll stop on the way out of town and get you one."

Gaze never leaving mine, Candice took the piece of paper and shoved it in the pocket of her worn-out jeans. "All right," she said to me.

Promises of also stopping for more food finally got Candice moving toward the Xterra. Barely concealing a look of begrudging tolerance that bordered on hostility, Morene stared Ty down for a tense moment. I walked them to the vehicle, Ty shadowing me much farther behind. There were no tear-filled good-byes, hugging, or even much more than a nod, but Candice's eyes told me all I needed to know. She was grateful but was trusting this woman only because I did. The moment the engine revved to life and Morene began to back the SUV out of the parking spot, I turned to Ty.

"Want to tell me why I'm placing that girl's life in the hands of someone you obviously can't stand?"

"She will be safe with her, you have my word."

Though the words were measured and controlled, his clenched fists gave away his fury. He started for the truck.

"Why don't you like that woman?" I pushed.

"It does not matter," he said as he got in and shut the door.

Determined, I jumped in the passenger side and turned to him. "It does if it affects that girl's life."

His hands clenched the wheel so tight I saw imprints. "It does not. She and I have history. It ended badly, that is all." As he spoke I saw the gleam of fangs.

Compelled by something I couldn't fight, I laid a hand on his arm. It was like placing my hand on a wood stove. Despite the sting, I refused to pull away. Breathing heavy, fangs bared, he turned to me, but it wasn't hostility that flashed in his eyes, it was pain. Damn if that didn't make him even sexier. It shouldn't have after what I'd been through. But where Raul's wolfiness had felt threatening and dangerous, Ty's made my blood heat up.

"I'm sorry. If you feel she's safe, then I trust your judgment," I said softly.

As a long breath eased from him, his fangs retracted. I was about to pull my hand back when his came to rest on top of it, trapping it in a wonderful cocoon of heat. "Thank you. I am sorry, I did not know they would send her."

"You wanna talk about it?"

His hand let go of mine to start the truck. "No."

Though I knew they were long gone, I glanced in the rearview mirror. "Do you think Candice will make it through the *verða*?"

He nodded without hesitation. "It is easier for the young. Their minds are resilient, malleable. The concept does not seem so foreign to them, therefore the risk of madness is less."

"How do you know that if there hasn't been a new *varúlfur* in so long?" If he was just trying to make me feel better, I needed to know.

"The *kennari* handbook."

"Seriously?"

Another nod.

"How did you find her?" he asked.

He shifted into reverse and I sat back in my seat, pulling my seatbelt on. "I saw her sitting in the coffee shop. Coincidence, I guess."

As he turned my way to look behind us, his doubtful gaze raked across mine. "Which is weird enough in itself. But how did you know she was a new *varúlfur*?"

I shrugged. "*Varúlfur* radar. I assumed that was a thing."

His brows knitted together as he pulled out onto the virtually traffic-free road. "It is, sort of. But only after you have gone through the *verða*."

The way he kept his tone guarded, it was hard to tell, but I thought he sounded mystified. Between the sunlight and dappled shadows caused by the trees lining the road and the way he kept his eyes firmly ahead, I couldn't tell much by trying to read his face, either.

"So I'm an early bloomer," I suggested.

"Maybe. I do not know. According to the literature it is not supposed to happen. But like I said, you are the first new *varúlfur* in my lifetime. Well, you and now Candice."

"Wait, there's literature on this? More than just the *kennari* handbook?"

Tension drained from his body and he relaxed back into the seat. "Of course." The playful tone of his voice suggested it wasn't so simple.

"Why haven't you let me read it?"

He shot a half grin my way. "It is in Icelandic."

"Oh."

A determination the likes of which I hadn't felt since my first year of college came over me. Crazy as it was, this was my life now—or would be if I survived. I had to know as much as possible. "Will you teach it to me?"

"Icelandic?"

"No, Chinese." I rolled my eyes upward. "Yes, Icelandic."

"If you really want to learn it."

Was that a challenge I heard in his voice?

"I do."

"All right then. We will start when we get back to the cabin."

I grinned at him, pouring all the challenge I could into it. "Excellent."

Sitting back, I crossed my arms beneath my breasts and turned my attention to the tree-lined roadside. It wasn't that I thought Ty was withholding information, quite the opposite. I needed answers to things I wasn't willing to ask him yet. Like, why was I drawn to a rune that looked like the birthmark on my hip? Why had I known that girl was a new *varúlfur* who'd yet to go through the *verða?* And more importantly, how had I known she needed my help? Me of all people, who could barely help myself.

CHAPTER FOURTEEN

SONYA

H ead still spinning from a two-hour lesson on a literally tongue-
tying language, I leaned over my outstretched leg to grab the
deck railing. The pull of my hamstring muscle helped me clear
my head almost as much as the view of the spruce and pine forest beyond
the deck. Clouds covered most of the blue sky above the towering
treetops, keeping the day pleasantly cool. Even now, rolling some of the
words around in my head, I couldn't get Ty's accent quite right. Breathing
the wet earth and fresh rain-scented air deep into my lungs, I whispered a
few of the toughest words, going over their meaning in my mind.

"See, you are a natural at it." Ty's voice came from the French doors a
moment before his soft footsteps sounded on the deck.

Laying the side of my face against my leg, I peeked at him through the
curtain of my black hair. Clothed only in a pair of loose gray sweats, he
looked as divine as a Norse god. With that smirk on his fine lips, the
expanse of chiseled chest, abs, and those bulging arms, I couldn't imagine a
finer looking deity.

"Hardly," I said a bit breathlessly, hoping he would think it was from
the stretch.

One of his legs came to rest on the railing beside mine, and he leaned
down to stretch. Seeing how my leg was at a ninety-degree angle and his

was barely at forty-five, it hardly seemed as effective for him. I was suddenly very interested in how flexible he might be. Shaking the thought from my mind, I pulled my leg off the rail, took a step away, and began stretching my arms. Sanity, I had to keep my sanity. Which made me wonder...

"You mentioned *varúlfur* who didn't make it through the *verða* being put to the reaper. Is that like a metaphor for a person, or just the killing itself?"

Eyes going so wide they practically bulged from their sockets, you would have thought I'd wrapped my hands around his neck and squeezed. "I should have known you would catch that. I did not mean to say it. Such dark talk is not exactly encouraging to a newly bitten."

I touched his arm, partially because it was growing harder and harder not to touch him, but mostly to make him look at me. Right, that was why, because that was so important. Dammit. "I realize it's been less than a week, but you still know me better than that already. My doctor brain wants all the facts. Tell me."

He met my gaze. "Hundreds of years ago, it was a person, chosen by the Gods, legends say. But with fewer and fewer being bitten in, there has been no need for the Gods to choose a reaper. So now, when necessary, it is carried out by the *lögreglu*."

"The police?"

He grinned. "Very good. Yes, the police, or the chief of police, rather."

"Tell me more about this reaper legend."

"My apologies, I do not know much more about it. It is one of our most obscure legends that is not talked about much. It is a dark part of our history, my father says."

Cocking my head at him, I put a hand on my hip. "Seriously? A history teacher that does not know the legends of his own people?" I teased.

Pink flushed across his cheeks. "I know of it, just not the details. Like I said, our kind do not like to talk about it. Besides, I have spent much of my time learning the history of the world, and there is a lot to learn."

I tagged him gently on one rock-hard biceps. "Forget it, teach. I'm just messing with you." Another thought occurred to me, this one almost as disturbing as thoughts of the reaper. "Do you think Raul had one of his people bite Candice as some twisted backup plan?" With two long phone calls between us in the last twenty-four hours, I had learned the girl liked to chat and had a million questions. Not that I could answer any of them.

Stretching over his leg to loop his interlaced fingers over his toes, he shook his head. "No, even Raul is not that sick. She is just a kid."

"I thought you said they—we—don't do this kind of thing without approval."

"We do not. I do not know who could have done it, or why. Unless... No that is not possible."

His eyes had drifted off into the distance, peering deep into the trees but seeing something else entirely.

"Unless what?" I prompted.

"There are old legends my mother used to tell me, about a time when our kind would bite those who had wronged them. The bitten ones became indentured to those they had wronged, often serving decades or centuries trying to redeem themselves."

Despite the constant flush that clung to me lately, chills crawled up my arms. "What could a teenage girl have done to deserve that?"

Gaze pulling back to me, he shook his head. "Nothing. That is not done anymore. It risks exposing us too much. It was outlawed around 1900."

Hip thrusting out a bit, I rested my right hand on it. "Yeah, well turning someone without *raðið* approval is outlawed too, yet here I stand." I almost nailed the accent, which made me proud despite the darkness of the conversation.

Ty fixed me with a stare so serious it drained the snark right out of me. "You do not understand. Since it was outlawed, the sentence for turning someone to punish them is death."

"Oh."

My chills multiplied until the cool morning air seeped right through my *varúlfur* temperature. "Who would risk that? And why?" My mind went to Raul, then to James—the one who had attacked us on the road. As pissed as I was at him, Raul didn't feel like the right culprit here. But James, I wondered.

Ty shook his head as he stretched an arm behind his back in a maneuver that looked almost painful. The movement made the muscles of his chest flex, which made me forget what we'd been talking about for a second. "No one in their right mind, which sort of answers the why too, I guess. But I do not believe that is why whoever turned Candice did it."

"Why do you think they did it?"

"I am not sure yet."

"What do we do about it?"

"Us?" A sort of helpless frustration clouded his eyes. "There is nothing we can do. It is Council business now. They will handle it."

The finality of his tone grated on my nerves. I got that he felt helpless, removed from the situation because he didn't belong to one of the packs, but how he could let something like this be, I couldn't get.

"And what will they do about it?"

He bent at the waist, reaching for his toes and hiding his face from me at the same time. But that toned backside was oh so visible.

"They will put a *lögreglu* on the case, sniff out whoever did it, and take care of them." The flat tone of his voice revealed that he was trying to hide something.

"And you trust them to do this?"

Expression guarded as it so often was, he stood to his full height and looked down at me. That careful guard slipped a bit as his eyes flicked across my low-cut tank top. Apparently I wasn't the only one distracted. "Yes. Now let us get to this, shall we?" he asked.

I was too emotionally drained to have the energy to pull any more information out of him, so I nodded. "Teach away." Part of me desperately hoped today's lesson involved running, or better yet, *chasing* something. The need to run something down burned through me. I didn't know if it was related to my desire to hunt Raul specifically, or if anything would do. The closer the full moon got, the stronger this impulse grew. Psychoanalyzing that should have helped me squelch the need, but it didn't. I prayed to any who would listen, even the Norse Gods, that it wasn't the madness clawing at the edges of my mind.

Without a word, Ty leaped over the railing and dropped the twenty feet or so to the grass below, making it look graceful and sexy as hell. No. I wasn't allowed to think of him that way, especially when he was acting like the unsanctioned creation of new *varúlfur* wasn't his problem. It seemed to me that should be every *varúlfur*'s problem. Lone wolf or not. He started down the flagstone pathway that wound through a backyard carpeted in as much clover as grass. After a moment he stopped and turned to look at me. A grin pulled his luscious lips upward. How could he frustrate and entice me practically at the same time?

"Are you not coming?"

"You dropped like twenty feet."

He shrugged. "You can too."

Sparkling blue eyes beckoned.

If I broke an ankle or something I was totally going to make him wait on me hand and foot. Preferably in only those sweats. Or less. I took a deep breath and jumped. My legs bent and absorbed the impact with an ease that left me breathless with shock. I didn't even stumble. Looking back up at the deck, I wondered if I could just as easily jump back up. When we came back, I was definitely going to try that.

"Told you," Ty said, drawing my attention back to him and the yard.

Hints of a dark blue lake peeked through the pine trees that bordered the edge of the large lawn. Most people would have cut those trees down to have a full view of the lake, but this way it was somehow more beautiful, mysterious almost. A smile on his face, Ty followed my gaze.

"There is a path that leads down to the lake. Maybe I will show it to you sometime." The hint of joy in his voice made me want to ask him to take me to see it now.

Then I realized he was likely trying to distract me from our earlier conversation. There was something he didn't want me to ask, didn't want me to know. I must have been close to touching on whatever it was. And here I had let him sidetrack me again.

Arms crossing beneath my breasts, I stopped when he did and faced him. I won't lie and say I didn't enjoy his gaze wandering down to the cleavage the V of my low-cut T-shirt revealed. "Maybe I'll let you."

A pointed pink tongue darted out to lick his lips. The sight made muscles between my legs clench and it was all I could do to will myself not to get wet. Would he smell it if I did? For some reason the idea sent a rolling tremor through my inner labia. He looked quickly away.

"You said you have taken martial arts," he said with a forced casual air.

"Yes." My attempt not to sound breathless wasn't much better.

Those glacier-blue eyes crawled back to me as if they couldn't stay away. "Full contact, light, or no contact?"

Seeing how my mind went somewhere completely different—somewhere his own resided by the hungry way he chewed on his bottom lip—it took me a moment to answer. "Light."

One after the other, he rolled his shoulders, the motion having a sort of cleansing effect that left his face blank. "Good. We will do a bit of sparring and work on your anger control that way."

I didn't want to tell him, but that would certainly test me. When sparring, my mind went to a place where the fight was real. My dad had always said we must train like we want to fight because when it comes down to it, we will fight like we trained. And the idea of anyone raising a hand to me really pissed me off. It was part of why I had never taken to the idea of sparring, and hence never gotten very good at fighting.

"So we're not going to work on controlling desire?" I asked, making my voice sound teasing to cover the disappointment.

He chewed on his bottom lip as his eyes traveled the length of my body. "Unfortunately, that is not your strongest emotion."

The measure to which his disappointment pleased me was so wrong. If only he knew. Ty led me to where the flagstones circled an area of sand. I had a feeling it was no coincidence the circle was the size of a standard fighting ring. With a wave of his hand, he invited me to step in first. Not knowing what to expect, I kept him in my peripheral as I moved past him. Despite being wet from last night's rain, the sand was pleasantly warm beneath my bare feet.

"*Varúlfur* fight for their place in the pack. Fighting comes as natural to us as breathing and hunting." As he spoke he paced around me, legs bent in a fighting stance, hands up at the ready.

I shifted into a stance of my own and moved methodically with him to keep him in my line of sight. "Great. I suck at fighting. No room for pacifists, huh?"

He took a slow jab at me, one easily blocked with a sweep of my right forearm. "Sure, at the bottom of the pack. But you do not strike me as one who enjoys being on the bottom." The gleam in his blue eyes as they flashed across my body revealed his double meaning.

The look alone heated me up more than the rise of my wolf ever could. I returned the smile, and the jab. He blocked mine just as easily, the skin of his arm sliding across mine in something close to a caress. "As long as the person on top is good at what they're doing, I don't mind."

The husky tone of his voice took my mind to places I couldn't afford it to go. Drawn by those thoughts, my eyes traveled the impressive V of his lower abs and external oblique muscles to where they disappeared into his low-slung sweatpants. The *verða* had to be setting my lady parts on fire because there was no way I wanted anything to do with sex after what had happened with Raul. Yes, that had to be it. Was this what madness felt like? The thought sent a shiver of fear through me.

Ty made a contented sound somewhere between a groan and a growl that made it hard to focus. "*Sanngjarn nógur*," he said as he prowled around me.

Impossibly, his voice sounded even sexier when he spoke Icelandic. Fingers curling into fists, I kept my stance low and stepped as he stepped, keeping him in sight.

"And that means?"

The right corner of his mouth quirked up. "You tell me."

"Seriously? A language lesson now, when we're about to fight?"

"Always."

Pulling in the scents of damp sand and grass, I thought hard. "*Nógur*, that must be similar to *nóg*, which means "enough. The other words I don't know."

Fast as a snake, he shot in, tapped my midsection with a punch that barely brushed my tank top, and threw a backhand toward my head. Our arms collided with a smack reminiscent of bodies slapping in a far more intimate setting as I blocked the backhand. Dammit, I had to get my mind out of the gutter. I barely knew this guy. Falling into bed with him just because he was hot could be an epic mistake, and I'd had my fill of those. This one, though, this could kill me.

"The first is actually one word, it means fair. But you got half of it, that is good," he said.

But was it? I couldn't help but wonder. No doubt the phrase was one he had taught me this morning, one I'd already forgotten. To get any of the language down before we went to Hemlock Hollow in a little over two weeks I was going to have to seriously step it up. My distraction must have shown because Ty grinned and kicked out at me. As I sidestepped it, he whipped his leg in the opposite direction, catching me behind the knees and sweeping my legs out from beneath me. Had the impact not knocked the air from my lungs, I would have cursed something colorful enough at him to make him blush. Or at least tried.

"Ah come on, you made that too easy," he said.

I glared at the hand he offered and stood on my own, my guard coming back up the moment I was on my feet.

"Yeah, well, I didn't realize you were going to play dirty."

He licked his lips, making me wonder what they tasted like. "It is no fun if we do not get a bit dirty," he said.

"*Sanngjarn nógur*," I threw back at him.

I threw a few punches and other strikes, testing his defenses and reaction times. He blocked swift and smooth in an almost effortless fashion, his eyes locked on mine all the while. The grace with which his movements flowed was something I hadn't possessed even in the height of my training years ago. But I found that as we danced, my reactions smoothed out, beginning to flow from that place within where no thought dwelled, only instinct. Our bodies collided, arms with arms, arms with legs, sometimes legs with legs in the dance of blocks and strikes. Some of them stung, especially on my shins and forearms where I lacked muscle, but none hurt. He was going easy on me. Oddly, that made me angrier than the occasional strikes that broke through my defenses.

I sped up and he followed suit. Still, he pulled his strikes, never landing them hard enough to hurt, or even knock the air from me. It made me feel inadequate, which fueled the very thing I was working to control. The combination of his speed and perfect form made it impossible to land even a single strike on him. It had been a very long time since anyone had made me feel like a helpless girl. My skin began to burn and my teeth began to ache. Growing desperate to land even just one strike, I sped up more. Again and again he tapped my side, stomach, back, with gentle strikes, proving my defenses were not keeping up with my speed.

"Dammit!" I yelled as his fist brushed my T-shirt below my breasts.

Laughter bubbled from him as he spun around me and landed another strike on my back, this one so feather soft it was obviously meant to tease. I'd had it. Fast as I could, I stepped back, one leg going between his. I slammed into his chest—which wasn't even slick with sweat, dammit—

dropping down the moment I felt the impact, and grabbed his leg. Wrapping my arms around it, I stood and threw my body back against his. Air left him in a whoosh and suddenly we were both on the ground. Releasing his leg, I spun around in a half crouch. Before he could get up, I straddled his waist and raised my fist high. Breath coming in gasps, lips curled back from my fangs, I stared into his eyes and realized I was about to lose it.

The burning beneath my skin intensified until I broke out into a sweat. I teetered on the edge of panic. My breath came in gasps, tongue brushing against the backs of my fangs with each gasp. My nostrils flared, not to draw in scents, but from the onslaught of them: Ty's delicious sweat and musk, the sweet clover and tang of evergreens. Colors grew brighter. The grass beneath Ty seemed greener. The blue of his eyes became downright glacial as they stared up at me, filled with concern. A soft, steady thudding drew my attention. It took me a moment to realize it was Ty's heart. The world began to slip away, or rather, I did.

Along with the panic came the expectation of that feathery touch of madness, but I didn't feel it. Curious, I searched my mind for it. It wasn't there.

"Easy, Sonya, easy. Breathe, relax. Just relax." Ty's methodical voice had an instant soothing effect. He kept talking, encouraging me in soft tones much like a hypnotist might use.

The sound slowly brought me back, working like the North Star to guide me to safe shores. While he had helped, I had been the one to bring myself back. I felt that down to my bones. Soon I could feel him beneath me again, his hips holding my legs apart, his groin scorching against mine. Damn, he was hot. Literally. Considering the pressure I felt against my opening, it wasn't hard to guess why. Well, it was hard, quite hard, and the length of that pressure was impressive. Heat spread from between my legs, rising upward through me like a tide. The desire to tear Ty's sweats off and uncover what lay beneath made my hands roll into fists at my sides. Skin crawling and teeth aching, I leaned my head back and tried to catch my breath.

"Whoa, easy, no jumping lessons here. Breathe and find your center, your place of control," Ty said.

Melodic and soothing though his voice was, it also sounded deep and husky with a desire he seemed to be struggling with too. That knowledge made me wet. So much for keeping him from smelling my desire. At the moment I had bigger problems, like how my vision sharpened and how I could suddenly hear not only my own heart beating, but his as well. Colors changed slightly. They didn't bleed out like I half expected them to, but shifted, as if I was seeing on a different spectrum now. Light became far more intense.

The moon pulled at me from its position below the horizon.

"Sonya." Ty grabbed my arms. "Sonya!"

Slowly, I forced my gaze from the sky and trees. Ty had sat up and now shook me slightly. His blond brows scrunched together over his worry-filled eyes. My gaze tried to stray down to his bare, broad, rock-hard chest...

"Sonya!"

Like a switch being flicked, my attention shot back up to his face.

"Good. Now tell me why it bothers you that you could not land a hit on me," he said.

My face scrunched up into a look that had to be unattractive. "What?"

"Why did it make you mad that you could not hit me?" he pressed.

I shrugged his arms off me. He gave in a bit too easily, letting go as if I were on fire. "What are you talking about?"

He shook his head slowly from side to side. "Do not get angry. You need to focus on the reason for the emotion, rather than the emotion itself. Understanding reason is what keeps us from getting caught up in our emotions. It will help you keep control, and your sanity."

Uncomfortable as the idea made me, it also made sense. Figured. Everything about this made me uncomfortable, except for the strong, wonderful-smelling man beneath me. In one awkward motion, I pushed up off my knees and flipped to my feet. He rose slowly, like a predator flowing to its feet, eyes never leaving mine. Damn it was sexy. From beneath my skin a slight hum started. I slammed my eyes shut and tried to focus on what he had said. Reason, it had been about reason...

The hum slowed and finally stopped. Thoughts became clearer. "I don't like to feel as though I can't protect myself," I finally said.

Careful to keep his distance, Ty slowly rose to his full height several feet away. "There is no shame in that. It is a bad feeling. See how thinking of that stopped the change?"

I nodded.

"Good. Keep that reason forefront in your mind when you feel yourself losing control. Knowing what triggers an instinct is the key to controlling it," Ty said, this time in his teaching voice rather than that soothing, sexy voice that was meant to calm me and did the opposite.

The way his eyes locked on my chest made me tug at my shirt, wishing I had worn a bra that concealed how much I was attracted to him. Was it really attraction, though? Or a response of the *verða*? I preferred to think the latter. The wonderful ache in my hard nipples didn't really care what the reason was, but I tried to focus on it anyway. Once I got through this process and shifted, I'd be in control again. And then, who knew, I might not be attracted to him at all. That both soothed and upset me. The resemblance to puberty wasn't lost on me. And much like puberty, I just had to get through it without going mad. Today I felt a step closer to that. And to achieve it, I could fight my attraction to him. I knew I could.

And I did. For a while.

CHAPTER FIFTEEN

TY

Than calm, happy place of meditation would not come to me today. Well, at least the calm part would not. The happy part, that was another problem altogether. Watching the sunlight play across the silky black strands of hair blowing across Sonya's closed eyes made parts of me all too happy.

Something new and wild was awakening inside her and the more it awakened, the more my wolf side was drawn to her. Much more than my wolf was drawn to her. Had it been only the wolf, I could have fought it easier. But fight it I would. I had to. Her brow furrowed after a while, and I had to resist the urge to kiss the wrinkles away.

"You are scowling," I said in my non-meditation-inducing tone.

Those gorgeous eyes of hers slowly blinked in the bright sun. "Scowling?" she asked in a lazy tone.

"Um-hum. Meditation is supposed to be relaxing," I chided.

A bead of sweat rolled down the side of her forehead along her hairline. Gods, how I wanted to lick it from her skin. Thor give me strength, or else I did not know how much longer I would be able to resist. I knew how wrong it was, and on how many levels. But why did it feel so right? Every part of me ached to kiss her.

"Well, my mind has too much to think about to relax. Besides, it's hot, makes it hard to."

Head cocking to the side, I looked up at the sun. "It cannot be much above seventy. What you are feeling is the alteration of your body temperature."

She fanned herself. "What do you mean?"

"We *varúlfur* run hotter than normal people."

One eyebrow rose into her dark hair as her gaze skittered across my bare chest. The attention threatened to give my lower abdominal muscles a workout. "Hotter?" Her breathy voice guaranteed it.

I took a moment to gather myself so I did not pant like an animal. "Much like canines run hotter than humans, so do we. But it is more than that. It has to do with the atoms in our body moving and rearranging themselves."

After a long drink from the water bottle sitting in the grass beside her, she nodded. "That actually makes sense."

I offered my hands to her and she grasped them both. Her small, soft hands gripped mine with a strength that thrilled me. Together, we rose as one, each helping to pull the other up. With a thrust of my head, I indicated the direction of the lake. "Shall we go for a swim?"

She groaned, a reluctant and completely sexy sound that made my blood pump south. "I don't have a swimsuit."

Head dropping, I gazed at her from beneath my brows—well, as much as a six-foot-five man can at a five-six woman. "No need, it is a private lake. No one will be there but us." I told myself it was only to help her get used to life as a *varúlfur*. The problem was, I was a terrible liar, even to myself.

Crossing her arms beneath her breasts, she narrowed her gaze at me. "I know what you must think of me because of what happened with Raul, but I am not some easy girl who drops her panties for every great set of abs. I did not have sex with him."

The mention of panties made me instantly hard. The reaction gave credence to her fears and made me feel like an ass. I pulled my hands from hers and held them up in a placating gesture. "Whoa, that is not what I think at all. Raul is a master manipulator. I do not think badly of you; I think you were a victim of his."

The wrinkles between her brows fell away, taking her scowl with them. "Then why..."

The turmoil broiling in her eyes made me feel horrible. I had to fix it, to ease her pain. I could not let her believe I looked down on her for this. It could not have been further from the truth. "Every time we shift, which is often, we take our clothes off. Our kind do not think much about being naked. I am sorry if it came across wrong," I said.

Her eyes widened and she straightened. "Point made. Lead on," she said as she gestured toward the lake.

"It is all right if you are not comfortable with that yet, Sonya."

She gave me a little push in the direction of the lake. "I'm burning up, we're both adults, and I trust you'll be a gentleman."

If only I could trust myself to be. But she needed the distraction. Each day that passed I noticed her aggression grew and she fought harder against her instincts. Hands up in surrender, I started for the tree line. "No pressure, huh?" I said with a laugh.

We wove down a pine needle–strewn path that went around towering ponderosas, which offered a refreshing reprieve from the glaring sun. Their sweet, earthy scent normally soothed me, but not today. Beneath it I smelled the lake water, cool and fresh, fed by an underwater stream. Birds sang to one another in the branches overhead. Pleasant though their songs were, they only served to accentuate my torment. I pasted a smirk on my face but Sonya kept giving me a look like she did not believe it.

"Your own private lake. Must be nice," she said.

"Hmmm, it is."

While I loved this place, it stirred up memories of my ex and all the havoc and heartache she had wreaked on both me and those I cared about.

"I would have loved a place like this as a kid," Sonya said.

I wanted to respond, but I could not force the words past the pain, the anger.

A rocky shoreline opened up before us, dark blue waters lapping only a few yards away. The lake stretched out a good distance, though not so far as to be considered big. Cooler air blew up off the water, taking some of the heat of the morning with it. Though it helped, it only made me want more. I longed to jump into that cold water but the ghosts of my past held me back. I should not have brought her here.

"What's wrong?" Sonya asked, her voice breaking through the haze of pain that had settled over me.

Slowly, like a man awakening from deep sleep, my eyes focused and my head turned toward the sound of her voice. She had removed her tank top and her hand was frozen on the clasp at the back of her bra. The contours of her back and abdominal muscles drew my eyes to the waistband of her cutoff jean shorts. Gods she looked amazing. The fact that she was undressing and walking toward the water helped break through my trauma, but not as completely as I would have liked.

"Maybe this is not a good idea." My voice was distant, distracted, and pissed, even to my own ears.

Sonya walked back to my side, stopping out of reach. "Ty, what's wrong?"

A long, slow growl slid from me as my eyes traveled over the smooth pebbles of the bank. "Morene and I used to come here a lot." I had to pull out of my own head, for Sonya's sake. She needed the distraction today's relaxing would give us.

Was that anger that flashed across her face? I was too distracted to tell, and not in the way I should have been.

"She likes to swim?"

A sardonic smile pulled at my lips. "No, she hated the water, said it ruined her hair. She liked to lie out here and sunbathe when we were in high school." My gaze dragged back over the pebbled beach, my mind recalling things I wanted desperately to forget.

"Well, you're going to have to get wet, because I like the water," she said.

More clothing hit the ground. My eyes snapped back to her, finding her stark naked. Standing with one hand on her bare hip, she gave me a playful smile. Nipples hard as bearings adorned breasts that would fit perfectly into my big hands. The short trimmed hair that covered her groin was the same beautiful black as the hair on her head. I exclaimed something highly inappropriate before I could stop myself—thankfully having the good sense to say it in Icelandic. So much for being a gentleman. The huge smile on her face made me think maybe she did not care.

She wiggled her eyebrows at me. "I didn't catch most of that, except for the part about getting wet."

Hot blood rushed through me. I had to bite my tongue against a reply. Gods, what had she understood? My fingers slipped beneath the waistband of my sweats and I began to push them down. Feigning disinterest, Sonya turned toward the water, but I could see her watching me through the black veil of her hair. Keeping my pace slow, I slid both my sweats and boxers off, hesitating only slightly to let my erection jump free. Grinning immensely, she squeezed her eyes shut and turned her head to the lake.

Not wanting to seem like a complete voyeur, I kept my eyes on the lake. To better distract myself, I tried to focus on the brilliant blue hue of the water, the contrasting green of the trees framing the opposite shore, even the multi-colored round rocks leading up to it all. It worked to keep my eyes occupied, but my mind kept returning to that delicious glimpse of her in all her glory.

Water splashed as Sonya took her first steps into it. By the time I got my feet to move she was up to her knees, rings of blue radiating out around her. Trying not to watch her out of my peripheral, and failing, I strode into the water until I stood beside her. Heat sponged from my skin, drawing a sigh of relief from me. Out of a need to feel that soothing coolness all over in hopes it would douse the fire building within, I stretched out my arms and plunged into the water. Only a few strokes out, the rocky ground fell away. The slight sensation of moving water beneath my feet revealed the stream that fed the lake.

All the heat of the morning melted away, taking my pent-up need and stress with it. Water had that type of soothing effect on me, the more of it I could be in, the stronger the effect. Until now my evening showers had been keeping thoughts of a naked and eager Sonya at bay. Now that I had seen the real thing, I would have to make dips into this lake a frequent occurrence. Preferably with her. Dammit, so much for cooling down.

Sonya dove into the water, surfacing a few yards out. Lips pulled up into a smile, she turned on her back and floated. Her breasts bobbed, water trailing off in rivulets from her hard nipples. It pooled down in the line that led to her belly button, making me want to lap it up.

"Odin, woman, you are out to test how much of a gentleman I will be, are you not?" I said, voice strained.

Laughing, she sank back beneath the surface and began to tread water. I swam up beside her.

"Sorry, forgot myself for a minute," she said in a tone that told me she hadn't forgotten for one second.

I groaned. "Oh, do not be sorry. I enjoyed the show."

Exasperated exclamations flew from her lips as she splashed water at me. Grin widening, I splashed back at her, starting a water fight that soon left us both laughing so hard we could barely stay afloat. The desire in her eyes had transformed into something almost innocent and fun. Seeing it was like glimpsing how she must have been as a child and it stunned me in more ways than one.

"So you were born a *varúlfur?*" she asked.

Hands fanning through the water before me, I watched the ripples as I nodded.

"How was it, being raised a *varúlfur?*"

This would take a while. Best to do it somewhere we could relax better. Besides, I had a sudden urge to take her somewhere I had never taken anyone else. A thrust of my chin pointed to a distant island in the middle of the lake. Two thousand or so square feet of land probably made it more of a mooring spot than an island, but the lone hemlock and a few bushes on it had always made me think of an island.

"Are you a good swimmer?" I asked.

She nodded. "I can make that."

Water splashed once again as we matched each other stroke for stroke, maintaining a good pace all the way to the island. In what seemed like no time at all, sand tickled my feet. The little island was covered in golden sand, making it into a small beach. To my disappointment, Sonya sat on the sandy bottom, the water reaching her collarbones. Though her breasts floated, the water was deep enough to keep anything submerged that a bikini would cover. In the crystal-clear water I could still see plenty, but the view was distorted, and the sun hit the water just right with each lap to hide more than it revealed. I sat down beside her, keeping my lower body well below the surface. I let out a breath as gently as I could in hopes she wouldn't hear it.

"This place is amazing," she said, eyes scanning the tiny island.

I followed her gaze and couldn't help but smile, recalling years of playing shipwrecked, pirates, and Gulliver here. "This was my favorite place as a kid."

Clouds a serious-looking shade of dark gray had moved in while we were swimming over. One sunbeam broke through and bathed Sonya in light. The sight tugged at me, hard.

One corner of her lips quirking up, she turned to me. "Thank you for showing it to me."

It took me a second to remember what she was responding to. "You are the first person I have ever brought here," I admitted. Helheimr, she was the first person I had ever wanted to bring here, though I was not about to admit that part.

Her face softened, taking on a gentle look. "I'm honored. Thank you."

The amazing thing was, I could tell she truly meant it. Too deep. I needed to keep this light or else I was going to start down a path I wasn't sure I was prepared to travel. Thunder rumbled in the distance as if Thor himself warned me against it.

Eyes forward, for the most part, I changed the subject back to the question she had asked before we swam over here. "I have never known anything but being a *varúlfur*, so I really do not know what it would be like to grow up normal. When both of your parents are *varúlfur*, you are born one. We still go through the becoming, it is just different. Our bodies are prepared for it."

"When did you first shift?" she asked.

Blood rushed to my face at the memory and I looked quickly down. "The ability manifests itself in those of us natural born during puberty."

When I had agreed to be her *kennari*, I had sworn to myself that I would withhold nothing from her. But this, Gods, did I dare tell her this? It was not that I was worried about what she would think of me. She was not the conservative type who would balk at such a thing. But I did not want her thinking I was trying to be forward.

"How did it happen? Tell me about it," she pressed.

My face burned and I knew I had to be blushing horribly. Damn, no hiding it now. "It was orgasmic, literally, considering I had just finished masturbating at the time."

"Oh my God!" Her hand flew up to cover her gaping mouth and she barely stifled a laugh. Just as abruptly, her expression turned serious. "I'm sorry, that had to be horrible."

In her excitement, she had turned to face me and the lower half of her body began to float. Her beautiful bare ass had broken the surface. My tongue darted out to lick my bottom lip while my eyes devoured her. Again a boom of thunder sounded, this time louder, closer. It felt as if Thor himself were laughing at me. Or encouraging me. A growing part of me preferred to think the latter.

"Not at all. I expected it. I had wanted it to happen like that the first time," I said.

"Why?" she asked, leaning in closer.

"You know how kids are. Everyone said it hurt the first time, so I wanted to make it feel good."

"Yeah, but weren't you worried about future orgasms triggering the shifting?" she asked.

I loved how quick she was to think of that. I waved a hand, sending water flying. Sunlight danced across the droplets, turning them a rainbow of colors. They slapped the water with a slight pop and sank back into it.

"No. It is impossible to shift during orgasm because your body is so focused on the act. I chose to shift right after, when all the endorphins were still in my system. It was not the first time I had masturbated, after all," I said.

The relief on her face turned to curiosity. Her gaze moved slowly from my lips up to my eyes. Gods if she was not tearing down all my carefully constructed walls. I needed to shut this down, to change the course of the conversation, but I could not bring myself to. She was amazing and perfect in her imperfections. After all they had done, what did I owe the Council anyways?

"So does it hurt?" she asked.

"No. It was warm and a bit uncomfortable the first time, but it did not hurt. Of course, that could have been because of the endorphins." Blood rushed to my groin when I realized how close I had made shifting sound to masturbating. But if Thor was indeed encouraging me, then maybe the Council was wrong about the emotions of new *varúlfur* being influenced by the *verða*. Gods knew they had been wrong about plenty of other things in the past. Eyebrows wiggling, I leaned in close. "We could test that theory if you would like," I said, lowering my voice a few octaves.

The rapid, strong rhythm of her heartbeat revealed the level of her excitement over my suggestion. I wasn't sure which disturbed me more:

her intense desire for me, or the fact that I reciprocated it. She leaned in so close her breasts almost touched my chest.

"Tell you what, I won't test your gentlemanly restraint if you won't test my attempt to be ladylike," she whispered close to my ear.

A groan that I knew would do exactly what she asked me not to vibrated behind my pursed lips. I drew away and stood. The surface of the water reached below my belly button. Her gaze followed the path of water droplets streaming between my abs. Lightning crackled across the sky not far to the north, making her jump.

"Fair enough. We should get out of here before that storm reaches us," I suggested.

Her eyes moved to the stormy skies brewing above and she nodded without even a hint of concern. "If you'd like. I've always loved storms. They don't worry me," she said, her expression close to longing.

I tore my eyes from her as another flash of lightning lit up the sky behind me. Any semblance of sunlight had fled completely in the wake of roiling, dark clouds. "Yes, well, they do me. We are tough to kill, but not impossible, especially you."

She shrugged, but thankfully raised her arms to start out into the water. Thunder boomed as a bolt of lightning hit the bank opposite us. The rocky shore seemed to glow for a moment. I grabbed Sonya's arm and started to pull her back onto the shore with me. The little island was not exactly safe, but it was better than the water.

"We have to get out of the water," I warned.

We backpedaled onto the sandy shore as fast as our feet would go. Holding tight to her hand, I led her away from the tree. I hated how exposed standing in the wide open space made me feel, but it was the safest place, and that was not saying much. To my amazement, Sonya grinned up at the sky without an ounce of fear. Thunder boomed again and she smiled all the wider, closing her eyes.

"My dad always called the thunder Thor's music. It holds a certain rhythmic beauty, don't you think?" she asked, eyes opening as she turned that smile to me.

Her irises appeared golden with lightning crackling in the distance. The sheer joy on her face moved me on a deep level. One hand going around her waist, I gravitated toward her, and she to me. Her fingers brushed the sides of my face, their touch hesitant. The look of desire in her eyes was anything but. Desire won out and she pulled me down to her. Gods help me, but I let her. Just before I closed my eyes to kiss her I smelled a metallic scent somewhere between copper and steel. Then I saw it coming for us: a massive bolt of lightning. My *varúlfur* speed was no match for the fingers of Odin.

Light erupted all around us. For a moment it seemed the entire world was made of it. I could not even see Sonya within it. Then it flung me backward. My back connected with something so hard that I had neither breath nor sight for a moment. When both came back I realized the rough texture at my back was the tree. Every part of my body ached and burned at the same time. Almost immediately, the burning in me faded to a warmth that meant my *varúlfur* abilities were working on healing me. I tried to rise to find Sonya but barely managed to turn my head. Even if I could have moved, the sight I saw would have frozen me in place.

The bolt of lightning still held Sonya in its white, crackling beam. But that was not possible. Lightning struck and was gone in an instant, or it was supposed to. She stood with her arms outstretched and lifted slightly toward the dark sky. Little strings of lightning crackled along her skin, over her arms and fingers. She began to laugh and dance like a child overwhelmed with delight. That's when I realized the lightning did not have a hold of her; she had a hold of it.

My power had done enough healing for me to rise onto legs that shook from both the injury and what I beheld. The impossibility and beauty of it —and of her—left me baffled despite my extensive knowledge in Viking and *varúlfur* history.

The lightning started to lose its crackle. The tiny veins of it playing over her skin faded away. The huge bolt sank slowly through her and into the ground. She turned her smile onto me and damn if her eyes weren't glowing with residual electricity.

"Are you all right? Did you see that?" she asked.

One eye on the sky and the other on her, I approached slowly. My balls tried to crawl back up into my body out of fear of residual lightning. Not the impression a man wants to make on a lady, but thankfully she was too distracted by the fact that she had channeled lightning to look at my shrinking cock.

"I most definitely saw," I said.

As I walked, I continued to check the skies. The clouds rolled on at an alarming speed—thankfully into the distance.

Eyes wide with joy, grinning like a fool, she practically skipped to me, breasts bouncing in a way that was enticing enough to distract me even after what had just happened. She took hold of my hands. Little shocks traveled from her up into me, like a strong static electricity. The slight pain it brought reminded me that my body was still trying to heal itself from the direct strike we had both taken. Of which she seemed to be suffering no ill effects at all. From her expression, I did not think it had hurt her. Yet it had blown me several feet away.

"You didn't tell me we could channel lightning! That was amazing, like being part of the storm," she exclaimed.

The painful little shocks continued to flow from her hands, but I didn't let go. "That is because we cannot."

Her brow scrunched up. "What do you mean?"

I shook my head, taking a moment to find the words through my shock. "I have never heard of a *varúlfur* who can channel lightning." I wanted to say more, to ease any concerns she might have, but I had no more words.

"Hmm. Well that's strange," she said.

The wrinkles between her brows smoothed out and her smile returned. "But it was amazing!"

I laughed, because what else could I do? Then I realized her hands felt smooth. I couldn't feel the edges of the cut from the beer bottle. I turned her hands over in mine. The cut was gone and the skin new and smooth, without a trace of the wound. It should have taken days more to heal.

"And it keeps getting stranger. Your cut is healed," I said.

She looked down at her hand. "It was the lightning. I felt it knit together while it coursed through me. What do you think it means?"

Unable to offer up anything else, I shook my head. "I do not know, but we will definitely do some research on it." A few fat raindrops fell on my arms. This storm clearly was not done, and I wanted out of it before a repeat occurrence. "Tell you what, how about we go back to the house, I will barbeque some steaks, you can tell me all about it, and we will research some of the old books for information on this," I said.

I didn't want to scare her with too much talk about how strange this was. It was best if I researched it before giving her yet another thing to worry about. We were lucky as Helheimr that the lightning hadn't caused her to shift. For now, distraction would be best.

She pulled her bottom lip in between her teeth and looked down at me. "With clothes on?" she teased.

I laughed and she looked quickly away. The demure way she did it made me instantly hard again. How could she do that to me so easily?

"Yes. Do you like scary movies?" I asked, desperate to shift the conversation and get her moving.

"Oh, if that isn't a line..." She rolled her eyes and shook her head as she led me back to the water by the hand. "But yes, if they are truly scary and not just the slasher kind, I do."

"Good. We will watch a movie then. And do not worry, I will sit on the opposite end of the couch, and even put on a shirt."

One corner of her mouth lifted into a crooked grin and she tilted her head to look at me from beneath her eyebrows. "No need for that. Lightning doesn't strike the same place twice." The sultry tone of her voice melted and hardened me all at the same time.

Another quick glance at the sky showed dark clouds being swept away by a brisk wind. The clouds grew brighter with a flash, but it was contained within them. For now. Just in case that changed, I had to get her out of here, at least until we figured out what this channeling lightning thing was all about.

I plunged into the water and let go of her hand. Kicking off, I turned and backstroked away. She squeezed her eyes shut but it was too late. I knew by how red her face grew that she had witnessed how much she affected me. It worked. She plunged into the water and started to swim after me. I swam as fast as I could, eager to get out of the giant conductor of electricity and back to the house and hit the books. I didn't even know which *varúlfur* history books to research in regards to this. The mystery of this woman kept getting deeper and deeper.

CHAPTER SIXTEEN

SONYA

The pale yellow light of dawn had only started to cast its glow over the forest as I put my earbuds in, turned my music on, and started down the path. Dew heightened the scents of sweet pine needles and rich earth, making me long for the deep breaths of hard running. Tightening my ponytail, I picked up my pace. While I didn't like to run if I wasn't being chased, I wanted to get into as good a shape as possible before going to Hemlock Hollow. My fighting skills sucked enough that I had to make up for it with a bit of stamina training. Now I made a point to run every morning. My wolfy side would have preferred to be chasing something, but I was so not ready to go there. Ty had agreed to let me jog on my own after I had insisted I needed a bit of "me" time.

Not that I didn't want Ty time. Oh how I did. That was the problem though; all I wanted was Ty time. Something existed between us, that was for sure. But we couldn't give in to it completely, not yet. Focus was vital more than ever. Now I had another reason not to go mad and be put down. Whatever might be between Ty and me was worth fighting for. I drew on the strict thinking and dedication that had gotten me through all these years of medical school so far. It helped. A little.

Anger management training was going well, according to him at least. I wasn't so convinced. The heat and vibrations had become easier to control already, but my fangs still extended every time I got pissed. Part of the reason for the progress, I feared, was that I couldn't bring myself to get angry with Ty. Though he fought hard and pushed me harder, he never tried to hurt me or humiliate me like a lot of guys would when sparring with a woman. What I had a harder time controlling was my growing desire for him. Hence the need for me time.

Miles down the evergreen-lined trail, just as I reached my running groove, I sucked in a few scents that brought me to a skidding halt. The somewhat tangy mixture of fresh air and asphalt mingled with leather and wolf in a way that was both appealing and alarming. A figure stepped out from the trees ahead of me. Black leather chaps and jacket hugged a frame that was too short and narrow to be Ty. And of course I hadn't seen a motorcycle jacket hanging in his closet. I tore the earbuds from my ears.

Deep in my gut the sensation of familiarity stirred. Not because I knew this person, but because part of me knew they were a *varúlfur*. Hands held up, he approached me. At first the dark hair stirred my anger, but a closer glance at the neatly trimmed beard and deep-set eyes proved this wasn't Raul. Something about him tugged at my memory. Then it hit me. He had been the guy back at the restaurant, one of Raul's pack. I wasn't sure if I should be relieved he was from the Reinhard pack and not the Arnoddr pack. Both wanted me for reasons that had little to do with my welfare.

"What do you want?" I demanded as I casually turned my side to him. I didn't want to run, but I didn't think I could beat this guy in a fight if it came to it.

Like a smart wolf, he stopped a little more than five feet away. "Only to talk. I come in peace."

Though I kept my eyes on him, I tried to reach out with my other senses to make sure he was the only one. The heady scent of greenery warming in the sun overlaid the more distant smells of stagnant water and a warm engine. Birds chirped and rustled through the trees while frogs croaked down by the lake a little less than half a mile away. It freaked me out a bit that I could hear the frogs and knew how far away they were, but I'd have to process that later. The important thing was that this guy seemed to be the only one around.

"Then talk, but make it quick," I warned.

"Raul wanted to be here for you. He wanted to be the one to help you through the *verða*. If Ty hadn't chased him off, Raul would have been there for you."

A sharp bark of laughter escaped me. "I wouldn't be going through the damn *verða* if it weren't for him. The bastard should have thought to ask me if I even wanted this."

The man stammered several times before he got his next words out. "He wanted to, more than anything, but things got...rushed. He knows how special you are and that things shouldn't have happened this way."

I laughed and put my hands on my hips. Clearly this idiot wasn't going to attack me. "Special? Really? That's his excuse? The bastard took my life from me. It may not have been much, but it was mine and he had no right." With each word of the last sentence I took a step closer to the man, poking him in the chest with a finger upon the final word.

His prominent Adam's apple bobbed, and he leaned back. To his credit, he didn't step away. "He doesn't want you to be forced into mating with someone else. It's part of why he had to bite you in how he did," he said in a voice that shook a bit too much for my liking.

The sound of it, meek and docile, stirred something inside me, something that wanted to throw him to the ground and put my teeth to his throat. Some badass biker he was. My fangs extended. *Whoa.* Shaking my head, I took a step back and turned to walk away. Eyes closing, I concentrated on my breathing while trying to appear casual. What reason would stir such a reaction in me, I couldn't figure. Then it occurred to me that wolves have reasons too. This man's submissive attitude was what elicited such a reaction in the wolf part of me. The realization gave me the control I needed to retract my fangs and turn back around to face him.

"That's disgusting. By biting me, Raul virtually turned me into his sister, or daughter, or whatever. I don't know how the hell that works. But I can assure you, we will definitely never be together in the way he wants, ever." Pride swelled through me over the fact that I managed to keep my fangs retracted through the rant.

The man's brown eyes widened and he swallowed hard, again. "Ty has brainwashed you."

"What the fuck are you talking about? The only thing Ty has done is help me."

He tilted his head, one eyebrow rising slightly higher than the other.

"So he's told you all about why he was kicked out of his pack, why he left the AVV?"

I pulled back a little, and he moved in as if he scented prey. The instinct to run reared its ugly head, but I forced it down.

"Of course he hasn't. Ty knows nothing about the importance of family because he has no pack. Don't let him brainwash you into being the same way. You have a family, our family, the Reinhard pack. Raul wants you to come home and be with us; we all want you to."

Not caring that it made me seem submissive, I took several steps back. A new family that wanted me was almost as disturbing as the old one that didn't want me. More so, in this case. Thankfully, he took a step back instead of forward.

"Ask Ty what happened, why he was banished. You deserve to know the truth about your *kennari*," he said, taking a step back for every few words.

Each step he took forced me to fight the desire to follow, not because I wanted to go with him, but because the wolf in me wanted to *chase* him. From within my chest a rumbling began. It sounded so inhuman it took me a moment to realize it was a growl. Fangs grew and my skin started to heat up. Reason, I had to think of the reason. Since I was little I had been told I had a type-A personality. Now I understood it for what it was: dominant. And this man was submissive. I had no need to prove I was stronger or better than him (which was good because I wasn't), and certainly no need to chase him, as he wasn't anything close to food. Those thoughts helped me retract my fangs and cool my skin.

The man shrugged. "Maybe he isn't an entirely bad teacher."

Twigs snapped in the trees off to the guy's right. I tensed, turning in that direction. Dammit, why hadn't I brought a weapon? Not that I would use it if I had one, but at least I would look more menacing.

"Who'd you bring with you? What are you trying to pull?" I snapped. I grabbed my phone from my pocket and sent off a quick text.

NW side of path. Got company.

Eyes going wide, the guy held up his hands and shook his head. "Nothing, I swear, and I didn't bring anyone. Whoever it is, they aren't with me."

"Shit," I muttered under my breath.

The guy turned in the direction the sound had come from.

"What's your name?" I asked him.

"Leo."

"Well, Leo, I hope you can fight better than you can argue Raul's case."

Sliding into a fighting stance alongside me, fists raised, he nodded. "I can."

"Good, that makes one of us," I muttered.

Pine boughs rustled. I recognized the unshaven face of the man that stepped out. "James."

"Sonya," he said through a sneer.

"What do you want?"

"You to come with me."

"Not happening."

Leo growled long and low. "Arnoddr has no claim on her."

Anger spiked my blood pressure through the treetops. Claws extended from my nailbeds, forcing my hands open. James responded before I could.

"I'm not here on behalf of Arnoddr."

"Then why? You can't possibly hope to claim her for your mate. Raul would kill you," Leo said.

A derisive snort came from James. "She is so not my type. I like 'em driven, strong, a leader with a vision."

"Then why?" I interrupted, tired of this guy's shit and hidden agenda. "Tell me and maybe I'll go with you."

Feces-brown eyes full of loathing turned to me. A harsh comparison, maybe, but this guy was pissing me off. "For the greater good. And pup, you don't have a choice."

The rustle of brush and pine boughs against flesh and fabric told me two more were emerging from the forest to my left and right. They smelled like men and wolves—*varúlfur*. Dammit, three against two with my fighting skills was not good. Chances were he had brought better fighters this time too, if he was smart. I really hoped he wasn't. I needed to keep him talking until Ty arrived.

"What does this leader of yours want from me?"

Wicked laughter spit from him. "You'll find out soon enough."

"What makes you think he won't want me as a mate instead of you?" I tried to goad him into revealing something, anything, about who might be behind this.

He threw his head back, laughter growing belly deep and loud. Good, it would help lead Ty to us. It wasn't that I needed rescuing, just that I knew I was outmatched, and I had no idea if this Leo guy was actually with these idiots or not. Nothing wrong with admitting when backup was needed.

"You aren't their type any more than you are mine," he said, giving me no hints.

Fine, I'd try a more direct route. "What is this person's name?"

Ignoring me, he started to advance. I felt the other two move in as well. Growls rumbled behind me as Leo faced off with at least one of the newcomers. Maybe he was on my side after all, sort of.

"Don't do this James," I tried once more. "You're in Ty's territory. He won't let you walk away this time."

The disturbing grin on James's face widened. "Ty isn't here."

And he lunged at me.

Arms tied to grab me from behind. I dropped to my hands and knees and kicked up and back. A crack sounded as I connected with my attacker's knee. From in front of me came James, reaching down. Using the same leg I'd kicked the other guy with, I whipped around and swept James's legs. He went down hard, head smacking against the ground. I launched to my feet before either could recover. The dark-haired guy behind me clutching his knee groaned and cussed. The hook kick I swung at his face connected with his shoulder instead.

Pain shot into my right kidney. Bringing an arm up, I turned in time to block a second punch from James. He threw several more strikes and I struggled to keep up. My kidney ached, making me want to bend over and favor it. I didn't dare. Anger burned within over being attacked. I let it build, using it to dull my pain at the same time it sharpened my edge. Coming off my next block, I slid an upper cut beneath James's chin. His teeth clacked together and his head flung back. I cocked my knee in preparation to kick him—and something slammed into my left side, bearing me to the ground. Claws scraped lines of fire down my left arm. Fangs snapped at my face. All I could do was hold my arms against the neck of the massive wolf trying to gnaw my head off. I kicked and squirmed, but he was too heavy.

Out of my peripheral I saw a booted foot slam into the wolf's side. It flew off me and rolled several times. All too quick, it regained its feet and started back toward me. James stepped in its way. "You idiot!" he screamed at it. "We need her alive!"

The wolf snarled and snapped at him in disagreement.

I scrambled to my feet. The sounds of fighting to my right told me Leo was too busy to be of any help. Anger, pain, and panic swirled in me, making it hard to think. The pointy tips of my canines extending pricked at my lips. If I lost it here and shifted I'd likely go mad, and then die because my emotions were so out of control. I could not let that happen. The unreal sight of the wolf before me didn't help.

Dappled light filtering through the trees played across his black, gray, and white coat. His head reached James's pectoral muscles and his shoulders were easily as wide as James's. Unreal—no, supernatural. I'd seen his like before, though, back at the winery Raul had stayed at when we'd dated. It hadn't been this wolf, but they were the same size. I hadn't been crazy then, and I wouldn't go crazy now.

With a few breaths, I found my calm center, retracted my fangs, and prepared to defend myself. Both the wolf and James turned toward me. Widening my stance and raising my fists, I got ready to go down fighting. Jaws snapping, spit and snarls flying, the wolf stalked toward me. Before I could decide if I should try to kick or dodge, a flash of blond and white fur shot in front of me—right into the other wolf. The two tumbled in a flurry of fangs and claws. James took one look at the fighting wolves, one at me, then ran for the forest like the devil himself was on his heels. Or would that be Loki in his case? He disappeared before my scream of frustration cleared my lips.

Leo limped to me, his opponent having run a second after James retreated. "Are you all right?" he asked.

The tickle of something running down my arm made me reach for it. My fingers slid in warm blood before brushing across jagged cuts. It stung, but not as bad as I thought it should. Looking down, I saw they either weren't as bad as they had originally felt, or they were already starting to heal. A vicious growl warned me a second before the blond and white wolf launched at Leo. I stepped in between them, forcing the wolf to pull up short.

He was so tall he nearly looked me right in the face. Pale blue eyes gazed at me with sharp intelligence—and concern.

"Ty?" I asked, unable to utter anything else.

The wolf tried to look around me at Leo. I held my hands up. "No! He helped me. They would have gotten me if it wasn't for him. He isn't with them. He is a friend of Raul's who came to try and plead Raul's case to me."

The wolf's attention returned to me, gaze going to my bloody arm. Suddenly, he dashed behind a tree. I was afraid he would run after James and the other, but a second later Ty emerged in human form, holding a tattered shirt over his crotch. "You're hurt," he said.

Relief flooded through me. I did not want to be alone right now, and Leo did not count.

"I'm sorry, Ty. I tried to defend her. If we had known James would come after her more of us would have come to protect her," Leo said. He leaned against a tree, taking more weight off his right leg.

The look of fury Ty shot him radiated heat and something else, an intense pressure. Leo flinched beneath it.

"Why is James coming after her? Why is Isak, or the Council, not stopping him?" Ty demanded.

"I don't know. James's been missing, along with Calder and a few others from various packs. The Council suspects they have something to do with the unsanctioned bitings, but that's all they know."

"You'd better not be lying to me," Ty warned. Menace radiated off him. How he could pull off the look with nothing more than a scrap of cloth covering his genitals, I had no idea, but I was impressed. And turned on.

"I'm not. I'll tell the Council. They'll get guards in place right away. You have my word. Raul doesn't want anything to happen to her any more than you do."

Growling low, Ty took a step toward him. "They can keep others away, but they do not step a foot on my land. If they do, as Odin and Frigg are my witness, I will invoke *landsvæði*. You tell them that."

Hands held up, Leo started to back away awkwardly. "I will, I swear."

With that, he turned and limped away. My muscles tensed again with the desire to give chase, but I resisted easily enough. He wasn't the problem right now. The problem was that Ty was keeping things from me and I'd had it with secrets, especially from someone I had begun to trust and thought I might actually be interested in. If he didn't come clean right now, my ass was getting in my Jeep and I was going to drive to Hemlock Hollow, *verða* be damned.

CHAPTER SEVENTEEN

SONYA

T he sweet scents of maple sausage and pancakes wrapped around me as I stepped into the house. For someone so fit, Ty had a ridiculous craving for pancakes. During the week I had been here he had already fixed them for breakfast three times. But he had told me a *varúlfur*'s metabolism was so fast it burned up carbs practically like they were air. The memory, along with the scents, almost banished my anger until I shut them down. This was one time I wanted to be mad. I needed it. It would be my armor, an armor I regretted ever shedding. I didn't try to fight it when my fangs extended.

After he had dressed, we'd gotten my wounds cleaned and bandaged with barely more than a few sentences spoken between us. Now I was ready for answers.

I strode up to the bar and slammed my hands down onto the marble top so hard I heard the wood supporting it groan. The sound made me realize I was overreacting—a lot—but my anger had pulled hard on that little rein I had given it and stretched it dangerously thin. "You're keeping secrets from me, something you promised never to do, if you remember," I snapped.

His brow wrinkled up into deep furrows. "What are you talking about?"

I knew he didn't mean the promise.

"Let's start with what does invoking *landsvæði* mean?" We hadn't covered anything like it in our language lessons and I had a prickly feeling about it.

He answered without turning around. "It means I have deemed all other *varúlfur* hostile and will kill them if they come on my property." The chill in his tone told me he'd been pushed far enough to follow through on that.

Part of me thought that was a bit extreme, but another part of me was sick of being threatened. I decided to move on to more pressing matters. "Okay. Then how about you being banished from your pack, having belonged to the AVV."

The spatula in his hand clattered to the countertop. His face went smooth as glass, the brittle kind that threatened to explode into millions of shards that would cut you to ribbons. A chill washed over me, taking some of my anger with it.

"Leo told you that?" he asked in a voice as chilly as I imagined the winds of Iceland would be.

The question threw me for a loop. After what had just happened, that's what he was concerned with? "Yes."

Lips curling back from his fangs, he stalked around the bar in a manner that made the hair on my arms stand up. Disturbing as the sight of him was, it was a bit more disturbing how much I was getting used to seeing a man with four fangs. Part of me thought I should be afraid of the tall mountain of muscle descending on me, but I was too pissed. Craning my neck back to keep eye contact, I stood my ground.

A slight hum began beneath my skin, but it didn't burn, so I didn't worry overly much. Ty spun back around to face me, his fists clenched so tight the muscles of his arms stood out in hard cords. Fangs bared at me, he stared through me with icy eyes. The look finally broke me down. In the wake of reason, my anger faded. I wanted it back, wanted to wrap myself in the comfortable yet cold feel of its armor. But I couldn't, thanks to his teachings. I knew the reason for it and that negated it. I felt betrayed.

"You promised not to keep secrets from me," I all but whispered.

The vulnerability in my voice made me cringe. The cold look in Ty's eyes melted and his fangs retracted. Blond hair fell down across his brow as he shook his head.

"My past is irrelevant; it has nothing to do with your training. And it would only be a secret if you had asked and I did not tell you." Like a switch being flicked, the fury was gone from his voice. And just as quickly, it fled me as well.

His gaze flitted back to the door, but he didn't move toward it. Though I knew it could stir the wolf in him back awake, I touched his arm. His words moved me in such a way that I had to risk it.

"It isn't irrelevant to me. You are the first person I've started to trust in a long time. Your past is a part of you, and you are relevant to me," I told him. Damn, that had sounded less vulnerable in my head.

I pulled my hand away, but he captured it in his own. The warmth, the rough calluses, they distracted me in the most delicious way. "It is not a good story. You might change your mind about trusting me."

Hardening my heart against the charms of his touch, I looked up into his eyes. "I will definitely change my mind about trusting you if you don't tell me, because I'm asking now." It was a bit low, but I had to say it. I had to know who I was putting my trust in.

He let go of me and ran his hand through his hair. With a sigh, he sat down on the barstool closest to me. Eyes fixing somewhere on the wall behind me, he began to talk in a carefully guarded tone.

"For eight years I was a *verndari* for the alpha of the Draupnir pack."

As he paused to gather himself, I took a guess at the word. "Guardian?"

One corner of his mouth almost turned up. "Yes. They are to the alpha what knights are to a king. While I was a *verndari*, I also belonged to the AVV. Many of my pack did. My uncle was the Draupnir male alpha, and while he was a good one, he was old and clung to the old ways. There were those that opposed him and his mate because of it." He stopped and swallowed hard.

A slight shine to his eyes suggested the depth of his pain, but the stoic expression in them assured me that tears wouldn't fall. Enthralled though I was by the story, guilt tugged at me for causing him such pain. As he fell silent for a moment, I got two beers from the fridge and removed the food from the stovetop. With the same ease he had shown a week ago, I popped off the tops of the non-pop-top beers, and set one before him. Already my strength had increased that much.

Sure, it was early for beer, but I had a feeling we were going to need them. Giving me a grateful look, he lifted it to his lips, tipped it back, and emptied half of it. I sipped at mine as I sat on the stool beside him, wishing the drink were something stronger.

"I should have seen it coming; it was my job as a *verndari* to see it coming. But I did not. One of his rivals, his own brother Bain, moved his pawns into place and challenged him."

"Pawns?" I asked.

Though his eyes met mine, I knew they didn't see me. "Those who would support Bain's challenge. My girlfriend at the time, Morene, was one of them. I never saw that coming. You think you know a person..."

The image of the uptight woman from the park flashed across my memory like a cold breeze. I wanted to bring down all kinds of hurt on that woman now. With a great effort, I pushed that desire aside. As I touched his hand, his eyes finally focused on me, but only long enough to give a sort of half shrug. After downing another long drink of his beer, he went on.

"Bain did not just defeat him. He used my uncle's own beliefs against him, challenging him by the ancient Viking rule, the one that allowed a fight to the death."

The way his fingers began to turn white around his beer bottle started to worry me. Gently, I extricated it from his grip before he could break it and end up like I had a week ago.

"He killed him? His own brother?" I asked.

Throat working to swallow something lodged in it, Ty nodded.

"Why would he do that?"

Head sinking down into one of his hands, Ty made a sort of groaning noise that tugged at me. "Because it is the only way to keep an alpha's *verndari* from challenging the challenger. The new laws allow an alpha's *verndari* to stand in for their alpha, or fight the challenger even if he defeats their alpha. Either way, if they are able to defeat the challenger, the alpha maintains his standing. The old laws determine the victor final, with no further challenges allowed by the defeated one's *verndari* unless they want to take over as alpha."

"I knew there was something about that bitch I didn't like," I said more to myself.

He remained silent for so long that I had to prompt him, but this time I was gentle. "What happened after that?"

"The old alpha's *verndari* were given the choice of submitting to the new alpha, or being banished from the pack. Since I was not allowed to kill the bastard without taking over, I chose banishment. And the banished cannot belong to even an umbrella pack, so I am no longer an AVV member, either," he said in a smooth, emotionless tone.

But I could feel his emotions boiling below the surface, like a kettle about to scream. It hit me with a sudden clarity that he had felt my emotions in much the same way when I had stormed into the room. That was how he had known I was behind him, and pissed, before he even turned around. Another *varúlfur* perk, no doubt.

"You don't want to be alpha?"

Clouds of anger moved across his blue eyes. "No. I have no interest in leading and playing politics. Politics are a noose that makes a wolf weak."

"How can you stand going back to that town?" I asked.

Pain shone in his eyes when they met mine. "My parents live there when they are not in Iceland. I still have friends there. The Council sees me as an asset they cannot part with, so they made me a *kennari* to keep me connected. Since I was never defeated in battle, according to the Viking way, I have not lost face, so it was allowed."

"Why would you do anything for those people?"

Sighing, he picked his beer back up. "Because I still care about what happens to our kind. And something more than one alpha being challenged is going on there. I can feel it. I just do not know what it is yet. But now I have a feeling it has something to do with you."

The thoughts that stirred made me take a long drink of my beer before answering. "So I'm likely walking into a viper's nest in two weeks. You think Raul didn't just bite me in to keep from marrying."

Eyes narrowing, he looked at me hard, not with anger, but with a look that suggested deep thought. "Exactly. Raul is not the type to think much beyond his own desires. But that does not mean he is not a pawn for someone else."

Head already buzzing from lack of food, I downed the rest of my beer. "In that case, we'd best eat and get to training," I said.

A shadow of a smile worked its way back onto his face, giving him a wistfully handsome look that made something deep in me ache. The smile infected me, turning my own lips upward. I quickly found the bottle of beer in my hand interesting. Picking up his empty bottle, Ty rose and walked back around to the stove. He put the pan back on the burner and picked up the spatula.

With his back still to me, he said, "You are relevant to me too, you know."

It took several hard swallows before I could answer. "Thank you."

Gaze glued to his strong back as he flipped pancakes and bacon, I began to question the wisdom of where this training was leading me. Better control of my anger was most certainly developing. Desire was something altogether different, though. Already it had built coals too hot to touch. And touch them I would have to if I was ever going to master my control of it. With Ty becoming more interesting by the day, I wasn't sure how I was going to fare at that lesson.

CHAPTER EIGHTEEN

SONYA

I'd never thought of putting Worcestershire sauce on steak, but it smelled so good I could hardly wait to find out how it would taste. But that could've been because I was absolutely starving. Trying to learn to fight—a losing battle, by the way—learning a new language, and channeling lightning the other day had taken a lot out of me. My head still reeled over the channeling lightning thing. None of the books Ty had pored over told us anything about it. But I wasn't worried about it like he was. For one, I loved storms, always had. I didn't possess the fear for them most people did. That fear was self-preservation, I knew, and it was probably stupid to be without it. But it was what it was.

Channeling lightning had felt amazing, almost as good as sex, chocolate, and the buzz you get after a really good workout all rolled into one. Anything that felt that good couldn't be all bad. At least that's what I was going with. Hell, this werewolf thing needed a perk or two, so I was taking it where I could get it. Amazing as it was, a huge part of me was disappointed that it had interrupted the kiss Ty and I had almost shared. Clearly he felt something for me. I still didn't know if the *verða* was heightening my feelings for him or not, but I was starting to think it might not matter. He was a good man, the kind a girl could have a future with.

Maybe it was time I actually went after a guy like that. And maybe, just maybe, it would work. First to make it through the *verða* alive.

Perched on a tall stool next to the bar, I kept a watchful eye on Ty as he cooked. Not that I had to worry. By all indications it seemed he would undercook the meat rather than overcook it. The sweet, buttery scents of both corn and potatoes roasting within tin foil on the top shelf drifted to me. Spatula in hand, Ty leaned over the grill, blond brows scrunched together in concentration. In a pair of khaki cargo shorts and a faded tan short-sleeved shirt, he looked a bit like a Viking slumming with mortals on the weekend. Sipping at my iced tea, I tried to tune out the voice in my head that told me to reach over and touch him. It was getting harder and harder. But that was in part due to the fact that I was losing my will to fight it.

Each day that passed made me more comfortable with the idea of becoming a *varúlfur*. That had to be the key to staving off the madness, didn't it? Watching Ty made me feel a bit out of control, and I wasn't sure that was a good thing. It wasn't that I was worried about him being outcast or any of that crap. That didn't matter to me. But how could I focus enough to stay sane while I couldn't stop thinking about him?

Since I had dressed in a low-cut red silk tank top that clung to my breasts like a second skin to pay him back for his display at the lake, I had to be careful. Beneath it I wore a skimpy lace bra with no concealing padding. If my body reacted to him, he would know it with one glance. Apparently, my subconscious had already decided on where I wanted this to go when I chose what to wear. Any remaining resistance I might have had melted the moment I laid eyes on a hot guy cooking for me.

"So why did the three packs leave Iceland for Montana?" I asked, needing a distraction to keep me from jumping him right there in the kitchen. If we were going to do this, I had to do it slow and right.

He set the spatula down and picked up his glass of pop. "What makes anyone leave their homeland? Religious oppression."

"Really? Not angry mobs with torches?" I grinned, though I was only half kidding.

Such ignorance wouldn't surprise me. Ty gave a little, humorless laugh.

"Nope, though that often goes hand in hand with religious oppression."

He winked at me, making me want to climb over that barbeque and sample some hot meat. Oh, man, I really was losing it. Fear flashed through me. How did they kill *varúlfur* who went mad? Hanging, burning, drowning? They couldn't exactly electrocute me. Yep, that line of thought helped cool my desire. But too late.

Eyes sparkling from probably smelling my arousal—damn *varúlfur* senses—he went on. "Christianity came to Iceland around 1300 and we were seen as heathens, pagans who were an embarrassment to the rulers who once relied on us to fight their battles," he said.

"That's sad. Hmm, the packs have been here that long?"

"Not quite. They held out for about three hundred years before finally leaving in the 1600s."

"Why Montana?"

Soaking in the scents of pine, hemlock, grass, and water, I thought maybe I knew.

Wood ground against stone pavers as Ty pulled out a stool and sat across the bar from me. "You can feel it. Our kind need the forest. It is good for our souls. But really, it is the isolation we have to have."

I sighed. "People destroy what they don't understand."

"Yes, especially if it is more powerful than them."

Even if they kept to the forests, I didn't see how *varúlfur* had stayed hidden for so long. "Are there many more of our kind in other parts of the world?"

His eyes softened. The hint of a smile hid in the tug of his lips. The look was part joy, part relief, and sexy in a vulnerable way that made parts of me tighten. Whatever I had said to please him, I wanted to say it again.

"We are all over, though there are fewer of us now than there has ever been. Like I said, we need forests."

For the first time since we'd come back outside, my eyes moved from Ty to the nearby forest. "That's so sad."

Silence fell heavy between us, broken only by the sizzle of fat hitting hot coals. I began to feel bad for putting a damper on such a nice night. I didn't know if what I had to say next would make it better or worse, but it had to be said. "Look, Ty, about what happened at the lake..." My voice trailed off as he went rigid.

He waved a hand and pasted on a badly faked smile. "Do not worry, we will figure the lightning thing out. I am sure there is an explanation in the archives."

When it looked like he was going to say more, I reached over and grabbed his hand. "I don't mean the lightning, Ty, I mean us. I know you want to do right by the Council, or *kennari* code, or whatever it is that makes you keep your distance. And I get that. But I also think maybe there's something between us, something good. I want to let you know, I'm willing to wait until after the *verða*, if that's what it takes."

Somewhere in the middle of my breathless ramble, his gaze locked onto mine and didn't let go. The depth of emotion in his blue eyes staggered me. "Gods know, I do not want to wait another second to be with you. But, yes, that is exactly what we must do. We are worth the wait; *you* are worth the wait," he said.

Knowing there might be a future for us sent a thrill through me so powerful that it tried to stir my wolf. Out of necessity, I let go and stepped back. A few deep breaths helped me regain control. I looked around the stone patio where the barbeque and bar sat, then up to the back deck.

"Do you have a sound system out here?" I asked.

He nodded and pointed out a few speakers that looked like landscaping rocks.

"Mind if I grab my music?" I asked.

His eyes lit up and he sat a bit straighter on his stool. "Go ahead. That sounds great."

I stood. "Not worried about my taste in music?"

The easy grin that came to his lips heated my blood. "You have great taste in music. Which reminds me, you should hear Kaleo. They are an Icelandic group that sings bluesy music. I think you would like them." His words heated it even more.

I loved that he had thought about this enough to recommend an artist to me. Not to mention, I loved finding new artists to get into. I returned his smile and started down the path that wound through the side yard of the house. When Raul got in my Jeep that fateful night he hadn't exactly liked my music, said it was too ancient. The one time I rode in that sleek sports car of his he'd been playing classical music—like Bach classical. To each his own, I guess, but it was really nice to know Ty could appreciate blues. There was something about a man that liked blues music that really did it for me. I hated that I was comparing Ty to Raul, not because Raul couldn't stand up to him in any way, but because of what I feared it meant. It had to stop. Years had passed since I'd been a college freshman prone to swooning, and I wasn't about to return to that. Hot for teacher I might be, but I was an adult. I would do this right, so if it did develop into something more, it had a chance of succeeding.

The smile remained on my face even as I left Ty's sight. On one hand, I didn't like what that might mean, on the other, it was nice to be happy for once. Even if it that small measure of happiness was derived from something as simple as good company at a backyard barbeque. I hadn't relaxed and hung out with someone like this since early on in college, and it felt good. Sure, we were chatting about werewolf politics and immigration, but hey, I would take what happiness I could get.

The sweet, almost cloying scent of roses drifted to me as I came around the front of the house. No rose bushes grew here. With my heightened sense of smell I would have located any on the property by now. My steps slowed as I breathed deep through my nose. I didn't smell anyone but Ty and my own lingering scent around the place. Still, icy dread raised bumps along the exposed skin of my arms and legs. Tucked under the driver's side windshield wiper of my Jeep was a bouquet of red roses. Surely Ty wouldn't have left me such a thing, not red at least. Not yet. That left only one other person. Teeth clenched, I stormed up to the vehicle and tore the bouquet from it. Nestled inside all the red buds was a five-inch-long white box, and a card.

My shaking fingers took a few tries to open the velvet-covered box. On a bed of satin sat a bracelet of gold X's and O's. Diamonds—half a carat each at least—dotted the O's. At over eight of them, I couldn't even imagine what the thing must have cost. The tiny hope that this was from Ty dashed away like spilled salt. He would never choose something so ostentatious and impersonal. To some a beautiful bracelet like this probably had deep meaning, but not to Raul and me. Quite the opposite, if anything. We had never professed any feelings for each other besides attraction, which made this a mockery of what should have been. I opened the card.

Dear Sonya,

You're in my thoughts every day. I hate that I'm not the one there with you, helping you through this. Please be careful of Ty. Don't trust him. He's an outcast, and among our kind there is no greater shame than being cast from your pack. He wasn't willing to stand up and take charge, make things change. I promise, once this is over and we're back together I will give you everything you have ever desired. Until then, I hope you'll accept this bracelet as a symbol of my dedication to you. I will spend the rest of our lives making it up to you for how all this happened if you will let me.

    Raul

The chill on my skin turned into a slow burn that started to build until it felt as though I was boiling from within. My hand crushed the card into a tight ball and a scream blew between my clenched teeth. The box snapped, popped, and shattered, falling through my fingers in pieces of wood, velvet and satin. Diamonds cut into my palm and expensive gold bent to the shape of my fingers. My strength surprised me on some sublevel that existed below my rage. I dropped the card and bracelet and tore the roses into tiny bits of red petals, thorns, and green stems. Through a haze of moisture I refused to acknowledge as tears, I saw Ty running around the corner of the house at what seemed like light speed. I couldn't look at him, didn't want him to see me so out of control. Gaze falling to my hands, I realized it wasn't just the diamonds that had cut me. Claws grew out from where my fingernails had been, wicked sharp and dripping my own blood. Inside my mouth my tongue brushed across fangs. And that wasn't all—colors were changing as well, scents growing impossibly stronger. My body started shaking.

The hint of madness waiting at the edge of my mind whispered to me. At least it wasn't an all-out scream. Still, fear coursed through me as I realized I had lost control too much to avoid shifting. And I so wasn't ready, not like this, not because of *him*. "Ty, help," I cried in a voice that was more growl than anything.

"Oh no, Sonya."

He grabbed my hands. I could barely see him through the dark haze of my rage. Then I was in his arms, pressed against his chest. I think he was telling me to breathe, to think of the reasons, but I could barely breathe let alone *think* of anything. He tilted my chin up and pressed his lips to mine in a hot line that scorched down deep inside of me. Gently, his lips urged mine open and his tongue slid between my fangs, inside my mouth. The amazing sensation of his tongue tangling with mine obliterated my rage like a tsunami taking out everything in its path. The hard lines of his incredible body pressed against mine swept me away from the brink and safely back into control. Of my anger at least.

My hands snaked around his back, and I couldn't stop them. No, I wouldn't stop them. I'd had it with resisting my attraction to him. This felt too good, too right. Our tongues thrust in and out of each other's mouths as if we could lap one another up. His full lips devoured me as much as mine tried to devour him. The heat coursing through my body changed, became desire. The desire grew and grew until it felt like it was trying to consume us both. Moaning into his mouth, I rubbed my hard nipples against his chest and pressed my stomach to his erection. Our desire felt hot enough to burn our clothes away. I wished with all my being that it would.

Tongue withdrawing, he pulled back before I did, leaving me gasping and wanting so much more.

"Sorry. I did not mean to take liberties, but I did not know what else to do to bring you back from the edge," he said as he turned away.

Staring down at my fingernails that only moments ago had been claws, I stammered out a reply. "It's all right. I...I needed that. I mean, I couldn't have gotten it back under control alone." Had he not felt the desire as strongly as I did?

Though he remained close, he no longer touched me, and I kind of hated that. At the same time, I knew if he did, I would risk losing control of another emotion.

"You have been doing so well. I did not think even something like this could rattle you," he said.

Gravel ground under his bare feet and I realized he was retrieving the bracelet and card. Amazed that I didn't feel any pain, I turned my hands over to look at my palms. The cuts had already healed.

"He's trying to buy my affection now. That's something I can't stand. My father did that crap when I was a kid, sent me gifts from prison as if that could make up for him not being there."

I really hadn't meant to say that. And I instantly felt guilty for it, especially now that I knew he hadn't gone to prison because of a drug deal gone bad—but because he had killed a man who had tried to kidnap me.

"Gods, Sonya, I am so sorry. I will get the son of a bitch that left this," Ty snapped as he turned away.

I snagged his arm, stopping him with a strength that surprised me. "Please don't leave me alone." More words that I hadn't meant to say. Damn but my control was really off today.

Jaw opening, I prepared to take the words back, but I couldn't. I *was* afraid to be left alone right now. "What if that's what they want? To lure you away from me," I said so softly only a *varúlfur*'s sensitive hearing would pick it up.

The fear that shook my voice made me feel weak, pathetic, and that began to stir my anger back up. It must have shown on my face because Ty nodded and took a step toward me. His hand found mine and locked around it. My anger melted away beneath the heat of his ice-blue eyes. The protective look in them stunned me.

"Sometimes you make me wonder who the teacher here is, Sonya," he said through the barest hint of a smile.

I made an attempt to smile back. "Thanks, I think."

Still holding onto my hand, he started for the side yard. "Come on. We should get our steaks and go watch that movie."

Gripping his hand tighter, I nodded and ground rose petals beneath my shoe. Despite my lingering anger, I thrilled at the feeling of Ty's big hand wrapped around mine. I was still determined to enjoy this evening. The kiss made me believe what we had could really be worth something. As much as I wanted to fall into bed with him, taking it slow so I didn't screw this up and get myself killed was too important. All Raul's warnings and talk about not trusting Ty made me realize he was afraid I would get too close to him. It almost made me smile when I realized his insecurities had brought about the very thing he feared. Served him right.

CHAPTER NINETEEN

SONYA

Anger management went well over the next two days. Too well, really. The better I got to know Ty, the harder it was for him to make me mad. And the harder it became for both of us to resist our attraction. We sat up late each night watching horror movies, most of which involved vampires. It struck me as hilarious, a werewolf who was a fan of vampire movies. He enjoyed how the irony made me laugh, and as much as I hated to admit it even to myself, I liked that he enjoyed making me laugh. During the day when we weren't training we walked around his expansive acreage and he told me stories about the history of the area. I loved listening to him talk. If I'd had professors like him in college, I might have gone to class a lot more, and I definitely wouldn't have taken a semester off. Of course, I might have gotten far more distracted as well.

While I thought it was the growing friendship with Ty that made it hard to get mad at him, he claimed I was simply getting that good. My fighting skills, not so much. We added other tactics to the sparring sessions for the next two days, such as having me focus on Raul, talk about him, how I felt about what he'd done to me. It worked at first, enraging me almost to the point where I lost control of my wolfy side. After the first day, though, understanding the reasons for my anger allowed me to control it, even where Raul was concerned. My resolve to attend his trial remained as strong as ever. While Ty didn't think Raul had anything to do with changing Candice, I wasn't so sure. I needed to see him not only pay for what he did to me, but make sure he never did it to anyone else again. Despite the fact that I was starting to enjoy the heightened senses, the increased strength and stamina, even the burn of power beneath my skin, the fact remained that Raul had taken my choice from me. For that he had to pay.

Trapped beneath Ty's body after he executed a particularly impressive leg sweep on me, I realized the problem. How could I not? Its clear blue eyes bore a hole straight through me. The press of all that muscle against my thin tank top and mostly bare legs made me dizzy. Pink lips with the slightly raised ridge lining them drew me in, making me want to lick, bite, and suck on them. All right, it wasn't really his lips I was thinking about at this point. By the feel of the hard line pushing against my groin, it became clear I wasn't the only one feeling the effects.

"I think I know what the problem is," I said between labored breaths.

It came out sounding as horny as I felt, but at the moment, I didn't care.

Ty smiled and ran his hand along my jawline. "Too many clothes?" he suggested in a voice deepened by desire.

My traitorous eyes fluttered closed but I forced them back open as I fought the instinct to lean into his hand. Just when I thought he might be serious, the pressure of his body against mine disappeared. One moment he lay on top of me, the next he stood over me, offering me his hand. I accepted it, not because I needed it, but because I wanted to touch him. Which led me right back to the problem.

"Precisely," I said as I stood and brushed pine needles from my jogging shorts with my free hand.

His guilt-filled eyes widened. "I am sorry. I should not have said that."

"No, Ty. I'm sick of fighting what might be between us, and sick of wondering if it's just the *verða* heightening my desire," I said, keeping my tone as matter-of-fact as I could. The last part wouldn't come out, the part about how I was terrified of going mad and sick to death of the fear. I thought I had it beat, but there was only one way to be sure.

Those delicious lips quirked up. "That is not how it works."

I raised an eyebrow at him. "It might be. The *verða* is heightening my desire, so I need to master it."

Shaking his head, Ty walked over and grabbed a towel that hung from a tree branch. Beads of sweat trickled down between his pectoral muscles, making me want to follow them with my tongue. His arms and chest flexed as he wiped sweat from his forehead and the back of his neck. The reaction it stirred deep in my center only confirmed my suspicions of this being a hormonal imbalance.

"Once you have mastered your strongest emotion, you hold the key to mastering them all. And anger was definitely your strongest emotion," he said.

From a nearby stone table, he picked up two water bottles and handed me one. "You think the *verða* is the reason for your desire, yes?"

I accepted the water bottle and took a long drink. When I lowered it he stepped deep into my personal space. Knowing a lesson was coming, I resisted the urge to step back and instead craned my neck to look up at him. Moments like this reminded me of how tall he was. This close his body heat radiated from him, reaching out to me as if it could draw me in. He caught a drop of water that lingered on my bottom lip and spread it across my mouth, teasing the edge of my teeth as he almost pushed his finger inside. Just like that I grew wet. Nostrils flaring as he took in my scent, his eyes fluttered closed.

"No, maybe, I don't know," I breathed. "Well, the reason it's so strong, maybe."

His finger moved from my lips to my arm, tracing a line down it that burned deep into me in the most wonderful way.

"Then knowing the reason, you should be able to control it, to banish it like you can the anger."

As he spoke his finger traced its way back up the inside of my arm to my waist, running upward until it outlined the edge of my breast. My nipples hardened in an instant, aching for much more than a grazing touch.

He leaned down and whispered in my ear. "So banish it."

The feel of his breath against the sensitive skin of my ear set me on fire, making me wetter without so much as a touch. A slight groan slid from him as he took in a deep breath through his nose. Gods the sound was sexy, especially knowing the scent of my arousal was what caused it.

Damn him. I wanted to tear his clothes off, throw him down, and ride him right there on the lawn. No, no I didn't, it was the *verða* making me horny as a teenager. Focusing on that reason, I attempted to fight the desire. When it didn't work, I took a step back.

"It's not working," I gasped.

Oddly, my skin had not begun to burn, or even hum, and my fangs hadn't extended.

Ty took a step toward me. "Maybe because the *verða* is not causing it," he said in a deep, terribly sexy voice that held a hint of hope in it.

I took another step back. Putting on my best haughty look, I placed a hand on my hip. "What? You think I'm just falling for you?"

I had only known the man thirteen days, less time than I had known Raul before I'd made the near-fatal mistake of letting him get too close. I would not allow myself to make that mistake again. The *verða* messed with me in so many ways. If my feelings for Ty was one of them, I needed to know before I let myself tumble down that rabbit hole.

A grin easily as sexy as his lusty voice tempted me to step into him. He began to trace his hand up my arm again. "I did not say that. Maybe you only want to ravage me."

Shaking my head, I pulled my arm away from his touch. But I didn't step back; I couldn't bring myself to. This had been a lot easier when he'd been fighting his desire as much as I had. "Despite what you might think of me because of my monumental mistake with Raul, I don't do casual sex. It's part of why I didn't have sex with him," I said.

Without touching me, he leaned in, his shadow falling across me. "I did not say it would be casual between us."

Bumps rose along my skin, spreading down from the ear he breathed on to the hard nipple of my right breast, and on down to my core. If his breath could do such a thing, I wondered what his hands could do. Oh did I wonder. My eyes closed at the thought alone. Grass and earth sighed beneath his feet as he took another step closer. I held my hand out to stop him, gasping when it ran into his hard, bare chest.

"Stop. I have to be sure it isn't the *verða*."

He complied, but didn't step back. Beneath my hand, his chest rose and fell with the rhythm of quick breaths that made mine quicker.

"It is not the *verða*, Sonya. And I am not Raul," he said, not quite sounding convinced on that first part.

"I have to be sure."

Possibly the sexiest laugh I had ever heard rumbled from him. "Open your eyes or move your hand lower; you will be sure. I shared a high school locker room with Raul. I know he does not exactly measure up to me. The bastard was pressed up against you hard enough the night I ran him off that I know you will feel the difference." His voice deepened on the last part, almost became a growl. The little touch of jealousy sent a thrill through me.

How well I knew that was true, thanks to his display at the lake. His words might have pissed me off if my mind could stop picturing him naked and wet. Before my body could betray my resolve, I yanked my hand off him and took a step back. "I mean I have to be sure it isn't the *verða*."

He waved his hand dismissively and took a long drink of water. Tension and doubt hid in his movements and in the lines of his face. As he moved, I watched sweat drip from his blond hair, trail down his neck, and work its way to his chest. My tongue was trailing across my lower lip before I even realized I had begun to lick it. When he lowered the water bottle and met my gaze I could still feel the hunger burning in my eyes. I had not wanted him to see that.

"That is easy," he said.

It took me a moment to remember what we'd been talking about. "How can I make sure it isn't the *verða*?"

"Shift and the *verða* will be over."

The way he said it so casually, as if it wasn't my greatest fear, made me wonder if he was trying to make light of it, or if he hadn't noticed how afraid I was. Or he chose to notice how badly my body wanted—no, needed—to shift. I absolutely ached with the desire. Each day the moon grew fuller made it harder to resist.

"I'm not ready. It's too soon." But was it? Part of me vehemently disagreed.

The playful, lusty look on his face transformed into one of his "teaching moment" looks—brows high, chin dropped so he stared at me through his sweaty bangs. "You are ready."

I started to shake my head and couldn't stop. Suddenly, he stood before me again, his hands gripping my arms gently. Both his touch and closeness soothed me. But they also touched the wildness that rose within me at the idea of shifting, excited it.

"I don't want to be out of control," I whispered, eyes on his bare feet, which were half buried in green grass.

"You will not be. You can do this."

One of his fingers traced along my chin, lifting it so I would look at him. Though a glimmer of the playful, sexy attitude remained in his eyes, his face was all serious.

"You are ready. I know you are."

The faith in his voice struck something deep inside me that had nothing to do with desire. I realized I wanted to do this not only to make sure my attraction to him wasn't the *verða*, but to make him proud. Unfortunately, it was the same reason I was afraid to fail. He had worked so hard preparing me over the last two weeks. Seeing how I was his first, I wanted to succeed almost as much for him as I did for myself.

"But the madness..." My voice trailed off so the last part of the word was barely audible, even to *varúlfur* hearing. The desire to let my wolf side through, to let my paws touch the earth, to run with the energy of the forest coursing through me, it was so strong that it took my breath away.

He shook his head slowly, eyes holding mine. "You are displaying all the signs of a well-adjusted new *varúlfur* and none of the signs of one slipping into madness."

I tried to return the smile but I was sure it came out looking horrific. "More from your *kennari* how-to book?"

"Yes, but it is more than that. You understand and accept the instincts of both humans and wolves. And you have a strong desire to help people, not harm them, as is reflected in your fighting skills." He took a breath to go on, but I halted his words with a playful punch in one hard bicep.

"Hey!"

He grinned and took hold of my chin again. "I would not encourage you to do this if I did not think you were ready. There is a connection between us, Sonya. Through that, I can feel that you are ready."

It felt like my cheeks literally tried to catch fire. With my chin in his hand, I couldn't look away, so I had to make light of the situation. "Is that some kind of *kennari-nemi* bond thing?"

"You are my first. I do not know." His body leaned closer and his voice dropped an octave. "But I really do not think so."

Time to woman up because shit was getting real. "All right, so how does this work?" I asked.

Smiling, he let go of my chin. "First you have to want to change, then simply will yourself to do it, and you will."

The near panic that gripped my heart must have shown on my face because he took hold of my hand. "It will not hurt any more than the burning you have already felt beneath your skin. Your bones do not break and reshape, your skin does not stretch. It is not like the movies. Your atoms transform from one solid body to another, simple as that."

To wet my increasingly dry throat, I swallowed a few times. "Will you shift for me?"

"Of course." His smile grew wider. "But I have to strip."

I pulled my hand from his and slapped his hard chest. "Be serious."

His brows rose in feigned innocence that looked anything but. "I am. Clothes do not magically dissolve and reform. This process is natural, not magical."

Laughter burst from me before I could stop it. "You do realize that shifting into a wolf is an impossibility, therefore it has to be magical," I asked.

Ty shook his head. "We are made up of atoms. Atoms are building blocks, simply put. Rearranging building blocks is complicated, but completely possible. Our brains are developed further—or in another direction, if you prefer—than other humans, based off our DNA, which is transferred through our venom when we choose to change another. This supports the theory of the *verða*."

"How do you know all of this?"

Cocking his head at me, he lifted an eyebrow. "Our kind live for five hundred years, giving us plenty of time to advance and learn. We are not all teachers; some are scientists, doctors, engineers. We are more than human, more than wolf."

Complicated as all that was, I followed it, and couldn't argue with it. I mean, seriously, how could I? I wasn't even finished becoming a *varúlfur* yet. What did I know? Besides, strange as it was, it did make a sort of scientific sense. That, or I was already mad to think so. No. I stamped that fear back down where it belonged. Ty said I was ready, and I trusted him.

My thoughts blew away as Ty pulled his T-shirt off and dropped it on the ground. Perfect pecs any runway model would be envious of filled my vision at eye-level. Resist though I tried, my eyes moved down the path of his hard abdominals, past his belly button, and snagged on where his hands worked at untying the drawstring on his sweatpants. All of a sudden this didn't seem like a good way to quell my desire. In fact, it seemed like a horrible idea, as it was having the exact opposite effect. Still, I couldn't look away, couldn't stop it, wouldn't. I prayed to any that would listen to make what we felt be something more than the *verða*.

Clearly for my torment, he pushed his sweatpants slowly down his hips. At last, he sprang free of the cotton confines to stand up fully erect. The moisture in my mouth vanished. I shook my head and forced my eyes up to his chest. Just because he was impressively hung didn't mean he knew how to use it. Or worse, that he cared to use it for more than his own pleasure. Of the two men I had been with in my life, neither of them had much interest in anything beyond their own orgasms. I had read enough romance novels and watched enough porn to hope that men existed who cared about pleasuring a woman, but never having met one, they seemed like a myth. Then again, so had werewolves a few weeks ago.

My eyes tried to slip back down but I forced them up to his face. If this was a ploy to make me not think about the risk of going mad, it was working, too well. The smirk turning up the corners of his mouth gave him an impish look that made me shake my head. Most guys would respond to such impressed perusal of their bodies with an egotistical overconfidence, but not Ty. No, he found it amusing.

"What's so funny?" I asked.

"I am about to shift into a wolf, something you did not even know was possible a few weeks ago, and you cannot take your eyes off my goods."

Some of the tension eased out of me. "Your goods?" I laughed, not derisive or making fun of him, but because the phrase was far too cute for such a hulk of a man to utter.

He stalked up to me, passing close enough that our shoulders brushed. As our skin touched he leaned down and whispered in my ear. "Would you prefer I use the word cock?"

A thrill of naughty pleasure shot straight down to my tightening core.

He let out a small, deep laugh. "I was merely trying to maintain our attempt at being a gentleman and a lady."

The temptation to lean into him overwhelmed me, but he moved past me before I could.

"I think that went out the window the moment you stripped naked in front of me, again," I said, brows rising on the last word.

I turned to keep him in sight as he crossed the open space of the yard, stopping beside a tree. Eyes on his face, I secretly reveled in all I could see out of the edges of my vision. Telling myself the *verða* made me feel this way didn't reduce the power of my desire one bit. It should have, but it didn't.

"The first rule of shifting is to make sure humans cannot see you. That means knowing your surroundings," he said, chin lifting to indicate the tree line.

His words worked like a splash of cold water in my face, dousing my desire in an instant. Some small part of me resisted the possibility of shifting, even though my fangs and claws had already proven it to a point. Instead of thinking about that, I tried to focus on the lesson of the moment.

"You moved over there so the trees hid you from the house across the lake," I said.

"Exactly."

"But it's too far away for them to see anything."

He shook his head. "Not in this day and age. Do not ever underestimate the nosiness of others. Always assume everyone is trying to watch you, and always keep satellites in mind. It is the only way to stay safe and keep the secret of our kind."

Fear danced across my skin as though it possessed the razor-sharp claws of a newborn kitten. As if worrying about shifting and going insane weren't enough...

"How do I do it?" I asked.

"Decide to shift, and you will. Your skin will grow hot, vibrate for a moment, then you will flow from a human into a wolf, like water moving from one glass to another."

The right side of my lips lifted. "You make it sound so poetic."

"It is, really."

"Will I still be able to think? Will I still be...me, inside the wolf?" I couldn't bring myself to ask if I'd go mad. He'd only say no to make me feel better, anyways. The truth was, neither of us would know for sure until I shifted.

The lecture on shifting put his desire on the back shelf, as was evident by his lowering erection. It bounced as if my gaze on him alone stirred him. I squeezed my eyes shut and tried to focus. The delicious distraction of his chiseled body was working well to ebb my fear of shifting. A plan of his, no doubt. The fear of going insane, well, nothing was going to reduce that.

"Of course, just with less inhibitions. It is a bit like being drunk in a way, that carefree feeling, but with your senses and reaction times improving instead of decreasing."

"That doesn't sound so bad," I said. My eyes drifted downward. "All right, I'm ready." It was a loaded statement considering my physical reaction to him, but to his credit, he didn't take the opening.

Some force I felt on a gut level pulled my eyes up and his gaze snagged mine.

"There is nothing to be afraid of," he said.

Then he shifted.

CHAPTER TWENTY

SONYA

Like air across an Arizona blacktop in summer, the image of him
wavered and flowed, just as he had described. His hands reached
for the ground and by the time they touched, they were paws.
That quick, he became a huge wolf covered in a blond and white fur coat.
He barely had to tilt his head up to meet my eyes, which put his shoulders
at about four feet tall. Anyone who saw him could easily mistake him for a
bear at first glance, especially considering he had to weigh over two
hundred pounds. But then, that made sense. His mass would be the same.

And I realized, I had seen his wolf before. Back when I'd been dating
Raul, I'd seen a man—who I was now certain was Raul—face down this
very wolf. Even then Ty had been protecting me. I had suspected, but now
I knew for sure.

"Holy shit." I stumbled backward several steps, nearly tripping over my
own feet.

The light crystal blue of his eyes captured mine. Crazy as it seemed, I
swore I could feel him behind those eyes, not like madness crazy. At least, I
didn't think so. But what if it was? When he took a step toward me, I took
another back. My feet tangled together and I fell onto my butt in the grass.
He followed me, nose reaching out to my hand. Every instinct in my body
told me to pull back, run, or fight, but I ignored them all and let him touch

me. Fur so soft it felt like silk brushed my skin as he rubbed his long canine face against my hand. If this was madness, I didn't mind it so much.

"You're gorgeous," I whispered.

His eyes sparkled and I swear one edge of his mouth quirked up.

"Don't let that go to your head," I warned.

A barking sound that might have been a laugh came from him. My fear began to subside, leaving a burning curiosity in its place. Along with something else, something that pulled at me like a magnet, urging me to join him. For the first time, I wanted to shift, truly wanted to with all my heart. The compulsion became stronger the longer I looked at him, dissolving my fear until none of it remained. My skin became stifling hot, graduating into the feeling of a bad sunburn. Gently, he took the edge of my tank top in his teeth and tugged on it.

"All right, all right," I said.

Pushing him away, I stood and peeled off my tank. My sports bra followed it to the ground a moment later. Exquisite cool air caressed my skin, leeching the heat away a little. For a second I thought I was shaking, then I realized my skin was vibrating. The movement tickled as it heated me. Ty took a step back, his four paws as quiet as his bare feet always were. Looking at him increased my need to shift to the point where I knew I couldn't hold out much longer. Fangs grew within my mouth. My fingernails formed into claws. Fear fled me in a rush, leaving me feeling buzzed and energized. Careful of my claws, I slid my yoga pants and panties down my hips and stepped out of them. Even though he was in wolf form, I instinctively turned a bit and held a hand over my birthmark to hide it from Ty.

I thought about being a wolf, how I wanted to be one right now. Deep inside, I felt it. The wolf wasn't a separate being within me like I had thought. The wolf and I were one and the same. It was the pure, instinctual part of me and it longed to be set free. The decision to let it felt like the most sane idea I'd ever had. I hoped like hell it was.

Like I had seen Ty do, I reached for the ground. The vibrations in my body increased, becoming white-hot for a fraction of a second. Green grass rushed toward me and suddenly my hands—no, my paws—were on it. Legs led down to the paws, not arms. Black fur that shone in the sun covered me. On instinct, I tried to say "Wow," but it came out as a guttural canine sound. Until that moment, it hadn't dawned on me that I wouldn't be able to speak. Dizziness rushed through me, leaving me feeling slightly disoriented.

This new body felt very different, yet somehow still right. I turned toward Ty and was surprised to discover how easy moving on four legs was. Out of the corner of my eye, I caught a glimpse of my own tail. It was solid black like the rest of me seemed to be. I wagged it experimentally, thrilling at how I could feel the movement all the way up my spine. The details of my shiny black coat jumped out at me. Everything looked different, not because of color, that was quite similar, but it was all sharper and more focused. Ty's wolf form was even more beautiful through a wolf's eyes. His fur was mostly blond with gray markings on his face, chest, shoulders, and tail. A weird compulsion to rub all over him until I was covered in his scent seized me.

So much for my desire being a product of the *verða*.

As for the madness, I had never felt so clear-headed in all my life. Not even my decision to attend med school had made me feel this...right.

The scents of a thousand different things poured down my nose— which was quite distracting considering its length. Each tree, bush, plant, and flower had such a distinctive scent that I had never noticed before. The only thing I could compare it to was the scent of the first grass cut during summer—but even that didn't explain it. So vivid were the smells that I could practically *see* scent trails left by deer, squirrels, even Ty and myself. It was heady, overwhelming, and I wanted to experience more.

A blond and white tail wagged in my peripheral vision. Ty's head tipped in the direction of the forest, gaze shooting toward the path. While I understood well enough, I realized Icelandic wasn't the only language I was going to need to learn. The body language of wolves would hopefully be a tad easier, though. Ty trotted toward the path and I followed without thinking. Then it dawned on me—I was walking on four legs. Not only was that something I hadn't done since being a baby, my back legs bent the wrong way. Oddly enough, overthinking it didn't trip me up or make it harder. My body simply did what I asked of it, one foot in front of the other in an easy rhythm.

We began to run side by side. All those wonderful scents poured down my throat with each breath, connecting me to every living thing around me, both plant and animal. Most powerful of all was Ty's evergreen scent with a pleasant underlying musk. It wrapped around me like a favorite sweater or throw blanket, comforting me and making me feel at home in an impossible situation. Less than a mile later, we left the path. The woods didn't slow us in the slightest. Fallen logs, thick underbrush of brambles and ferns, none of it impeded me, much to my surprise. I leaped, ducked, and dodged through it all at a blinding pace as if part of me intuitively new the landscape before me.

Everything about it, from the ground beneath my paws to the air moving across my fur and down my tail, felt amazing and natural. Why I had worried so much and feared this for the last two weeks, I couldn't understand. Deeper into the forest we went until I couldn't smell or hear any sign of human life at all. Ty kept shooting gazes my way, his eyes filled with joy and pride. Odd that I could tell that about a wolf's eye, but really, they were still Ty's eyes. In them I could see him. Just as he was a huge, fine specimen of a man, he was a gorgeous wolf. My wolf self was very attracted to him, so much so that I had to resist the urge to rub against his side and nuzzle my nose into the fur around his neck.

In this form it wasn't as hard to resist my desire. I had a feeling that had more to do with the discomforting thought of having sex with another creature—even if we wore the same form—than it did with a reduced desire for Ty. Maybe the idea would become more comfortable with time, maybe it wouldn't. Regardless, I wasn't even remotely tempted to cross that line right now.

Though he led the way with a nod or thrust of his head now and then, Ty kept his pace so that I ran alongside him. Such chivalry made me grin a big wolfy grin. We crossed meadows and thickly forested areas, running without tiring. For a moment, we stopped at stream to drink and nibbled at a few berries before starting back. In every move, sound, scent, and taste I felt the instinct he had been talking about. It made the transition from human to wolf easier, but I also felt how it could get out of control if I let it. The wildness in me reveled in the experience. It awakened something wonderful and free.

Each scent amplified a thousand-fold, each sound a hundred. Large and small animals scurried about the forest. The prey drew my attention and elicited the urge to give chase, to hunt. I resisted.

By the time we made it back to the house, dusk had settled over the landscape, casting everything in deep shadows. Under the cover of the huge pine trees that lined the edge of the back lawn, Ty shifted back to human form. His body blurred, then ran like water, becoming that of a man once again. He sat down in the grass and watched me. Seeing him as a man made me want to be human again. The moment I decided to shift, my body reacted by warming up and flowing. Colors changed a little, scents and sounds retreated slightly, and the wildness within tucked away, sated for the moment. My paws became hands, my legs arms. Long black hair spilled down into my vision. I still felt like me. Hell, I felt more like me than I ever had. The same went for my sanity. Of course, it wasn't likely that an insane person knew they were insane. But if this was insanity, I was good with it.

Not caring that I was naked, I rolled onto my back in the grass and threw my arms out wide. "That was amazing!"

The grass was cool and refreshing against the bare skin of my back. Its rich, heady smell poured into me, soothing and relaxing me. A slight chill in the air hardened my nipples, but it wasn't enough to actually make a *varúlfur* feel cold. Even in the dark, Ty would be able to see much of me, erect nipples included, but I didn't care. That wasn't true, exactly. I wanted him to see me. Low in his throat rumbled something that sounded like a growl filled with desire instead of menace. On all fours, he crawled toward me. Even in human form as he was, it looked as though he stalked me.

"You shifted and adjusted to it as if you were born to it. Clearly, nature meant for you to be a *varúlfur* from the start," he said as he drew closer.

The light of the rising moon reflected off his eyes like an animal's, making them seem almost electric blue. It had always been disturbing to me to come across an animal in the dark and see such a thing. This was different. Oddly, I found it sexy as hell on Ty. For a better view of him, I pushed up onto my elbows. The darkness hid more than I liked, but it also created some interesting shadows that played over his chest and gave me a peek-a-boo view of his goods. His scent changed, the musk deepening in a way that made my mouth water. Moving in that sexy stalk/crawl, he straddled me, working his way up my legs until he hovered over me. Looking up into his ice-chip blue eyes, I found I couldn't breathe. An exquisite lightheadedness seized me.

"Tell me, Sonya, do you still think your desire was caused by the *verða?*" he asked.

I wanted so badly to say yes, to fight the tide rising inside me. My breath caught in my throat when I tried to give voice to the lie. With a great amount of effort, I mustered up my control and ignored my body's burning need.

"No, but a pheromone thing maybe," I whispered.

He laughed and shook his head. "*Varúlfur* do not give off any more pheromones than humans."

Pink flashed as his tongue slid out and licked his lips. His eyes bore into mine in a way I wanted other parts of him to. "Face it, new wolf, it is me, and only me you are reacting to."

The deep rumble of his lusty voice made my mouth dry and my outer labia moist. He was so close to touching my naked body, and I wanted him to so badly. Bumps rose all over me. My breasts ached for his touch. I closed my eyes, but the sight of him hovering over me was burned into the back of my eyelids. His soft breath on my face and the warmth of his skin so close to mine didn't help either.

The determination not to make the mistake of casual sex burned through me. But would it be? In two weeks I had learned almost nothing about Raul, and what I had learned wasn't true. In less than that I had come to know Ty more than I had anyone in the past seven years. I hated that I was trying to rationalize it. Such things only opened me up for pain. Yet Ty felt different from any other man I had ever been attracted to, and not because he was a *varúlfur*.

His body shifted, lowering down onto mine in a deliciously hot line. "I am not Raul," he reminded me, his breath close to my lips. "I want you because you are amazing, funny, and the sexiest woman I have ever met, not because of anything you can give me or do for me."

The raw honesty in those words flung my eyes open. Face only inches from mine, he stopped. I searched for the hesitation, the turmoil that always lay within him when we got anything close to being intimate, but it was gone.

"What about the Council? What about the law, or creed, or whatever against *kennari* getting involved with their students?"

"You are through the *verða*, safe. That was all that mattered to me. I do not care what the Council thinks anymore. What I feel for you is too strong to allow them to govern. My family would understand. They would not see it as being disgraced."

Knowing it might be the last chance I had, I took it.

"I don't do one-night stands," I warned.

One of his hands slid slowly up the side of my body, along my arm, and around the back of my neck to cup it. "Neither do I," he said before pressing his lips to mine.

His kiss was every bit as thrilling as I had tried to forget. The gentle exploring of his tongue, which both gave and took, held the possibility of so much more. From his warm, wet mouth to the hardness pressed against my pelvis, he felt amazing and oh-so-right. The contrast to Raul's cocky danger was so stark it was almost painful. That rightness appealed to me in a powerful way that tried to stir up fear and self-preservation. For once, I shut the instincts down, believing in the reasons why I was attracted to Ty.

Being in his arms felt good and right. One of his legs nudged between mine. I opened them for him. The slight scruff of his five-o'clock shadow scratched at my hand, thrilling me. His pine and lake water scent surrounded me, melding with my own scent to become something even more amazing. He tasted like the wild blackberries we had eaten during our run as wolves: rich, sweet, and tart enough to make him delicious. Tongue thrusting deeper into his mouth, I tried to crawl down inside him. But that wasn't what I wanted, not exactly. I wanted him inside *me*. My legs lifted to wrap around him, when the night exploded.

CHAPTER TWENTY-ONE

TY

A loud boom, like thunder colliding directly overhead, broke the quiet night and shook the ground beneath me ever so slightly. Almost as one, Sonya and I leaped to our feet. The sound had come from around the front of the house. For a moment it sounded like hail falling. A piece of blue metal landed not far from my feet. Gods, my truck. The snap and crackle of flames—a lot of them—made me realize the "hail" sound was probably shrapnel from an explosion. Unfortunately, it was not a sound I was unused to. Yellow light flickered from around the edge of the house. Wide eyes on Sonya, I took a step toward the path leading around the house.

"Go, I'll be right there," she said as she scooped her clothes off the ground.

No way was I leaving her. Gaze scanning the darkness around me, I stepped to where my pants lay on the ground when I saw something moving in the trees at the edge of the lawn. Eyes shone in the black: yellow and bright. They held a sense of malice that made me start toward them. I felt the press of two more figures moving in behind me. Dammit. The bastards had lured me away from Sonya just enough to cut me off from her. The soft brush of shoes against grass behind me stopped me. I turned to see Sonya wrapped in the arms of a man.

Growling, I took a step toward her, but the two men who had been flanking me cut me off.

Instead of struggle, Sonya found her footing and settled her weight down into the ground. She stomped, hard, coming down on her captor's foot. The man grunted in pain. Arms thrusting out before her lightning fast, she shoved her butt backward at the same time. The second higher pitched grunt of pain told me she had slammed right into her captor's scrotum. I laughed as she spun out and away from him.

My own problems moved in on me. Dark as it was, I couldn't see much more than the shine of his eyes. By concentrating, I adjusted my eyesight to that of my wolf, thereby seeing better in the dark. It was not as good as night-vision goggles, but it was good enough to make out the men's tall frames. Sliding into a fighting stance, I glanced in the direction of the other set of eyes I had seen in the trees. A second man approached from that direction, shorter than the first, but broader. I growled and bared my fangs at them in warning, but they attacked anyway.

I sidestepped the attack of the man who had first approached, driving a roundhouse kick into his kidney as I moved. He let out a cry of pain followed by, "Bastard!"

Having no time to respond, I thrust a back kick out with my other leg that caught the second man in the gut. Air left him in an audible rush as he doubled over. Before he could even think about grabbing my leg, I whipped it back in to my body, chambering it like an arrow preparing to fly again. No easy feat when your balls were swinging free, but I managed without pinching anything vital. The first man took another step toward me and I let that arrow fly in the form of a front kick that drove the ball of my foot between his pectorals. He stumbled back, arms flailing. Movement out of the corner of my eyes told me I did not have time to watch and see if he went down. The second man started to straighten back up. Leaping into the air with one knee to get more lift, I brought my other leg up high and slammed my heel down toward the man's shoulder. When the strike connected, I whipped my hip back and down, putting all the power and speed into the move that I could, which was a lot.

The kick was so dangerous that it was illegal in most martial arts tournaments. An axe kick, some called it. It was aptly named considering it could split a person's skull or crush their spine. In this case, it drove the broad man to the ground, but his bones did not break. It took a lot more than that to break the bones of a *varúlfur*. I spun back toward the other man, only to find him fleeing into the trees. On instinct, I started to give chase, halting before entering the deeper darkness of the trees to turn back to Sonya. Her attacker had a hold of one of her shoulders and was rearing his fist back.

Swooping in, I grabbed the man by his fist and hauled him backward. He was shorter than me by at least half a foot, but I didn't stop once his feet were off the ground. I lifted him as high as my reach would allow, letting him dangle, choking, legs kicking at the air. It forced me to hold him out away from myself so he could not reach my balls, but my *varúlfur* strength made it easy. Nor did it hurt that I spent at least an hour a day in my home gym.

"You son of a *hóra*! How dare you come to my home, threaten my *nemi*, and blow up my truck!" I roared.

Letting out a vicious growl, I threw the man to the ground, following him down to pin him there with a hand on his chest. My fingernails grew into claws that punctured the man's shirt. The material around each claw began to darken and the tang of blood mixed with the smoke that flavored the air. His heart pulsed directly beneath my hand. Pissed as I was, all it would take was closing my fist. Eyes so wide I could see the whites around them, the man whimpered and went very still.

"James and Calder made me. I didn't want to come after you, never you, but we had to," the man said in a voice that shook so badly I barely understood it.

"Isak did not send you?" I demanded in a cold, calculating voice.

If it was Isak, his alpha, I would kill the man, regardless of what that meant.

"He doesn't even know we're here," the man said.

My fingers clenched a bit and flesh tore beneath my claws. The man cried out, his legs twitching, but he did not try to get up. "And are you prepared to die for what these two want? Neither of them is your alpha."

"No, but they'll hurt someone I care about if I don't help them," the man groaned, the word laced with more pain than I would have thought only one word could hold.

"Why are they doing this?" Ty's words held a weight of compulsion.

"Because she's special. They want to use her to change the world. That's all I know, I swear it. Calder because he's bat-shit crazy, and James because he wants to live in the open, have the same rights as humans," he whined.

The shine of his eyes disappeared as his lips slid closed. His chin lifted a bit as if he were preparing to die with honor, or bracing for the pain. Despite being pissed at him, a reluctant respect bloomed.

"Ty, don't, please. I don't want anyone to die because of me, not even this bastard," Sonya said.

I heard her soft steps approach a moment before she laid a hesitant hand on my bare shoulder. The warmth from her skin and power seeped inside, brought a sense of calm. A sigh shuddered through me. I withdrew my claws and rose to my feet. Her hand slid from my shoulder as my height took it out of her reach, but she let it slide to the middle of my back and rest there. Her touch continued to soothe me, helping me to breathe easier, to think past the rage.

"She saved your life today. Remember that, because I will not spare it again," I said through clenched teeth.

The man crab-crawled backward. He did not pause to roll over and scramble to his feet until he had reached the trees.

"Oh God, Ty, your truck," she said, a piece of metal in hand.

She turned and ran for the front of the house. Hesitating, I scanned the trees, listening hard and smelling the air. It was difficult to tell over the crackle of a raging fire and the scent of the smoke, but I didn't think anyone else was around. Barefoot but not even feeling the rocks, I ran onto the gravel drive after her. Flames engulfed the front end and cab of my truck, their orange and yellow fingers reaching high into the night, banishing the darkness. Sonya stood before it, fire extinguisher thrust too close to the flames. I could smell that the heat was searing her flesh. The white foam disappeared into the roaring flames, hardly making a dent. I ran to her, clamped hands around her waist, and hauled her back.

"Sonya, no, it is only a truck," I said.

Her lips curled back from fangs. "But it's your truck and it's my fault," she protested.

I picked her up and carried her back several feet. She threw the useless fire extinguisher on the ground and turned to me. Fire reflected in her angry eyes. I rubbed my hands up and down her already healing arms, lending my power to hers to help speed the process.

"It is just a truck. We are not immortal, only hard to kill. Fire is one of the things that can do a good job of it, though," I said.

Her gaze flicked to the impossible inferno that now engulfed my truck, then to her Jeep parked on the other side of the circular drive. "We should at least go after them."

I shook my head. "Their scent is all over the hood of your Jeep. I am sure they disabled it so no one could follow them."

"But..."

My brows drew together and I took her face in my hands. "But nothing. The truck can be replaced, you cannot," I said.

She dropped her gaze. I moved closer, acutely aware that I was still naked. My relief over her being all right morphed into something deeper, more profound. Her eyes bore into mine and her hands started to work their way up my bare back as she leaned closer. The loud blare of a fire engine's siren echoed from somewhere far away.

"Dammit," I swore as I pulled away.

I took hold of one of her hands as I started to return to the backyard. "I have got to get some clothes on before they get here," I said.

Throwing a last glance back at my burning vehicle, she followed without a word. The now mostly risen three-quarter moon lit the backyard in an eerie glow, revealing the shape of my sweatpants on the grass where I had left them. Orange and red flames reflected off a metallic garden ball, casting foreboding lights on the flagstone pathway. The sight sent a chill through me, along with a sudden desire for this night to be over. It had started out so promising. While I dressed I did my best to recall the names of the men who had attacked us so that when I saw them again in Hemlock Hollow, I could make them pay. For now we had more pressing matters, though. The wail of police sirens joined the fire engine sirens, promising that this was going to be a very long night in all the wrong ways.

CHAPTER TWENTY-TWO

SONYA

T he distance the sunlight had traveled across my bed told me it was hours past dawn when I finally woke. Little surprise considering how late we had stayed up dealing with the fire department, Ty's truck, and talking to the cops. Having been raised with a deep-seated distrust for law enforcement, I'd been more than happy to let Ty do all the talking. He was good at it. Too good. It made me think he'd had to do that kind of thing a lot. But then, he had belonged to a speed-hungry group. Umbrella pack, whatever. The story he fed them about an irate student who was failing summer school and in jeopardy of losing his scholarship appeased the cops. They even seemed to buy that he only knew the kid's first name. But they had only left after Ty promised to come down to the station in a few days to give a more formal statement.

Sadly, we had fallen into our separate beds after all the chaos settled. As much as I had wanted to spend the night in his arms, we were both too shaken up. The desire was still there, but the timing was off. He seemed more worried about watching the security monitors and windows than jumping my bones. Disappointing as that was, it helped me sleep soundly knowing he watched over me.

Having already showered before going to bed, I rushed through my morning routine. The desperate need to see Ty, to make sure he was all right, sped each movement. It was silly, I knew. Clearly the man was more than capable of taking care of himself, but knowing that didn't make the need go away. After running a brush through my long black hair and putting on a pair of cutoff blue jeans and a yellow tank top, I made my way to the kitchen.

Gaze going every which way, I checked the hall, the open floor plan of the living room. The second I stepped into the kitchen I knew something wasn't right. The air smelled like that coarse, orange soap mechanics liked so much when it should have smelled like breakfast. Then there was the guy bending over and digging around in the fridge. He was muscular enough to be Ty. But he didn't smell or feel like Ty. The feel of his power told me he was a *varúlfur*.

I lunged for the counter and snatched the biggest knife from the knife block that I could. The man in the fridge stood up so fast he smacked his head on the freezer.

"Ouch, shit!"

He turned toward me, rubbing his head with one hand and holding a beer in the other. Overly long, wild blond hair thrust up in every direction, stuck in a few places with something dark, grease maybe. His stance remained relaxed, so he didn't exactly look threatening. Still, I wasn't about to let go of the knife. My fighting skills were progressing at a snail's pace, so I needed every advantage I could get.

"Whoa, easy there, little wolf. I'm a friend of Ty's," he said.

"A friend? To an outcast, lone wolf?"

The man's brows bunched together. "Helheimr yes. We lone wolves have to stick together."

Pace and stance casual as could be, he walked from the kitchen and planted himself in a bar seat. The fact that I held a knife as long as my forearm apparently didn't faze him. That, or he was really good at hiding it. He popped the top off his beer with one thumb and took a long drink.

"Lone wolves sticking together. You seriously expect me to swallow that?"

The man grinned. "I don't care if you spit or swallow, darling. Gorgeous as you are, I'm not one to mess with a friend's woman."

Whoever he was, his quick wit made me like him a bit despite my caution. I sat the knife on the counter, but didn't let go of it. "So you're a friend of Raul's?"

One side of the man's lips rose to bare a fang. "Never. I didn't mean him, because clearly, you aren't his."

My eyes widened. "Oh." I gathered myself and cleared my throat. "Why are you here?"

"I brought Ty some parts for your Jeep. Those bastards did a number on it." One eye remaining on me, he took another drink of his beer. "I like that you're cautious, means you're smart. No wonder you've brought him out of his hiatus."

"Hiatus?"

"On women."

It was a good thing I didn't blush easily.

"Really, little wolf, you can relax. I'm one of the many that left the Draupnir pack with Ty. You won't find more loyal wolves to him than us."

I sat down on the stool farthest from him. "Left with him?"

Blond eyebrows rose until they disappeared into his unruly hair. "He didn't tell you. Of course he didn't. He's too damn modest." He sat his beer down and leaned his elbows on the bar top. "Almost half the pack left with Ty in a show of support. Helheimr, we'd even follow him if he wanted to start a new pack, but he has no taste for leading. Can't say that I blame him with all the shitty politics."

The shock made me take a moment before responding. "Half the pack? Even though he didn't fight?"

"Because he didn't fight. Our alpha wouldn't have wanted him to fight, and he respected that, honored his memory by not doing it."

It took a special kind of man to walk away from a fight. I respected the hell out of that. "That's pretty amazing."

"It is. I'm Lars, by the way." He extended his hand and I accepted it. As much as I didn't want a stranger touching my hand, it was better than sniffing my ass. Okay, that wasn't fair. But I had only met a handful of *varúlfur* and I really didn't know what the norm was.

"Sonya."

"I know."

I groaned. "Guess everyone knows."

Lars shrugged off my discomfort. "People don't know shit. I know what

Ty's told me, not bullshit rumors. And you've nothing to worry about. He says only good things about you. Incessantly." He rolled his eyes at the last part.

Heat rushed up my neck to my face. The impulse to ask what he'd said about me swelled, but I clamped my teeth together, determined not to embarrass myself.

The gentle tug of Ty's power pulled at me a second before he walked in the front door. His eyes widened as they went from me to Lars. In the next stride, his muscles relaxed so much his shoulders dropped and he managed to put on a casual smile. Concern lingered in his eyes and tinged the feel of his power.

"Well, Lars is still upright, which means you two meeting could not have gone too badly."

I smiled, partly because I liked Lars, but mostly to ease that look of worry from Ty's eyes.

Lars clapped Ty on the shoulder as he walked by. "Don't worry, *félagi*, I told her nothing but good things."

I looked to Ty. "*Fél...*" I stopped because I couldn't get the word to come out sounding right.

At the sink, Ty squeezed some of the coarse orange soap beside the faucet onto his greasy hands. "It roughly translates to 'mate', as in packmate, which he should get out of the habit of calling me seeing how we are no longer packmates," Ty said, glaring at Lars as he spoke the last.

Since he was turned sideways to me, it was hard to tell, but I thought I saw Ty smile.

Head back, Lars downed the rest of his beer in one drink. Bottle in hand, he stood. Rather than go for the trash, he took it to the cabinet where Ty kept his recycling. "Oh, before I go, I heard from Vidar yesterday, said he tried to get a hold of you."

As Ty turned around, Lars handed him the towel from the fridge door. The guy knew his way around so well it was clear he hung out here a lot. Yet I hadn't met him. It made me wonder how much of his life Ty had put on hold for me.

"Really? Damn. I have not been checking my messages since I brought Sonya here. We could not risk the distraction."

Lars gave him a crooked grin. "Riiight. Well, anyway, he said there's something he has to talk to you about. He's coming back to do it."

Ty's eyes popped open wide. "From Iceland? I thought he was studying at the temple and could not leave. All because I did not answer my phone? Did you tell him I was all right?"

"Of course. That's not why. He said it's something he has to talk to you about in person, before you go to Hemlock Hollow again."

"Meaning, before I take Sonya there."

Some of the color drained from Ty's face.

"Obviously he didn't want to say that, but yeah, that's the impression I got. He said he'd meet you here and ride up with you for the trial."

Face going blank, Ty folded the towel neatly and hung it back on the handle of the fridge. Though he grinned and tried to look casual, tension sang through his power like a tuning fork being plucked. The two men exchanged a look and Lars shook his head. "He said don't call him, he wouldn't be able to talk about it on the phone."

Ty nodded.

Grinning, Lars slugged Ty in the arm. "Don't do anything I wouldn't do." His brows wiggled as his gaze darted between Ty and me.

"There is not much you would not do," Ty said.

"Exactly! I'm off while the trail's still lukewarm." He tipped his head to me. "Sonya, a true pleasure meeting you." With that, he strode out the door.

I stared after him, needing a moment to process all the info he dropped in my lap.

Dishes clanked as Ty began to prepare breakfast.

"Should I be worried about that?" I asked.

"No. Vidar probably has information about who bit in Candice. That is all, I imagine." He sounded sincere enough, but the way he kept preparing and didn't turn around made me think there was more to it.

I had the sudden urge to call Candice and make sure she was all right. "I'll be right back."

Turned out Candice was fine, a bit bored, but that was it. I picked her brain about Hemlock Hollow. Sleepy and boring was the length of her description. Her *kennari* was an older man, who she also described as stuffy and boring. But she was having fun with her new abilities. I grilled her a bit on how she was adjusting and decided she was probably doing better than I was. I should have known. Kids always adjusted to change fast. I grilled her on the description of the guy who bit her. Tall, wiry, and creepy. No she hadn't come across him in Hemlock Hollow. With promises to call back soon, I hung up and headed for the kitchen.

The delicious aromas of crackling bacon and browning pancakes drew me in. I yawned long and deep. Nightmares about Ty having been in the truck when it blew up plagued me all last night. I hated the idea of him getting hurt because of me. Suddenly, I wanted to get to Hemlock Hollow to put an end to people trying to make me a pawn in their politics. But first thing was first. In a pair of cargo shorts tight enough to accentuate his fit ass and a brown flannel that set off his blond hair, Ty looked so amazing he made me forget anyone existed but him.

"I am sorry breakfast was not ready when you woke. Did you sleep okay?" he asked without even turning around.

His deep voice both soothed and thrilled me. "Not bad," I lied.

He made a short grunt/laugh sound that clearly expressed his disbelief. When he turned to set a coffee cup in front of me my breath caught in my throat. The brown flannel hung open, not a single button done up to hide his sculpted chest. The only thing breaking up the perfection was his triple triangle pendant that he always wore. Desire burned right through my hunger and anxiety, igniting an entirely different kind of hunger. A thin trail of light blond hair led from his belly button into the low-slung waistband of his shorts, dragging my eyes with it. Reaching for the ceramic brown coffee cup, I pretended my gaze had gone to it instead of Ty's goods.

"I was able to fix your Jeep, thanks to Lars," he said as he turned back to the stove.

Guilt helped dampen my desire. How could I have gone all night without wondering what they had done to disable my Jeep? Another thing I would have to make those bastards pay for.

"What'd they do to it?" I asked.

The coffee was perfect. Just enough flavored creamer sweetened it to take off the edge. Ty impressed me by how quickly he had come to know my likes and dislikes. Most guys took years for that kind of thing, if they ever got it.

"Removed the battery, messed with a few other things, nothing permanent," he said.

Heat coursed through me at the thought of him elbow deep in the hood of my Jeep. Dear Gods I was going to need another set of panties. "Thanks, but you didn't have to go to all that trouble."

He set a plate of bacon, hash browns, and eggs before me. The mingled aromas made my mouth water almost as much as his bare chest did.

"No trouble. I needed to talk to Lars anyway, or he needed to talk to me rather, it seems. And he was coming over to help me with my new security system anyway, so it worked out."

Carrying a plate of his own, he walked around to my side of the bar and sat beside me.

"Security system?" I asked.

He nodded as he chewed and swallowed a bite of food. "Twice rival pack members have come onto my property threatening you. It will not happen again."

I was almost afraid to ask. Was violence really the answer? "What kind of security system?"

"If you want to go for a run after breakfast, I will show you."

Taking the time to chew a bite of perfectly peppered hash browns, I nodded. "That'd be great."

I had a lot of pent-up energy I needed to run off. Only one other thing sounded better, and I wasn't about to indulge in that on a whim. The timing needed to be right, and distracted as we both were, now was not the time. For the most part we ate in silence. Attention on my food, I tried to think of anything but Ty. Halfway through breakfast I realized I wasn't as hungry as I normally was. It seemed shifting had fixed the ravenous hunger. We finished breakfast, cleaned up, and went outside. The scorched portion of gravel where Ty's truck had sat made my stomach turn. He'd had it towed last night to a local shop. The dark spot served to remind me of all I had brought down on this man.

"Why are you still helping me after all that has happened?" I asked as we walked.

The corner of his mouth I could see turned up, but he didn't look at me as I was hoping he would. "Is it not obvious?"

Maybe it should have been, but it wasn't, partly because I refused to see it. "No."

We reached the back deck and he turned around to lean back against it, arms crossed over his chest, those blue eyes boring into me. "I care about you, Sonya."

I tried to make light of it. I had to because the alternative kind of scared the hell out of me. "Well you may not survive long if you care this much about all the new *varúlfur* you have to train."

Smiling, he shook his head. "I will not feel this way about any other new *varúlfur*, of that you can be certain. They will not be you." With that, he turned and leaped over the railing to the grass below.

All those mesmerizing tattoos winding across his shoulders and down his spine captured my attention as he took his flannel off. I remained frozen in place for a heartbeat as he pushed his shorts down over his perfect ass. The man was going commando. Knowing he had been sitting next to me, facing me at times, his legs propped up on the bar at the base of the stool, with no underwear on, drove me a little mad. If I hadn't had such an iron grip on my control, I could have caught a glimpse of his dangly parts earlier. Shaking my head to get it out of the gutter, I leaped over the railing and landed next to him.

"I thought we were going running," I said.

I may have sneaked a peek and he may or may not have been sporting a partial hard-on. The lapse in control over my eyes had been too short to know whether he was really excited or whether my imagination made him look that way.

"We are, as wolves." His voice dropped so low on the last two words that anyone without *varúlfur* souped-up hearing wouldn't have heard it.

When his voice dropped like that it became deeper, rumbling on the edge of a growl that made muscles in my pelvis clench. Dammit. So much for my control. The idea of a run as a wolf sounded even more appealing. Problem was, running wasn't what I wanted to do anymore. It seemed wrestling for control of my libido would be taking place of wrestling for control of my emotions. Great. I couldn't get away from the whole internal struggle crap. I looked down and fumbled with the button on my cutoff shorts.

"Two runs in two days. Aren't you worried the neighbors might report a wolf sighting?" I asked.

"We are on over a hundred private acres. Besides, wolf sightings are not that unusual in Montana," he said.

That logic was hard to argue with. Not that I wanted to. All night I'd had to fight the desire to shift again, not from a deep-rooted need, but simply because I wanted to. Touching that wildness within had been so thrilling that, second only to Ty, it was all I could think about. But I was afraid of people seeing me, or more to the point, I was afraid of seeing people while I was in wolf form. I wasn't sure what I would do. Eating them wasn't an issue. At least I didn't think it was. But if they threatened me I wasn't sure I'd be able to fight the instinct to hurt them. Ty's hands came to rest on my shoulders, pulling me from my thoughts. Knowing he was naked and only a step away made it incredibly hard not to look down.

"We will be fine. We will not come across anyone, and if we do they will never even see us," he said.

The heat of his body teased me, making me want to step into him. Before I could cave in and do just that, I stepped back, turned half away from him, and pulled my tank top off. Using the excuse to place it on one of the lounge chairs, I walked several feet away. The rest of my clothes quickly joined it, bra and underwear included. Ty's gaze was so heavy on my ass it may as well have been a caress. My eyes slid closed and I had to repress an indulgent sigh. If I didn't make this quick, we would end up entangled in each other instead of running.

Thrills of an entirely different kind—yet no less powerful—raced through me at the thought of shifting. The desire to shift strengthened until I felt the vibrations begin beneath my skin. All fear of madness was gone now, leaving me feeling only free and excited. Unlike before, the vibrations now brought pleasure instead of burning, anticipation instead of fear. A quick glance around and I moved beneath the covered deck where I would be blocked from the sight of any distant neighbors who might be nosy. From deep inside I called up the wildness, and set it free. Turning back to Ty, I reached for the ground, shifting as I did so. Fur covered my nakedness but did little to banish the feeling of exposure. At eye-level to Ty's crotch I got a perfect view of his hard-on. The attraction was still there, but it was different, subdued, as if part of me knew mating wasn't an option with us in different forms. Mating. Oh God, had I really just thought of sex as mating?

When I was ready to turn away, Ty's body shimmered and flowed into that of a huge blond wolf. He seemed to smile at me, canines flashing. With a shake of my head, I took off running across the lawn. In only a few strides Ty caught up to me and we ran into the forest together, paws eating up the path in an effortless gait. Soon after entering the shade of the trees, we left the path behind for the deeper forest. After a little less than a quarter of an hour of running we came to a post and rail fence like the kind wealthy ranchers liked to put around the entrance to their driveway. The difference was, this fence was slightly taller at five feet, and went as far as I could see in both directions, stretching for acres and acres.

Unable to speak my surprise, I looked at Ty with wide eyes. His nose lifted, gaze going to a tree not more than three feet from the fence. I followed. My ears found the device before my eyes did. A slight buzzing emitted from a little pan-tilt zoom camera mounted over twenty feet up in the tree. Impressed, I cocked my head and nodded. For a while we ran along the fence line, checking cameras that were mounted high in trees every fifty feet or so. Such a system had to have cost a small fortune, but then, if this fence surrounded Ty's property, it seemed his family likely had much more than a small fortune.

Soon we cut back into the heart of the property, starting back for the house. Though the trees and valleys all looked alike, I knew we were headed back toward the house as surely as I knew from which direction the sun rose. Not only could I smell the trail we had both left and the lake next to us, it was an instinctual thing. Instead of taking us back to the main pathway, Ty turned into the forest. He stopped inside a familiar ring of huge spruce trees, the very ones I had been drawn to my first day here. The ground beneath my feet pulsed ever so slightly, kind of like the air at a loud concert or movie. It didn't smell and I couldn't hear it, but it energized me in a way I couldn't understand.

The overcast day made the shadows thick beneath the boughs of so many huge trees, but it was still warm enough to be pleasant. Which was crazy considering it couldn't be barely sixty degrees, a temperature that normally would have had me reaching for a jacket. The fur coat I now wore helped, sure, but that wasn't it. Deep inside heat roared within from a well that felt as though it would warm me in the coldest of climates. Part of being a *varúlfur*, I guessed.

A very human-sounding sigh issued from Ty. The moment I saw him in human form, naked and magnificent, I shifted on instinct. It took me until I was rising to my feet to realize I had done so because I wanted to speak to him, touch him, and so much more. Naked and not caring beyond placing a hand casually over the birthmark on my hip, I approached him. The stone altar blocked my path to him, which I took as a good thing. My long hair hung down past my breasts, covering them for the most part. Not that I wanted to hide them from his roaming eyes, but a little mystery can be a very good thing. Judging by the way he couldn't take his eyes off me, it was working well in my favor.

"That fence, does it go all the way around your property?" I asked.

"It does."

He stalked around the stone altar until it no longer stood between us.

His naked body called to me, driving out all other distractions until my feet moved closer to him seemingly on their own. I made one last attempt.

"Why come here?" I indicated the rune-carved trees with a wave of my hand.

My mind plummeted as the word *come* left my lips, drawing my gaze down with it. Already he stood at attention, impressive, and oh so tempting. Only a few feet from him, I forced myself to stop. Slowly, my eyes worked their way back up to his face, enjoying every hard mountain and valley of the journey. The man could have been carved from the very same steel as his Norse gods. I couldn't imagine Thor or even Odin himself being built better. Maybe it was a sacrilege to think that, but surely they'd forgive one as naive as myself. My eyes locked onto his and in them, for a moment, I swore I could see the glaciers of his ancestral homeland.

Moving slowly, giving me all the time in the world to pull away, he reached up and cupped my chin. But I could no more move away from him than a compass needle could move away from true north. I leaned into his hand, craving the heat, the feel of his rough palm, and something more. The splattered shadows of spruce boughs cloaked us, crisscrossing over our skin in patterns that hid much, but not enough. It wasn't that I didn't want him to see me. No, it was more that I didn't want to see him. He was too much of a temptation for me, especially now that I knew my desire wasn't a result of the *verða*. It had been so much easier when I'd had something to blame it on. I closed my eyes to try and block out the thoughts of all the things I wanted to do to him, and let him do to me.

"This is a mistake. I'm trouble. You shouldn't get involved with me," I said.

Deep laughter rumbled from Ty. The sheer masculinity of the sound, the way it pulled at something deep inside me, forced my eyes to open, to look at him.

"Trouble and I have been bedfellows for as long as I can remember," he said.

Despite my inner struggle, I smiled. "You're my *kennari*. You said there is some kind of teacher/student code against having sex with me, didn't you? I don't want to get you in trouble."

"I do not care, not now that we know your sanity is safe and that our mutual attraction was not caused by the *verða*."

His hand moved down my neck, around the outside of my breast, and to my waist.

"Are you sure?" I asked in a breathy voice.

That hand moved around to rest on the small of my back. "Very sure. If the Council disapproves that much, I will give up being a *kennari* to be with you."

The depth of commitment in his eyes frightened me a little, and excited me. "You've barely known me for three weeks. You can't be serious." Though I kept my tone light and joking, even I could hear the hope in it. Damn.

Gentle pressure on my back moved my body against his. "Sonya, I felt something for you the first moment I saw you, and I would give up the world to be with you," he said, lips hovering over mine.

The emotion in both his voice and his eyes should have scared me, but it didn't. Just under three weeks shouldn't have been long enough. You couldn't even really get to know a person in that short amount of time. But then I thought of our nights on the couch, laughing and jumping at horror movies, our days meditating, and the long afternoons hiking, swimming, and talking about history and Norse mythology.

"How can you know that already?" I whispered.

Unable to pull my eyes from his, I simply stared into their light blue depths, caught like a moth. His arms worked their way around me until he cradled me against him, secure and gentle as though he'd never let go.

"I think you know," he whispered.

And I did, oh how I did. The double meaning wasn't lost on me at all. His lips descended to mine and all resistance melted away in an inferno that ensured it would never return.

CHAPTER TWENTY-THREE

SONYA

I rose up on my toes to meet his kiss, the movement causing his long erection to rub against my bare stomach. The sensation made me moan as our lips met. His opened, inviting me in with a press and pull back of his soft tongue. Unrestrained, I delved into the warmth of his delicious mouth, losing myself in it, until I wasn't sure who devoured whom. My hands ran up the taut muscles of his back to his broad shoulders. The electric feel of his bare skin against mine, running the length of my body from my breasts to my legs, carried me to a place I never wanted to return from.

Those strong arms that I had so often admired wrapped around me, cradling me gently, and at the same time holding so securely it seemed he'd never let me go. Our kiss deepened, became something more like shared breath, as if he could breathe for me and I for him. His hands roamed down my back, cupped my butt, and lifted me off my feet. On instinct my legs wrapped around his waist, trapping his erection against my pelvis. We began to move, to where I had no idea, and didn't care so long as he didn't stop kissing me.

Finally, he sat me down on something cool. Dried flowers crunched beneath my right cheek. The altar. I drew back from the kiss enough to give him a questioning look.

"Isn't it a sacrilege or something to do this here?" I asked through a half smile.

Though I didn't want to say it out loud in case it was disrespectful, I had to admit, the altar was the perfect height. Ty's long legs were almost straight and my legs still wrapped around his waist easily. The desire to lean back on my hands and appreciate the view was so strong I almost did it, but I didn't want to crush any more of the lavender flowers. Grinning at me, he traced my cheek and the line of my jaw.

"Not at all. The Norse Gods appreciate offerings of all kinds, sex included," he said.

My tongue lashed out and caught the tip of his finger as it ran along my lips. "I think I could come to really like these Norse Gods of yours."

When he didn't pull his finger away I leaned forward and sucked it into my mouth. Head falling back, he moaned. The sound made me wet and for once I didn't care if he smelled my arousal. I moved his finger in and out of my mouth, tongue flicking along the end of it like I longed to do with other parts of his anatomy. To my dismay, he withdrew his finger and shook it at me as if I were being naughty.

"Before this night is over, you will *come* to like many things about me," he promised, his voice deep and throaty.

He reached down and slid that finger over my mound of shortly trimmed hair, teasing the outermost folds which were already slick. That one little touch sent dozens of sparks flying through my pelvis like lightning bolts that shot their way to muscles within. My sheath clenched, drawing a moan from me. Gods, I wanted him so bad I couldn't think. Finger poised over the folds that hid my clit, he leaned down until his lips nearly brushed my ear.

"You are amazing, Sonya. So open to new ideas, so caring. I want you for who you are," he whispered.

The feel of his breath against my ear made me shiver. I giggled. "I know, Ty. You don't have to wax poetic to me. Though it is nice."

A sound between a hum and a contented growl issued from him, exciting me in ways I hadn't known was possible.

"In that case..."

His voice trailed off as his finger slid inside me. Our lips crashed together and we both moaned into each other's mouths. His finger found a rhythm, pushing in and out of me in a way that left me dizzy. In my mouth his tongue did the same, breath becoming wonderfully ragged, as if pleasing me excited him. I reached down until I found his erection and squeezed the base of it. It was so long, I would need both hands to take hold of it all, and it likely still would poke out through my fists. But my second hand was busy holding the back of his neck, and I wasn't about to let go. A gasp tore from him as I began to pump my hand slowly up and down all eight-plus inches of him.

Shock stilled my hand as his finger slid from inside me to rub at my clit. The rhythm he picked up, steady circles around and over it, soon had my pelvis muscles fluttering. Gasps tore from me one after another as he brought me closer and closer to a crescendo I had only ever reached on my own. No man had taken the time to try and make me reach orgasm this way—or any way really for that matter. Sometime during the waves of sensation he had stopped kissing me. I only noticed when his mouth was suddenly over my right breast, his tongue teasing the hard nipple. Arching my back, I pushed my breast into his mouth. With a grunt, he sucked hard, teasing it with his teeth, rolling his tongue over it. All the while his finger worked over me in a furious rhythm that brought me closer and closer. Another of his fingers slid into me and shoved me over into orgasm. My muscles convulsed in tantalizing waves as I came so hard my eyes slammed shut.

Ty's mouth moved from my breast to my neck. I tensed but he only nuzzled and licked me before moving up to my ear.

"If you do not let go of my cock with that karate grip of yours I am going to come, and I really do not want to do that yet," he whispered.

Dancing back from the delirious edge of bliss, I released my grip, rubbing the head of him as I did so. He moaned and muttered something dirty in Icelandic. A giggle slid from me as I realized he had called me a dirty goddess. Lips hovering above mine, he groaned.

"Gods, I love your laugh."

Too choked up to respond, I pressed my lips to his in a slow, sweet kiss. One hand behind my head to cradle it, he laid me down on the altar. Lavender crushed beneath me, the slightly oily but wonderful scent wafting up around us. After a moment, Ty's lips moved from mine. He kissed and licked my skin from my neck down to my navel, moving slow and steady. My muscles clenched and quivered as my skin ignited from the attention. Tongue flicking down my belly, he moved lower.

Pausing at my hairline, he looked up at me. "I need to taste you," he murmured.

A man had never taken the time or effort to go down on me. I'd only ever seen it in porn and dreamed about it. Yes, I'd had horrible, thoughtless lovers. Rather than respond, since my voice failed me yet again, I pulled my feet up until they rested on the edge of the altar and spread my legs for him. Ice-blue eyes locked on mine, he sank down between my legs. His tongue licked over my opening, making my body buck up off the stone. The moment I settled back against it, his tongue slid inside me. That wonderful, soft probing over my most sensitive parts drew a cry from me that sent birds flying from the trees overhead in a flurry of shadows.

Uttering a very pleased sound, his tongue withdrew and his head lifted. He took hold of my hips and gently pulled me down closer to the edge of the stone until my legs were hanging off. Licking his lips, he gave me such a pleased look that it sent a shudder through me. Poised only inches from my opening, he paused. My tolerance for waiting and resisting fled. I wrapped my legs around him and pulled him to me. He slid slowly into me, easing in until he was buried balls-deep inside. Never had I felt so full, so complete. Thoughts scattered out of my reach as he began to move in and out of me.

At the height of every thrust his tip touched a place deep inside that felt so amazing it made my vision go white. It began to drive me wild. Unable to hold myself up any longer, I lay back on the rock, head held up enough to watch him work. Gripping my hips, he pumped in and out of me. The lengthening shadows of twilight played across his glistening chest. One of his hands moved up my body, across my stomach, to caress my left breast. His hungry eyes devoured me as if he couldn't get enough of the sight of me. That look drove me almost as wild as the feeling of him moving inside me.

My breath soon became ragged and I realized with a start that I was nearing orgasm again. That new spot he kept hitting deep within was about to throw me over the edge of something entirely new and powerful. I cried his name.

Hand moving back to my hip, he growled through a smile. His thrusts sped. Gasping now, I arched my back up off the rock. Ty leaned over me, a hand going behind my back to hold me against his chest. Two more hard thrusts and the world exploded as an orgasm tore through me that started deep inside and rippled all through my sheath, pelvis, and even my abdominal muscles. In the midst of those waves, Ty followed me.

He nuzzled against my ear. "Sonya, oh Sonya."

We lay like that for some time, clinging to each other as if reluctant to allow the moment to pass. Impractical as it was, I didn't want him to withdraw from me, ever. After a while, he gathered me up in his arms. I wrapped my legs tighter around him, not ready to be separated yet. Without withdrawing from me, he lay me down in the grass and nuzzled into my hair, his weight barely settling on me. The guy was freaky talented. Or maybe it was a werewolf thing. Either way, I wasn't about to complain.

"We will have to do that again soon, and much slower next time," he said.

The sound of his voice, all euphoric and spent, made me happier than I could ever remember being. Arms going around his back, I pulled him tighter against me.

"Slower? Why, Ty, do you intend to torture me?" I teased.

Pushing upright enough to meet my gaze, he gave me the most devilish grin I had ever seen. "I do indeed."

He quieted my laughter with a languid kiss. As he drew back from the kiss, his body lifted and he pulled out of me. I let him go only because my arms were too weak to hang on anymore. To my surprise, he lay down beside me, put an arm around me, and drew me in against his side. I'm not sure what I expected, but cuddling had definitely not been it. A few moments later he propped himself up on an elbow and began playing with my hair. The thoughtful look on his face worried me a little.

"You are a wonder, and I do not just mean the amazing sex," he said.

"I've been called a lot of things, but never that."

He laughed as his hand began to trail down my arm. "I mean it. You captivate me, make me think and feel things I have never felt before. And you took to shifting as if you were born to it, a true natural."

The vulnerability in his tone made me want to look away, but I didn't. Partly because his eyes were following his fingers, and partly because I couldn't look away from his face. The lack of lines between his brows and the grin told me he was completely at ease with saying such a thing to me, and that he didn't expect an answer. That relaxed me in a way I hadn't expected.

"Well, it's nice to be a natural at something, considering my fighting skills suck as bad as my grasp of Icelandic." I took a breath. "You think I'm safely through it, then? No risk of insanity?"

"Quite safe."

Fingers splayed across my hip, he went tense and suddenly sat up. Dread filled me as I realized I hadn't even thought to cover my birthmark.

"What is this?" he asked in a mystified tone.

My hand went to cover it, but he caught it, stopping me.

"Nothing. Just a birthmark." I tried to make the words sound light but panic crept into them.

He leaned over me, getting a closer look.

"No, it is more than that."

Gentle fingers traced over it, making me both want to cry and scream. No one ever touched it. Hell, no one ever wanted to. I froze, terrified of what he would say next. The silent perusal stretched on far too long.

"Some call it a port wine stain, but really, it's just a birthmark. Not a rash or anything. You can't catch it," I said.

He shook his head. "This is the *Sowilo* rune. You are marked, Sonya."

Chills worked their way through me. "Marked?"

The gentle touch of his fingers over the mark almost seemed to burn. I pulled away, sinking deeper into the grass, but he didn't notice.

"It means something, the *Sowilo* showing up as a birthmark. I cannot remember what exactly, but this coupled with the fact both of your parents descended from old bloodlines is not a coincidence. There is a book in my office back at the university that might tell us more. I will have to get it. I wonder if this is what Vidar wanted to talk to me about? But how could he know..."

It took a moment for his words to sink in. He wasn't fearful or disgusted by my mark, he was *fascinated* by it. The two other guys I had got naked with in my life both thought it was weird, or ugly, a flaw to be covered.

"Means something?" I asked.

Taking me back into his arms, he pulled me close. "Yes, but I cannot remember what right now. It is something from an ancient text. All in time. Vidar will be here soon enough. Hmmm..."

He nuzzled my hair.

"Must be the endorphins from the fantastic sex making my mind foggy."

I couldn't argue there. As the fear of his disgust or rejection over my birthmark faded, the high of the endorphins kicked back in, leaving me feeling as though I floated in a sea of pleasure. This man was so amazing on so many levels that I wasn't entirely sure he wasn't a dream. But then, I had become an entirely different species to find him. Despite all I had been through, if Ty was a dream, I didn't ever want to wake up.

CHAPTER TWENTY-FOUR

TY

T he light pouring through the sunrise-style window on the wall beside the tub caused red and blue to dance across the bubbles of Sonya's bath. Her gaze was cast out over the view of the back gardens with the lake stretching out beyond it. Soap bubbles teased her chin as she repositioned within the claw-foot bathtub that sat in my loft. The image of her blurred, then disappeared. I wiped the steam from the glass shower walls yet again, desperate to watch her a little longer. For at least the fifth time that afternoon, I was tempted to go to her and ravish her again. But after last night's amazing sex and the marathon session this morning, I did not want her thinking that was all she was to me.

So I forced myself to stay put, rinse the shampoo from my hair, and be content with the memory of our multiple sex sessions. And oh what memories they were. This morning proved that she already possessed a *varúlfur*'s amazing endurance. But it was more than endurance. It was like we were synched.

The harsh ring of an ancient rotary-style phone cut through the quiet of the loft. My cell ringtone. I shut the shower off, grabbed a towel to dry the side of my face, and picked up the phone. It was the police getting impatient about my statement regarding the truck bombing. I promised the man on the other end of the phone that I would be in within the hour.

I could not have them getting suspicious that I might seek out my own justice, especially since I would. I toweled off, ran a comb through my hair, and pulled on a pair of boxers and shorts.

My eyes drank Sonya in without the steamed up wall between us. The bubbles were enough to make me ache. My tongue slid out and ran along my upper lip, dipping between my fangs.

"Damn, woman, you look fine."

I shook my head, grabbed the towel off the leather chaise, and held it out to her. "As much as I would love to spend the entire day making love to you, I have to go to the police station. How do you feel about a ride on my Harley?"

For a moment, her eyes widened, a vulnerable and touched look came over her, but it disappeared too quick, as though she were trying to hide it. Grinning, she rose from the water and stood there a moment with suds rolling down her body. I cursed softly in Icelandic and took a step closer. Just before the towel I held could slip from my hands, she grabbed it from me. Very slowly, she wrapped it around her body and tucked the end between her breasts.

"I'd love to go for a ride with you," she said, making it sound deliciously dirty.

Groaning, I grabbed hold of her hips and pulled her to me. We melted together for an intense moment. Long before I was ready, I forced myself to draw back, knowing if I did not, I would not make it to the police station yet again. The look of desire and almost pain in her eyes made me feel a little less desperate for not wanting to let her go.

"Damn *lögreglu*. I really did not want to leave this room today," I said as my fingers ran along the edge of her towel.

She laughed and turned away. "Best get it over with. Besides, I'd like to see this book you have. Maybe we can stop by your office," she said as she began to towel off.

Now there was an idea. I had been itching to reread that book ever since I saw her mark. It bugged me that I could not remember much about the legend, but then it was hundreds of years old and was scarcely told anymore. The book had sat on my shelf in my office for the better part of a decade. Despite my beliefs that Raul was a raging idiot, I could not pretend her having that mark was coincidence. He might not have chosen her because of it, but someone more calculating might have pushed him in her direction. Just before she got her shorts to her hips, my hand brushed across her birthmark.

"Sure thing," I whispered in a thoughtful voice.

She rose up on her toes, full lips reaching for me. I bent and kissed her, long and sweet. So I didn't lose control and tackle her, I kept my fingers tucked into the belt loops of my shorts. The clean scent of soap and shampoo mingled with her spicy scent in a heady concoction that almost made me lose control. Breath coming in short gasps, I spun away, grabbed my T-shirt, and pulled it on. Sonya made an appreciative sound as I walked away.

How was it I had become so good at controlling all of my emotions except for those involving her? We would be lucky if we made the ride to town in one shot without having to pull over.

The second I pulled up to the single-story, red brick building, Sonya began to breathe harder. Thanks to my *varúlfur* hearing I could hear it despite my helmet. In a heartbeat, she was off the bike. She all but tore her helmet off. Her eyes darted from the police cruisers parked out front, to the hint of razor wire around the corner, and back to the road we had pulled off of. I killed the ignition and got off the bike. She jumped when I laid my hand on her arm.

"Are you all right?" I asked.

She shook her head and swallowed hard before answering. "I don't like police stations."

I moved my hand to rest on top of hers, which gripped her helmet so tight it flexed beneath her fingers.

"Because of your dad?" I asked.

A few measured breaths later she answered. "Yeah. I was just a kid when he was arrested for murder. Too many prison visits when I was little."

Gently, I peeled her hand from her helmet, draped it over one of the bike's mirrors, and wove my fingers through hers. She gripped my hand as if it were a lifeline.

"I am sorry, I cannot imagine how hard that had to be," I said. Not to mention the fact that she had only recently found out her dad had not killed a man in a drug deal gone bad, but had killed him to save her from being kidnapped.

She shrugged. "It was what it was. I wish I had trusted that he was the man I had always thought he was, and not the one the police made him out to be."

I glanced around us, eyes going from the parking lot to the road, then back to her. No one was around. I did not want to leave her here alone, but I could not expect her to go inside with me either.

"I'll be fine here. If anyone at all pulls into the parking lot I'll come inside," she said.

"If you even smell someone strange—"

She stopped my words with a quick kiss. "I'll come right in."

I drew in a long breath, considering my words carefully. "I know you can handle yourself. It is not that. Even with Lars and the others out looking for who did this, I still worry. The truck bombing makes me worry about how far they are willing to go."

"Not as far as I'm willing to go to stay by your side," she said.

The level of conviction in her words thrilled me for more than one reason and made me smile. Nodding, I rose from the bike and stared at her a moment before leaving. Those brown eyes, so full of confidence, stared at me from behind a half curtain of her ebony hair. If it came to a fight she would be in trouble. A few weeks of training to fight was not enough for someone who had no natural inclination or desire to do so. I hated the way my chest tightened at the thought of anything happening to her. A bad feeling tried to tug at me, but I wrote it off as an overprotective instinct resulting from having mated with her so recently. I would only be gone a few minutes.

CHAPTER TWENTY-FIVE

SONYA

The quick, aggressive stride he took to the police station almost made me feel sorry for the officer who would have to take his statement. Part of me wanted to follow him while another cringed at the thought of walking through those doors. Memories of seeing my dad in a sterile visiting room with tables and attached stools that were bolted to the concrete floor quickly made me look away. Even if I were being chased I wasn't sure I could go in there. It wasn't the same as a prison, I knew, but it was associated closely enough to bring panic to the surface.

More to look away from the station than out of any real suspicion, I checked the parking lot and the street behind me. Nothing, not even traffic. It hit me that someone might not approach by car, but by foot. Birds sang from within the trees that lined the sidewalk and framed a green space that went around the side of the building. I gravitated toward it to get away from some of the city smells. Sunlight found its way through the yellow and green leaves of the many trees to dapple the sidewalk. As soon as I could, I stepped from the concrete onto the soft cushion of shortly trimmed green grass. The energy of living things worked like an instant balm on my nerves. While the feeling was still a little weird, I would take what I could get right now.

The sidewalk kept going, turning into a wider pathway that cut between the greenspace on the side of the police station and a grouping of buildings. From one of those buildings wafted the aroma of baking dough, cheese, and spices. It didn't quite drown out the asphalt and exhaust scents, but it helped. The cut grass beneath my feet and swaying leaves overhead helped far more. I leaned against the trunk of a small maple to wait. More to keep Ty's scent close than out of any need to block out the breeze, I pulled his brown flannel close, burying my nose in the collar.

Minutes ticked by and though a bit of traffic moved along the road, no one pulled in to either the police station or the brick buildings next door. Something unsettling stirred deep in my stomach, awakening both urgency and what I could only associate with a motherly type of instinct. One of my own was close, someone newly bitten. The certainty with which I knew that bugged me. I raised my nose into the breeze and breathed deep. A very slight musk mingled with an aloe-scented soap drifted to me. Along with it came a sniffling sound from around the corner. On a picnic table beneath two pine trees hunched a figure in a gray hoodie. From this distance I couldn't make out any more. But I knew all I needed to know. They were a new *varúlfur* and they might need help. I had to do what I could, however little it might be.

Maybe Candice had run away from Hemlock Hollow. I thought she would have called me, but I couldn't be sure. If it was Candice, I had to talk to her. The full moon was tomorrow and my instincts told me she shouldn't face it alone. Hell, even if it wasn't her, I had to talk to this person. I glanced back at the police station. This constituted as smelling someone strange, but not someone Ty had been worried about. The instinct deep inside pulled harder at me until I finally took a step in the person's direction. With a great amount of effort, I stilled my feet and concentrated on the reason for the instinct. Letting instincts of any kind control me weren't an option anymore.

Sympathy weighed heavy in me, along with a desire to make sure no one went through the *verða* alone, or with someone who had forced it on them. All in all, the reasons behind the instinct didn't seem like anything bad, certainly not anything to fight against. As a precaution, I checked the air once more. When I didn't smell anyone else besides the person on the bench, I started in their direction. They didn't look up until I was almost next to them.

The wide, bloodshot eyes of a young man who couldn't have been more than twenty shot up to me. Shine that was part tears and part predator in transition made his green eyes almost translucent looking. Not Candice, then, but still someone who needed me.

Trying to look friendly, I smiled. "You look like you could use someone to talk to."

His eyes traveled across my body, halting at my cleavage. I didn't take it personally. The guy was barely out of his teens, and he had to deal with raging *varúlfur* emotions on top of that.

"Do I?" he asked, a note of humor in a voice that was thick from crying.

"Mind if I sit?" I asked.

He shrugged. "Be my guest."

Giving him as much space as possible, I sat down on the far end of the wooden bench. I decided to go with the direct approach. "You've been bitten."

He sat up straight and pushed his hoodie back. Spiky black hair tipped in bright red held my gaze for a moment until I noticed the jagged pink scar on his neck. Whoever had bit him had been almost cruel, like it was an act of anger and not a decision to make a new *varúlfur*.

"How did you know?" he asked as he leaned away from me a bit.

Best to take it slow considering his darting eyes and shaking limbs. "Because it happened to me too."

Brows pulling tightly together, his eyes filled with moisture. "You seem nice. I didn't want to do this."

He shook his head, then buried it in his hands. Horrible deep sobs tore from him, turning into thick, messy crying. Scooting closer, I put an arm around his shoulders.

"It isn't as bad as you might think. There are people who will help you through the transition. Everything will be okay," I told him.

The sobs became louder, as if my words had made him feel worse. Something settled over my mouth, a cloth of some kind. For a second I smelled an odd mixture of sweet and fruity, then the fruity part of that scent began to burn. The young man beside me scurried to his feet and moved away. If it wasn't him, then who held a cloth to my mouth? I tried to pull away and found myself against something solid, a hand pressing the cloth tighter over my mouth and nose. Attached to that hand was the muscled arm of a man spattered with dark hairs. The harder I fought, the more I breathed in the toxic, burning scents of the wet cloth. My muscles responded slowly to my commands to fight, my strength ebbing away with each breath. My claws extended, but a second after they sank into the arm of the person holding me, my vision went black.

CHAPTER TWENTY-SIX

SONYA

W rists bound behind me and legs trussed up to them like I was going to be cooked over a fire, I woke in the back of an SUV. Nothing covered my mouth but I held my tongue anyway. It wasn't easy with all the curse words streaming through my head. Tucked into that small spot behind the seats intended for cargo, I couldn't see much. Forward motion and road noise told me we were on the move, seriously breaking the speed limit from the sound of the engine. The darkly tinted windows didn't allow me to see out at this angle. The scents of pine and earth in the carpet didn't tell me anything either, but the sound of two men breathing and another talking did. I recognized the voice but couldn't put a name to it.

"—not a good idea. If she's this *leitar* you think she is, won't she kill us all when she wakes up?" asked one tremoring voice.

"No, you idiot. The *leitar* is the one who finds those that have been bitten and are about to lose their shit. They try to help them, save them from themselves. The reaper is the fighter, the killer. Besides, I don't even think she's shifted yet. We've got nothing to fear from this one," said another voice, a familiar one.

"Aren't you worried about Ayra after her power awakens?"

A loud smack—like flesh against the back of someone's head— sounded. "No. She's too afraid of her brother to give us any shit."

None of them smelled like Raul, but that didn't mean they weren't from his pack. I knew I would know him by smell, and that was a bit disturbing, yes, but I was getting used to disturbing. The whole hog-tying thing told me they probably weren't from his pack. Even Raul wasn't stupid enough to stoop to a tactic he knew would piss me off beyond repair. Which meant they were from the Arnoddr pack, who really didn't want me spoiling the whole arranged marriage thing. I wasn't sure if they much cared whether or not I made it in one piece. *Shit.*

Almost on instinct, I started to struggle against my bonds. Several sharp objects bit into the skin of my wrists and hands, sending heat shooting into me as if I had been stung by a hornet from the Jurassic era hopped up on steroids. A gasp escaped me. The talking from the front seat stopped. Holding my breath to try and stay quiet, I struggled harder. Pain exploded into me from dozens of little stings, making me see spots of bright light. It almost felt like razor wire was woven into the damn ropes.

"Fuck, Dustin, I told you to keep an eye on her. The chloroform already wore off. Put more wolfsbane on the rag this time," came that second voice I had heard when I woke.

Recognition struck. It was James, the ring leader of the group that had cornered Ty and me on the side road coming to Missoula. Chloroform, wolfsbane... My mind spun at what that meant. A bearded face appeared over the backseat, along with a huge hand holding a rag that reeked of that fruity sweet concoction that had knocked me out before. I knew him too. He was the man Ty had caught and released when his truck was blown up.

"No, don't." It was a demand instead of a plea, fueled by the rage against my helplessness.

"Sorry, *Leitar*, but if I don't knock you out, I can't guarantee James will get you there in one piece," the man whispered.

I recognized his voice as one of the men from the roadside attack too.

"Just fucking do it, Dustin. You don't need to be nice about it," James said.

"If she's the *leitar*, James, we need to show some respect," Dustin snapped.

A short bark of a laugh sounded. "Who cares? Our pack will soon have the *uppskera*," the third man said.

"Yeah, thanks to her," Dustin grumbled as he pressed the rag to my mouth.

I struggled and fought but it only made me breathe harder, pulling the noxious, burning smells into my nose and mouth all the faster. It hurt. Shit, it hurt. Like breathing in broken glass. Seconds later I blacked out to the sound of the three men arguing about whether or not it mattered that I was bitten or born in. I made a mental note not to hurt Dustin as bad as the others when I got loose. Whether or not I would remember that through the haze of the drugs remained to be seen.

An erratic dripping woke me. Gone were the stuffy smells of the SUV and the three men who had been in it. The pungent smell of old wood and moldy hay worked its way into my abused nostrils. A hard surface beneath my ass and back told me I sat upright. The warm feel of sunlight on my mostly bare legs, which stretched out before me, suggested it was around early evening. Just like the moon, I was beginning to be able to judge the position of the sun by the feel of its light alone. The ability felt like part instinct and part something mystical. That meant hours had passed. My hands lay in my lap, ropes still wrapped tight around them. The position—comfortable in comparison to how I'd been trussed up in the back of the SUV—suggested Dustin had been the one to leave me here.

The man would definitely retain his balls for that. I wouldn't be so kind with the others. Not hearing or smelling anything else living save for a few mice, I slowly opened my eyes. Light poured through the gaps in the vertical boards that made up the walls of my prison, pooling on the old hay that covered most of the dirt floor. The structure was somewhere around twenty by thirty feet with a few structural posts throughout reaching up to beams in the roof. My bound hands were attached to one of those posts by a long rope.

Getting free would be a cinch. Had Dustin wanted me to? Another look at the ropes dashed that thought away. Thorns wove through the fibers, several of which dug into my flesh. It hurt bad, and seeing it made it worse. That horrible fruity smell wafted up from the rope, making me suspect it had been soaked in something similar to what they had drugged me with. Wolfsbane, they had called it. So that myth was at least partially true. I twisted my wrists slightly to test it out. Not only did a fiery pain shoot through me in a ring around both wrists, but my strength felt horribly diminished. Even as sturdy as they were, these ropes should have snapped with a simple twist and pull. Whatever they had been soaked in had to be sapping my *varúlfur* strength.

I tried to slow my thundering heart and think. If they wanted me dead, I would be. They must want to hold me here until after Raul's trial. My lack of attendance there might be able to sway the Council into forcing Raul into marrying the woman from this pack. It sort of made sense, I guessed. But what if it had nothing to do with Raul? It could have to do with them thinking I was this *leitar*. The fact that they may not be planning on killing me didn't make me feel any less murderous toward them. Raul's trial was still six days away. If they kept me in here for five days it wouldn't end well for any of them, including Dustin.

The rumble of Harley engines reverberated up through the floorboards beneath my feet. They grew louder, then shut off. From a distance came the sound of heavy weeping broken by an occasional plea. Soon the words became clear as the sound drew closer. Along with it I heard the shuffle and drag that indicated someone was being forced in this direction. Three other sets of footsteps accompanied it. Through the gaps in the barn wall I could smell James, Dustin, and the third man who had been with them.

"Please don't do this. I don't want this, I've never wanted it," sobbed a woman.

While the voice had been distorted from crying, I was sure it wasn't Candice. Who could it be? What the hell were those bastards up to? Why did they think I was this *leitar* thing? Wait, *leitar*... Maybe it was Icelandic for something. They had said the *leitar* was the one who found those who had been bitten and tried to help them. Like I had found Candice and the guy they had used to lure me out. Find...no, seek. *Leitar* had to mean seeker. The birthmark on my hip... Chills raced across my skin as if in hot pursuit of one another.

Were these guys the ones biting people? If so, why? The mark, could it be why Raul had bitten me? I leaped to my feet, putting my back against the post I was bound to. The muscles in my legs protested, proving I hadn't been unbound and out of the back of that SUV for long. The post was rough enough that it might wear at the cotton ropes. Cursing myself for not thinking of it sooner, I turned and began to rub the ropes binding my wrists against the wood.

"Shut up, *ylva*. This is your duty. The moon is nearly full, the *leitar* is here, it's time," a man's voice that I recognized from the SUV said.

"Yeah, and since the moon ain't up just yet, that means your power ain't fully awakened, so you can't stop us," said another voice, dropping off into cruel laughter after the last word.

One of the ropes around my wrist popped and broke. Three more to go. I sawed faster. The footsteps drew closer, the crying louder and more desperate, pleas melting away into incoherent sobs. That horrible, defeated sound made me want to hurt the men even more. Another of the ropes broke, freeing my left wrist. The thorns and blood kept the damn thing glued to me, but I tore free easily enough. A few twists of the rope and my right wrist was free as well. Angry red gouges peppered both wrists, but the moment the thorns left my skin the pain began to fade.

The footsteps paused right outside the barn. I grabbed the rope and wrapped it around my wrists. Sunlight poured in as a huge door—more the size of one wall really—slid open on rails of some kind. Eyes adjusting, I had to blink several times before I could make out the figures silhouetted by light. Dustin pushed the huge sliding door the rest of the way open while James and the third man, a broad blond, dragged a young girl into the barn. The men all wore black leather jackets with AVW on the top rocker. At odds or not, they belonged to the same umbrella pack that Raul did, and that worried me.

Thin to the point of being almost waif-like, the woman couldn't have been a hundred and ten pounds. Long, almost white-blond hair obscured her face, hanging all the way down past her B-cup chest to her tiny waist. In an admirable show of defiance, she yanked away from James, flung her hair back, and bit the third man's arm. From the Norse tattoo on the back of her neck to her mature blue eyes, she looked fierce, and far older than I had first thought. Small as she was, she was no girl. This was a woman of at least twenty years old. And the long fangs embedded in the man's arm told me she was a *varúlfur* as surely as the strong pull of her power.

Cursing in Icelandic, James backhanded her so hard it sounded like a thunderclap. Head snapping to the side, the woman went flying to the ground, tearing a good-sized chunk out of the blond man as she went. Blood flavored the air. Part of me was proud that the girl didn't make a sound, while the man screamed bloody murder. Growling, he moved toward her, leg rearing back as if to kick her.

"Leave her alone, you son of a bitch!" I yelled.

It took every ounce of control I had not to run to her side. His leg halted, relaxed, and returned to the floor. If he had kicked her I wouldn't have been able to hold myself back. As it was, my fangs and claws had extended. Knowing I might need them, I didn't try to retract them.

"The Reinhard's little *leitar* is awake. Good, she should see this," James said.

Dustin moved to help the young girl to her feet, putting himself between her and the man who had been about to kick her. For that he moved up on my list of people not to kill.

"I've never seen anyone burn through chloroform and wolfsbane so fast. It's amazing," Dustin said in an almost reverent tone as he stared at me.

The third man kicked Dustin in the back hard enough to make him stumble as he helped the young woman to her feet.

"She's to be a Reinhard, you idiot. Don't sound so smitten," the man said.

Fangs extending, Dustin growled at him. "You know I don't swing that way, Calder. She's the *leitar*, she belongs to all packs and none, just like Ayra here will. They are above even the Alpha Council. You would be wise to remember that, because she'll soon be far more powerful than you. You shouldn't treat her the way you do," he snapped.

Hands curling into fists, Calder took a step toward Dustin. "Don't tell me how to treat my own sister, mutt."

"Someone should, *ylva*," Dustin said, sneering at Calder upon the last word.

I recognized the word. It was Old Norse for female wolf. Probably his way of calling Calder a bitch, which I was torn between wanting to applaud and taking offense to. Detestable as he was, I cringed to think the man treated his own sister so badly. Now I really wanted to hurt him.

Something Dustin said struck a chord and distracted me. Ty had an old book he wanted to check after he saw my birthmark. Oh Gods, Ty. He had to be half out of his mind right now. This was all my fault. I took a deep breath. One problem at a time.

Calder growled, baring his fangs as he stepped toward Dustin. "You're calling *me* a *ylva*? In your fucking dreams, queer!"

Though he stormed toward Dustin, it was Ayra who cringed as though she expected a beating. Abusing his own sister and now insulting the sexual orientation of one of his own pack members, I'd had it with this guy.

"You want to hit someone? Hit me, you son of a bitch," I snarled.

Light reflected off his eyes as his head whipped my way. His lips pulled up into a grin that showed fangs. "You want some of me, *Leitar*? That's fine, we don't need you in one piece. Until your first full moon, you won't be at full power, and I'm guessing you haven't even shifted yet. Which means you're that much weaker. We've got a few more minutes before it rises."

Steps light, he strode up until he towered over me, broad chest heaving with pants that hinted at more arousal than anger. Then again, by the dark look in his eyes, I had to guess the two went hand in hand with him.

He brought his face close to mine, breathing in deep as if savoring my scent. "I'd love to ruin what the legendary *verndari* of the Draupnir pack has been dipping into," he said, low and husky.

Oh, this guy had so much pain coming. A low growl began to rumble in my chest as I bared my fangs at him. It was all I could do to keep my hands low and twined within the ropes that were supposed to be restraining me. The moment was not now. It was close, but it wasn't now. My control almost slipped when Calder took a lock of my hair and held it up to his nose.

"You even smell like power. I can't wait to see the look on Tyler's face when he learns that I split his little wolf in two," he said.

I pulled back from him, not out of fear mostly, but because I was too close to losing my temper. This was testing me in ways I had never been tested before, not even by the *verða*. At the very least I worried that I would give away my element of surprise too early. Not only did these assholes not know I was loose, they thought I hadn't shifted yet. The problem was, I hadn't figured out fighting as a human, let alone as a wolf.

While moving as one was instinctual, fighting, probably not so much. But I had to try it. Or maybe something in between...

"Calder, no. Even you wouldn't stoop to such a level," Ayra spoke in a voice that held far more confidence than I expected from her.

She thrust her head up, her long white-blond hair spilling back over her shoulders like fine silk. The defiance on her face was mixed with surprise, almost as if her own words and boldness shocked her. Calder's dark gaze shot to her.

"To teach that packless son of a bitch a lesson, yes I would," he said.

Threatening me I could take, insulting Ty, I couldn't.

"Clearly you haven't seen the size of Ty's cock, because trust me, yours is bound to be smaller and totally incapable of splitting me in two," I snapped.

Even before his face burned red with fury I knew it was the exact wrong thing to say. From what he had said, though, I needed to distract him until the moon rose. I didn't know if he was crazy or telling the truth about me becoming powerful. That was a risk I was going to have to take. The other option would be to let him hurt his sister again, and I wasn't about to do that.

He leaned closer, his bodybuilder bulk blocking out all light. I knew I couldn't take this guy. Being stronger and faster than I had ever been as a human had given me a little more confidence than was healthy for me at the moment. This guy at least doubled my weight, and from the looks of how his shirt fit, it was all muscle. The element of surprise alone might not be enough. I suddenly felt very underdressed and vulnerable in only my cutoff shorts, tank top, and Ty's flannel. The hard-on bulging out the crotch of Calder's jeans didn't help either.

"I'll split you in two no matter what I have to use," he snarled.

As he reached for me, I sidestepped and moved around the post I was pretending to still be tethered to. It was too soon. I needed James away from the door before I fought and tried to make a break for it.

"Is this really why you brought me here, James? To threaten me and try to rape me?" I called out to him, letting my anger fill my voice so it hid my fear.

Finally, he came closer. "No, it isn't. Back off, Cal," he said.

A muscle in Calder's right cheek twitched. "I will take what I have earned."

Long fangs bared, James leaned into him. "Becoming monsters wasn't part of the plan, Cal. We're doing this to take our rightful place in the world, in the light."

Chest puffing out, Calder's hands closed into fists. "You don't even know the whole plan."

I could hardly believe my luck. They were going to do half my work for me. They growled and began circling each other. Though Calder bared his fangs right back at James, he did so through a huge grin. I had a bad feeling he was going to win, and then I would have to fight him. And if I lost... A shake of my head dislodged the thought. Couldn't let my mind go there. That way led to fear, which would dissolve my control. Hopefully James could put up a good enough fight to at least wear Calder down so I stood a chance. They launched at each other and my attention shifted to Dustin, but the man only watched them with wide eyes.

"Dustin, please, get me out of here," Ayra said, her small voice holding an authority that hinted at a hidden power.

Eyes filled with indecision, Dustin looked from the small blond woman to the fighting pair, and back again. I had a feeling if she had made it a command and not a plea, he might have complied.

Overly long dark hair brushed his brows as he shook his head. "I'm sorry, Ayra, but you know my standing in the pack. I can't disobey Calder."

The only reason I could hear their soft voices over the growls and curses of the two men fighting was because they stood close to me. Too close. They were now in the way of the door as much as James and Calder. Oblivious to the three of us, the two men punched, kicked, cursed, and growled at each other, using not only their fists but their fangs and claws as well. Blood spilled from more than one wound on both, its coppery scent filling the air.

"Calder only said to bring me here. You've done that, now take me home," Ayra said with a bit more force.

Good girl.

Like a rat in a cage, Dustin's eyes traveled between them all again. "I'm not sure it's enough, just having brought you to her."

"But I don't want this, Dustin. Please, you were my friend. Don't do this," Ayra begged.

The desperation in her voice, the catch at the end as her words turned into a sob, tore at me. What possible reason could they have for bringing her to me, even if I was this seeker they talked about? My eyes flicked back to James and Calder. Sweat and blood poured from James's brow. He seemed to be dodging and blocking a little slower than the last time I had glanced their way. On the other hand, Calder bounced on the balls of his feet, dodged and wove with a seemingly endless flow of energy.

"Calder is going to win. She doesn't need to see what happens after that. Get her out of here," I said.

Dustin's wide eyes landed on me. A glimmer of sympathy in them suggested I might have an ally. Too bad he was too submissive to do any good in a fight.

"Do it, now," I commanded.

Just as I had suspected, he began to move toward the door as if unable to go against a command. But it was too late. A cry of pain followed by the grunt of air expelling from lungs came from the direction of the fight. James writhed slowly on the ground. The amount of blood on his shirt, arms, and dripping down his forehead ensured he wouldn't be getting up any time soon. Breathing hard and grinning like a maniac, Calder turned toward me.

"You're mine now, *ylva*," he said as he approached.

Holding my ground and keeping my hands before me as if I were still bound, I let him come. An easy calm settled over me while I watched him walk, assessing his energy level and injuries as he came. Dark blood flowed from a long gash on the inside of his right arm. He favored his right leg a bit. Little things, considering how much stronger he was than me, but they'd have to do. The smug look on the bastard's face made it clear he didn't expect me to put up a fight. Shit, the man's biceps alone were intimidating. Eyes wide, I did my best to look scared. It wasn't hard. He ate it up, grinning all the wider, baring his fangs as he scented the air.

"You have his stench on you. But I'll fix that," he said as he reached for me.

I cowered and flinched. As he took that last step I pretended to step back, using the motion to draw my leg back for a kick that I drove into his groin as hard as I could. Beneath my foot I felt soft bits slam into his pelvic bone. Air left him in a groan that sounded as if it wanted to be a scream but lacked the ability. He hunched over and covered his crotch with his hands, but didn't go down. Without hesitation, I turned, cocked my leg, and threw a potentially deadly hook kick that whipped my heel into the side of his face. His head snapped to the side so fast I expected to hear his neck break—and didn't, dammit. He went down hard. Guilt tried to rear its head at the death wish, but I forced it away, knowing I may still have to do worse.

I stood over him in a fighting stance, waiting for him to move. After a moment of stillness, I dashed for the door. Dustin stepped in my way. As he did a power tugged at something deep inside me, stirring it to life, awakening it. But it wasn't my wolf. This was something impossibly stronger, deeper. I could feel the moon like the pressure building before a storm, but instead of pushing, it pulled at that thing inside me. Trying to ignore the sensation, I shook my head.

"Don't do this, Dustin," I warned.

He swallowed hard and straightened. "I have to at least try to stop you or Calder will kill me."

Having seen Calder's chest moving, I couldn't waste time. The man would get up eventually. Dustin's fists shook as he held them up. Faster than even a snake could hope to move thanks to my wicked *varúlfur* skills, I planted a palm heel strike solidly into Dustin's left cheek. He went down almost as hard as Calder had. Leaving him groaning on the ground, I ran for the door again. James stood in my way, silhouetted by the pink light of early evening. In his arms he clutched Ayra.

"Don't hurt her," I demanded.

He shrugged. "Fine, here."

With a mighty shove, he heaved her at me, his *varúlfur* strength lifting her easily off the ground. It was either catch her or let her fly across the barn and slam into a wall. I caught her. The moment we touched, that energy the moon had been pulling at erupted from me in a golden glow and poured into her. Warmth spread over my skin, not like the heat of fighting the change, but more like the buzz from far too much whiskey. The mark on my hip burned slightly. Though it felt kind of good to me, it must have hurt her because she screamed like a banshee. Not wanting to hurt her any more, I let go of her and stepped back. Her screams turned into sobs as she slumped to the ground and clutched her head in her hands.

"I'm so sorry. Did I hurt you?" I asked, taking a step closer to her.

When she didn't answer or even lift her head I took another step and started to reach out a hand. "Are you all right?"

Head bowed as it was, she couldn't have possibly seen me, but she flinched nonetheless. At first I thought it was a *varúlfur* thing, scent, sounds, or something. Then I felt the push and pull of her energy as if somehow we were tied together in a way that allowed me to feel her without needing to see or smell her. In an instant, I knew she wasn't hurt. The opposite, really. She felt like a fountain of that golden energy that had burst from me. Not even Ty felt this powerful. Bumps rose along my skin and I took a step back.

Hands covering her face, she shook her head. "No, I'll never be okay again," she said.

Something red against her pale skin on her lower back caught my eye. At first I thought it was a bruise from her brother's rough handling, then I realized it was far different. The bumps that had risen on my skin spread until it felt as though they covered my entire body. Her mark was a port wine stain, a birthmark exactly like mine, the rough shape of a crude *S*, as if someone had stamped it on her skin. I reached a hand toward it and it started to glow the same gold color of the energy that I had seen pass from me into her. The mark on my hip began to heat up again.

"What the...?" I stumbled backward. "Look, I don't know what's going on, Ayra, but we need to get out of here while these guys are still down."

But deep down, I did know. Both of our powers had just awakened. The feeling was undeniable. In my gut, my heart, I knew I was this seeker they spoke of. I held my hand out to her, far enough away not to be intrusive, but close enough that I knew she'd feel it. The sobbing stopped and her hands moved slowly away from her face. She looked up, hair falling away from a pale face from which topaz blue eyes peered.

"You really don't know, do you?" she asked.

I shook my head. "I didn't, and I didn't mean for it to happen. Please, let's get you somewhere safe."

Her head turned as she looked at each of the men, then back to me.

"Might as well. There is no going back now," she said in a sad tone that told me she didn't think that was a good thing, not at all.

Looking at the men lying on the barn floor, I couldn't blame her. Family wasn't exactly my strong point either.

Slowly, she took my hand. An almost electric charge that wasn't entirely unpleasant passed through us. It felt more like residual energy than anything else this time, like a powerful static from clean laundry.

James blocked our way.

"What just happened? What did I do to her?" I demanded. Part of me needed to hear it said out loud.

The smirk that turned up the corners of his lips made me want to tear him a new one. "She has become what she was always meant to be, thanks to you."

"What the fuck does that mean?"

"For every *leitar* there is an *uppskera*. It takes one to bring the power of the other forth during the full moon," he said.

I knew what *leitar* meant, well, the word at least. But the other word... Swallowing hard, I glanced at Ayra before I asked. "What does *uppskera* mean?"

His grin melted away. "Reaper."

My mind chewed slowly over that but couldn't make any sense of it. Right now, especially in present company, I didn't care to think on it anymore.

"You got what you wanted. Get out of our way," I said.

One hand pressed against his left side, James widened his stance. "You can go. She stays with us."

"That's not happening," I said as I moved between him and Ayra.

Reaper or not—whatever that meant—this young woman was in no condition to fight, and I wasn't about to leave her with these men. Gravel crunching beneath tires sounded from outside—two motorcycles from the whine of the engines. Footsteps pounded toward the barn a second later. Whether it was backup for these guys, or Raul, both were trouble that I couldn't afford right now.

A door slid open to our left. Two men rushed in from the dark. "Get Ayra before she realizes what she can do," James commanded.

I tried to pull Ayra to my other side to shield her, but she tore her hand free. "Can you fight?" I asked her.

From the corner of my eye I saw her smile, but it was not a pleasant expression. "Unfortunately for them, yes," she said.

I couldn't wait to see if she was right. This had to end quickly. Her image wavered like a heat mirage, then became a white wolf. With a thought, I grew my fingernails and toenails into claws, and made my fangs extend. The two men rushed Ayra and I lunged at James with a sidekick that was meant to look like I put all my power into it. He deflected it with one hand and stabbed the other at me, claws extended. Pretending to be off balance from the kick, I let myself fall in the direction my movement was going. Hopping on the leg I had just kicked with, I whipped my left leg toward his abdomen. It collided with his thrusting hand and I felt a claw dig into my knee, but the roundhouse kick followed through and struck him solidly in his bloody gut. At least two of the claws on my toes dug into flesh. With my *varúlfur* strength behind it, the kick would have sent anyone else flying, but it only doubled James over.

He caught the second one and twisted my foot swift and hard. To avoid my leg getting broken, I went with the movement, spinning in midair and sprawling to the ground. Claws dug deep into my abdomen when I landed. Oddly, it didn't hurt. I didn't have time to worry about that right now, though. From a crouched position I kicked out at his left knee and connected hard, claws raking straight through his jeans and deep into his flesh. He cursed at me in both English and Icelandic, and paused long enough that I was able to launch to my feet.

He stared at me with wide, dumbstruck eyes. "What the hell? You can extend your claws?"

It was the last moment I was going to get. A kick beneath the chin sent him flying backward. He landed hard and writhed, but didn't get back up. The almost overwhelming urge to follow him to the ground and take his throat in my teeth raged through me. The desire nearly made me shift, but then I thought about the reason for the instinct, and the need disappeared. I had to stay in human form. With my claws and fangs, I had more of an advantage in this form than I would as a wolf.

Something warm flowed down my shin and my chest, distracting me. Blood, dark in the fading evening light, ran from a gash in my knee that showed enough bone to make me queasy. Heat drew my attention to my right side. Below my ribs four long gashes had torn open my tank top and were leaking blood in steady streams that darkened the waistband of my shorts. Those weren't the worst part. Four wicked-looking holes sat below my ribcage. Damn. The world swayed. Ignoring it, I shifted my stance, hands held at the ready, and checked to make sure no one else stood in our way. The urge to take James's throat in my fangs and make him submit completely didn't leave, but I didn't give in either.

Steps pounded on hard ground, coming at a pace I wouldn't be able to outrun even if I were willing to leave Ayra behind, which I wasn't. Ayra stood over the still forms of two men, her naked chest heaving. Blood dripped from her hands and ran down from her lips to drip off her chin. I couldn't think about what that meant. More were coming. Slowing my breathing, I turned to the door and prepared to fight again. The person that ran through it wasn't at all who I expected.

"Damn, Sonya. And here I thought you needed rescuing," Ty said in a voice filled with relief.

My arms sank down and the tension drained from me in a rush that left me feeling light-headed. His head turned as he swept the area, taking in the downed men. It looked more impressive than it was since I hadn't exactly taken them out all on my own. They had helped with their little pissing match, and Ayra had clearly beat two all on her own, but I was too tired to voice that right now. In fact, now that the threat was over, the room began to sway, a lot.

"Ty..."

The world fell out from under me, leaving only darkness.

CHAPTER TWENTY-SEVEN

TY

I registered the other people in the dingy barn, but they did not matter. Not the prone but breathing body I leaped over, not the groaning man in the corner, not even the dainty blond woman rising to her feet. Only Sonya, collapsed and bleeding out on the musty hay-covered floor mattered. There was so much blood, dark and spreading its coppery scent throughout the barn. It surrounded her in a growing pool that I had no choice but to step in to get to her. Her eyes were closed and they did not even flutter when I knelt and pulled her carefully into my lap. The slow rhythm with which her chest rose and fell was only slightly encouraging.

Up close the wounds in her abdomen looked so much worse. They had the scent of impending death on them. I did not know if new *varúlfur* could survive wounds like that. Helheimr, I didn't know if seasoned ones could. Soft footsteps padded on the brittle hay toward us, but I couldn't look away from Sonya.

"We cannot let her die," said a level, feminine voice in what sounded more like a command than a statement.

"I do not know what to do," I whispered.

Thunder sounded off in the distance. Sandaled feminine feet came into view. "I do," said the female voice. I looked up at her, more because of her words than any sense of fear of a threat.

Long, white-blond hair plaited into a loose, frazzled French braid hung over a dainty shoulder strapped with sinewy muscle, down across her meager breasts, and reached all the way to a thin waist. An almost elfish-looking face with high cheekbones gave her a slightly severe yet lovely appearance. Sapphire-blue eyes, filled with a sense of purpose and confidence that was slowly eclipsing the fear in them, looked past me. She regarded Sonya in a calculating manner that I didn't like. Despite her delicate frame, the woman's expression and stance made her look like a force to be reckoned with. More than that, it made her look like Frigg, the wife of Odin. She was not, of course.

I instantly knew her for what and who she was: Ayra Valdísdóttir, now one of the most powerful *varúlfur* to walk the earth, the *uppskera*, or the reaper. The power rolling off her was staggering. Vidar had told me all about the legend during a phone conversation on my drive here. He had known exactly what was going on without me even having to mention Sonya's mark, making me feel like a complete idiot for not calling him sooner. But he had put me at ease by telling me the monastery didn't allow him to have a phone, so I wouldn't have been able to reach him anyways. That, and he said people were listening and watching every communication and interaction he had. When I finally did reach him, he'd been in an airport on his way here. Since it was too late to warn me, he didn't see the harm in telling me over the phone.

I clutched Sonya closer and bared my fangs. "You will not take her from me. Odin help me, I will kill you or die trying before I let you finish her off," I all but growled.

From what Vidar had said, the *uppskera* was powerful beyond their appearance. I knew I'd likely die if I tried to fight her. But I would do it anyway. My arms convulsed around Sonya. A brief flash of sadness lit Ayra's eyes and she shook her head and looked to the side.

"Already they fear me," she said through a sigh. When she looked back at me any hint of sadness was wiped away from her face. "That's not what I meant, Tyler. Bring her," she commanded and promptly turned to leave.

All signs of the hesitation she had shown while approaching were gone. She stood tall—rigidly so, almost—and walked with confidence, as if she had undergone a change in that short trip across the barn. But then, I suppose she probably had. According to Vidar, the *uppskera* was fully awakened by the touch of the *leitar*. Meaning, Ayra had likely just come into her full power. James had probably brought Sonya here for that reason. He had found out about her. Her bloodlines, the Cherokee pack trying to kidnap her, the signs were there for anyone who knew to look.

James. Shit!

I looked around as I rose with Sonya in my arms. He had been lying over...somewhere. But he was gone. So was the other man who had been groaning in the corner. Finding and killing them would have to wait. Saving Sonya came first.

"What can we do for her?" I asked Ayra as I followed her small frame out of the barn.

Darkness waited for us. I had not been in there that long, had I? Then I smelled the moisture in the air and looked up at the pregnant, charcoal clouds. In the distance, flashes of light lit them in dancing spots from high above. Thunder rolled near the horizon. I knew before Ayra said it.

"The lightning can heal her. We need to get her to the bridge."

The words forced my eyes in the direction of the bridge. I remembered all too well where it was. All important events involving the packs of Hemlock Hollow took place there to be witnessed by the Gods. My alpha had been killed there. The storm clouds seemed to be concentrating over that very spot. Flashes in the clouds highlighted the tree-covered hills now and again. It beckoned and taunted me at the same time. That was one place I had sworn I would never step foot or paw on again. One look down at the bleeding woman in my arms and I realized I would go anywhere for her, even Helheimr and back if it came to it.

"My car cannot get through the forest and I do not think we will make it in time if I carry her," I said. My voice broke, but I did not care. Much more of me would break if Sonya did not make it.

Ayra strode out into the cloudy dusk with long steps that should have been impossible for a woman barely over five feet tall. She called over her shoulder as she went, "We'll stop by my place and get my parents' Polaris."

I nodded as she opened the passenger door of my borrowed truck. Gently as I could, I lay Sonya down on the leather seat. She groaned, and her lashes fluttered, but her eyes did not open. I put her seatbelt on to hold her in position then leaped over the hood of the truck to reach the driver's side. Hand on the door handle, I looked over the hood at Ayra. "Are you riding with us?"

"No. I can cut through the forest and beat you there," she said.

One of my eyebrows rose in an involuntary show of disbelief. "I'm the *uppskera*, remember?" she said with a touch of irony darkening her tone.

I did not bother protesting. It would take up precious time we did not have. I jumped in and turned over the ignition. As it roared to life, Ayra took off like a bullet from a gun—literally so fast that one moment she was standing there, the next she wasn't. I'd never even heard of a *varúlfur* being that fast. Once this was all over and Sonya was healing, we had some serious research ahead of us. On the phone, my father had told me the seeker and reaper had faded from memory because there hadn't been one awakened for over three centuries. Which meant this was all new territory.

I threw the truck in reverse and tried not to whip back toward the road too fast. Sonya slumped over in her seat but did not awaken. It became painfully clear that being gentle about it was not as important as getting there as fast as possible. Gravel flew as I shifted and tore off down the road. An eternity seemed to pass before I finally pulled into Ayra's driveway—though only minutes actually ticked by. Each minute was precious time as Sonya's heart pumped more of her blood out. As I took her out, the roar of a Polaris motor sounded over the building storm.

Not twenty feet away loomed a two-story Colonial-style house with massive windows that reflected the distant flashes of lightning. Two figures stood on the big covered porch of the house, arms around each other, watching. I nodded to them, having no words or heart for a greeting, especially since they stood there as if too afraid to approach and help. A big black and red two-seater Polaris screeched to a halt in front of my car. Ayra jumped out of it and my mind blew a little. My speedometer had rarely dropped below one hundred. No shortcut could have been short enough for her to beat me here on foot. Yet here she was.

I did not question it or even overthink it as I sat Sonya in the seat and belted her in.

"I'll ride on the back to help hold her in place. Can't have her head bouncing around too much," Ayra said.

With her directing me, I found the path along her parents' house that led into the woods. All the homes in Hemlock Hollow backed up to this forest, and all had paths—visible or scented—that led to that bridge. Normal towns had a hall or a courthouse. This one had a bridge. The deeper into the forest we went, the slower I had to drive to avoid the fir, pine, and hemlock that covered the mountainside. Their sweet scents poured down my throat with each breath. Moisture hung heavy in the air, making the smells stronger. They reminded me of a home and loved ones I had either left behind or lost. It infuriated me that I had to bring her back here of all places to save her.

The trees flew by in a blur but it did not feel fast enough. Rain began to pour down in big, fat drops that soaked my shirt through in moments. It soon made it difficult to drive by scent. The growing darkness ensured driving by sight was not much easier. Once we broke through the trees and the hollow opened up I was able to go mostly by memory. Every now and then a strike of lightning turned the hollow white, illuminating the massive bridge that spanned its hundred-foot depth. The bridge was made mostly of steel that had been treated to create an anodized rainbow effect that was admittedly stunning. At the bottom of the hollow, several hundred feet down from the center of the bridge, a stream cut through a bed of jagged rocks.

Chills of anger, trepidation, and a noxious mixture of half a dozen other things I did not want to feel raced through me. I took the path that led to a ridgeline that ran up along to connect with the bridge. It was rough traveling across steep rock slick with rain, but I managed to keep the Polaris on four wheels most of the time.

The trees and rocky incline soon made forward progress impossible. I climbed out and together Ayra and I maneuvered Sonya out of the roll cage of the four wheeler. Even when the rain pelted her face and ran down it in rivers, she did not stir. Fear threatened to drive me to my knees, but I would not let it. Clutching her to my chest, I started to climb. Her weight was so slight, and I swore I could feel her grow colder with each beat of her heart. The rhythm was a song in my ears that slowly wound down as if each beat grew closer to her last. Shale rock gave way beneath my left foot, causing me to fall to a knee. Ayra grabbed my arm and stopped me from sliding any farther. I thanked her, but the sound of the rain punctuated by the occasional thunder covered my words.

The world went white, then turned to sparks as electricity danced along the bridge not five feet from me. Ayra held up a hand, stopping me from stepping on the bridge. Heedless of the snapping arcs, she walked out onto the bridge without hesitation. They swallowed her whole. For a desperate moment I thought for sure it would kill her. Then the dancing arcs began to flow inward, toward the middle of the bridge where she stopped. She stretched her arms up to the dark sky. Lightning shot from her hands into the clouds. It flowed from the bridge, through her, and back up to the storm until every last crackle of it left the bridge. She beckoned to me.

The moment the bridge stopped crackling, I strode out onto it. Ayra's eyes sparkled as they took me in. Bumps rose all over my skin. It was as though Odin himself looked through her at me. I hoped he did, prayed for it, because if so, maybe he would save Sonya. I lay her at Ayra's feet.

"Get back...don't know...keep it from striking you," she yelled over the storm.

I took one big step back, but that was as far as I was going. If it looked like this plan was going south, I needed to be close enough to stop it. One blond brow of Ayra's rose and she shrugged. She knelt down beside Sonya's prone form and began to chant in Icelandic. It was a prayer beseeching Odin. The skies rumbled overhead, but another bolt of lightning didn't come.

I took up the prayer with her. "Odin, I beseech you—" My next word was shattered by the thunderous crackle of lightning as it shot down from the sky and struck Sonya not five feet from me. My body hummed from being so close. Little shocks traveled up from the bridge through my feet. It felt like someone was driving nails into my feet, but I didn't move. Nothing could make me leave her side. Ayra lay her hands on Sonya, right in the middle of all that crackling light. The bolt continued to flow down from the sky as if Ayra had hold of an endless source of energy. That thought started to worry me. Would it kill her if she held it too long? Would it kill Sonya?

I moved a step closer.

Suddenly, Ayra poured the lightning into Sonya's abdomen. The pressure of it held me back no matter how hard I struggled. It was like trying to swim against a riptide. Sonya's body lifted up off the bridge, her head hanging limp, long hair still touching the steel. I screamed to the Gods. No matter what I said, promised, or threatened, Ayra ignored me. Hell, I wasn't sure she could even hear me within the pressure of the lightning.

Slowly, Sonya's body sank back down onto the bridge. The lightning faded to small snakes that moved across her and Ayra, then sank into Sonya. I stumbled forward as the pressure disappeared. Ayra rose to her feet and moved back a step. I skidded to my knees beside Sonya as her eyes fluttered open. The wounds in her abdomen were gone. The only sign they had even existed was the dried blood on her skin and torn clothes. Electricity snapped in her eyes the same as it did in Ayra's. After a few blinks it faded away, leaving her amber irises slightly aglow. I pulled her to me, needing to feel her against me, solid, breathing, and real. Little snaps of electricity danced from her into me. I endured them gladly.

She was alive. Nothing else mattered.

CHAPTER TWENTY-EIGHT

TY

For two days and nights Sonya recovered from her blood loss and read the book. I helped as much as I could, lending my power to her to heal, and my assistance with the Icelandic words she didn't know. What we learned fascinated me, but worried me at the same time. The fine print said Sonya would be drawn to new *varúlfur* strongest right before their first full moon, and that she would only have until the day after that moon in which to get them to master their strongest emotion, and thereby their control. Three days wasn't much. Then the reaper would step in to stop them before they became too dangerous. Though I tried to convince her this didn't mean she was responsible for their salvation, I was not sure she bought it completely.

Knowing all that made me itch to get out and do something. I wanted to help her, to be a part of the solution. If it hadn't been for the careful planning of whoever had bitten Candice and the boy, they might be dead right now. The book said Sonya's awakening meant there were far more than two in need of her help. That had to mean someone had been biting people in for years, at least as many as Sonya had been alive. I wasn't sure how much longer she would sit around and heal. The 'call', as the book described it, to go to someone hadn't happened again yet that she had told me, but she was still anxious.

Worse, the closer the full moon drew, the stronger her desire to shift became. I remembered the first full moon after my *verða*. Resisting the call was hard, to say the least. But a wound from another *varúlfur* was one of the worst wounds we can suffer. Hard as we are to kill, that is one of the things that can do it. We could not risk her shifting and messing up the healing. Still, the only thing that stopped her from shifting was my assurance that she would tear the wounds right back open if she did.

Cozy as the cabin was, I knew she had seen enough of the inside of it after three days of recovering. I hadn't allowed anyone to disturb her, and I began to fear she was growing tired of my company alone. But there were things she needed to know before all the politicking started. Standing in the living room, staring out the huge picture window at the vast forest that filled the view, she looked amazing and utterly tense. I knew she needed to feel the earth beneath her paws, drink in the scents of pine and greenery, and revel in the wildness slumbering inside. It was time. Her knee had healed completely and all that lingered of the wounds in her side were four long, pink scars that were swiftly fading.

"Something seems wrong about me finding you sexy in my mother's old clothes," I said as I began down the stairs.

She fingered the edge of the gauzy red top she wore as she watched me descend.

"You sure she won't mind?" she asked for at least the fifth time.

I crossed the room in a few long strides and swept her carefully into my arms.

"Of course not. They left this cabin to me a long time ago, and haven't used anything left in it since for three years. She would want you to have them."

Part of me was disappointed they were in Iceland visiting relatives and would not get to meet her. But another part of me was relieved she would not have to worry about that right now. I was not sure what to tell my parents about us yet, and that complicated things. I did not want to push Sonya to define us.

Entranced by her scent and the feel of her curves against me, I dropped my head and began to nuzzle her neck. We had not made love again and it was killing me.

"What happens tomorrow during the full moon? You still haven't told me," she asked.

I sighed and lifted my head. "The packs run, hunt, and gather together."

"They do that every full moon?"

My body tensed despite my attempts to remain relaxed. "No, not exactly. This one is different. They will all be gathering together in one place to honor and discuss the awakening of the first *leitar* and *uppskera* in over three hundred years."

"Honoring, not celebrating," she said.

There had not been a seeker and reaper in over three hundred years because they had not been needed. Only in dark times, when newly bitten *varúlfur* either were not being taught properly, or were deserting their *kennaris*, were the pair needed. Sonya and Ayra were the equivalent of a supernatural backup plan to make sure *varúlfur* did not rage out of control or turn into rabid beasts that threatened to expose all of us. She knew this from the book, but what she did not know was how frightened my kind would be of her.

"You are like the master of all enforcers, above the *verndari* and *lögreglu*, above the alphas, and even the councils that govern the AVW and AVV. You alone can tell who made a *varúlfur*, it is one of your gifts, just as being drawn to them is. This gives you the power to pinpoint anyone who has illegally changed someone. People fear that," I explained as gently as I could.

She grunted her disapproval. "Only the ones who break the law need to fear that."

I kissed her forehead. "True, but I am afraid we are headed into dark times with more people like that than we may care to think about."

Eventually she slid her arms around my waist and leaned into me. "I'm still not sure what to make of all this."

I held her close and stroked her back. "You will not have to face it alone. I will be here with you every step of the way."

Moisture pooled at the corners of her eyes. "You don't have to be, you know. I don't want you to feel obligated just because of this new complication," she said.

My devotion must have shown in my eyes because her breath caught. "I want to be there. It is too late to get rid of me now," I said through a half-grin.

She rose up on her toes to kiss me but I did not go down to meet her. As much as I wanted to take her right there up against the window, I could not.

"Look, if I can't get rid of you, then I intend to have my way with you. I'm almost completely healed. You don't have to worry," she said.

My grin widened. "I know. Tonight you can have your way with me all you want. It is just that we have a visitor coming."

"A visitor?"

Mouth agape as I searched for the right words, I hesitated. I was not sure how she was going to feel about this. There was no avoiding it, though. Thankfully, the doorbell rang, saving me from having to explain myself. Sonya's eyes popped wide open.

"If you are not ready to see her yet, I can send her away," I said.

The way her brow pinched, I realized she didn't know who I meant. Slowly, comprehension dawned in her eyes.

"Ayra. No, I mean yes, of course I'm ready to see her. I want to see her."

With a reluctant look that made me want to clutch tighter to her, she let go of me and drew back a few steps. I planted a quick kiss on her forehead and went to the door. I both felt and heard her move away from the window to stand behind the couch, resting her hands upon it. Tension sang in the air, rolling off her in waves. A similar tension tried to constrict the muscles of my own body, but I didn't dare let it. Sonya needed me to be strong for her, and I would, no matter what it cost me.

My smile felt genuine enough when I opened the door. With her hair pulled back, it revealed a dainty, almost elfish-looking face with high cheekbones that gave her a slightly severe, yet lovely, appearance. Sapphire blue eyes filled with a sense of purpose and confidence looked past me to regard Sonya in a calculating manner that I did not like. Despite her delicate frame, her expression and stance made her look like a force to be reckoned with. And I knew her for what she was: one of the most powerful *varúlfur* to have walked the earth, and an active member of the AVV. Her gaze moved from Sonya only to exchange polite and slightly formal greetings with me, then moved right back.

Stepping aside, I let her in but stayed close at her back. I had heard the stories about her not wanting to be the *uppskera*. While I had not known her growing up, I had known of her. She had always been a quiet, gentle girl, but one with a dark side if the stories from the AVV were true. There was a good chance she resented Sonya for being the final trigger in fully awakening the power within her. If that was the case, I would throw her right back out on her tail. Or at least try. To protect Sonya, I wasn't afraid to reckon with the force that was the *uppskera*.

"Sonya, it is a pleasure to meet you under better circumstances," she said with a slight bow of her head.

I detected a hint of honesty in her formal tone that made me relax a notch. Sonya must have too, because she came out from behind the couch and approached her, stopping a few feet away.

"I'm so sorry you were forced into something you didn't want. And I'm even more sorry that I had something to do with it," she said.

Sonya cringed at her own words, but didn't look down. I had to fight the instinct to leap to her defense. I knew she wouldn't want that, but it was difficult not to, seeing how hard this was for her. The cold, detached look on Ayra's face softened a bit.

Her gaze shot to me before returning to Sonya. "Ty tells me you didn't have much of a choice in the matter either," Ayra said.

Sonya shrugged. Realizing she needed a moment, I invited Ayra to sit in one of the chairs while I pulled Sonya down on the couch next to me. She clutched my hand tight for a moment then sat up straighter.

"It's my fault this happened to you. I'm so sorry," she whispered.

Ayra shook her head. "No. It is the fault of my brother, him and whoever has been biting in others against their will. You are as much a victim as I am."

I liked this woman more by the minute.

Sonya still did not relax. "But our power didn't fully awaken until we touched. James and the others brought me here to awaken you, to make your pack more powerful."

Their eyes locked but it was not a show of aggression. At first glance, I caught a glimpse of something tender in Ayra's eyes, then the look in them grew so cold I had to fight the instinct to move between them.

"Yes, they are the ones to blame, not you or I. Remember that at the full moon, and remember you and I are equals, but we are above the others. All of the others," Ayra said.

In a flurry of white gauzy fabric, she rose and stood before the door in less than a blink. Equals like hell. With her air of danger and menace, this woman spooked even me a little. I could not put it any other way. But at the same time, I liked that she seemed so accepting of Sonya, that she did not blame her.

"As a mated pair, you are strong, but I will stand together with you at the festival, if you will have me there, ensuring no one tries to take advantage of either of us again." She bowed slightly to us both. "Thank you for having me over." With that, she opened the door and left.

Mouth agape, Sonya stared at me as the door closed. I traced a finger along her lips.

"Let us shift and go for a short jog, come back and make passionate love, then we will talk about the festival," I said in a low voice.

She hummed against my finger, eyes fluttering closed. "I'm not about to argue with that, save maybe for the order of the events."

My finger drew away and trailed down to tease her in other, far more sensitive areas while my lips covered hers. Though my body became lost in the sensations of enjoying her, my mind could not stop going over part of what Ayra had said. She had called us a mated pair. The implications were far deeper than I knew Sonya understood just yet. Whether she was ready to define us as such or not, others were already. I was not sure if I had properly prepared her for the implications of that, but we were about to find out.

CHAPTER TWENTY-NINE

SONYA

W rapped in Ty's arms was quite possibly the best place I could imagine ever waking up, even if it was on a bed of slightly damp grass and crushed wildflowers. Bits of frost clung to the star-shaped purple flowers, yet I didn't feel cold in the slightest. Our love-making session—his words not mine, though I have to admit, they fit how we spent the night—lasted so long we had collapsed into sleep on the spot afterward.

The full moon festival had indeed been an aggravating political dance that we had fled from the moment we found an excuse to. Alphas had tried to entice Ayra and me into joining their packs, appease where their shortcomings were concerned, and assure us they had no knowledge of the wrongs done to us. The alphas of the Arnoddr pack—Ayra's birth pack— had even given me a gift, offering up one of the guys who had helped abduct me and one who had torched Ty's truck for me to punish. I gave the one guy to Ty, who after a brief fight had diplomatically sentenced him to helping restore his dad's '73 Shovelhead. Considering the guy was the alpha's son, that had gone a long way to making them respect Ty a bit more since he'd been fully in his rights to beat him within an inch of his life. It had gone even further with me.

Most of the alphas treated Ty with a disdain that pissed me off, a big reason for our early departure. The only good part about the party had been that I got to meet another friend of Ty's, Vidar Balderson—who seemed to share some steamy history with Ayra if I was picking up on their vibes correctly.

The warmth of the first rays of the sun breaking through the trees hinted at something I was supposed to be doing. Birds sang in the trees overhead, tempting to lull me back into sleep. Then it struck me. Raul's trial was this morning.

I sat bolt upright and cursed. In a fraction of a second that made it seem as though he simply appeared, Ty sat up beside me, an arm going around me.

"What is wrong?" he asked.

"Raul's trial."

He cussed far more colorfully in both English and Icelandic.

Laughing, I reached for my clothes. "Don't worry, we'll just go straight there. Ayra said it is in the same place as the celebration was, right?"

He started pulling his clothes on so quickly I feared he may tear them. "Yes, but we have to go back to the cabin and shower first."

Fingers on the buttons of my shirt, I paused. While he always maintained great hygiene, Ty had never struck me as the vain type before. His hair was a bit tousled giving him a wild look, but it was clean enough. And he smelled amazing... Oh. He smelled like sex, with me. We had taken a quick dip in a stream last night before collapsing, but it hadn't been enough to get rid of the scents completely.

"You don't want anyone to know we had sex," I said, voice sounding far harsher than I had meant to let it.

The frantic race to dress stopped and he took my face in his hands. "Not for the reasons you are thinking. I would love for everyone to know. But they will think that we belong to each other, that we are mates, and I do not want to force you into that corner."

I smiled, loving the feeling of how it brushed my cheeks against his hands. "Ty, that isn't a corner, it's a road leading somewhere amazing that I very much want to travel."

Moisture brought a shine to his ice-blue eyes. "Really? But are you ready?"

"Yes, I'm ready." I breathed the last word into his mouth as he leaned in and kissed me.

Our tongues met and twisted together in a delicious push and pull that had me pressing my body to his, needing to feel more of him. His hands started to work under the edge of my shirt. Laughing, I pulled back.

"That will definitely make us late."

Letting out a huge sigh, he drew away. Though I worked on putting on the rest of my own clothes, my eyes followed him as he stood and adjusted his erection so he could zip up his shorts. For the first time since I had been bitten, this trial wasn't the most important thing in my world. That realization sent a thrill through me, one that would have to wait. Keeping a safe distance between us, I finished dressing as quickly as I could. I spared the little meadow with its tall green grass and purple flowers one last glance before we left.

The euphoria I'd felt upon waking slid away with each step closer we came to the hollow. For weeks I'd been eager to face Raul, to take my rage out on him at having my choice stolen. But now... I didn't know what I felt, and I had no idea how I was going to react when I saw him. From the book I had learned trials were often by combat, a show of who was dominant, stronger, and had the right to judge. But during that early morning walk I didn't feel dominant or strong. I just wanted this over with.

The terrain began to feel familiar and the scents of others soon drifted to me. One in particular that I was beginning to know well approached from our right. Looking like a slender ghost of pale light in the shadows of the forest, Ayra stepped out from behind a tree and nodded to us. I nodded back, as did Ty. Seconds later, Vidar stepped out and moved to her side, a stark contrast of shadow and muscle to her light and lithe form. They didn't hold hands, or even touch, but I could feel a connection between the two of them. My mind buzzed with a million different things, but I didn't feel much like voicing any of it. Thankfully, Ty didn't push or question me, just held my hand as we walked, offering up his silent support.

Compared to last night, the hollow looked abandoned now, which brought me a great measure of relief. Only a few dozen people were scattered about, sleeping in the grass and beneath the trees. Most were naked. Sunlight spilled into the gorge that cut through the two hills, highlighting something I hadn't seen last night in the dark. Far beyond where the bonfire and fighting rings were, a bridge spanned the hollow, connecting the two hills. At only fifty feet or so long, it wasn't overly large, but because of the depth of the hollow at that point, it was a few hundred feet high. It shone in the sun like a prism. Something about that bridge pulled at me, made my feet turn toward it.

"That's where the trial is, isn't it?" I pointed to the bridge.

"Yes, that is Hemlock Hollow's ode to the *Bifröst*," Ty said in a hushed tone.

"The burning rainbow bridge to Valhalla," I said.

Pale brows rising high, Ayra regarded me with the closest thing to shock I had seen on her face since the barn. "You know our eddas?"

I shrugged as if it were no big deal. "I've been working on reading them again."

Reading them was one thing, understanding them was another altogether since they were in verse and ancient as dirt.

I looked to Ty. "The rainbow bridge is supposed to be a bridge between Midgard, which is this world, some think, and Asgard, the world of the Gods. Right?"

He smiled like a proud teacher and nodded. "Well, between all the worlds really."

"It's a metaphorical thing, right? I mean, that's not really a bridge to another world, is it?" I asked, voice low so those scattered about wouldn't hear.

Even if they were asleep, I didn't want to sound like a lunatic. That said, I half expected Ty and Ayra to say yes and half expected them to laugh. I mean, really, it wouldn't surprise me all that much. A month ago I wouldn't have believed people could turn into wolves either. Head cocking to the side, Ayra regarded me with deep interest. Vidar grinned and nodded to Ty with an impressed look.

"Metaphorical, yes, for now. Theoretically it is designed with the proper materials and positioned over a place of power so it could be activated as a bridge between worlds I guess, but someone on the other side would have to activate it as far as we know," Ayra said.

I waited for the shock, but it never came. Not knowing what to say after that, I fell silent as the terrain grew steep. We wove through a few sleeping people, some entangled pairs that reminded me of how Ty and I had awoken.

"Looks like we missed an interesting part of the party," I said.

One corner of Ty's mouth quirked up. "Only if you are into the group kind of thing."

Though his expression was all humor, I detected a bit of concern hiding in his eyes.

Making a face, I shook my head. "Definitely not."

Group sex, or sex among a group, hit far too close to casual sex to appeal to me. Hemlock Hollow was looking more and more like a place I couldn't wait to leave. The hill became more of a hike than a climb as we neared the bridge. The bridge looked like it was made mostly of steel that had been treated to create a rainbow, anodized effect that was really stunning. At the bottom of the hollow, several hundred feet down from the center of the bridge, a stream cut through a bed of jagged rocks.

Looking at the full expanse of that bridge, I wondered, "Could our kind survive a fall from there?"

Ayra nodded. "Some of the more powerful could, alphas, us. But most, no."

"Aren't they worried about being seen by satellites?" I asked.

"Einstein," Vidar said, which answered nothing.

Eyebrows raised, I looked to Ty.

"He is a member of the Reinhard pack. Einir is his real name, but a lot of people call him Einstein because he is one of the most brilliant people of our time. He invented a device that blocks satellites much like blocking a radio wave," he said.

"Why don't we have this everywhere?" I asked.

"Because no one knows about it but our kind. If the government got a hold of such technology, well, you can imagine what they would do with it, and Einir. They will invent it on their own in time, but for now, it keeps us safe in Hemlock Hollow and that is enough."

I had a feeling that was part of why this 'trial' was being held there. That and it would create a fantastic spectacle for those watching. As far away as it was from the place the bonfire had been held, *varúlfur* hearing would ensure those gathered heard everything. Long before we reached the top of the hill—which at this point had really become more of a cliff side— I heard the voices of the alphas. Like a switch being flipped, the feeling of euphoria I had awoken with disappeared, replaced by tension that stirred my power awake. Upon cresting the cliff side and reaching level ground, Ty took my hand in his and gave it a good squeeze. Letting out a long breath, I squeezed back and did my best to relax. He tried to let go as we moved through the trees toward the group of people waiting at the start of the bridge, but I wouldn't let him.

Only Isak and Iona, Ayra's old alphas, and Vidar's, I assumed, waited beneath the hemlock trees framing the entrance to the bridge. Out in the middle of the bridge four more waited, Ander and Gyda, alphas of the Reinhard pack, my would-have-been in-laws, along with two who weren't alphas. It surprised me that Bain and Morene—alphas of the Draupnir pack—hadn't shown, but it definitely didn't disappoint me.

Three people approached from the opposite end of the bridge. Bain's acrid scent—similar to that of freshly turned dirt—mingled with Morene's rosewater smell told me who the two figures on the outside were. I didn't need to smell the leather and pine, or see the confident swagger of the middle figure to know who it was. Had my five senses been blocked, I would had known him by the feel of his power alone. It was a power too similar to my own to mistake—not in strength, but in origin. Strong, yes, he was that too, possibly even alpha strong, but not *leitar* strong.

Breath coming in ragged gasps that I sucked through gritted fangs, I stormed into the circle and forced myself to stop and wait. I wanted him to come to me. As they reached Isak, Bain gave Raul a good shove. At the same time, Raul took what looked like a stumbling step forward, he kicked back at Bain, connecting hard. The smaller man doubled over, gasping for air. When he found it, he bared his fangs and started to move in on Raul.

Ayra was suddenly between them, one hand on each man's bare chest, a low growl rumbling from her small body, fangs flashing behind all the white-blond hair. Though Vidar tensed, massive biceps flexing as his fists closed, he didn't move. The potential for this to go really south thickened the air like smoke.

"He is not yours to judge or punish," she warned.

Hands held up, Bain took several steps back and flung the long braid of his dark blond hair over his shoulder. The shaved sides of his head revealed rune tattoos along what would have been his hairline. Despite being sinewy and thin, an air of menace and danger surrounded him that made the hair on my arms stand up.

Morene's glaring countenance made me think she might challenge Ayra, but she only took hold of Bain's arm and pulled him back another step. He shrugged her off and crossed his arms over his chest, trying to pretend he wasn't still struggling for breath. The hate-filled look he stabbed Raul's way made me think the man might actually detest Raul as much as I did. Everyone else faded away into an angry haze as Raul's attention shifted to me and he started to approach.

Awe filled his wide eyes as he gazed at me, that and something close to worship. It was completely unexpected and I hated it. I wanted remorse, fear, not this. Anger choked my words so that the only thing I could get out was a growl. But it was enough when it melted that look off his face and sadness filled those amber eyes. He stopped less than five feet from me. One lunge and I could have his throat in my hands. I started to shake, not from the desire to shift—though that boiled within as well—but from fighting back the urge to hurt him. Power crackled out from me, making Raul flinch as it passed over him.

"You took my choice from me," I finally managed to say.

"I never meant to do that. I'm so sorry, I was desperate—"

"Not to have to marry another?" I cut him off.

He shook his head and cast his eyes to the ground.

I advanced on him, letting my power roll over him, shoving him to his knees with an ease that would have shocked me if I hadn't been so pissed. Part of it was the fact that he didn't resist, only looked up at me with a reverence that made me want to strike him.

"Why then?" I demanded.

Mouth opening, his gaze flicked into the crowd. His eyes settled on Morene. His mouth closed, he swallowed, and opened it again. "With the *uppskera* coming from Arnoddr, they would have had enough power to swallow the Reinhard pack whole. It wouldn't have been an alliance, it would have been an annihilation. I couldn't let that happen to my pack, to my alphas. I wanted to ask you, but I was running out of time with Tyler on my tail." A sinking suspicion tugged at my stomach. That hadn't been what he was going to say before he looked at Morene.

A glance at Ander and Gyda revealed wide-eyed looks of shock that looked genuine. One hand covering her gaping mouth, Gyda turned a tear-filled look full of tenderness to Raul.

"You knew the *uppskera* was in Arnoddr, but others didn't," I said to Raul.

He nodded. "She was good at keeping her unwanted mark covered. I think the only people that new about it were her parents, Calder, James, and me."

"So you were in on this with Calder and James?" My voice grew gravelly as I had to force it out between my fangs.

Suddenly I was standing over him, claws brandished, not recalling the steps I had taken to get there.

Eyebrows rising into his dark, brownish-black hair, he looked the picture of innocence. "No, never. Ayra and I made out once, when we were younger, I saw it then. Ever since, I've been searching for you, knowing you were the only way to keep my pack from being absorbed into Arnoddr."

I wanted badly to disbelieve his innocence, but I could feel it in his power, smell it in his scent. He'd never meant to hurt me, to take away my choice. It pained him, deeply. But there were volumes he wasn't telling me. Which led my mind down another path.

"In a world of millions, how did you find me?" I asked.

His eyes darted about, then he leaned close and whispered, "The *leitar* and *uppskera* are always of the same blood line. I found your bloodline, and it led me to you."

"How did you know the *leitar* would be awakened? It has been hundreds of years since the last one."

Pink tongue darting out to wet his lips, he looked past me. "Because I suspected Calder was biting people in against their will, trying to force the awakening of the next *leitar* and *uppskera*."

Prickles of anger worked beneath my skin. "Why the hell would he do that?"

"Because the *uppskera* is from his bloodline."

I fought the urge to glance back at Ayra, back to where Raul was looking. "He wanted to be the next *uppskera*, but it fell to his sister instead."

Raul's gaze returned to me. "Yes."

The pieces clicked together. Many of the names of *leitars* in the book that had surnames were the same. Most of them didn't have surnames listed, so I hadn't made the connection before. I was destined to be this. If Raul hadn't been the one to change me, it could have been Calder, and that would have been so much worse.

I pulled my power back from Raul. He breathed easier but didn't rise to his feet. Having him kneeling before me, willingly, should have felt better than this.

Behind him Ander and Gyda stiffened, their hands intertwining, as if they knew I had reached a decision about their son. Not wanting to draw out their pain any longer, I straightened and took a deep breath.

"Raul Anderson, you bit me in against my will, and without the Council's consent. However, you did so to protect your pack and for that, I will spare your life."

A sob of relief tore from Gyda. Giving me a grateful look, Ander drew his mate into his arms. I gave them a moment before I went on.

"You will serve as a *kennari* for ten years, one that will work exclusively with those who have been bitten-in against their will. And I will hold you personally responsible for each of your charge's successful integration." I looked to the gathered Council members, who nodded their approval.

Hope filled Raul's eyes and I knew what he was going to ask before the words left his lips.

"I will be your *kennari*, then?"

I took a wicked pleasure in crushing that hope. "No." I leaned over him and whispered. "If you had asked to bite me in, I might have said yes, to both of those questions." Taking maybe a bit too much pleasure in the pained look on his face, I turned and walked away from him, my eyes gravitating toward Ty.

He stood rigid and motionless beside Ayra and Vidar, his face blank but his power screaming of tension and fear. I took his big hands in mine and raised them to my mouth. Lips almost twitching up into a grin that belayed his confidence and enough cockiness to make my stomach flutter, he sank to his knees before me as was apparently customary in this situation, so the book said. Having such a powerful man kneeling before me sent a thrill of excitement straight to my core. Though it kind of weirded me out—and honestly, excited me a bit—I turned his hands over and licked his palms. Another odd custom.

"I choose Tyler Viðarsson as the *leitar's kennari*, and as my mate, if you want the job," I announced loud enough for even those gathered an acre away to hear clearly, which really wasn't that loud considering their heightened sense of hearing.

A gentle tug on his hands and Ty rose.

"It is the only job I want, and you are the only person I will ever want." He pulled me into his arms, leaned over, and kissed me long and sweet, claiming me right there in front of everyone. Tongue pushing through his lips, I turned the kiss into something far more intimate, making it clear he wasn't the only one laying claim. Whispers started all around us, some carrying up from the valley below, though I couldn't make out what those were saying. I pulled back from the kiss.

"Let's get out of here," I said.

He put an arm around me, resting his hand on the small of my back as we walked. Ayra and Vidar fell into step beside us. I couldn't get off that bridge and leave those other people behind fast enough. Once we were on the ground and had scaled down the cliff side people and wolves poured in around us, reaching out to touch us, tongues licking at our hands. Not one for physical contact, I had to force myself not to flinch or draw away. Words of praise and awe spilled from their lips. They called us Valkyries, heralds of a new age, some even whispered the word *frelsari*. None of those titles felt right. I was just an out of work bartender-turned-*varúlfur* who had no family to miss her.

With Ty on one side and Ayra and Vidar on the other, I realized that wasn't true, not anymore at least. I had Ty, and maybe even Ayra. And messed up as it was having a reaper for a friend and a werewolf for a boyfriend, it felt right. Finally, I had found who I belonged with and what I was meant to be.

***

Thank you for reading! Did you enjoy? Please Add Your Review! Every review helps authors and encourages readers to take a chance on a book.

And don't miss more in the Children of Fenrir series with book two, TEMPERED & TURNED, available now! Turn the page for a sneak peek!

You can also sign up for the City Owl Press newsletter to receive notice of all book releases!

SNEAK PEEK OF TEMPERED & TURNED

VIDAR

Being chosen wasn't an option. It was necessary, essential, vital. I had to get back to her. For every *uppskera*—reaper—there has always been a *verndari* monk from the Order of the *Verndari* at their side. I had to be that *verndari* for Ayra. I forced myself to go faster, until my legs were no more than a blur as they flew over the forest floor. Pine needles and twigs tickled at my bare feet, feathery boughs brushed at my arms. The wonderful, sweet, heady scents of the forest poured down my throat, but something else came right behind them—the musky odor of my rivals. Their feet brushed the ground behind me, and their breath touched my shoulders.

The rocky terrain grew steeper. Fighting the instinct to slow, I forced myself faster through the ferns and brush clinging to the mountainside. From somewhere nearby, the clean, fresh scent of a waterfall carried to me. The trees thinned the closer I drew to the top, letting the afternoon sun break through in large, warm patches, too warm on my sweaty, ebony skin. I concentrated on trying to outrun the light itself.

I reached the top of the plateau I'd been ascending and launched across it. A hundred feet away stood three raised stone-encircled platforms, the fighting rings. The slightly salty scent of the sun-warmed sand within them drifted to me. Close to a dozen men and women clothed in simple linen uniforms stood at attention in an arc on another raised area around the platforms.

I went straight for the highest ring. My feet slapped on the stairs in a few heartbeats. Sand gave way beneath my feet, a welcome relief after an hour of running barefoot on rock and dirt. The brows of a few of those waiting rose, but otherwise, they didn't react.

The smaller ring would be the most challenging of the three. Three winners would emerge at the end, and the waiting priests would choose one of us based off how well we performed and how much risk we took.

I would take every risk I had to for her.

Chest pumping like a bellows as I regained my air, I turned to see who else would make it. I found my calm center and sank deep into it. My breathing slowed. Clarity filled me, followed by determination. One by one, my muscles relaxed as I willed them to. Power hummed beneath my feet, and the ground vibrated slightly. That power tugged at my own, encouraging it to rise and rejuvenate me. The Order had chosen this place for the trials specifically because of that power. It ran deep through the earth and fed our kind as surely as the air that filled our lungs.

The others soon burst up over the edge of the plateau, men and women all eager to be chosen, eager for the wrong reasons. To them it was an honor, one that would bring them fame and renown. I saw it in their wide eyes, smelled it on their sweating skin.

My fangs sprouted from my top and bottom jaws, and a growl forced my lips apart.

In only running shorts—and sport bras in the women's cases—the strengths and weaknesses of each were on display. One ran with a limp, another sucked air so hard his chest looked in danger of collapsing, and another bled from a gash across her abdominals. They all glared at me with a ferocity that made my hackles rise.

I bared my fangs at them out of instinct.

The first four went to the other two rings without hesitation. Out of the corner of my eye, I watched as they rested, some bending over to put their elbows on their knees, others collapsing onto the sand. Only one remained standing, and she looked as though she may fall over at any moment. Despite our training, not one of them calmed themselves or drew on the power of this place to replenish their energy.

Fools.

They weren't worthy of her.

At last, the sixth and seventh candidates burst over the plateau edge, both tall, broad, blond men native to the Icelandic soil we stood on. But then, so was I. It made no difference that my ancestors had been stolen from English slave traders and brought here over a thousand years ago. I was just as native as these lot were. Some didn't see it that way, these two included. Even now their expressions tightened with judgment. My ancestry, coupled with the fact that I wasn't born in Iceland, rubbed their fur all kinds of wrong ways.

One of the final two took one look at me, hung his head, and collapsed on the rocky soil. For once, my reputation served me well. Or rather, it served Ayra well. She deserved someone far more determined to protect her than that man. They were good monks, each one of them, but that didn't mean they were what she needed. I smiled, enjoying the furious snarl of the remaining man that strode to my ring.

Mat Matheson.

Despite his swagger, the reluctance in his eyes and stiffness in his gait made it clear he would have rather gone to any ring but mine. For that alone I would have to beat him. He sauntered up the steps at a leisurely pace. Clearly, he meant for me to think he was confident he'd win, but I could see right through the ruse. Each slow step gave him more time to suck in air and recover a little. Fine by me. I wanted him at his best, or as close as he could get.

No wounds covered his pale skin. He didn't limp or favor any part of his muscled body as he moved. Sweat plastered locks of his shoulder-length hair to his glistening skin. He rolled his neck as he climbed the steps. Slipping into a fighting stance, he swung his arms out and around to loosen them, then flexed his pectorals until each bounced in rhythm. One of my brows rose as I swallowed a humorous quip.

A man and a woman leaped onto the outer rock ring that surrounded my fighting pit, two of the monks who had been waiting for us. They walked to opposite sides of the circle and stood at attention, waiting to serve as judges. From the raised arc surrounding the three rings came the voice of the High Priestess.

"Welcome. Congratulations on being the top six to complete the second round of the physical trials. The very fact that you have made it here means you are favored by the Gods."

Keeping Mat in my peripheral vision, I gave the priestess my attention, as was proper. Back straight, muscled arms behind her, blond hair woven into a single, massive plait that trailed over one breast and down to her waist, she looked every bit the priestess of Frigg and Odin. The knotwork tattoos on her bare upper arms and trailing down her neck into her cleavage completed the image. Still, she was nothing compared to Ayra.

The remaining competitors began to climb—and in some cases, crawl —their way up onto the plateau. They sat on the rocky ground around the three rings, eager spectators for an event that would go down in our kind's history books.

The priestess went on. "There can be only three potentials. You will fight by the old rules until a winner is declared. Judges, ready?"

Six collective affirmatives shouted out.

"Begin!" the priestess announced.

Out of the corner of my eye, I saw Mat move. Fists rising, I shadowed him. We danced back and forth, around and around for several moments. Kicks, punches, jabs, and more flew as we blocked, spun, and sidestepped in an attempt to gauge one another's skill. With the blinding speed that only our kind can manage, Mat kicked for my abdomen. That one move signaled the dance's end and the fight's beginning. The kick was fast enough it was going to hurt, but I didn't block it. Instead, I raised my hands to block the second kick that I knew would come for my face.

Sure enough, the first had been only a good fake, and the second one, even faster, came at my jaw. I caught it easily, cupping my hand to grasp his heel and throw Mat's leg back at him. Rather than let the motion jam his own leg into him, Mat used the momentum to backflip away. When he landed on all fours, it was as a brown wolf. Almost before his paws touched the ground, he lunged with teeth snapping.

Instead of sidestepping, I crouched and grabbed his furred throat, holding those sharp teeth at a distance. Continuing with Mat's momentum, I rolled onto my back and placed my foot in his chest to throw him past. As I turned to face him again, I saw him skidding to a stop in human form, teetering on the edge of the circle.

His display had blown his running shorts to pieces. Bits of them fluttered down to the sand. Most wouldn't have thought to try shifting back to catch themselves from falling over the edge, or even been fast enough. Stepping or being thrown out of a circle meant losing.

His ability to shift in mid-fight meant he had the power of an alpha's *verndari*, or possibly even an alpha. I hadn't expected that. I smiled as our eyes locked again, and this time Mat bared his fangs at me. That look told me he knew I had underestimated him. But I wouldn't do it again. We paced around each other to the sound of a cheering crowd.

Then we were on one another in a flurry of kicks, blocks, and strikes, too fast to see. I had to feel, instead, to open myself up to instinct. I kicked for Mat's chest. He sidestepped and caught my leg, locking an arm around it. Unable to pull it back, I pushed against him and jumped into the air, twisting and kicking. He let go, but too late. By the time he ducked, I shifted into my hybrid form—half man, half wolf—and the different angle of my leg allowed me to land the kick solidly into his back. He collapsed, the air forced from his lungs with a loud grunt. He rolled to the right, escaping my second blow and getting closer to the center of the circle.

The crowd gasped and cheered louder. The hybrid form wasn't something many of our kind could do. Even those that could had to practice long and hard to pull it off, something I did daily. I was lucky to have a father who could also shift into the hybrid form, and he had taught me well.

I leaped for Mat, my hybrid form giving me the extra reach I needed to grab him by the shoulders with my black furred arms. I spun him around, and with deadly four-inch claws, marked him across the chest with shallow gashes. Mat's eyes shot open in shock as blood trickled down his chest. I had moved far too swiftly for him to even begin to block. Speed was another thing I worked on incessantly.

The crowd fell silent as we straightened and stood looking at one another. All knew I could have opened Mat's chest and torn out his heart. The fight was over. No judge could challenge that. But I remained ready, just in case they did, or Mat got any ideas to keep fighting.

"Match!" both of our ring judges called at once.

Mat fell to one knee and bowed his head nearly to the ground. Sweat and blood dripped into the dirt. With a thought, my body flowed back into that of a man.

The judges turned their backs to us. As they deliberated silently with hand signals, the other fights to our left and right slowly came to an end. Mat rose but kept his head bowed and his eyes averted. It was no less of a submission. The stench of defeat—a mixture of a sour, sweaty smell and tangy rot—hung heavy on him. Our judges approached us at the same time the others approached their fighters. Mat's gaze finally lifted to mine. Respect shone in the depths of his blue eyes, and his shoulders slowly drew up. We smiled at each other.

Just because I was the clear winner physically didn't mean the judges would pick me. The match was won by skill, creativeness, and passion. He had fought well and earned my respect. There was a good chance he had earned the judges' favor as well.

The winds of anxiety and doubt attempted to blow me out of my calm center. Controlled breaths and years of discipline helped me stand fast.

One judge took hold of my left hand while the other took hold of Mat's. My breath caught in my throat, making it feel as if my chest was about to collapse.

"Judges, choose your winners," the priestess commanded. The judge holding my hand thrust it high into the air. A triumphant howl rose from me before I could stop it. The howls of the other two winners soon joined mine, reminding me this wasn't over yet.

After the howls died down, the priestess said, "Winners approach."

Quelling the urge to keep howling, I found my calm center again and gathered my wits. I bowed deep to both the judges and my opponent. The new respect in Mat's eyes as he bowed in turn heartened me. I leaped down from the fighting ring and approached the base of the steps where the priestess stood. The other two winners, a man and a woman whom I knew to be excellent fighters, joined me. The woman smiled and nodded while the man glared with a ferocity that tried to call both my anger and my power up. Being sure to retract my fangs, I grinned at him. He glared all the harder.

Tall and broad as I was, these two were not diminished in the slightest standing beside me, not even the woman. At less than three inches shorter than me, she possessed the muscular build of a big-boned Norse woman who dedicated her days to the gym. The other male finalist was cut to the point that he probably possessed zero body fat. All well and good if it were a bodyguard Ayra needed. But she needed much more than that. Her body wouldn't be the only thing in danger.

The judges joined the priestess on the raised platform before us. Their solemn gazes weighed heavy on each of us in turn. Snowcapped peaks of jagged mountaintops rose behind them in an arc that hugged the horizon. As it so often did, the beauty of this place added to the poignancy of the moment. One way or another, I'd be leaving tomorrow, and I'd miss this magnificent island deeply. It had a way of digging deep down into one's soul and nesting there. But I had to go. Whether it would be as the chosen, or as only a friend, I had to return to Ayra. Not even my love of this island could keep me from her. Four years away was too long.

Behind me, I felt the press of the other competitors' power as they gathered to witness. My fighter's instincts didn't like them at my back, but I couldn't turn away from the council in front of me. I didn't need to see the other competitors anyway. Their defeat and acceptance of it weighed heavy in their power.

The priestess stepped forward, her glacial gaze sweeping over me and the other two winners with an impartial air. To my left, the other potential fidgeted as if disturbed by that gaze. It comforted me. Impartiality meant she would choose based on logic, not favoritism. I could only hope the other six would do the same. The priestess's gaze settled on the woman to my right.

"Why do you want to be the *uppskera's verndari?*" she asked her.

The reaper's protector. The very phrase seemed an oxymoron. The reaper of those *varúlfur*—werewolves—who'd gone mad and started killing people. My Ayra, my childhood best friend, had become the thing all monsters fear. But the *uppskera's verndari* was only an oxymoron to those who didn't understand why the reaper needed a protector. Sadly, many of today's competitors didn't. That knowledge was lost to the ages in which we didn't have an *uppskera*. But I had found it, I knew. These competitors just wanted to be her *verndari* for the glory it would bring their family, their pack. Which was part of why it had to be me. Ayra was more than just the *uppskera* to me. So much more. "To honor Odin and his plan for our kind," the woman said.

Giving no reaction whatsoever, the priestess turned her head to me. "Why do you want to be the *uppskera's verndari?*"

I swallowed to wet my throat and loosen my words. "To ensure both the *uppskera's* physical and mental health." Not a grandiose answer, but it was mine nonetheless. Raw honesty was always my policy.

The priestess asked the man to my left the same question. He puffed his bare chest out. "To help protect our kind from both discovery and persecution." His overconfident tone made him sound like a student who knew he had the right answer.

Each time one of us answered, the council of six would scribble in the small notebooks they removed from their belts. I tried desperately to discern what those notes might be by the sound of the writing. Who was to know, though, if less or more scratching was good or bad? Their power weighed heavy on us. It crawled across my skin like a prickling breeze, searching, feeling, judging. With practiced control, I kept my own power from flaring up in reaction. The others didn't do quite as well. Whether mine or theirs was the proper reaction was hard to say. But I found comfort in my discipline, so I was sticking with it.

Still looking at the man, the priestess asked, "Would you kill for the *uppskera?*"

"Yes," he answered far too eager for my liking.

Both myself and the woman answered yes when the priestess asked us. For the third question, the priestess looked to me first. "Would you die for the *uppskera?*"

"Absolutely," I said without hesitation. Now who was too eager? Dammit. I hadn't meant to jump on the question like that.

The priestess's eyes widened just a touch, the only reaction I'd seen her give so far. She moved on with the same removed air she had possessed before, making me wonder if I'd imagined the look. She asked the others the same question. They both answered yes, but slower, and with a touch of hesitation in the man's case. A powerful protective instinct rose in me at his reaction. If they chose him, I wasn't sure I'd be able to walk away from here without another fight.

The seven turned away from us to gather and compare notebooks, not saying a word. As *varúlfur*, we possessed the sharp hearing of a canine, so to speak would be to give away results. Tension started to build up a terrible pressure in my chest. The last four years of training and learning came down to this moment. If I wasn't chosen, all that time away from Ayra would be wasted. True, I had learned about what she was becoming and what I needed to do to help her, but if I wasn't chosen, what good was it? If that happened, leaving her four years ago would feel like I'd abandoned her when she needed me most. My power became a steam kettle threatening to explode, or at the least make me scream.

Just when I feared I couldn't take it anymore, the six turned around and took their places before us. Their stoic expressions gave away nothing. The priestess's gaze settled on me, and my heart felt like it stopped.

"Vidar Balderson, you have earned the right of First Impression. You will have one moon to impress the *uppskera*. If she does not choose you as her *verndari* by the new moon, Birna will have the second opportunity to impress her. If Birna fails, Seth will have the third opportunity of Impression," she announced.

The relief that coursed through me made my knees weak. I bowed low, grateful the motion hid my reaction and gave me the opportunity to draw in a few deep breaths. It wouldn't be good for the council to see the depth of my emotion.

"Thank you, honored council. I will not let you down," I said in a voice far steadier than I felt.

The priestess gave a very slight shake of her head. "Our opinion is inconsequential. It's the *uppskera* you can't let down. May you go with the speed and blessing of the Allfather," she said.

It was all the dismissal I needed. I bowed low to the council, turned, and ran for the edge of the plateau. If I hurried, I might be able to catch an earlier flight out. Every moment counted. Already, I hadn't been there when her power awoke. For that I would never forgive myself. But I'd had to come to Iceland. I'd had to learn everything I could about her ability and the history of those like her. Now that I was armed with the knowledge, I would help her survive this. I had to. Whether I survived or not remained to be seen, but mattered far less.

I leaped from the plateau and plunged headlong over the edge into an uncertain future.

Don't stop now. Keep reading and grab your copy of TEMPERED & TURNED today! And find more from Heather McCorkle at www.heathermccorkle.com

NOTES & GLOSSARY

PACK BREAKDOWN:

Reinhard: Raul's pack.
Alphas: Ander and Gyda.
Draupnir: Ty's old pack.
Alphas: Bain. Morene is his first *verndari* and stands in as the female ruling voice until he finds a mate.
Arnoddr: Ayra's pack.
Alphas: Isak. Standing in as ruling female until he finds a mate, is his mother, Iona.

GLOSSARY:

Asni: donkey, ass
Varúlfur: werewolf
Ráðið: council
Verða: becoming. It is the process of transition from human to shifter.
Lögreglu: police

Verndari: protector. The inner circle of wolves closest to the alphas who protect the pack.

Kennari: teacher. A term used most often to describe someone who is dedicated to teaching newly bitten wolves about being *varúlfur.*

Konunglegur: royalty. Used among *varúlfur* to mean the families of alphas, council members, and the seeker and reaper.

Uppskera: reaper. One who is imbued with power by Odin and Frigg to hunt down and kill condemned shifters.

Leitar: seeker. One who is imbued with power by Odin and Frigg to seek out and help those on the precipice of madness due to being bitten in.

Landsvæði: Territory. To shifters, once it has been invoked it means they will kill any trespassers that come into their territory.

Frelsari: liberator

Read book two, TEMPERED & TURNED, available now, and find more from Heather McCorkle at www.heathermccorkle.com

Ayra is the monster that slays monsters—a fate she never wanted. Forced on her by her brother Calder, a man who bit in countless new werewolves to awaken the power of the reaper, she now has no choice.

The responsibility falls on hers. Not only does she have to put down rabid werewolves, but she must stop Calder from exposing them to the world, and thereby risking the annihilation of their kind.

But she won't be alone.

Vidar, the crush of her childhood, has returned from Iceland. Trained by monks to help guide and protect her, he insists on traveling with her. But is it her, he wants, or the reaper?

It shouldn't matter, but it does, even as her family promises her to a man she does not love. As they are dragged deeper into a plot involving the fate of the Norse Gods, Vidar is all she can think about.

He deserves a life, a mate, a pack. Ayra only brings death.
If they can't get past their would-have-been romance and focus on the future of their kind, there may be no future...for any of them.

Please sign up for the City Owl Press newsletter for chances to win special subscriber-only contests and giveaways as well as receiving information on upcoming releases and special excerpts.

All reviews are **welcome** and **appreciated**. Please consider leaving one on your favorite social media and book buying sites.

For books in the world of romance and speculative fiction that embody Innovation, Creativity, and Affordability, check out City Owl Press at www. cityowlpress.com.

ACKNOWLEDGMENTS

It's true, we owe much of a book's success to luck and timing. But the deeper truth is that success is hard work, dedication, and belief in something—and not just from the author, but the entire team that brings it to life. So I must thank the amazing team at City Owl Press for believing in this series and breathing new, amazing life into it.

To those who love to read paranormal books, you rock my world and make my dreams possible. And fans who review, you make that world spin. Words cannot express the gratitude I feel toward you all.

And, of course, a huge thank you to my better half for putting up with the endless questions, research hours, and brainstorming. He never tired of the many discussions while driving or sitting on a ski lift, but then, he couldn't exactly get away. You are the best unpaid plot consultant anyone could ask for.

ABOUT THE AUTHOR

HEATHER McCORKLE is an Amazon bestselling author of paranormal romance, historical romances, urban fantasy, and steampunk. She lives in the Great Northwest with her amazing husband and horizontally challenged cat. As a Native Oregonian, she enjoys the outdoors as much as the worlds she creates on the pages. When she isn't writing, reading, or editing, you can find her on the ski slopes, or prepping for ski  season by hiking, mountain biking, and paddleboarding. She has been known to play an excessive amount of disc golf, but still claims to be mediocre at it.

www.heathermccorkle.com

twitter.com/HeatherMcCorkle

instagram.com/heathermccorkle

facebook.com/authorHeatherMcCorkle

pinterest.com/heathermccorkle

ABOUT THE PUBLISHER

City Owl Press is a cutting edge indie publishing company, bringing the world of romance and speculative fiction to discerning readers.

Escape Your World. Get Lost in Ours!

www.cityowlpress.com

facebook.com/YourCityOwlPress
twitter.com/cityowlpress
instagram.com/cityowlbooks
pinterest.com/cityowlpress